Evie Blake is from Londo... is currently busy writing her next novel. For more about Evie Blake visit her website: www.evieblake.com.

SURRENDER YOURSELF
Evie Blake

headline

First published in Great Britain in 2014 by
HEADLINE PUBLISHING GROUP

1

Cataloguing in Publication Data is available from the British Library

ISBN 978 0 7553 9891 1

Typeset in Sabon by Avon DataSet Ltd, Bidford-on-Avon, Warwickshire

Printed and bound in Great Britain by
Clays Ltd, St Ives plc

HEADLINE PUBLISHING GROUP
An Hachette UK Company
338 Euston Road
London NW1 3BH

www.headline.co.uk
www.hachette.co.uk

I will kiss you like no other.
Make your heart spin
Touch your fingertips with such care you know you are safe.
I ask you to let go.
And you trust me,
Leap off the cliff into my arms
I carry you down, down
Two bodies melting into one
As I let you come into me.

Noëlle Harrison, *The Secret Loves of Julia Caesar*

$\mathcal{T}$ina

1989

VALENTINA'S HAND IS IN HERS. SHE SQUEEZES IT TIGHT. HER daughter's tiny, cold palm is cooling her hot hand, for Tina is sweating despite the fact it is a bitter day in mid-November. Anticipation courses through her body, heating her from within, making her skin damp, as if she and Valentina are melted into each other. They are as one as they weave through the crowd, Tina scanning it for his face among them. It may have been five years since she last saw Karel but she will never forget his shocking beauty. She is sure she will spot him.

Now this moment has come, finally, she cannot bear to wait one second longer. She sees the East Berliners pouring through the Borholmerstrasse border crossing, and she is sure he will be among them. For had they not promised each other? If the wall came down, no matter when, no matter what, she would be waiting for him. She had said she would be at the first crossing that opened, five days after it opened, at midday. She glances at her watch. It is now five minutes to twelve; in a few minutes Valentina will meet her father.

* * *

1

The last few days have been surreal. She will never forget the moment, as she sat down to watch the evening news, that she saw the interview with the journalist from ANSA. It was a day like any other: packed with work and mothering. She had done a shoot in the morning for *Elle* magazine, and in the afternoon she had taken Valentina to the park, where she had pushed her in the swings before it had got too cold. She had bought some food on the way home, and stopped to chat to her neighbour outside the apartment. She had called up her son, Mattia, in America to talk to him while her tomato sauce was simmering in the pot and Valentina was drawing pictures with her crayons at the table in the sitting room. She was such an easy child, never demanding her attention.

She said goodbye to Mattia, took the sauce off the stove and had just settled into a chair, staring aimlessly at the television while sipping on her pre-dinner glass of wine, when the programme cut to an interview with East German Politburo member, Gunter Schabowski. A journalist was excitedly asking when exactly the new regulations for free passage by way of all border transit points from East to West Germany and to West Berlin would come into effect. Schabowski's words in response were still spinning inside her head:

If my information is correct, to the best of my knowledge, immediately.

She had dropped her glass on the floor and it smashed to pieces, spraying red wine all over the carpet, a stain she was never able to remove.

Immediately.

She jumped up from the couch clasping her hands, letting out a small cry so that Valentina looked up from her drawing in surprise. The Berlin Wall was coming down. She *had* been right.

She had told Karel to hope and now he would finally be free. Nothing in the world would stop her from being at that border crossing in five days' time. It was not because she loved Karel any more. Surely by now he was with another woman? And that was fine; she had Phil. It was not for herself she was going, but for her daughter. This was Valentina's one and only chance to meet her real father.

'I'm cold, Mama.' Valentina is shivering next to her.

'Not long now, darling,' she says to her.

'But why are we here?' her daughter whines. 'I want to go home.'

She doesn't want to tell Valentina about Karel until she sees him. She couldn't bear to confuse her unless absolutely necessary. She needs to know that Karel still wants to know them first.

She moves right up to the barricade, watches the East Berliners as they walk across the bridge in their throngs. Most are obviously just crossing for the day, to have a look at the other side, before going back home again. But some are going for good, staggering under big cases, pushing bikes with packages strapped on the back, or crawling through in laden Trabants.

She waits and watches as the minutes tick by. By half past twelve she begins to doubt; by one o'clock Valentina is so cold her teeth are chattering. What can she do? Maybe he got held up. If she leaves now, he could come and they would miss him. She looks around her and spies a stall selling hot drinks and pretzels.

They shiver as Tina gives Valentina a sip of her hot chocolate, raising it to the child's blue lips. Valentina is so cold that she has stopped complaining. Instead she is tugging at her mother's

3

sleeve every now and again, but Tina cannot take her eyes off the crossing. She cannot risk missing him. The hours tick by. East Berliners come through: people cheering as they cross over, others crying, cars beeping, jubilation and emotional out-pourings. Families are reunited, hugging and crying, and still she waits for Karel. She begs him to come. Yet the crowd keeps on flowing across the bridge and he is not among them. She glances at her watch and to her dismay it is three already. She had been so certain that he would be here. Her situation begins to dawn on her.

When Phil had got home late that night, after the announcement about the Berlin Wall on the news, she couldn't wait to tell him.

'Did you hear?' she said, charging into the hall to greet him before he had even taken his coat off.

'What?' He looked grey in the face, and terribly tired. She felt a stab of concern for him. 'The Berlin Wall . . . it's over.'

'Really?' His eyes lit up, and he walked over to the television and turned it on. There were images on the screen of East Berliners bursting through the border at Borholmerstrasse, and walking across the Bösebrücke Bridge.

'This is amazing,' he said. 'We are watching history unfold.'

She put a hand on his arm, and he turned to look at her.

'Let's go to Berlin,' she said.

'What? Now? To watch the Wall come down?'

'No, I mean to live for a while. You said we should get out of Italy . . . and, well, now the border is open . . .' She nodded over at Valentina. 'I can bring her to meet him.'

Phil looked at her incredulously. 'You're not serious, Tina?'

'Of course I am serious,' she said. 'I promised Karel I would be there, five days after the borders opened, with Valentina.'

'But she doesn't know him, Tina; as far as she is concerned, I am her father.'

'But you are *not* her father, Phil. He is. I have to take her to see him. It's not right.'

Phil had looked hurt. 'You know I love her,' he said.

'I'm sorry; I know that,' she said, realising she sounded harsh. 'And you are a brilliant father, but don't you see I promised Karel I would bring Valentina to him . . . ?' she said, softening her voice.

'Can't he come here?'

'He won't . . . because of you. I know he won't.'

'This is madness, Tina. How will you ever find him? It will be like finding a needle in a haystack.'

'We have an arrangement . . . We promised each other.'

'How romantic,' Phil said, sarcastically.

'Phil, I want you to come too. All of us . . . to be together.'

He shook his head. 'No way. If you want to go and meet this young gigolo of yours, then go ahead, but I am not going to share you with anyone any more.'

'What do you mean, "any more"?'

He gave her a cold look but said nothing.

She was confused by his behaviour. This wasn't her Phil, who was usually so unpossessive and easy-going.

'Well, I *have* to go, Phil, for Valentina's sake. Please come with me.'

'No; it's either him or me.'

She couldn't believe he meant it. Surely Phil understood how important it was they went to Berlin?

'That's not fair. Think of Valentina. Don't you think she deserves to meet Karel?'

'She doesn't care or know who the hell he is,' Phil said hotly.

'I'm her father, as far as she is concerned. But if you don't value me in your lives any more, that's fine. I'll bugger off and leave you to it.'

He had stormed out of the room, slamming the door behind him. She had been stunned by his reaction. Where had it come from? She had expected Phil to come back to her that night so they could talk some more, but his side of the bed remained cold and she slept alone. In the morning, he had left a note, saying he had gone to London for a while. She had been so hurt and a part of her was angry with him. How could he be so selfish? She had promised Karel she would bring his child to meet him. That was not the sort of promise you break.

And yet it seems that Karel has broken it. That is unless he literally isn't able to come. Maybe he is sick or not living in East Berlin any more. The only way she will find out is if she goes to his apartment.

It feels strange to be walking the streets of East Berlin again. Everyone seems to be on the move, heading west, either for the day or for ever. She finds the building in Prenzlauer Berg, where Karel lived, easily. After the last time, she would never forget the way. Despite its one-time grandeur, the façade looks even more dilapidated than she remembers: dirty, cracked windows, peeling paintwork and plaster crumbling off the walls to expose the brickwork. She walks through the front doors and up the stairs. Valentina is tired, dragging her heels and whining.

'Come on, there's a good girl. Not much further now,' she encourages her.

Tina remembers the last time she was here in this building. Karel carried her up the staircase, the two of them covered in snow, the wet chill settled on her lap, yet she had been warmed by the heat from his chest, his heart beating against the heart of his baby girl inside her, his breath upon her forehead as he blew snowflakes off the top of her head. His presence in this building feels so real now that Tina imagines she can hear the strains of his cello floating down the staircase. Yet, when they get to Karel's apartment, his name is no longer on the door. The music has gone and, instead, the doorbell echoes eerily out into the empty landing. She grips Valentina's frozen hand tighter and says a silent prayer, yet she knows she is hoping against all hope. The door is flung open by a robust woman, probably about the same age as her, although her hair is completely grey. Tina speaks in English, since she has no German: 'Does Karel Slavik live here?' But the woman shakes her head, giving her an unfriendly look. Before Tina can ask if she knows where he is, she slams the door in her face.

Mother and daughter trail back down the stairs and into the street. It is beginning to get dark, an unpleasant drizzle of rain blowing horizontally into their faces and penetrating their coats. She can't believe it's over, that she will never see Karel again. And now she has lost Phil too. She is on her own. She shivers suddenly, her body jerking violently.

'What's wrong, Mama?' Valentina asks, looking up at her with her big baby-girl eyes.

'I feel a little sad and lonely,' she tells her.

'Don't be sad,' her daughter says. 'You're not lonely; you have me.'

Yes, but it's not enough, she feels like saying. *I need a man in my life to make me love myself, to make me feel whole.*

Back in the hotel, she is so exhausted that she falls asleep still in her clothes, while reading a bedtime story to Valentina. In her dream, she finds Karel. He is living with those poor punks in one of the abandoned buildings on Schönhauser Allee. He is sitting on top of a pile of rubble, quite calmly, as if it is the most comfortable place in the world to be sitting. His cello is propped between his legs, and he is waiting for her and Valentina. She waves to him. 'We're here!' she calls. 'I brought her to you.'

Karel smiles back, looking down on Valentina with pride. He has such a magnanimous smile, full of understanding, compassion and love. He is a good father. He picks up his bow and he starts to play. Oh, it is the song he composed for Tina! She knows immediately. She stands beneath his rubble castle and listens to the sound of his love. It lifts her and Valentina up, so that, for a moment, their feet are no longer touching the ground. And as she watches him play his cello, she feels his bow across her naked body – the strings sawing across her breasts and catching on her nipples as he plucks her down below. He is playing her, his dexterous, nimble fingers sensing the inner vibrations of her body and bringing forth the music of her soul.

And, as he plays, she sees the shadows in the derelict buildings turn into people she once knew in East Berlin: Sabine and Rudolf, Hermann and Simone, and Lottie. Karel is the warmth and he is the light around which they all gather.

She wakes in a sweat again, her clothes soaking through to her skin. Valentina is fast asleep. She gets off the bed, and strips off. What could that dream mean? And then it occurs to her, there is one last possible route to finding Karel. She turns on the table lamp by her bed and hunts in her bag for her address book. She pulls it out and flicks through it until she finds Lottie's old address in Berlin.

* * *

When Lottie opens her front door the next morning, Tina recognises her instantly. Her punk looks are slightly toned down – the black hair not quite so spiky, and her eyes not as heavily made up – but even so she still has that edginess that attracted Tina to book her as one of her models in the first place. Lottie gawps at her for a moment, speechless with shock at seeing her. It has, after all, been over five years.

'My God, Tina!' she exclaims. 'And is this your daughter? Hello,' she says to Valentina, bending down and offering her hand.

'Hello; pleased to meet you,' Valentina says, politely, in Italian.

'Oh, so cute,' Lottie says, straightening up. 'So what are you doing here in Berlin?' she gushes. 'Well, of course, the Wall coming down . . . isn't it so exciting? Since the ninth, every day has been one big party.'

She leads them into a messy kitchen. 'Sorry, the place is in a state. Do you want a cup of tea?'

'No, I'm fine, thanks. Have you been over the Wall yet?'

'Of course; I went over at Brandenburg Gate on the ninth at exactly nine thirty p.m. It was incredible. I cried.'

'Did you meet up with Sabine? You must have had such a family celebration!'

Lottie looks awkward, her pale cheeks blush. 'Yes, my parents went over to see their family,' she says, changing the subject. 'The atmosphere in the city is so great . . . Finally, all Germans together . . .' She beams.

'And Hermann? Did you meet up with him?' Tina asks her.

Lottie clutches her hands, her smile wiped off her face. 'Hermann is dead,' she says, looking away from Tina and out the smudgy window of her kitchen.

Tina bites her tongue. How could she have been so tactless?

'I'm so sorry, Lottie. What happened?' she asks her, softly.

'That's why I lost contact with my cousin, Sabine,' Lottie says, offering Tina a chair at the table and sitting down opposite her. 'I always suspected that her creepy boyfriend was Stasi, but it turns out that Sabine was an informer too.'

'But she was such a lovely girl,' Tina says, remembering the sweet Sabine.

'She was weak, not lovely,' Lottie says sourly. 'That's how she knew Rudolf, in fact. He was interrogating her and I guess he got some kind of mental control over her . . . terrified her into being an informer.'

'But what has that got to do with Hermann?' Tina probes.

'I made the mistake of telling Sabine about Hermann and Simone, and the fact I brought them music to listen to and stuff to wear. She told Rudolf and next thing you know they were rounded up. For some reason they picked on Hermann. They let Simone go. The Stasi locked him up and started mentally torturing him. When they finally let him out he was really damaged –' she taps her head – 'he ended up killing himself. Slashed his wrists with a piece of broken glass.'

She turns away from Tina, suddenly noticing Valentina standing by her and staring at her with big, horrified eyes.

'Sorry, I forgot about the kid . . .' she mumbles.

'It's OK; she doesn't understand English,' Tina says, gently. 'I'm really sorry about Hermann. And what happened to Simone?'

Lottie sighs, shakes her head. 'You saw how sick she was . . . After Hermann was gone, she just gave up . . .' Lottie's voice breaks. 'They are both dead, Tina. That's why I stopped going to the East. I couldn't bear it . . . I felt that somehow I was responsible for their deaths.'

Tina reaches out and puts her hand on Lottie's arm. 'You know that's not true.'

Lottie shrugs, picks a packet of cigarettes off the kitchen table and offers Tina one.

'No, thanks,' Tina says, shaking her head.

Lottie lights up, puffing on the cigarette meditatively.

'Does she want to sit down?' she asks Tina, indicating Valentina, who is still standing motionless and staring at Lottie as if she is regarding an exotic creature rather than a person.

Tina turns to Valentina and, speaking in Italian, she tells her to stop staring and to sit down at the table. Valentina reluctantly slips on to a chair, but still she cannot pull her eyes away from the vision of Lottie.

Tina quells the butterflies in her stomach, takes a breath. She has to ask Lottie about Karel and yet she is scared of what she might tell her. She changes her mind and grabs Lottie's cigarette packet, helping herself.

Lottie looks at her curiously, sensing that Tina is building up to something.

Tina takes a long, slow drag on her cigarette. 'So, do you know what happened to Karel Slavik, the cellist?' she finally spits out as casually as she can.

'You don't know?' Lottie asks her.

'No.' She shakes her head, feeling a cold dread creeping into her stomach.

'I knew about you and him,' Lottie says, crushing the butt of her cigarette into an empty saucer on the table. 'I watched that night in the car . . .'

'Not in front of Valentina,' she whispers, despite the fact that Valentina doesn't understand a word they are saying.

'Oh, sorry.' Lottie scrutinises Valentina, meeting the child's

11

eyes for a moment. 'Jesus!' She whistles under her breath, looking back at Tina. 'Now I know why you'd want to find Karel. She is the image of him.'

'So do you know where he is?' Tina asks, suddenly impatient. She can't bear it any more, the not knowing.

Lottie is looking at Valentina, transfixed. She shakes herself, as if breaking from a trance, before looking over at Tina and speaking so slowly it seems as if the words are being dragged from her.

'Yes, I know where he is. I'll take you.'

$\mathcal{V}$alentina

2013

SHE IS RIGHT ON THE EDGE OF THE CLIFF, LEANING OVER, MORE SO than is safe. Yet Valentina doesn't move. She is hypnotised by the clear blue sea, drawn into its glittering depths. Theo is down there somewhere.

The ocean mocks her, its hue the exact shade of her dead lover's eyes. She feels such an intense loathing for this island, so wild and elemental, a place that she always loved before, and yet this very shoreline swallowed up Theo, took him away from her and left her broken.

The wind pushes into her back as she leans even further forward. It would be so easy just to slip off this cliff edge and drop into the sea below – so easy to join Theo in his watery grave. Seagulls circle above her head, crying out as if to warn her and yet she doesn't step back to safety. Today is a year to the day that Theo disappeared into the Mediterranean Sea, off the island of Capri.

They never found a body. She heard that his parents had a memorial service for him in his home city of New York, but she refused to go. How could she meet Theo's parents for the first time in such circumstances? To think that she had been worried about meeting them when he was alive, fearful of the commitment! She is ashamed to face them now.

Valentina cannot believe that she is still standing; that her heart is still pumping despite the fact Theo is dead. She twists the engagement ring on her finger, rubs the cut edges of the sapphire stone against her fingertip, an action that gives her comfort. She should take it off, bury it in the bottom of a jewellery box, but she just can't let go of the last thing Theo gave her. She stares at that blue sea, and sees Theo's eyes within it. 'Speak to me,' she begs, but the only sounds are those screaming gulls and the sea crashing on to the rocks below.

She sighs, and turns her head to look up into the sky. She sways on the edge as she watches the seagulls flying in and out of the blue void above her. She remembers another blue-sky day: she and Theo lying on their backs in the grass in Parco Sempione in Milan. It was a hot June day, not long after they had first started dating, nearly two years ago now. The two of them were staring up into the perfection of the blue abyss above them, holding hands.

Valentina remembers she had suddenly been filled with a spontaneous need to be intimate. She had rolled on to her side and climbed on top of him, closed her eyes and kissed him on the lips. She remembers they had been eating ice creams, and he was still sweet to taste. His lips were cool and creamy against hers.

'Open your eyes,' Theo had whispered.

She had not wanted to. She shook her head, burrowing her face into his tender neck and inhaling him.

'Please, Valentina,' Theo insisted. 'Let me look at you.'

She had felt a little bullied. She didn't want to break the trance of their bodies melting into each other under the hot sun. If she opened her eyes it would be like a separation.

'What is it?' she had snapped, whipping her head up and flashing her eyes at him, unable to hide the annoyance in her voice.

Theo looked back at her, unblinking, white heat glinting within cool blue, and her irritation seeped away. He said nothing, just held her with this gaze that spoke a thousand words. Deep down she knew then how he felt about her. It frightened her to the core. No man had ever looked at her in this way; no man had *seen* inside her. She knew right then that he loved her, months before he ever said it to her, and nearly a year before she could admit it to him. And yet, as his face broke into a smile, her heart had lurched and she too had fallen.

Those were the moments, she now realises, on a random June afternoon in a park in Milan, when we first fell in love.

'Don't look so serious, Valentina,' Theo had teased her, wrapping his arms around her and pressing her tightly against his chest so that she could feel his heart beat against hers. She had let herself sink into him. She had bathed in the golden warmth of his comfort. For the first time in her life, she had not felt alone.

Valentina drops her head, looks back down at the tempestuous sea crashing off the Capri coast, its demons calling to her. She inches even closer to the edge of the cliff. She is so close to giving up, and yet the memory of that June day reawakens and she hears Theo's voice again: 'You are special, Valentina,' he had said.

'*Everyone* is special,' she had retorted.

'Of course,' he said patiently, 'but what I am trying to say is that you are special to me. I have never met a girl like you before.'

She had rolled off him on to the grass, sat up and looked down at him.

15

'You do know that is a very corny line . . .'

He shaded his eyes with his hands and looked up at her. Shadows fell across his face. 'I mean it,' he said, sounding serious. 'You are everything: beautiful, clever and talented . . . You are sexy, *so* sexy.' He smiled. 'But what makes you even more attractive to me is who you are, and what you do.'

She had looked back at him in surprise, unable to think of what to say in reply. No other man she had been with had ever been interested in her work; in fact, they had usually been threatened by her drive and focus, and especially by her successes.

'Promise me something, Valentina,' Theo had said, raising himself so that he was leaning back on his elbows. 'No matter what calamities in life you have to face, you will always take photographs.'

'But I am just doing the same thing that my mother did: fashion shoots . . . I am just copying her.'

He shook his head, with a face that said he knew better. 'There's more to you than being Tina Rosselli's daughter. There is a depth to your pictures that she doesn't have. I have every faith that your work will go through many incarnations . . .'

She gave his arm a friendly pinch, a little embarrassed by his belief in her. 'You are beginning to sound like an art historian,' she protested.

'Well, now, that would make sense, wouldn't it, seeing as that is precisely what I am?'

When they first met, Valentina had been surprised to discover that Theo was a Professor of Art History at the University of Milan. He had struck her as the least fusty academic she had ever met – always so lively and witty, and wanting to discover new art in Milan. He was forever taking different perspectives, looking at art in a different way, and he encouraged Valentina to break out of the boundaries of her profession as a fashion photographer. He had taught her so much and not just about art, but about films, books, music, politics, history. Valentina remembers now that even in those early days she had been a little confused by this dynamic man, always on the move, disappearing off on lecture tours and consulting with art dealers all around the world. He had not seemed what he claimed to be. And she had been right. Sure, Theo was an academic, but he was something else too, something dangerous and clandestine, a profession that had ultimately led to his death.

It should have been her, she thinks, who drowned this day a year ago. She nearly had. But Theo had saved her. It seems that he had given his life for hers, yet she wants to tell him so badly that her life is worth nothing to her without him by her side.

She wants to jump off the cliff. She feels herself pulled towards the edge again. She wonders if her body will be battered by the rocks below. Would they kill her first, or could she fall clear of them and drop into the sea? Could she sink to the bottom like a stone, gulping in sea water until her lungs burst? The urge to let go is so strong inside her and yet Valentina finds herself stepping back.

Promise me something, Valentina. No matter what calamities in life you have to face, you will always take photographs.

She had promised him, that's the problem. She sighs, opens her bag, digging around in it until she finds her digital camera. She turns it on, looks at the small screen, directs it down at the raging blue sea and takes a photograph. She turns around, with her back to the sea, stretches out her arm and turns the camera on herself, not sure what she might come up with as she spontaneously clicks. When she looks back at the photographs she has taken, she sees parts of her face – her windblown hair, her sorrowful eyes – against the startling blue backdrop of the Mediterranean, and the chalky cliffs behind her. She feels a little better already. By taking a picture of herself, she is able to step out of her emotions and document a process. Is it the process of her grief? For surely this is why she is in Capri in the first place? Her friends had thought she was maudlin coming here; in particular, Leonardo, who had written her a long email advising her not to go back.

Leonardo had been with her that desperate week a year ago. She had phoned him to tell him that Theo had gone missing and the next day Leonardo had just turned up. She had been so relieved to see him. He had not left her side, accompanying her all the many times she took rowing boats out to the blue grotto to scan the cave for signs of Theo. The water had looked floodlit from below, the refracted daylight beaming up through its blue sheets. When she dipped her hands into its azure glitter, they became silver. This magical, iridescent place was now transformed into the gates of hell for Valentina. She could see right to the bottom of the sea in the blue grotto and there was nothing there. What more could she find that the police hadn't? Yet Leonardo traipsed the island of Capri with her as she spoke to the fishermen and the shopkeepers, the other tourists and the owners of the trattorias. She could not believe that Theo had drowned. And yet it was the only logical conclusion, for she knew he would never have run away from her. It was inconceivable. They had just got engaged.

She remembers the last night of her search. Over dinner, Leonardo had told her, as gently as he could, that it was time she went back to Milan. The police would contact her if anything turned up. She had been furious with him, and yet in her heart she knew he was right. She had drunk too much wine and it had fuelled her anger.

Back in the hotel room, she had been cruel to her friend, and accused him of having ulterior motives for being there with her. She will never forget the hurt in Leonardo's eyes; yet, at the same time, there was a flicker of his eyelashes, a blink that told her she had hit a nerve. She had seen a shard of his feelings for her.

'You want me to give up on Theo,' she had said.

'Valentina, I am trying to help you,' Leonardo had protested. 'Theo was one of my best friends.'

'Don't talk about him in the past tense,' she had screamed at Leonardo. 'He could still be alive . . . he could be hurt . . . lost . . . Glen could have kidnapped him.'

'From what the police said, it sounds like, after Theo and Glen fought in the sea, they both ended up . . . well . . .' Leonardo bravely stumbled on.

Valentina shivers at the memory of Glen. She slumps down onto a rock by the edge of the cliff, cradling her camera in her lap. Why is it that as each day passes Theo's face becomes more shadowy, and yet she remembers Glen's face so clearly? Those sculpted yet cruel features like a Roman Emperor, and dazzling blond hair that looked like a halo. And yet he was the most sinister person she had ever met. She could not understand the man's deep hatred for her. Every time she was in his company she could almost smell it, the loathing, and yet he was practically a stranger. Glen tried to destroy her and Theo. And it seemed he had succeeded, although it appeared to be at the cost of his own life.

Perched on her rock, Valentina gazes out at the endless blue and wonders where Leonardo is now. Has she driven him away? She bites her lip, her throat tight with shame at her behaviour as she remembers that last night in Capri with Leonardo. Her friend had been firm. She should go home to Milan. Over that dinner table of untouched food Leonardo and Valentina had stared at each other, and in her friend's eyes she had seen the truth.

Theo was gone. Suddenly all her energy, her fervent searching for Theo, her hounding of the police, her anger at Leonardo's suggestion she should give up, was swept away by a tidal wave of grief. A sound had come out of her that was hard to describe – a deep, guttural wail.

'I don't want him to be dead,' she had begged.

Leonardo had taken her in his arms and held her tightly. She could not cry, yet she was shaking uncontrollably, the shock of Theo's loss only hitting her then.

She had asked Leonardo to sleep with her in her bed. He held her all night long. It was a small comfort to hear his soft sleeping breath, and feel his chest rising and falling against her own, yet she could not sleep. All night she had repeated in her head the words like a mantra: Theo is gone. Theo is gone.

As she watched the sun rise through their open window, its fuchsia bloom infusing her tired body, making her soul scream for intimacy, she had turned to Leonardo and begun to kiss him. He stirred sleepily and instinctively took her into his arms. She pushed herself against him. She was afire with the need to block out the pain. She could feel Leonardo's cock stirring against her belly. Yet, as her friend woke up properly, he pulled away from her and shook his head, looking at her with doleful eyes. She had immediately felt ashamed of what she had been about to do. She had been embarrassed, and grateful that he never said a word. Instead, he got out of the bed and padded into the bathroom, giving her a chance to collect herself.

A week after they'd returned to Milan, Leonardo had announced that he was heading off to India to study yoga. Valentina has often wondered whether she had anything to do with his decision. He knew that she was vulnerable. But so was he. Had he run away from her? At times she had felt angry with him, let down. She missed him. And yet, deep down, she knows that Leonardo is doing the best thing possible to protect their friendship. If he had let the two of them make love when she was in such a raw state of grief, it would have ended in disaster.

Valentina gets up from her rock and turns away from the cliff edge. Slowly she begins to wind her way back down towards the centre of Capri. Every now and again she stops to take a photograph: a tiny windblown wildflower surviving against all the odds; the jagged coastline of the island; the empty sea with just one white sailing boat in the distance; an islander riding past on a moped. She is keeping busy. This is how she has survived the past year: taking photographs, working non-stop. She thinks that Theo would be proud of her. As she turns the corner, she looks back once more at the edge of the cliff, acknowledging how close she has come today to slipping off the edge of her life. She will live, for Theo's sake, but can she ever love again?

$\mathscr{T}$ina

1984

THE WHOLE FLIGHT FROM MILAN TO BERLIN, TINA WONDERS WHY she lied to Phil. It was the first time. And yet how easily the lie had popped out of her mouth.

'I have to go to Berlin. They've no one else to do the shoot. I've no choice.'

She'd felt as if the words *liar, liar* were emblazoned upon her forehead, and yet Phil didn't question her. Why should he?

'Oh, that's a pity. I was going to take you out for dinner tomorrow night for our anniversary.'

'Phil, we're not even married . . .'

'The anniversary of the first time we met,' he said, grinning at her. 'Remember? You, driving like a lunatic in that little Triumph. I thought my last day had come.'

'I wasn't that bad,' she grumbled.

'And I know we are not officially married, but we've been together so long it feels like it . . .' Phil continued to say, 'so that's why I thought we should go out, because it's been fifteen years.'

She had turned her back on him, pouring herself a small cup of thick, black espresso from the pot.

'Is it so long you feel trapped?' she asked.

'Of course not,' Phil had said, coming to stand behind her, putting his arms around her waist and kissing the back of her neck. 'Although I do miss those early years when we couldn't keep our hands off each other.'

She shifted away from him, sipping her espresso. 'Having a baby changes a woman . . .'

'I know, I know,' Phil sighs. 'I've read all the books. But now, don't you see, with Mattia away at school and nearly grown up . . .'

'He's only twelve, Phil . . .'

'Yes, but since he's gone to boarding school it's like we can start over again.' He nuzzled into her neck, started bringing his hand down her backside. She used to love Phil touching her like this, and yet she moved away from him again.

'I've got to go,' she said.

He frowned at her.

'What is it, Tina?'

'Nothing,' she said, looking away from him.

'Have you gone off me?' he asked.

'No . . . It's just I don't feel like sex right now. Is that OK?' she snapped.

'Hey,' he said putting up his hands in defence. 'I'm just asking. It seems to me you haven't felt like sex in a long time. What's up?'

He had offered her a chance to open up and tell him how she felt, but she hadn't known how to begin, how to tell him that she just wasn't interested in sex at the moment. He would take it personally, see it as a reflection upon him, but it was nothing to do with him. She loved Phil. He was her partner. It was just she didn't want to be touched by anyone at the moment. She wanted to be on her own. That was why she had lied about Berlin. She had asked for that fashion shoot, not the other way around.

'Nothing,' she said, shaking her head. 'I've just got a lot on; I'm very busy.'

Phil had put his head on one side, given her a sad smile. 'You know, every man needs a little attention from time to time, otherwise he can be tempted . . .'

'Are you threatening me?' she said, her voice rising. 'Are you saying you are going to fuck someone else if I don't have sex with you?'

'Christ, Tina! Calm down . . . I was joking.'

She gave him a glare and stormed out of the kitchen, grabbing her small suitcase and camera bag by the door. 'I'll see you in a few days,' she said.

'Hey, Tina, I'm sorry,' Phil said, following her down the hall. 'Don't walk out angry. I just miss you.'

'How can you miss me? We live together.'

'You know what I mean, love.'

She had hated herself at that moment. Any warm-blooded woman would have fallen into the arms of her lover and shown him how much she cared for him. Yet she felt cold inside, completely switched off. It was disturbing and frightening. For about the last two years, every time they had made love had been an effort for her. She just couldn't get turned on, no matter what. She now understood the term frigid; that was what she was: a cold bitch, pecking him on the cheek and walking out the door. Her behaviour was going to push him into the arms of another woman. The idea of it filled her with panic, with dread. Yet she couldn't keep pretending. The way she felt at the moment, she would quite happily never have sex again.

* * *

24

The plane begins to descend for landing. Tina looks out of the cabin window but she can see nothing of Berlin, just a thick layer of cloud concealing the whole city. She wonders if they are flying above the East or the West at this particular moment. She takes out her compact and fixes her face, reapplying her lipstick. Already she feels better to be out of Italy and preoccupied with her fashion shoot and all the details she has to get right. She can put Phil, and all her worries about their relationship, to the back of her mind, and face them when she comes back. She knows deep down that she has to do something. Phil is not a monk. She might choose to be celibate, but it's not fair on him.

Tina wonders if what her friend Isabella says is true. She refuses to commit to any long-term relationship because she says the passion always dies, eventually, no matter who you are with. Tina teases her that it just gives her an excuse to be pro-miscuous, but Isabella is adamant that marriage, or long-term commitment, is the death of desire. She says that no two people are supposed to be locked in a monogamous relationship for ever. If that is true, what is Tina to do? Tell Phil it's OK if he wants to sleep with other women? The idea of that makes her feel sick. Or should she let him go? Should she end things between them? The prospect of breaking up makes her feel even worse. She may pretend to be a strong, independent career woman, but she needs Phil in her life. He balances her.

The taxi speeds into West Berlin, and gradually Tina starts to feel better, the adrenalin of being on a job and all that entails lifting her spirits. She has always wanted to come to Berlin. It is a city that has fascinated her since she was a child. Her father had been a lifelong Communist, and yet she remembers his reaction the day they put up the Berlin Wall in 1961. She had been her son Mattia's age at the time, and beginning to develop an interest in the world outside their daily lives in Milan. It was clear that she had taken after her father in this regard, although she didn't look a bit like him. Her mother had seemed determined to teach her good homemaking skills – baking, knitting, sewing – all of which Tina hated. She preferred the company of her father. Sometimes he would take her to some of his Communist party meetings, and she would sit at the back, her book unread on her lap, listening to all the debate and wishing so fiercely that she could be one of those passionate, chain-smoking young men with big ideals. Yet, when they built the Berlin Wall, her father began to change his opinions about Russia and the Eastern bloc. It became personal for him. He began to realise that ideals are all very well, but people are imperfect, and rules need to be flexible.

She remembers the story he told her about his friend from Rome, Alfredo. By this time she was fifteen and the story of Alfredo had a huge impact on her. Alfredo was living and working in West Berlin as an engineer. One day he went to a wedding party in East Berlin, where he met a beautiful young woman, Ursula. They fell in love, and soon enough they decided they would get married. They imagined that, having become engaged, she would be entitled to leave as the future wife of a foreigner. However, her applications were refused. Alfredo could not live in East Berlin because he worked in West Berlin. As far as the couple could see, they had two choices: to say goodbye to each other for ever, or for her to try to escape to the West. They were both so deeply in love that the first choice did not seem like an option to either of them.

Alfredo planned Ursula's escape meticulously. He observed that the horizontal wooden pole at Checkpoint Charlie, which was raised to let each vehicle through, had no vertical struts, and he had also noticed that a certain type of sports car, once its roof was down, would actually fit under the barriers at one of the border crossings. One day, he hired one of these cars in West Berlin and drove over to the East to collect Ursula. They waited until two in the morning, when they hoped the guards would be less vigilant. Alfredo put Ursula in the boot of the car and made his way to the checkpoint. The first barrier pole was raised, and the border guard merely checked his passport. He was flagged towards the vehicle inspection area, but this was the crucial moment because it was at this point that they would check to see the boot was empty. He pressed his foot on the accelerator, despite the warning cries and then the shots, but he did not stop. He will never forgive himself for that mistake. He threaded through the three concrete walls and ducked his head as the car went under the last pole; all the while, the border guards were firing at him. He made it to the West all right but, when he opened the boot, Ursula was dead, riddled with bullet holes. He blamed himself. He had killed the love of his life.

This story sickened Guido Rosselli for, despite his political principles, he was also a man who believed in love. He tried to counsel his friend, to comfort him that it was not his fault his fiancée had been murdered so ruthlessly. It was to no avail. About three months after the disastrous escape attempt, Alfredo threw himself in front of a train at Friedrichstrasse train station.

The more stories Tina's father heard about people being killed trying to cross the Berlin Wall, the angrier he got.

'You can't cut a city in half with a wall!' he would rant. 'What is wrong with this world? Can East and West not come to some kind of arrangement? Are we barbarians? Where is the humanity of our civilisation?'

* * *

27

Driving through the streets of West Berlin, Tina can't see any sign of conflict, or unease. It looks like any Western city – in fact, even more opulent than most, with shop windows stuffed with luxury goods and foods. She supposes it is the emblem of the West for the East, since West Berlin is geographically isolated from the rest of Western Europe. But how must that make its citizens feel? Perhaps they are used to the division by now. It has, after all, been twenty-three years since the Wall went up – a wall that has been transformed from the concrete blocks and wooden poles of Alfredo's days to a sophisticated construction of death strips, watchtowers, minefields, tank ditches, automatic guns, and dogs. There is a whole generation of young people who have known nothing else.

The taxi turns right and she gets her first glimpse of the Berlin Wall. The Western side is surprisingly innocuous looking: a plain concrete wall, covered in graffiti. Yet the more she looks at it, the more menacing it becomes. Although high, it is still low enough that you might hope you could actually get over it, and yet it's a deathtrap, so smooth that there is nowhere to get a foothold, and with a roll-top making it impossible to get a grip.

She looks up to see a watchtower just behind the Wall. She sees the shape of two border guards inside, the chilling sight of a gun strapped to one of their backs. Everything this side of the Wall looks so ordinary and yet on the other side, if she were to try to walk across, if she happened to be born the wrong side of that Wall, they could shoot her in the back. Her life would have no value.

Tina wishes she could tell her father that she is in Berlin, but he is long dead. Both her parents were killed nine years ago in a plane crash. It occurs to her how very alone she is. No siblings, no aunts or uncles. Her father's family was Jewish and were all killed during the Second World War, and her mother was an only child. All she has is Belle, her maternal grandmother, still miraculously alive and living in Venice, Mattia, her son, and Phil, of course. No wonder she needs him. She is an orphan, has been since she was in her twenties. It makes you resilient, but maybe a little too tough. She wishes sometimes she could be softer, more feminine, like her mother, she guesses.

As the taxi pulls up at her hotel, Tina's spirits begin to lift. Maybe the reason she lied to Phil was because she knew they needed this break, that sometimes you should be separated from the one you love to appreciate them. Distance makes the heart grow fonder, as they always say. If she had stayed in Milan, things were bound to have come to a head on their anniversary night. It is better to be apart. And yet, beneath her reasoned logic, there is another sensation: a buzzing taste of freedom in her mouth. She is on her own, free of her partner and her child, in a city where no one knows her. What might happen now?

$\mathcal{V}$alentina

VALENTINA WALKS THREE TIMES AROUND THE CHEST BEFORE approaching. When she returned from Capri, it was waiting for her in the caretaker's office of her apartment building, having been delivered while she was away. Antonio, the caretaker, brought it up to her apartment in the lift, and handed her an envelope that had been delivered along with the chest, before shuffling out again.

She has already read the letter. It is discarded on her kitchen table, flapping in the breeze from the open window, like a bird with broken wings.

Dear Valentina,

    It has taken us a year to go through our son's things. This chest was shipped to us from an art gallery in London. Apparently Theo bought this collection of work before he left England. We are sending it on to you because we feel they might be of more value to you. Or that you might be able to use or sell them again. We would also like to again extend an invitation to visit us in New York. We would love to meet you.

    With very best wishes,

    Walter & Rachel Steen

It is just a box of paintings, she tells herself. Why is she so afraid to open it up? When she and Theo had got back together again in London, at the time of her exhibition, he had not mentioned any paintings but then he was always acquiring random art, one way or another. They had left for Italy in such a hurry it had probably slipped his mind.

As she kneels down and begins to prise the lid off the chest, it occurs to her that inside could be secrets about Theo that she never knew. This could be a hoard of stolen art. What would she do then?

She pauses, takes a breath. She is being stupid. Theo only took back art that had been stolen in the first place, and returned it to its rightful owners. His focus had been on the Nazi hoard of paintings that his grandfather had lost during the Second World War. He had been a type of Robin Hood. A good thief.

The lid suddenly pings open and she pulls it off the top of the box, rummaging through the bubble wrap to grab hold of the cold, hard edges of a frame. She pulls it out and almost drops it with shock. She is looking at one of her own photographs from the exhibition of erotic photography that she was part of in London last year. It is a particularly explicit one of her friend, Antonella, and her lover, Mikhail. She pushes her hands back into the bubble wrap and pulls out another framed photograph, and another . . . It goes on and on until she has emptied the box, and the floor of her hall is littered with every single erotic photograph she exhibited in London last year. The gallery owner had told Valentina she had sold out, but not that the same person had bought every single picture. Theo had never mentioned it to her.

She sits back on her heels, clutching her hands, her heart squeezed tight. At the time of her exhibition, they hadn't even been together. They had reunited afterwards and yet here is

31

evidence that he never stopped loving her. He had gone into that gallery and, at great personal expense, he had made sure that every single one of her pictures had a red sticker by it. She is stunned by the sheer grandness of this gesture. And yet, strangely, there is a little part of her that feels piqued. She had believed that she had sold her work to strangers off the street who had come into the gallery and liked her photographs for what they were. It turns out that in fact Theo had bought them all. Was it because he loved all the pictures? Or did he do it to protect her? His reasons don't matter now. All she knows for sure is he did it because he loved her.

She picks up the self-portrait in Venice. She had made this image before she knew Theo. She looks at the girl in sepia shadows, the water reflections of her nudity, and it is as if she is looking at a previous incarnation of herself, as if it is not Valentina but one of her ancestors looking into the canal. Was she happier then, before she had lost her heart to Theo?

She places it on the hall table and sits down on a chair, chewing her nail. No, she had not been happier because she had not actually experienced the kind of joy she felt when she and Theo were together in Sorrento, before he went missing. She realises that all her pain now is worth it, for those glorious few days together with the love of her life.

'Oh, Theo,' she whispers. 'Where are you?'

The door of the hall bangs open and the letter from Theo's parents is blown off the kitchen table, coming to fall at her feet. It dawns on her that Theo's parents have seen all these photographs. Her throat goes suddenly dry at the thought. She is not ashamed of her work: erotic photography is not pornography, she is quite passionate about that, and yet it is hardly the introduction she imagined. How can she ever go and see them now that they have seen these hard-core pictures of Antonella and Mikhail, or even the nude photographs of herself?

She picks up the black and white close-up of Antonella's lips sucking on Mikhail's cock. She is quite shocked at how outrageously open they had all been, taking that shot. At the time, she had been the artist, considering tone, light and shadow, composition and texture, but now, looking at the image, she is seeing it through Theo's eyes. Did he imagine her sucking his cock when he looked at this image? She closes her eyes and takes a shivering sigh. She sees an image she wishes she had been able to immortalise in print, yet she can only imagine it: she and Theo lying on that enormous bed in the hotel room in Sorrento, with the doors of their French windows open and the pale yellow curtains billowing into the room. They have just drunk a bottle of champagne and eaten strawberries dipped in chocolate. She is now licking his cock, her tongue thick with sweet cocoa, as he presses his lips against her pussy. They are in adoration of each other. There is no other word for it.

She feels the tip of his tongue circling her clitoris and parting her lips, kissing her in the most sensitive part of herself, and she shudders as she squeezes his cock with her lips. It is slow, oh so languorous, and luxurious. They felt like they had all the time in the world to make love to each other. It was, in fact, the last time they ever did.

Valentina grits her teeth, opens her eyes and sees herself in the hall mirror: white face, hands clenched tight, pursed lips. She had no idea that loss could be such a physical sensation: the raw ache of it, the throbbing pain in her chest, her belly and her groin, the tightness in her throat, the heaviness of her skin and bone. She has to stop torturing herself with memories of her and Theo together.

He is gone, she tells herself yet again.

Her phone begins to ring. She hopes it isn't her mother. Since Theo died, she has been ringing her more often. Each time she rings, Tina asks her daughter to come out to New Mexico and stay with her. Valentina can't think of anything worse than spending time with her mother at the moment. She is still furious with her, although her mother doesn't know it, for lying to her about who her father is. Tina's behaviour is unforgiveable. Besides, how can she understand the extent of her daughter's loss when, as far as Valentina can tell, Tina has never valued the men in her own life?

The truth is, though, there is another reason she doesn't want to visit her mother. Deep down, she is afraid that, if she and her mother are alone, she might start needing her again and where would that leave Valentina? Her mother is bound to let her down. She always does.

She picks up her phone and, to her relief, she sees it is her friend Marco's number.

'Hello, darling! How are you?' Marco says, his voice a welcome breath of warmth.

'I'm OK.'

'You sound a little down,' Marco says. 'How was the trip to Capri?'

'Hard.' She swallows. Should she tell him how close she came to jumping off that cliff?

'I told you not to go,' Marco says gently.

'How's New York?' she asks, briskly changing the subject.

Despite her friends' efforts to make her talk about Theo, she has been adamant that she doesn't want to talk about what happened. Only Leonardo has seen her so exposed. She doesn't want to become a charity case, a drag, or someone that people avoid.

'Well, that's why I'm ringing you,' Marco says, sounding excited. 'How would you feel about doing a job here in New York?'

New York. Theo's home city. Her chest tightens at the thought.

'Valentina, are you still there?'

'Y-yes,' she stutters. 'What kind of job?'

'I have got a fabulous feature for *Harper's Bazaar*, and I asked them if I could bring in my own photographer . . . the one and only Valentina Rosselli. The art director was very excited about it. She said they would pay for your flight and give you a nice fat fee. What do you say, darling? You could come over for the shoot and then, if you like it, try to get more work and stay on in New York for a while.'

'Are you sure they want me and not my mother?'

'Of course they want you, Valentina! Sure, your mother's not a photographer any more, anyway. I showed them some of your recent work. The art director, Taylor, said – and I quote – "She is one of the best."'

Valentina can't help but feel a little buzz of pleasure at the flattery.

'So,' Marco continues to say, 'will you come? You can stay with me and Jake. We've plenty of room.'

She looks around her apartment in Milan, at the scattered photographs on the hall floor. She had always felt safe here, yet, since Theo died, her apartment has felt like a morgue. Indeed, she feels like a ghost living here. She has tried her best to move on. She even had a couple of drunken encounters on nights when she tried to escape her heartache in bed with a stranger. She never brings anyone back here but she has gone home with three or four different men she picked up at parties or clubs. She has tried to resurrect the old, free-spirited Valentina but always she has stopped, just at the crucial moment, and pulled away, horrified by how wrong it all feels. He tastes wrong; he smells wrong; he feels wrong. *He* is not Theo. Leaping from the bed, ignoring the astonishment of the man she was only a few minutes previously stripping for, Valentina flees. She would find herself breathless on the deserted streets of Milan at the cusp of dawn, marching in unison with the rising sun; but, as more light seeped into the sky, more life awakened – birdsong, cars starting up, people emerging on to the streets – her heart filled with dark, deathly solitude. She had become convinced that no one could ever replace Theo, for her home city was full of him. And yet maybe, just maybe, she could have a chance of new love if she left Milan.

'I'm not sure; when is the shoot?' she asks Marco now.

'Next Tuesday, so that gives you four days to get over here.' Marco pauses, sounding a little more subdued. 'Darling, it might help,' is all he says, and she knows what he means without him having to spell it out. If she stays in Milan right now, she might completely unravel. And yet, will New York remind her even more of Theo, Brooklyn born and bred? And what about his parents? Will she feel obligated to visit them?

'I don't know,' she says uncertainly.

'Come on,' Marco says. 'Where's my intrepid Valentina?'

And even though it is Marco saying this, it is just the sort of thing Theo would have said. She feels a surge of power course through her. She promised Theo she would keep taking photographs. She promised him she would live.

'OK,' she says. 'I'll come.'

$\mathcal{T}$ina

THE MODEL DOES NOT LOOK UNLIKE HER YOUNGER SELF. IN FACT she is a dead ringer for the silent movie star, Louise Brooks. However, the girl is not American like the actress, but German. Her name is Lottie and she is one of the stars of Tina's Berlin fashion shoot, inspired by the liberal and easy-living society of the Weimar Republic in Germany in the twenties. Pre-Hitler and the Nazis, the nineteen twenties in Germany had been a time of openness, or some would call it promiscuity, creativity and liberalism. Tina had felt it was the perfect backdrop to show-case some of Zandra Rhodes' new dresses, which hark back to that era.

It had been hard to find the right location. There were hardly any buildings left in Berlin that predated the war, such was the devastation of the Allied bombing. She could have shot it in a studio in Milan, re-created a Berlin cabaret interior, but she had wanted some authenticity. Tina likes to be in control of as much as possible on her fashion shoots. That is why she usually chooses the setting for the shoot, and works in conjunction with her own stylist, Octavia. It is Tina who makes the final selection on which models to use, and what they will be wearing. Lottie had appealed to her immediately; her features came from another time.

For her Berlin shoot, Tina has settled on two principal locations: one interior and one exterior. The first is a large coffee house, somewhat in the Viennese style. In this location she has dressed her two models, the dark-haired Lottie and a blond Marlene Deitrich lookalike called Freida, in outerwear. Lottie is wearing a long military-style coat with a peaked cap, and Freida is in a black and white pin-striped suit. For her second location she has used the backdrop of the façade of the Reichstag building, one of the last symbols of the grandeur of old Berlin, and against which rubs the interfering presence of the Wall, so that the girls, in their sequined and fluttery Zandra Rhodes dresses, look like ghosts from the luxurious twenties. They are all that is decadent in the West, harking back to the new liberalism in feminine fashion, contrasting with the brutal affront of the Wall and the Soviet regime.

Again the division of the city hits her. Yet the few West Germans that she has spoken to about the Berlin Wall seem reluctant to discuss it. There appears to be a resigned acceptance of its presence. Or maybe they are just careful not to let their true feelings show.

'Have you been to East Berlin?' she asks Freida.

The model shakes her head, looking at her with her cool, green eyes. 'Why would I want to go there?' she asks her, shivering. 'Those border guards just give me the creeps. They are always staring.'

Tina can see two of them now, looking down at them from a watchtower. And, sure enough, they are staring at them. Is it with longing, she wonders, for all the goodies of the West? Or is it with disdain? Her father had told her they shoot to kill anyone who tries to escape over the Wall. His friend Alfredo's story was testament to that. It is hard to believe that something like that could happen so close to where they are standing, in what appears to be a civilised and modern city.

She wishes she could have brought Mattia with her. Her son would have been fascinated by Berlin, watching the border guards and going down to Checkpoint Charlie to look at the American soldiers. When Mattia was very little, she used to bring him on the odd shoot, but for years, since he was a toddler, he has stayed home with Phil when she's been away. Now he is growing up so fast.

If Tina is honest with herself, she regrets her decision to send him to boarding school. She misses him. It was as if, as soon as her little boy put on the oversized school blazer (that he would grow into), he was no longer her boy any more. She sensed already that detachment. She had tried to hug him, tell him how smart he looked, and he had shrugged her off. It stung, and she wondered, not for the first time, why she and Phil hadn't had more children. It had been her choice. And yet she missed being the centre of a child's world.

She remembers summers in Sardinia, herself and Mattia, hand in hand, beachcombing, he with his little fishing net in one hand, and she with the bucket of shells. She and Mattia would spend hours on that beach, building castles and decorating them with his shells, paddling in the sea. They were blissful holidays. Later, when Mattia was sleeping, she and Phil would make love on top of the tousled bed by the open window, the scent of the sea spilling over them. She would still be in her bikini, and Phil would untie the little strings on either side, push his fingers through the curls of her pubic hair, peppered with sand from the beach, and softly, slowly, stroke her pussy so that she would almost be purring with indolent desire. Those days were so slow, and lazy, and filled with pleasure: she, Phil and Mattia in their

2CV, driving along the coast roads, stopping to eat fresh fish dinners, or simply to look at the sun set as it sank beneath the waves. It was in the days when they did not have much in material terms. She was still establishing herself as a fashion photographer and Phil had just taken up a new teaching position at the university. He hadn't started the journalistic work yet. But they were happier. She knows it.

Do all couples eventually grow bored with each other? she wonders. Does desire for each other wane no matter what, just as her friend Isabella claims? Why exactly *is* it that she has gone off sex? She feels as if she and Phil are always rushing, as if there is almost not enough time for sex, their lives are so filled with goals, and plans, and objectives. It is hard to slow it all down. But that's not the real reason. It is a combination of things. Getting older is part of it. She is becoming more conscious of her body, and about two years ago she put on some weight. She had relaxed, just for a few months, indulged in the odd pastry, the second glass of wine or slice of cheese, and before she knew it she had put on ten kilos. Phil claimed she looked great, said he loved her big tits, but she hated being that size. It made her feel awful, out of her body almost, and out of control. She went manic trying to lose it, cutting down on everything and fasting some days. The whole process made her irritable and tired, and not interested in sex. She lost the weight, in fact she is probably the thinnest now that she has ever been, but she never got back that feeling of relaxed satisfaction about her body, as if it might let her down again if she takes her eye off the ball. She is an intelligent woman and she knows it is stupid to be so obsessive about her weight, and yet she can't help it. She has always been this way. When her parents died, her obsession got dangerously out of control. She was so thin that her grandmother, Belle, brought her to the doctor, where she was told unequivocally that she must eat, otherwise she would end up dead like her mother and father.

The light is beginning to go, and Lottie is shivering in her flimsy Zandra Rhodes design. It is a beautiful dress, as finely stitched as a couture garment from the twenties. But it is not Tina's style; too floaty and feminine. Lottie comes down the steps of the Reichstag building, the security official watching her like a hawk, but *Vogue* has permission to shoot here. After all, their fashion shoot is promoting West Berlin. The temperature has dropped within the last half an hour and Lottie looks almost blue she is so cold. Tina offers her a jacket to put over the dress, and a cigarette.

'*Danke*,' Lottie says, hooking her with her big, silent-movie-star eyes. Really the girl belongs in the past.

She reaches over and strokes Tina's hair. 'We have the same hair,' she comments.

'Yes, we do,' Tina says, taken aback by the sudden intimacy. 'Have you heard of the old movie star, Louise Brooks?'

Lottie shakes her head, delicately puffing on her cigarette. She has the same quality as Louise Brooks: elegance, and yet there's something dangerously alluring about her languid expression – a nonchalance that Tina had always hoped she could aspire to.

'You look just like her. Actually, her most famous movies were with the German director, Pabst. I always cry when I see *Pandora's Box*.'

'I have never heard of these films,' Lottie says. 'I'm not that interested in movies.'

Tina is surprised by her response. It is rare to find a model who is not interested in the film industry. Most are aspiring actresses. 'What are you interested in then?' Tina asks her. The girl intrigues her; she is different from most of the other models she meets.

'Music,' Lottie says. 'I am studying the violin. I do this work –' she sweeps her hand rather dismissively behind her at Octavia who is packing up after the shoot – 'to pay the rent.'

Tina takes another drag on her cigarette. She feels a little dizzy. She has forgotten to eat again, yet she is not hungry.

'Do you like classical music?' Lottie is asking her.

'Of course, most,' Tina says. 'I love Debussy and Chopin, but I also like Dvorak and Shostakovich.'

Lottie's eyes light up and she looks the most animated that she has all day. Tina is tempted to grab her camera again and take some more pictures.

'You do? Well then you must come with me tomorrow to a concert! That is if you don't have to go back to Italy.'

'No, I'll still be in Berlin,' Tina says. 'I'm not going back until the day after.'

'Good,' Lottie says, finishing off her cigarette. 'I am going to bring you to a concert of Karel Slavik, the most exceptional cellist in the whole of Germany.'

'I don't think I've heard of him. What is he playing?'

'Shostakovich's Sonata for Cello in D minor; that's why you should come.'

Lottie starts to walk away from her, heading towards the costume tent set up by the River Spree. In the Berlin dusk she looks like a phantom girl from a forgotten age. She doesn't look like she belongs in the grey, Cold-War Berlin of now.

Tina follows her over to the tent. 'Where is the concert? What time?' she asks Lottie.

'Meet me at the border-crossing pavilion at Friedrichstrasse station, tomorrow morning at eleven.'

She grins at Tina's puzzled expression.

'The concert is in East Berlin,' she explains.

'You've been there?'

'But of course, all the time,' Lottie says. 'My cousin, Sabine, lives in East Berlin. And I also have some friends who live in Prenzlauer Berg.'

Tina feels a little thrill of excitement. She is going to go beyond the Wall. She is fascinated to find out what it is like on the other side of the city. Maybe it won't be that different at all: the same, only more dull and dour. Or maybe it will be completely different, like being in another continent. But she has to see. And there is another feeling as well, a deep sense of anticipation, as if this trip to East Berlin will turn out to be more than just a day trip to see a concert.

All that Tina has seen of the East so far has been deserted S- and U-Bahn stations. Last night she took a trip on the underground just to explore the city. At one point the underground train emerged from a dark tunnel into a deserted station. The train slowed to a crawl as it went through, tantalisingly slow, but it never stopped, of course. She had been confused for a moment. Why wasn't the train stopping? The station was barely lit, and roughly finished with concrete. Just as they were leaving the station, she glimpsed a lone guard with a gun. Of course, they were actually travelling through the East. These stations had once been so full of life, and now they are hidden from their residents. She wondered if the people in East Berlin even knew that they were down there, under their feet, moving below them. How can a city be cut in half like this? Could it have happened in Milan? The idea of it seems impossible.

So tomorrow she is going to East Berlin. Octavia tells her that there is nothing much to see and not to bother to go. 'The food is terrible, and there are no decent shops,' she says.

But Tina has never been that interested in food or shopping. She wants to see what the people are like. How could they stand it, she wonders, to be trapped in the East? It would be her idea of hell never to be free to go where she pleases or when. She turns to look at the concrete mass of the Berlin Wall. Would she have tried to get over it, if she had had the misfortune to be on the wrong side of the Wall when it was built? She likes to think she might have tried, but how can she say for sure?

Tina walks towards the Wall, standing back a distance, afraid that something might happen to her if she stands too close. She hears the River Spree's swirling current, and she thinks of all the desperate people who have tried to swim across to the West, so many of them drowned or shot in the water. This Wall is an affront to all that she stands for in her heart: the freedom to be true to yourself. She can't wait to see the other side of it tomorrow, and to meet Lottie's cousin and talk to her. She can take or leave the concert, but it will be nice, she supposes, to hear some music.

Apart from her excitement at crossing over to the East tomorrow, there is another feeling as well: a deep sense of anticipation as if what happens tomorrow will turn out to be more than just the contents of one day. Her skin is tingling, her throat feels dry and her eyes are itching. It is exactly the same physical sensation she gets when she feels a storm approaching.

$\mathcal{V}$alentina

SHE IS IN A FLOCK OF YELLOW TAXICABS FLYING FROM NEWARK into the city of New York. The island of Manhattan appears in front of her. It looks like it should be inside one of those plastic snow-dome ornaments, a perfectly mythic microcosm of a city with its miniature skyscrapers in the distance, their heights seemingly balanced in steps: up and down, up and down. She notices a new skyscraper, its summit sliced with shining silver angles.

'What building is that?' she asks the taxi driver.

'That's the One World Trade Center, to replace the World Trade Center,' he tells her. 'It's the tallest building in New York City, but it's not open yet. Next year.'

Now they are in Manhattan and the taxi is forced to slow down as they weave through early-evening traffic. She looks down at the crumpled piece of paper on her lap with Marco's address, or rather the address of his lover, Jake: 448 East Twentieth Street – Midtown, east side, according to her guidebook.

She is surprised by how old Manhattan looks once you are on the island itself. There are not many modern buildings on their route, mainly red brick, with black fire escapes facing out on to broad streets. It looks straight out of a movie set in the twenties. It is quieter too, not the surging crowds she had envisaged. Why had she thought New York was going to be all high tech and high speed? It was, after all, a city whose skyscrapers were first created in the twenties and thirties, the era of her idol, her great grandmother, Belle. Even so, she tells herself, she isn't actually downtown; Times Square is surely as glitzy as Piccadilly Circus in London. The taxi turns off First Avenue and they are driving into a looping road, cutting through a vast estate of apartment towers. It is the last place in the world she thought that Marco would be living.

'Darling, you're here!' Marco pulls her into a tight embrace. She breathes in the comforting scent of her old friend, realising how much she has missed him this last year.

'Yes, I'm here,' she says, retreating to pull her huge suitcase across the threshold.

'Jake isn't home right now, but he sends his love, and welcomes you to our apartment.'

'I never expected you to live in a place like this,' Valentina admits.

'I *know*,' Marco rolls his eyes. 'But, darling, it's free! Jake's grandmother used to live here and, bless her soul, when she died last year she left him the apartment.'

'That explains it,' Valentina gives him a teasing nudge. 'You were always a freeloader.'

Marco puts on a mock hurt face. 'Darling, how could you say such a thing? Besides, if I am a freeloader . . . so are you! And most welcome to stay as long as you like.'

Marco takes her through the apartment. There is a small kitchen with a huge gas cooker, a decent-sized living-cum-dining room, a bathroom and two large bedrooms. Most of the rooms are dominated by heavy, dark, oriental-style furniture. In her bedroom there is a huge bed, a dramatic wardrobe with carved doors, and a myriad of ornaments and sculptures, from frogs and china dolls to Venetian masks.

'Goodness! Does all this stuff belong to Jake?' She can't imagine clean-cut Jake being much of a hoarder.

'No, it's his gran's. He wants to get rid of it, but his father keeps saying he's going to come by first and go through it. His father lives in San Francisco, so I can't imagine when that might happen. Thus we have to live with all our creatures,' Marco says, patting the head of a large statue of a rhinoceros in the living room. 'You know, I've become quite fond of some of them now.'

Everything in the apartment smells a little musty. It's run-down, Valentina can see that – the big, old heating pipes, the cracked walls – but it is also a homely space.

'Do you want a drink? Something to eat?'

'I'd love a glass of water, actually. I'm really thirsty.'

Marco goes into the kitchen and opens the giant fridge, taking out a jug of filtered water and pouring her a glass, before helping himself. They chink glasses.

'Welcome to New York, Valentina,' Marco says.

His phone buzzes. She follows him back out into the sitting room as he scampers to pick it up, putting on a pair of Armani glasses to read his message. Valentina has never seen him in glasses before. She wonders if he really needs them or if it is just one of his fashion phases.

'Oh, darling!' he squeals as he reads the message, his cheeks flushing with excitement. 'How are you feeling?'

'Tired . . . Well, it is two in the morning in Italy.'

'Of course,' he soothes, 'but really it is better to keep going and not fall into bed . . .'

'I suppose.' She recognises that look on his face and is not surprised by his next statement.

'And the best way to stay awake is to go to a party!'

She shakes her head. 'No, I really don't feel like partying, Marco.'

He looks crestfallen. 'But we've been invited to the coolest party this month. You have to go because all the people you will be working with at *Harper's Bazaar* will be there.'

'I don't want to be around crowds right now. You go, Marco. Honestly, I am quite happy to stay in on my own.'

She sits down on the couch, looking out of the open window. The evening is surprisingly quiet. All she can hear is the rustle of the wind in the trees. She is so tired, all she wants is to lie down on this couch and listen to the sounds of the neighbourhood.

I will talk to Theo inside my head, she thinks.

But Marco is not put off so easily. He slides next to her on the couch and grabs her hand, squeezing it tight. 'You are *not* staying in on your own,' he says emphatically, 'all mopey and lonely. This is your first night in New York . . . You are coming out with me. This is a new beginning, Valentina. You have to start living again.'

'I am living,' she insists.

'Darling, you haven't had sex in months!'

'How do you know that?' she says defensively.

'It's obvious . . .'

'Well, what if I don't want to have sex with just anyone? Is that OK?'

'Not when you've turned into a moody bitch.' He sighs, lets go of her hand and gets up.

'I'm not moody, just sad, that's all,' she grumbles.

'Whatever, you've got to stop looking so miserable. Don't you know it ages you, V? What you need is to abandon yourself

48

to pointless passion, just for one night. You will feel so much better.'

'I don't want to meet someone else; I'm not ready.'

'I am not talking about love, baby; I am talking about sex. You can separate the two, can't you?'

Of course she can. Before Theo, that had been her thing – sex with no strings – but since his death, she is not sure. If she sleeps with another man, will it tarnish her memories of Theo? How could anyone else begin to compare?

Marco pulls her up from the chair. 'Come on, darling; no more protests. We are going to get on our glad rags and have a good time tonight. You are going to forget about everything. I promise you.'

Three hours later, Valentina is swaying to some reggae beats at the private party in some trendy club in Chelsea she has already forgotten the name of. She has no idea whose party it is. She feels woozy from the jet lag, and from the two glasses of red wine she has just drunk. She just wants to go to bed, but she can't. Marco and Jake have disappeared into the throng of dancers on the floor. Every now and again she catches sight of them boogieing, and waves to indicate she wants to go, but either they are ignoring her or they haven't noticed her signals. She should just go, but she has no key to Marco's apartment.

He had promised her that she would forget about everything but he couldn't have been more wrong. In fact, she can't stop thinking about Theo. New York was his home city. Had he ever been to this club? Stood right here, where she is standing? She wants to ask him. *Where did you live? Where did you hang out?* She wants him to show her. She closes her eyes for a second, the throbbing music permeating her skull. She has to stop thinking. She will go crazy if she can't get her mind to stop racing.

The music changes and Valentina is thrust violently into the past. A song she shared with Theo begins to seep into her: the dreamy ethereal Elysium sung in haunting tones by Lisa Gerard. She and Theo had made love to this music so many times, in slow measured rhythm, just like the waves of Gerard's song, aware of each tantalizing touch between them. Valentina opens her eyes, and yet she can see nothing of the present; only the past. As if in a trance, she pushes her way through the dancing crowd but they are swaying in a tangle to the music like swishing reeds in a thick hot breeze. They are trapping her. The music is too haunting, too resonant for her pain, and she feels panic sweeping through her.

'Are you OK?'

A man stands before her, blocking her way out. He is tall, with auburn hair and concerned brown eyes.

'Yes, I'm fine,' she says, trying to get past him.

'It's just you looked like you were going to faint. You were sort of falling over.'

'I was just on my way out, that's all,' she says, defensively. Thankfully the music has changed again and the spell she was under is broken.

There is an awkward pause. Valentina's first instinct is to walk away from this man, pull down the shutters yet again. She thinks about what Theo would want her to do. She knows that he loved her so much he wouldn't want her to be this sad and lonely.

'It's my first night in New York,' she offers up. 'I'm a little jet-lagged.'

'Where are you from?' he asks, looking at her with interest.

He is very tall, in fact, and she can't help feeling drawn to his powerful physique.

'Italy. Milan.'

'I thought you looked too stylish to be local.' He grins.

She notices that he has a nice mouth, plush lips and even teeth.

'I'm very tired,' she says. 'It's five in the morning back home.'

'Well, what you need is a pick-me-up cocktail.'

'I'm not so sure; I don't usually drink cocktails.'

'You're from Milan? And you don't enjoy a cocktail? I thought you guys practically invented cocktail hour? *Aperitivo*, right?'

He takes her by the elbow and steers her towards the bar.

'Now, cocktails are my thing,' he says. 'I used to work as a bartender and inventing cocktails is a hobby of mine. I try to customise them to who a person is, how they are feeling.'

'It sounds like an art.'

His hand on her elbow sends shivers down her arm, making her whole body come awake.

'It is,' he says emphatically. 'By the way, my name is Russell.'

'Valentina.'

'Beautiful name; beautiful woman,' he murmurs.

She feels a little flutter of panic in her chest. She can tell this man likes her. He is extremely good looking, almost too much so. She should be enjoying his attention, but she is afraid. She has never felt scared before of being chatted up, of what might happen later.

Just have fun, Valentina, she can hear Theo whispering to her, his voice inside her head.

'So, Valentina, tell me,' Russell asks her, 'how would you describe yourself? What do you do?'

51

'I'm a photographer. Freelance, mostly fashion, but I also do some of my own work.'

'OK, so you are creative, stylish, a little edgy . . .' He looks her up and down. She is wearing one of her mother's numbers from the sixties: a micro-minidress in red with an open back, and a chain belt around her hips. 'I can see you are quite an individual. Would I be right that you usually don't follow the crowd?'

She shrugs. 'Maybe.'

'OK,' Russell says. 'I think a base of gin with some limoncello, because that is Italian and it's zesty and spirited . . . like you.'

He winks at her and she finds herself blushing in response.

'Last question,' he says, as they elbow their way to the bar counter, stopping suddenly and turning to face her. 'Have you ever been in love?'

She flinches. His eyes are gleaming amber in the murky light of the club.

'That's a very personal question.'

'OK, so that is a yes, I take it . . .' Russell says softly. 'Sorry, I didn't mean to be intrusive; but, you see, a person who has been in love . . . well, they are a risk taker . . .' He looks down at her and smiles. 'So we need something that is a little bit of a risk to mix with the gin, and something that will create an interesting contrast with the limoncello. Yes, I think I know what we'll use. There is this black raspberry liqueur, called Chambard. I think it will mix perfectly,' he says, triumphantly.

'I don't like sweet drinks,' Valentina protests.

'Trust me,' Russell says.

She notices that people make way for him. He has a certain presence. Girls turn around and look at him for just a second longer than normal.

Russell asks the bartender to mix up the cocktail, giving him exact measures of each component. They watch as the guy expertly shakes it all together in his cocktail mixer, pouring it into two martini glasses on the bar-top for them. Russell hands her the cocktail with a flourish. 'I hereby present you with your very own bespoke cocktail – gin, limoncello and Chambard – which, of course, I shall name "The Valentina".'

She takes the stem of the cocktail glass in her hand, looking at it suspiciously. It sounds very strong. And yet it looks so fascinating. The raspberry liqueur has turned the drink the colour of blood. What will happen if she drinks this? On top of her jet lag, the wine, her loneliness . . . what might she do next? And, for one fleeting second, the weight of her loss lifts and she feels a surge of her old self, her free spirit and her abandon.

'This should wake you up,' Russell says, taking the other glass. 'Cheers . . . or, what do they say in Milan?'

'*Salute*!'

She takes a tentative sip. At first the cocktail tastes a little sweet, but then the limoncello hits her, its citrus flavours lifting the sweet raspberry. The gin is subtle enough not to dominate and yet she feels it warming her from her belly to her heart. It certainly seems to have had a restorative effect. She takes another sip, and another.

'So?' Russell asks his head cocked on one side.

'It's good,' she says. 'It's not too sweet.'

'Yeah, I reckoned, if you like red wine, you wouldn't want a sugary, girly cocktail. You want something richer, more layered: a woman's drink.'

'Who would have thought there was so much to making a cocktail?'

'As you said before, it is an art form.'

There is a crowd around the bar and Russell is standing even closer to her. She is aware of his long, lean frame, the deep blue of his shirt attracting her to him.

'So what do you do, apart from inventing cocktails?' Valentina asks, the effects of the drink making her feel more gregarious.

'I'm an artist, of sorts,' he says.

'All bartenders are artists, or actors, or writers, or musicians . . .' she says cheekily.

He lifts her chin with his finger and pins her with his liquid brown eyes. 'Oh, I'm the real deal, baby,' he says.

Valentina feels a shiver of energy from his touch. How long has it been since a man touched her in such an intimate way?

'It looks like you need a refill,' Russell says, looking down at her empty glass.

In the end, Marco and Jake leave the club before her. Surprisingly, Marco tries to persuade her to go with them, but now that she has woken up the last thing Valentina wants to do is go home, get into an empty bed and remember she is all alone.

'Are you sure, darling?' Marco had taken her aside. 'Maybe you should meet him another night. You just got here.'

'But, before we came out, you gave me a lecture on letting go of the past . . . moving on.'

Marco nods. 'Yes, but I know about this guy, Russell.' He licks his lips nervously.

'What is it? Is he some kind of pervert?'

'No, not at all; it's just he is a bit of a womaniser, darling.'

'Good; he sounds perfect for me. Isn't that just what you told me I needed right now? Sex with no strings?' She doesn't know what has come over her. It must be the cocktails. She feels bold and wanton for the first time since she lost Theo.

Marco pats her hand. 'OK, darling, but be careful, and call me anytime if you need me. Here's our address again, and a key. Be sure to take a cab home.'

Russell's apartment is just how she imagines Theo's might have been if he had stayed in New York and lived a life in America – a life without her in it; one that was not cut short. Russell lives in Chelsea and, although Valentina knows little about New York, she knows enough to realise that he must be incredibly wealthy or successful as an artist to live in such a place. His apartment is all exposed brick walls and dark wood flooring. There is one large living space, with an island kitchen. He has a French window opening out on to a small terrace; in the dark, it is hard to make out how big it is, but she can just about see the outline of some plants and what looks like an armchair, positioned with its back to the apartment. Past his terrace, she imagines she can see more plants, tiny trees and is that a glimmer of water in the distance?

'I look out at the High Line,' he tells her, taking her hand and leading her away from the window.

'What's the High Line?' she asks him.

'The High Line is old rail tracks that have been transformed into grassy walkways up in the sky. It is so cool. I'll take you there.'

Again she wonders how he can live in an apartment with such an amazing location. Did his grandmother die too and leave it to him? She wonders what his history is; has he been married? Is he brokenhearted like her?

Valentina sits down on the huge cream leather couch.

'Can I mix you up another Valentina?' Russell asks her, picking up a bottle of Chambard and showing it to her. 'I just happen to have the right ingredients right here.'

'OK, thanks.' She suddenly feels nervous. What the hell is she doing here? She should have gone home with Marco and Jake.

He slides on to the couch next to her and hands her a cocktail. She takes a big gulp to fortify herself and almost chokes.

'Sorry –' he gives her puppy eyes – 'I made it a little stronger than the ones in the club.'

He picks up her hand, as if to inspect it.

'Not married?' he asks.

She flinches. She had been so close to marriage with Theo. 'No, and you?'

He shakes his head, examining her other hand.

'Is that an engagement ring?' he asks her. 'Are you being a naughty girl, Valentina?'

She stiffens clenching her fist. 'No, it's over.'

'Really, you should give back the ring,' Russell says. 'It's not very—'

She kisses him to shut him up. The last thing she wants to do is explain about Theo.

Russell immediately pulls her into his arms. She doesn't want soft caresses or a slow, gentle build-up. Now his skin is upon hers, she feels fury rising inside her. At last she is angry. How dare Theo leave her? She clutches on to Russell's shirt, pulls it so that it rips open. He catches her rhythm and responds, unzipping her dress. She slides it down her body and slithers out of it. She opens her eyes, careful not to look into Russell's face. Instead, she focuses on his waist, how firm it is, a tiny crease of fat just above his belt line. She unfastens his belt and tugs at his jeans, pulling them down so that he is just in his shorts; he springs free as he slips out of them, too. She cradles his cock in her hands, fingering its silken length. She feels such a deep ache in the pit of her. She wants this man to fill her, like Theo used to. She wants him to take away her loss, even if it is for a few moments. She wiggles out of her G-string and lies back on the leather couch. What a cliché, she thinks, as she sees Russell's glowing face just for second; in the dim light of his flat, he does look quite like Theo, apart from his eyes. But he isn't Theo. He is some random man she has picked up at a party. Panic fills her. What is she doing? She has to stop this. And yet her body won't let her stop.

She reaches up and pulls him down towards her as he rips open the condom packet.

She is closing her eyes and lying back. She has never before been so passive, yet she doesn't care. She is going into her fantasy world. She opens her legs wide, wraps them around Russell's waist as he pushes into her. She raises her pelvis to meet him as they begin to move as one. Deeper, she is begging inside her head; take me deeper. The sensation of Russell's cock inside her, of their unity of movement, his deep penetration, begins to open up her fantasy world. Now she is free to meet her love.

She sees Theo. He is as he was in Sorrento. Again they are in the hotel bedroom, making love, naked and entwined. Theo's thick dark hair is curled around her fingers as she holds on to him. They are looking into each other's eyes. His winter-blue eyes are speaking to her. It is everything she needs to hear. Those few days before he disappeared, they had made love in a way she had never made love before. In fact, they did not make it, they were love. Their sex became them. They completed each other, as if they ran into each other, one complete, perfect ring of golden light. Time ceased to exist; it was as if it was elastic. They were flowing off the bed like water – a cool, delicious, fragrant stream. They were the core of life itself, together. She is kissing Theo now; she is receiving his love inside her; she urges him on. She wants to feel him come. She is so lost in her fantasy that she doesn't see or feel the moment approaching, yet all of a sudden she is convulsing, climaxing, and so is Theo. It is just perfect. They are complete.

'Valentina?'

A strange voice breaks through, like a light in the fog.

'Valentina, are you OK?'

She opens her eyes, and stares in shock at the strange man in front of her. What is his name again? Who is he? He doesn't look a bit like Theo. She clenches her eyes shut again and sighs.

'Hey, Valentina?'

She opens her eyes again. Russell – that's his name, of course – is sitting back on his heels at the end of the couch. He grins at her.

'That was amazing,' he says.

'Yes,' she agrees. She does feel better, as if she has opened a small door on her grief and let some of the anger, some of the pent-up frustrations and loneliness pour out.

She looks at Russell and thinks he is much younger than she had originally believed. Although toned, his body has a spoilt softness, too. He didn't have any scars – not like her Theo. She looks at his cock, meek now, limp inside the milky condom.

She staggers to her feet, naked still, but she doesn't care.

'Where's your bathroom?'

When she comes back into the living room, Russell is at the kitchen island, dressed in boxers and a white T-shirt, brewing coffee.

'I thought you might like a cup of coffee,' he says, twisting round to give her an appreciative glance.

'Thanks,' she says, walking over to the couch to retrieve her clothes.

His eyes trail her. 'I *love* your body,' he says, in a way that makes Valentina think there is something different about her naked body.

'It's just a regular woman's body,' she says dismissively, picking up her dress to quickly cover herself.

'Oh, no; not just any woman's body.'

'What do you mean?' she says, clutching her dress to her stomach and turning round to face him.

'I really love the fact you are so natural. I mean, nowadays especially, in my line of work the girls you meet are so worked out that they are all bones and hard angles. There is no softness any more. Their butts are so muscled and tight because of all the aerobics they do. Even the tits – they get them pumped up with all that silicone and they are not nice to touch.'

'Theo used to say that,' Valentina murmurs.

'Who is Theo?' Russell asks.

'My ex.'

'Well, he's right,' Russell continues, not at all bothered by the mention of her ex-boyfriend. 'I love the fact that you haven't tried to change your shape. Everything about you is natural and that doesn't mean you are some kind of hippy because you look so chic when you dress up, but underneath . . .'

'It's all soft and falling apart?' Valentina jokes weakly.

'Oh, no,' Russell says. 'You are all woman, with curves, your own tits and an incredible butt.'

'I haven't had my body analysed to such an extent for years,' Valentina says, slipping on her dress.

'I'm not offending you, am I?' he asks.

'No, not really. It's just my mother was obsessed with body image. Made my adolescence a nightmare. She was always trying to get me to diet.' She perches on a stool by the island in the kitchen.

'Your mother is a crazy woman,' Russell says, coming over with the coffee and giving her a cup. 'You are perfect the way you are made – that's my point.'

Valentina feels a rush of gratitude for Russell.

'Well,' he says, sitting on a stool opposite her and leaning over to give her a gentle kiss on the lips, 'that was really great.'

She blushes. She has never been into post-coital discussions.

'I had better go home,' she says awkwardly. 'Can you call me a cab?'

She waits for him to ask her to stay over, but he doesn't.

All the way back to Marco and Jake's apartment, she tries to convince herself that she wouldn't have stayed over even if Russell had asked her to. Yet she knows in her heart that this isn't true. For what she misses most of all is not sex, but intimacy. She misses being held all night long in her lover's arms.

$\mathscr{T}$ina

AT FIRST, TINA DOESN'T RECOGNISE HER, THE TRANSFORMATION is so complete. She looks like some kind of punk princess, all traces of Louise Brooks gone. Lottie has backcombed her jet-black hair into a spiky, dishevelled mess, her eyes are outlined with thick black kohl and her ears are adorned with a crescent of tiny silver studs. She is dressed in an outfit somewhere between Madonna and Siouxie of Siouxie and the Banshees: all black, with soft, feminine touches – lacy fingerless gloves that go halfway up her arm, skintight ripped jeans, black Doctor Marten boots and a sort of black corset worn on top of a ripped black top. Tina hates her outfit, especially the big, heavy boots. It makes the girl look trashy and goes against all her fashion rules. The way Lottie is dressed makes Tina feel a little middle aged in her favourite classics: little black dress, bolero jacket and high-heeled boots. Tina is conscious of the age gap. Her body might still be youthful, but what about her face? Is she gaunt from all the weight loss? Does she look her age, all thirty-five years of it? She hopes not.

'You're late,' the German girl accuses her.

Tina glances at her watch. It is just six minutes past eleven.

'Not really,' she says.

'My cousin is waiting for us at her apartment. She is on a

61

break from her work, so we have to get there on time. She really wants to meet you. She is in a photography club at her work.'

'What does she do?' Tina asks her.

'One of those state office jobs,' Lottie says, shrugging her shoulders. 'I think she is in the mail room. She never talks about it.'

They join the queue at the border-crossing pavilion at Friedrichstrasse station.

'We call this *Tränenpalast*, Palace of Tears,' Lotties tells her. 'It is the most used crossing because of the trains . . . A lot of sad goodbyes have been said here.'

Tina's heart rate begins to quicken as soon as she sees the border guards. Seeing men with guns always makes her feel quite sick. She believes she gets it from her father, who had a hatred of all guns and any kind of aggression.

It is so hard to believe that her parents have been dead nearly ten years. Some Sundays, she still catches herself waiting for her mother's weekly phone call – her checklist, as Tina used to tease her. Had she got in enough food for Phil and the baby? What was she planning to cook them? Had Mattia had his vaccinations? What was she reading to him in bed every night? She'd never asked Tina about her work. Her mother had been obsessed with Mattia. One of the worst things about their untimely deaths is that her parents never saw Mattia grow up. And Tina has lost the help and support of her mother, although she is certain Maria Rosselli would not approve of her gallivanting around rather than staying at home and looking after her family. She would be disappointed that Tina and Phil have never married. But Tina believes that the best way she can be a good mother is if she is a happy mother. And, to be happy, she needs her freedom, and her career. Phil understands that, of course. It has been a double-edged sword. In the early years, she had been a little jealous of the fact that Phil got to spend more time with Mattia. She remembers being terribly hurt one time when Mattia was about two and half. He had fallen off his scooter and cut his knee, but it wasn't her he ran to, but Phil. When she complained, she remembers Phil saying, 'You can't always have it your way, Tina.'

But there was something inside her that rebelled at that comment. Why couldn't she make her life exactly as she wanted it? Career woman and mother? Was it so impossible to be successful in both spheres?

They are at the front of the queue and, just before they go through, Lottie turns round. 'Do you have twenty-five Deutsche Marks? There is a compulsory exchange; I forgot to tell you.'

'Yes, I've money on me.'

'As soon as we go through, we can get our one-day visa. It lasts until two in the morning.'

The border guards take one look at Lottie in her punk outfit and turn her bag inside out, but they find nothing, and reluctantly let them through.

Friedrichstrasse station and the railway tracks are behind them now, and immediately Tina's surroundings feel different, as if she has stepped back in time to an older Berlin of the sixties and seventies. Practically all the cars are the same, most of them tinny-looking Trabants in white and blue. They walk down the street and Tina can't help but notice people looking at them, particularly at Lottie in her outfit. It is obvious they are from the West.

'How did your cousin end up on the other side of the wall?' Tina asks Lottie, as they walk down the street.

'Originally my family is from East Berlin, an area called Prenzlauer Berg. Later, I will take you to the street to show you the old house where my father and his brother grew up. All those houses were turned into flats; they are falling apart now. When they built the Wall, my father and my mother decided they didn't want to stay in East Germany, so they escaped.'

Lottie has dropped her voice to a whisper, although Tina can't imagine who might hear them talk.

'They got over the Wall?' Tina asks.

'Under,' Lottie says. 'They went through a tunnel. My mother was pregnant with me at the time. She was very frightened she would get stuck in the tunnel. My father had to push her through it.'

'My God, it sounds very dangerous.'

'It was. They were among the last ones through. Some of those behind them got caught.'

Lottie pauses, standing on the street; the concrete hulk of the Wall is behind them now. Tina hears the rattle of trains passing through Friedrichstrasse station on their way to the West – trains the East Berliners can hear but not see.

'My parents swear they will not return until East Berlin is free. They never thought the Wall would still be up after all these years. They haven't seen their families for years, apart from my grandparents. They can get passes to the West because they are pensioners. But my parents have never met my cousin.'

'And when did you first meet her?'

'As soon as I was eighteen, I wanted to cross into the East and see with my own eyes what it was all about. When I met Sabine, it was like meeting the sister that I had never known. We are the same age and we have nearly all the same tastes – although she doesn't dress like this, of course. That would attract too much attention.' Lottie glances at her watch. 'Come on; we don't want to miss her.'

She hurries Tina along the street. It is less colourful in the East, for sure. Instead of advertisements and billboards, Tina notices plain white signs with black text in German on them. They are Communist slogans, Lottie tells her, translating one for her: 'Continue to strengthen the socialist order, discipline and cleanliness.'

The idea of living in such a limited regime makes Tina feel sick. She has always hated any kind of rules. She used to drive the nuns at school crazy coming in late every day and not doing her homework on time, yet always scoring top grades in class tests.

'Of course, I would never want to live here,' Lottie tells Tina, 'but they do have a lot of fun, you know. Sabine went to way more discos when she was a teenager . . .' She pauses and gives Tina a cheeky grin. 'And she claims that they have better sex lives than we do.'

Tina raises her eyebrows. 'Really? I would have thought that a liberal approach to sex would have been frowned upon by the state; it doesn't seem to fit with Communist ideals.'

'I think it is officially frowned upon, but Sabine says that, because there are less capitalist pressures on them – like making money, or having a big fancy career – they have more time to flirt, fantasise, fall in love . . .'

'Yes, but I would imagine, if you stepped outside the box – let's say you're gay, for instance – then you wouldn't be tolerated so easily.'

'I suppose, but then gay people are persecuted all around the world, aren't they?' Lottie asks her. 'Sabine says that even things that you would think are negative about living here, such as food shortages or power cuts, can aid romance. For instance, she met her first boyfriend while standing in a food queue.'

'How touching!' Tina says, her tone caustic, for it certainly isn't her idea of romance.

'And you know what they say . . . Apparently men from East Germany have bigger cocks than those from the West!' Lottie giggles. It makes her look really young, despite all the make-up caked upon her face.

'Well, now, how would you know that?' Tina asks.

'That would be telling.' Lottie winks at her.

The apartment block where Lottie's cousin, Sabine, lives is pristine. No graffiti or vandalism, but perfectly uniform blocks of buildings. It looks like some kind of futuristic vision of utopia from the sixties – as if it is a movie set and no real people actually live here. Lottie enters the second block and, as they ride up in the lift, she explains that this is actually Sabine's boyfriend Rudolf's apartment. Apparently he has a very good job, although Lottie is vague about what that might be.

'It's all very clean,' Tina comments, thinking how sterile the whole place is. It gives her the creeps.

'This is one of the best places to live,' Lottie says, again dropping her voice to a whisper. 'He has a very important job,' she repeats, looking at Tina knowingly. 'He is a good socialist. He doesn't like Sabine seeing me; that's why I visit her in the day. He thinks I might taint her with capitalist dreams.'

Sabine is as beautiful as Lottie, although what she is wearing could not be more different. She is dressed in a plain white shirt and an A-line brown skirt.

'Oh, your clothes are horrible!' Lottie exclaims as soon as she sees her cousin.

'Work,' Sabine grimaces, showing them into the apartment.

Like the exterior of the building, it is pristine, although devoid of much character.

'This is Tina Rosselli,' Lottie says to Sabine, dumping her bag on the coffee table. 'She is a famous fashion photographer from Italy. She has come for the concert this evening.'

'You're from Italy?' Sabine turns to Tina, her eyes brimming with excitement. 'And a photographer?'

'Yes,' Tina says, taking her Kodak Duaflex II out of her bag, as if to prove it.

Sabine takes the camera in her hands as if it is a precious jewel and examines it. 'I wish I could get hold of a camera like this,' she sighs.

'It's very old,' Tina says. 'I've had it since I started out.'

Sabine hands back the camera. 'I'm sorry; I have to go back to work now,' she says, looking at her watch. 'I shouldn't be here at all. If Rudolf knew I was missing work, he'd be angry.'

'Come on, then,' Lottie says, taking her arm. 'I don't want to get you in trouble.'

'Where do you work?' Tina asks Sabine.

'I work in the mail room in the cultural state department. That's how I got to hear about the cellist, Karel Salvik.'

'Luckily for your government, he is a committed socialist, otherwise I am sure the West would have snatched him up by now,' Lottie says.

'Sush,' Sabine says, looking alarmed. 'Don't talk about such things . . . not in *here*.'

'Don't tell me Rudolf's apartment is monitored? Surely not someone like him?'

Sabine's cheeks flush. 'You never know,' she whispers.

* * *

67

'Do the Stasi really bug so many ordinary people in their homes?' Tina asks Lottie as they walk down the street, away from the complex of apartment blocks.

'Apparently, although Sabine is a little paranoid – but then her last boyfriend ended up in the Stasi prison . . .'

'My God; what did he do?'

'Apparently they suspected him of helping some neighbours of his to escape.'

'And was Sabine involved?'

'She told me she had no idea about his involvement. But she still got dragged in for interrogation. She won't talk about it. All she says is that someone must have informed on him.'

'Informers? Like in Stalinist Russia?'

'That's the biggest problem about living here, according to Sabine. You can't trust anyone completely. Someone might take a dislike to you and, next thing you know, they are telling the authorities all sorts of rubbish, just to get you into trouble.'

'God, it must make you very neurotic . . .'

Tina has never really thought about how lucky she is to live somewhere where she is never censored. How many of her fashion shoots would be considered antistate? It is not even a consideration to Tina whether she offends her government or not. She has always felt free in her work to express herself however she wants.

Tina made her debut as a photographer with *Vogue* in 1968, when she was just nineteen years old, with a feature inspired by Jane Fonda in the sexy sci-fi movie *Barbarella*. She dressed her models in Paco Rabanne: skintight vinyl catsuits, silver and white PVC, and aluminium panels. It got her attention – and another feature. This time she dressed her models in see-through

Yves Saints Laurent chiffon trimmed with ostrich plumage. Before she knew it, she was the name on everyone's lips: Tina Rosselli, talented new photographer, as beautiful as the models she shoots. She wore the clothes she shot – designers gave her pieces; they said she looked as good as the models, and she did. She had the body for the clothes of that era, and the hair: a Louise Brooks black bob. Tina was invited to every fashion show, exhibition opening and cool party, not only in Milan but in the south of France, Paris, Rome, London and New York. She was the girl every man wanted to date and yet she stayed single. She was, in fact, a shy Catholic girl at heart. After all, she had been *so* young. It had been a vibrant and heady time for her with all the new freedom and creativity that she had in her life. She moved out of home (much to the consternation of her mother, who wanted her to go to college) and shared a flat with her best friend, Isabella, a fashion journalist. They worked hard, and partied even harder. She had met Phil through Isabella, who had invited him to Milan to participate in a journalism conference at the university. When Isabella had unexpectedly had to dash off to Verona to collect another delegate, she had asked Tina if she could pick up the English academic in her Triumph and bring him to his hotel in town.

Phil had not made a particularly good first impression. She thought he was fusty and old in his English tweeds, and smoking a pipe, for God's sake! Who, under the age of thirty, smoked a pipe, unless it was weed?

She had driven her usual way – too fast and weaving in and out of traffic. By the time she had pulled up at the Hotel Principe Savoia, Phil was green in the face. Yet he called her up that very evening and asked her out for dinner. To this day, she really doesn't know why. Was there something in the way she drove that turned him on? Or did he just call her because she was the only girl he knew in Milan? She had nearly turned him down – he had seemed very boring – but she had been curious about Englishmen, and also, to be honest, wanted to practise – or show off – her English.

Something had happened to her as soon as they sat down to eat. For one thing, she had forgotten about the meal itself. She was eating without thinking about it or measuring what she was spooning into her mouth, because she was hanging on every word Phil said. He knew so much about art, politics, film, culture, history. He reminded her of her father, Guido. There was something about his geeky academic style, his glasses and formal suit, that turned her on. She wanted to dishevel him, mess up his neat hair, throw off his glasses and rip the starched shirt off him.

She had managed to hold back for three more dates before she made her interest clear. But once that barrier was down, once they kissed for the first time, there was no going back. Behind the bedroom door, Doctor Phil Rembrandt was on fire. Inexperienced as she was, she knew this was something special. No man had ever given her an orgasm before, and not just any kind of orgasm . . . This was a deep inner climax in a part of her where she felt she had never been touched before. Phil turned on the tap, and she was hooked. She couldn't get enough of him. It's hard to believe that nowadays she will stay up late just to make sure he is asleep before she goes to bed, so she can avoid having sex with him.

Tina had only been twenty when she and Phil began their affair. It was the end of the sixties and the beginning of a new decade. They were brimming with love for each other, with hope, with self-belief. The world truly had felt like it was their oyster. What a contrast to where she is now, standing in a street in the repressed East Berlin of 1984. She had been so naïve when she met Phil. She had only slept with one other man: her old college tutor – a mistake and an embarrassing cliché. Phil was still older than her, but not that much older. Just six years. He had plenty of experience. Right from the beginning, he'd spoken as if they were going to be together forever, and yet it didn't make her feel trapped – quite the reverse. When she became pregnant with Mattia, quite by accident, Phil didn't suggest even for a moment that she get rid of the baby. He was so into her being pregnant. In fact, some of the best sex they ever had was when she was pregnant. She would never have believed that she and Phil could lose their spark.

They have been together fifteen years, for all of her twenties. She has only ever slept with two men in her whole life, and she is thirty-five. She doesn't want to break up with Phil – of course not, she adores him – but she can't help feeling a little resentful. He had nearly all of his twenties to play the field and experience lots of different partners, but she met him at twenty. What are you supposed to do if you meet the love of your life so young? Never ever sleep with anyone else? Isn't that what lots of women do? Because women are different from men – they don't need such variety. Yet she knows this is rubbish – the sort of demeaning thing her mother might say, and which she had spent her teenage years rejecting. So, is the reason she doesn't want to sleep with Phil the simple fact that she is bored? Does she need some diversity in her sex life? Yet she doesn't want to cheat. So what are her options? Up to now, her only option seemed to be to stick her head in the sand and shut down, but she knows in her heart she is repressing a part of herself – the part her grandmother, Belle, called their 'Louise Brooks spirit', as if that signature haircut was a statement in itself:

I am free as a blackbird. I will give you my body, heart and soul, but don't ever cage me.

Lottie is ahead of her in the street; she turns around.

'You look a million miles away,' she says. 'Come on, I'll take you to Alexanderplatz to see the Fernsehturm – the TV Tower – and the world-time clock. They might not be able to go to all those places, but at least East Germans know what time it is in other countries.'

'Can I take pictures?'

'Sure you can. You're a Westerner. They want you take pictures and show the rest of the world what a success the DDR is.' She snorts derisively.

After they have visited the tourist spots, stopping off for a cup of inferior coffee to spend some of their hard currency, Lottie offers to show Tina her family's old house in an area called Prenzlauer Berg.

They walk in a northerly direction into a district that could not be a more stark contrast to Alexanderplatz, the showpiece of the German Democratic Republic, or the uniform perfection of the apartment blocks where Sabine lives. Most of the houses in Prenzlauer Berg are decrepit. She can see that they were once beautiful, grand old buildings, but now their façades are falling apart, literally, as plaster crumbles off brickwork. It is hard to imagine that they are inhabited. Yet she sees people going in and out of buildings, and the atmosphere is different from anywhere else she has been so far.

'A lot of artists live here in Prenzlauer Berg,' Lottie tells her.

They stop at a flower shop, filled with carnations and gerbera daisies, and Lottie buys a bunch of the daisies, 'For a sick friend.'

They turn down a street that, to Tina's eyes, looks little better than it must have looked after the Allied bombing of Berlin. She can't believe that people actually live here.

Lottie comes to a stop outside a particularly derelict-looking building. 'Here it is,' she says, pointing up at the house. 'This is my family's ancestral home. A bit run-down.' She turns and gives Tina a sad look. 'One day, we'll get this place back. And I'll do it up.' She sighs. 'Shall we go inside and meet my friends?'

'You know the people who live here now?'

'Yes, it's a funny thing. I came here one day a few months ago, just to look at the house, and I met the people who live in it. We just clicked.' Lottie opens the front door, which almost falls off its hinges. 'It's in a real state,' she says. 'Don't be shocked.'

They climb over some assorted debris at the entrance of the doorway, old broken bottles and tin cans. Tina follows Lottie down a dank corridor and up a rickety staircase that looks like it might fall apart any day. At the top, Lottie bangs on a battered old door, the paint peeling off it. There is a terrible smell of damp and decaying earth. Tina wonders how anyone could live here.

The door is opened by a young man with short bleached-blond hair, wearing a string vest and skintight, bleached jeans with braces. He has old army boots on.

'Lottie!' his face lights up as he gives her a big hug.

'Hi, Hermann,' Lottie says in English. Tina notices that the girl is blushing. 'I brought Simone some flowers. How is she?'

'Oh, that is so kind; they will cheer her up. She is OK . . . yes . . . Well, you will see for yourself.'

They follow him into a dark entrance hall as Lottie says, 'And this is a friend, Tina; she is Italian, and a photographer . . .'

Hermann looks at her with interest. 'Are you a journalist?' he asks.

'No, fashion photography. Lottie was a model on my shoot.'

Hermann pokes Lottie in the tummy. 'Ah! You, a model, of all people – buying into all that superficial Western lifestyle,' he says, but he is grinning and Tina can see that he is joking.

Lottie swipes his hand away. 'Well,' she says coyly, 'if you think the West so superficial, maybe you don't want your present?'

'I didn't say that,' says Hermann.

Lottie zips open her bag and rummages around inside the lining.

'Ta da!' she says, whipping out a cassette tape.

'You are a wonder, my darling Lottie,' Hermann says, giving her such a kiss on the cheek that Lottie is blushing.

'It's a post-punk tape of some sounds I thought you might like. I wrote the bands on the cover.'

Hermann grabs the cassette off her and opens it up. 'Oh, this is great,' he enthuses. 'All my favourites: The Fall, Joy Division, Lene Lovich, My Bloody Valentine, Suicide, Nick Cave, Violent Femmes, Nina Hagen – you know she's from round here, don't you? Lucky bitch got out in the seventies—'

'Yeah, I've seen her in concert,' Lottie says. 'She's brilliant.'

'Thanks, Lottie. I really appreciate this.' He hugs her again, and Tina sees the shine in Lottie's eyes when she looks at Hermann.

'I brought chocolate and cigarettes as well,' she says, tipping more out of her bag on to a rickety table propped up against the wall.

'That there is a magic sack. I don't know how you managed to hide all this stuff at the border,' he says. 'Come on in and say hi to Simone, give her the flowers.'

He pushes open a door and they walk into what must be the main living room. The state of it is shocking. As with the hallway, there is no carpet and no rugs – just bare wooden boards. There's a sofa with broken legs, covered with a dingy-looking throw, a few wooden chairs and a table. The windows are cracked and dirty, with raggy old curtains hanging from them. Outside the sun has come out, illuminating the room and showing up how wretched it is. On the walls are huge canvases splashed with violent abstractions of colour. A very skinny punk girl is sitting at the table mixing up some paint. She has black spiky hair and huge eyes rimmed with black kohl, like Egyptian eyes. She is so pale her skin is almost translucent. She is wearing a ragged T-shirt, a chain looped several times around her neck, and threadbare jeans, covered in paint.

'Hello, Lottie,' the girl says, not looking up from her palette.

'Hi, Simone; how are you?'

'OK.' The girl shrugs, looking up at her. 'Bit of a cold.'

As if to confirm this fact, she starts to cough. But it is no harmless cough. It turns into a disturbing hack that goes on for several minutes – the kind of cough that needs medical attention.

The others seem not to want to make a fuss. In fact, Hermann lights up one of the cigarettes Lottie brought and goes to look out of the window at the street below.

'This is Tina.' Lottie introduces her to Simone. 'She is a photographer.'

'Do you want to take a photograph of me?' Simone asks her, looking at her with such a doleful expression it almost breaks Tina's heart.

'Sure,' she says. 'Are these your paintings?'

'Yeah,' Simone says. 'I'm trying to paint . . . Not sure, though, if I'm any good.'

'They're great,' Lottie encourages her. 'Don't stop painting.'

'I might have to,' Simone says.

Tina has her camera out. She realises that she really wants to record these two young people here in their run-down apartment in Prenzlauer Berg. It seems to her that to be a punk in East Berlin is a very different thing from being a punk in the West. Here it is a defiant rebuke to the socialist state. These kids are expressing that they do not want their future mapped out for them from cradle to grave. They are true rebels. In the West there is little left to rebel against. Punks nowadays are more followers of a trend than anything else.

They say their goodbyes and walk away. Lottie is quiet the whole length of the street. Tina wonders what the deal is with her and Hermann and Simone. Are the other two a couple? Hermann and Lottie had kissed on the lips when she left, and she could see how much the girl was into him, but she wasn't sure about Hermann. He seemed fond of Lottie, but distant as well. She takes out her cigarettes and offers Lottie one.

'What is your dream, Lottie?' Tina asks the young woman as she lights her cigarette.

The girl shakes her head, exhales slowly. For a second, her face is obscured by cigarette smoke and Tina can only see her lips.

'I don't know. Not to be a model, anyway,' Lottie replies as the wisps of smoke softly melt away.

'But it's good money . . . You could travel the world.'

'Yes, but I would rather do something creative. Like you.'

'Photography is just a job to me.'

'I don't mean the fashion photography in the studios; no, I don't really like that world. But I like the fact you take it outside of the studios and use different places. The photos you took of me, Hermann and Simone – I really liked that. It was expressive. I like to express . . . For me, it would be to play music.'

'Would you like to be a famous musician?' Tina asks her.

Lottie shakes her head. 'Not really.'

Her answer surprises Tina. She has always had this desire to be recognised, appreciated and known for what she does. She has always worked towards that, and she thought it would satisfy her but, if she is honest, she still feels like she is looking for something more in life, despite the fact she has the job of her dreams, a good man and a child. She lives in Milan, one of the coolest cities in the world, in a huge apartment that once belonged to her parents, right in the heart of the city. She can afford to do whatever or go wherever she wants. Her lifestyle could not be in more stark contrast to Lottie's cousin, Sabine – trapped in an office job, living in a tower block in East Berlin, with her whole life plotted out in grey uniformity – or to those subversive punks in Prenzlauer Berg, fighting the system.

Lottie drops her cigarette on the street and puts it out with her boot. 'I think what I want the most is to find my soul mate,' she suddenly announces.

Tina couldn't be more surprised by her answer. 'Do you believe in that?'

'Yes, I believe I do.' Lottie gives her a wonky grin; she looks so young beneath all the punky make-up. Tina has an urge to get out a tissue and wipe it all off – reveal the pretty face beneath; the Louise Brooks face.

'You know, you shouldn't cake yourself with all that stuff,' she tells her. 'It hides who you are.'

'It *expresses* who I am,' Lottie says, defiantly.

'I suppose,' Tina demurs.

'Come on, we should go to the bar,' Lottie says, glancing at her watch and picking up her pace. 'Sabine is meeting us for a vodka before the concert.'

As they cross the street, Tina notices a parked car pulling out behind them, yet it doesn't speed up and overtake them. Instead, it just trails behind them the whole way back towards Mitte. Tina has a distinct feeling that they are being followed, although she has no idea why.

$\mathcal{V}$alentina

VALENTINA HAS BEEN WALKING ALL MORNING, CUTTING ACROSS Manhattan from east to west. Now she is back in Chelsea, wandering the streets of boutiques, cafés and galleries, and wondering where exactly Russell lives in this maze.

She shouldn't be wasting her time like this. Tomorrow she is starting the shoot with Marco. Right now, she should be with her friend, checking out the location, the clothes and the models, yet she has asked him for the morning to herself. Sleeping with Russell has opened something up inside her and she is not sure if it is good or bad. All it makes her feel is restless and unusually unfocused when it comes to her work. She keeps hoping Russell might call her and yet she never gave him her number. Why exactly does she want him to ring her, anyway? Marco had told her he was a womaniser. Why would she want to see someone like that? And yet her one night of passion with Russell had taken away some of her heartache over Theo. She had begun to feel more alive again.

She has to keep walking, one foot in front of the other. She has to walk her confusion out. On Twenty-Eighth Street, she enters the Subway, deciding to visit the World Trade Memorial. However, as she sits on the train, examining her Subway map of New York City, her gaze can't help wandering to the coloured

79

lines linking Manhattan to Brooklyn. On an impulse, at Chambers Street, she gets off and changes lines. She knows exactly where she is going now. Maybe her intention had been to go this way all along. She has examined her map of New York enough times to know which Subway station is closest to Orange Street in Brooklyn Heights, and it is at Clark Street that she stands up and exits the train, as if on automatic pilot.

It is a bright spring day. Valentina tries to take strength from the sun's light, yet, for May, it is chilly. She shivers in her light jacket, wrapping her chiffon scarf around her neck twice. She is dreading this meeting. Yet she should go through with it. It is the least she can do for Theo. When they lived together in Milan, he wanted so much for her to meet his parents. She had always resisted, afraid of the commitment it would imply. In retrospect, her behaviour now seems pointless.

She walks down Orange Street; it is eerily quiet. There is row upon row of old redbrick houses with elegant stoops, the street itself lined with trees. She had not expected this gentrification. When Theo told her he grew up in a place called Orange Street in New York, she had imagined a street that was like the colour: jazzy, juicy, full of life and bustle. But this road is deserted.

Valentina stands at the bottom of the stoop, looking up at the front door and the large windows in the front of the house. She should have written or called beforehand. Probably nobody is in, anyway. But it is enough, she convinces herself, just to look at the house Theo grew up in. She half closes her eyes and, in the soft focus of her vision, she imagines she sees Theo as a boy, running down those stoop steps with his pet dog. It was a Scotch terrier, that's what he had told her, and he'd called him Fergus. Theo the boy is a tall and gangly kid, with the wild locks of a true thespian's child. She wants to scoop him up and swing him around. She wants to whisper in his ear: *I am the woman of your future.*

Valentina closes her eyes and takes a deep, ragged sigh. She should leave now. This was a bad idea.

'Hi there! Can I help you?'

She opens her eyes. A woman stands at the top of the stoop, peering down at her. She is tall, with hair as white as snow. Her eyes tell Valentina who she is: they are the same as Theo's – that piercing arctic blue.

'Are you looking for someone?' Theo's mother says.

'No . . . I . . .' Valentina begins to back off. She has no words to introduce herself.

'Valentina?' Theo's mother asks, uncertainly. 'Is it you? Have you come to see us at last?'

Shock courses through Valentina so that she is paralysed where she stands. How does Mrs Steen know it's her?

The other woman comes tumbling down the steps. 'It is you, isn't it?' she says, picking up Valentina's cold hands and warming them with her own. Without pausing to hear her answer, Theo's mother bustles her up the stairs and into the house.

Valentina sits in the room with the big window, looking out at Orange Street, where she just stood. She shakes herself. How did she get inside Theo's childhood home and how does this woman, who is putting a mug of coffee down in front of her, know who she is?

'My husband is out at the university at the moment, but I have called him. He is coming home as soon as he can,' Mrs Steen says.

'How did you know it was me?' Valentina asks in a small voice.

'Why, Theo sent us so many pictures of you. Of course I recognised you. You are very distinctive, my dear.'

Valentina stares down at her coffee mug. Her cheeks are burning. Of course, Theo's parents had seen those erotic pictures of her that Theo had bought at her exhibition in London and they had sent on to her in Milan. And he had sent them other pictures too. She remembers Theo offering to show her photographs of his parents, his childhood and college years in New York, but she had always refused. She had not wanted him knowing about her own mother and so she had denied him sharing his parents with her. Her behaviour seems utterly idiotic to her now.

'I am staying in Manhattan,' she begins, 'and I thought I should call by . . . but, I'm sorry, I should have rung or written . . .'

'It is such luck I was in!' Mrs Steen exclaims. 'Imagine if I had missed you! I have wanted to meet you since Theo first told us about you.'

'When was that?' Valentina asks, with curiosity. For so long she had resisted telling her mother about Theo.

'I will never forget it, Valentina. It was when you first met, before he moved in with you,' Mrs Steen tells her. 'We used to speak on the phone every week, talk about the paintings he was trying to recover for my father-in-law in Holland . . . Well, these were usually pretty serious conversations, but this one time he was different. I swear –' she pauses, smiling nostalgically – 'he sounded almost like a kid, you know, who's won some kind of prize. "I found her, Mom," he told me. "I found the one."'

82

Valentina stares at Mrs Steen in astonishment, her coffee untouched. She had no idea that Theo had had this conversation with his mother. She had no idea that he believed in *The One*.

'Oh, he was crazy about you, and I was so happy for him. It was terrible when you broke up; such a relief when you found each other again . . .' Mrs Steen's voice trails off. Valentina can see her eyes welling with tears. What has she done, turning up in this poor woman's house out of the blue, stirring up memories of her dead son?

She stands up suddenly, nearly sending her coffee mug to the floor. 'I am so sorry. I really shouldn't just have called in like this. I just wanted to pay my respects.'

'Please, sit down, dear.'

Valentina hesitates, then reluctantly sits down again.

'Is that why you came?' Mrs Steen asks her. 'To share your sympathies? It's a little late, dear . . . The memorial was over eight months ago.'

'No,' she admits. 'I wanted to meet you – see where Theo grew up.'

Inside her head, the words throb: I miss him I miss him I miss him.

Mrs Steen shakes her head. 'I told him to stop. I never liked those jobs he did for his grandfather. I warned my husband. It wasn't safe, was it?'

Valentina clutches her hands. 'He saved me,' she whispers. 'He died because of me.'

Mrs Steen's face creases with concern. 'Oh, no, my dear, you mustn't think that.'

She leans over and pats Valentina's hand. Neither of them speaks for a moment. They look at each other, both of them thinking it: this could be my family now. If only. We could be

83

here with Theo, and his laughter – his very life – would fill the cavity between us. Valentina can feel her chest is tight, her breathing shallow. She feels as if she is being buried under the weight of her and Mrs Steen's grief. She has to get out of here. She cannot bear to meet Theo's father as well. She looks into Mrs Steen's clear blue eyes, just like her son's eyes.

'I have to go,' she says, stirring. 'I'll come back.' She says this, although she is not sure she will.

'Are you sure? Can you not wait for Walter?'

Valentina stands up and shakes her head. 'I'm sorry; I have a work appointment; I have to go.'

'Theo told me you were strong. I can see what he saw in you,' Mrs Steen remarks, standing up as well.

'It's hard,' Valentina squeezes out.

'Yes,' Mrs Steen agrees, 'but there is a way through. You'll find it.'

'Have you found it?' Valentina asks the other woman, but instead of answering her Mrs Steen touches Valentina's engagement ring with her hand.

'You're still wearing it,' she says in a quiet voice.

'Yes,' Valentina replies, not knowing how to explain herself.

'My father gave that ring to my mother,' Mrs Steen says. 'And I gave it to Theo to give to you.'

Valentina colours with shame. She begins to pull the ring off her finger. 'I'm sorry; I should have sent it back to you . . .'

But Mrs Steen places her hand on Valentina's. 'Please keep it. I know how much you meant to Theo. We have no other children so . . . we want you to have it.'

'I couldn't . . . I . . .' Valentina feels humbled by Mrs Steen's generosity. So this is the lady from whom Theo got his big heart. 'I can't keep it,' Valentina says, shakily.

'Please, Valentina,' Mrs Steen says. 'It makes me glad to see it on your finger. It reminds me of how happy you made my son.'

'Thank you,' Valentina whispers, finally giving in.

'You will come back, won't you?' Mrs Steen asks, her eyes pleading.

'Yes,' Valentina says, but still she is not sure.

She hurries back down Orange Street, her body screaming with longing for Theo, her heart cracking inside her and her mind so full of memories that she feels as if she is blind. She has lost her bearings, bumping into people, tripping on the pavement. She cannot bear the thought of being on the Subway in a crowd, so she walks across Brooklyn Bridge. The chill of the spring day is even more intense on the bridge, and a sharp wind cuts into her, but she ploughs on, putting as much distance as possible between her and Orange Street. Halfway across, she stops. She could end it now, like she nearly did in Capri – just climb up on to the railings of the bridge and dive off – like a bird into the blue sky. But, instead, she would be going into the grey water, just like Theo did. Could she meet him again, down there?

She clutches her shaking hands, twirls the ring around and around her finger, remembering the moment he slipped it on. She has not taken it off since. Each time she looks at the sapphire, she remembers the blue of Theo's eyes, and his love for her. At last, she realises something: she is lucky. Yes, she has lost Theo for ever, but all this suffering now is worth it for the love they shared, even if it was short lived. Some people never find that kind of love their whole lives. Now she has to let go of Theo and say goodbye. She has to move on and hope that she might find a similar love again one day.

* * *

By midday, Valentina is sitting between Marco and Taylor, the art director, at a lunchtime meeting at *Harper's Bazaar*, surrounded by their creative team. She is no longer the girl she was a couple of hours ago, shaking with emotion in the front room of Mr and Mrs Steen's Brooklyn home. Now she is her professional self, all poise, with her dark glasses perched on top of her head as she clicks through images of the location for the shoot on her laptop.

'So,' Taylor is telling her, 'we are using the interior of the Neue Galerie, on the corner of East Eighty-Sixth Street and Fifth Avenue, by the park.'

'It is an old Rockefeller mansion that houses early-twentieth-century art from Germany and Austria,' Marco adds. 'In particular, Klimt.'

'So there is the connection,' Taylor says. 'We are doing a feature on prints – not pretty, floral prints, but bold, decorative prints, with lots of gold detailing . . . I think that Klimt's semi-abstract paintings go really well with the clothes.'

Valentina looks at the images of the interior and it appeals instantly. A huge sweeping staircase, a gallery with marble cornices featuring the work of the Austrian artist, Gustav Klimt, a grand landing with white pillars, black and white tiled floors throughout, and a dark-wood-panelled café in the old Viennese style.

'It looks good,' she says. 'I'll take a look this afternoon, before it closes.'

'That's not necessary,' says Taylor, taking a sushi roll with her chopsticks from one of the containers on the table and waving it around as she speaks. 'I've worked out where I want all the shots taken.'

Valentina turns to Marco, giving him a questioning look. Her friend knows full well that Valentina, as the photographer, likes to make those decisions.

Marco licks his lips nervously. Taylor is quite an intimidating figure: a tall, muscular woman, with very short black hair and a severe face.

'I think I explained to you that Valentina likes to have creative input on the shoot,' Marco says to Taylor.

'That's not how I work,' Taylor says, shortly.

'Yes, but it is how I work,' Valentina says, softly, looking the art director in the eye. 'And, if you want the best of what I can do, you have to give me the flexibility to have more control on the shots that I am taking for you.'

Taylor gives her a cold stare and for a moment Valentina thinks she is going to order her out of the room and on to the first plane back to Milan.

'All right,' Taylor says, gruffly, much to Valentina's surprise. 'I guess you may as well go down to Neue Galerie and take a look. We are shooting tomorrow, when the gallery is closed to the public.'

'I'll take you down in a minute to see the clothes that we've picked for the shoot,' Marco says. 'I've been working closely with Lori, who is doing the make-up. We are going for quite a luxurious look.'

'Heavy eye make-up,' Lori tells her. 'Either smoky or with bands of gold, and nude lips, mostly.'

'OK,' Valentina says. 'And who are the models?'

'We're using two girls and one guy. We want to feature some of the men's clothes in the collection: rich brocade patterns and decorative cravats.' Taylor slides over three portfolio shots.

Valentina picks up the images. One girl is from Russia, and

one from the Ukraine; they both have cliff-edge cheekbones, full lips and almond-shaped eyes. One has long, straight dark hair, and the other has short blond hair. Valentina can see that the two girls will contrast well. She picks up the last photograph and almost gasps out loud in shock, for the smiling face staring up at her is none other than her one-night stand, Russell. He told her he was an artist, a bartender . . . He had never mentioned male modelling.

She hands the picture to Marco.

'Oh dear,' she hears him whisper.

'Is there a problem with my selection of models now?' Taylor asks her, obviously having noticed Valentina's reaction.

'No . . . Well . . .' She wonders if she can convince this woman to drop Russell but, before she has a chance to continue speaking, Taylor talks over her.

'These models are booked and I insist that we use them so, whatever your issue is, you will have to deal with it.' She gets up, looking at her watch. 'I have another appointment now. See you tomorrow.'

Valentina grits her teeth. She is not sure how she is going to be able to work with Taylor as her art director. Most of the art directors she has worked with before have been much softer, and given her way more creative freedom. She can't imagine Taylor being so open. She seems much too pedantic.

Marco brings her down in the lift to look at the clothes he has picked for the feature.

'Did you know that Russell was a model on this shoot?' she asks Marco.

'Of course not,' he says. 'But I did know he was a male model. He has a reputation . . . Valentina, I did warn you . . .' He doesn't finish his sentence.

'I thought I was never going to have to see him again,' Valentina moans.

'Don't worry, darling; he has probably forgotten who you are, anyway,' Marco says, patting her back.

'Thanks a lot,' she says, sarcastically. 'That really makes me feel a whole lot better!'

The Neue Galerie is three blocks up from the Metropolitan Museum of Art, and housed in a building that looks as if it has been transported from nineteenth-century Paris. As soon as she steps through the doors, Valentina feels as if she is back in Europe – not Italy, but Vienna. The lobby is dominated by a sweeping marble staircase, the kind you trail down in a sumptuous ball-gown to be greeted by your dashing escort for the evening. She can already envisage a shot of the dark-haired model in one of the long, gold-brocade gowns, standing on the staircase. The gallery exhibits purely German and Austrian art of the early twentieth century and describes itself as aiming to bring a sense of perspective back to Germanic culture of the early twentieth century.

Ever since she first saw Gustav Klimt's art, Valentina has loved it. In the context of the modern world, it doesn't seem that unique – ornate, semi-abstract decorative panels of vibrant colour and gold leaf with a figure emerging, a perfectly realistic rendition of the subject's face, and parts of her body – yet Valentina likes to combine the real world and fantasy in her own photographic shoots. There is something so accessible about Klimt's abstraction – maybe it's all the jewel-like colours, the glittering gold; you just want to reach out and touch a picture. Valentina finds it exciting to think about the world that Klimt was a part of in Austria at the turn of the twentieth century – this coming of a new age, this intoxicating free spirit.

Klimt loved women. That much is clear. Nearly all of his paintings take them as his subject. But he never objectifies them. Klimt's women are real. They are not aloof and untouchable, and nor are they demeaned or judged. Valentina believes that, through his art, Klimt portrayed the goddess within. She is using her friend Leonardo's terminology and the thought makes her smile to herself. He is always saying that every woman has a goddess inside her. She teases him over it, and yet she finds his awe, his reverence for women, attractive. So many men are misogynistic, deep down. They would never express this overtly, in fact they would believe that they respect women as much as men, but there is always this implication that somehow women are the foe.

Theo brought Valentina's goddess out of her, and made her shine.

She sighs, trying to focus her attention on the paintings. Is it not possible for her to pass one hour without torturing herself over Theo?

Her eyes rest on a colourful composition, a magical kaleidoscope of orange, red, green, yellow, blue . . . The subject of the painting is a dancer. The dancer turns away from the viewer, almost shy, her dark hair pulled off her face, her skin pale and delicate, and her chest bare, her breasts a delicate proposition. It reminds Valentina of her discovery that her grandmother, Maria Rosselli, had been a dancer, despite the fact no one in the family ever mentioned it before. As she gets older, Valentina is learning that every family, no matter whose, has secrets – often huge ones. There is the issue, of course, of her father. The fact that Phil Rembrandt, the man she believed was her father all these years, is not. It is over a year since she found this out and she has been left in limbo with this vague information about who her father is: a Czech cellist called Karel. She doesn't even know his second name and has no idea where he is now, or even whether he is dead or alive. She had meant to confront her mother but, what with losing Theo, she couldn't face any more emotional complications in her life and so she has left it. She has survived this long without a father, why should she need one now?

Valentina turns her back on the dancer painting and crosses the room. The large ornamental portrait of Adele Bloch-Bauer I dominates the gallery, but it is in fact a smaller picture, of a woman wearing a black feather hat, that she is drawn to. Unusually for Klimt, this painting is much more muted: greys, white, browns and black dominate his palette. The woman leans forward, resting her chin on her hand, looking away from the viewer, a cigarette clamped between her lips. Valentina can't tell if she is angry or sad. Her eyes are narrowed, her expression guarded. What dominates the whole composition is the black feather hat: a monstrous black cloud upon her head. The plume, of course, reminds her of the black feather that tickled and tortured her naked body in Leonardo's Dark Room, the room at his club where clients can act out their deepest desires. It was the very same day that Theo revealed himself to be the architect of her sexual fantasies – that it had been his idea all along to involve Leonardo and his fetish club. Theo understood her free spirit. He knew what she wanted, needed, what would satisfy her. He never had to ask.

She glides away from the *Black Feather Hat* painting and enters a second room. This is a smaller chamber with soft lighting, the walls covered in drawings by Schiele, Kubin and Klimt. It is Klimt's erotic drawings that she is immediately drawn to.

She reads the titles: *Seated Woman with Spread Thighs*, *Seated Woman in an Armchair*, *Woman Reclining on a Sofa Wearing Fur*.

Not only are these drawings extremely explicit, but Klimt has captured the most intimate and secret moments of his subjects. She can detect the close relationship between artist and model for, in several of them, his model is touching herself. Her eyes closed, she could be lost in her own ecstasy, yet, at the same time, her legs are spread, all revealed – she is offering herself. These drawings are far more voluptuous than the angular nudity of Schiele's drawings. They are elegantly erotic. She wonders if she could get across this same quality in a photograph.

Turning away from these sensuous pictures, Valentina's attention is drawn to another drawing by Klimt. It is a portrait of a child, head and shoulders, leaning over a wall and looking right at her. It could be a boy or girl, for the child has a bob of messy dark hair and fine features. She suspects it is a boy because of the date on the drawing: 1885, an early work by Klimt, and no girl would have such short hair at that time. The child is asking a question with his eyes; curious, yet at the same time wary. He reminds her of someone; the feminine features: fine nose and delicate mouth, the pertinent stare. As she walks back down the staircase of the gallery, she realises who it is the child looks like: it is herself.

The café in the Neue Galerie is decorated in the style of a Viennese coffee house: dark-wood-panelled walls, marble-topped tables and waiters dressed in black with long white aprons. She chooses a corner table by the window, sunlight streaming on to the seats and warming the soft fabric cover of yellow roses. This spot will be perfect, she thinks, for a shot of one of the girls sitting with Russell and looking out of the window at Central

Park. The yellow roses against the red background will contrast perfectly with two outfits that Marco is styling in shades of blue and gold brocade print. She wonders what story she will tell with the couple in her shot. Will they be distant? Arguing? Or will it be a loving shot, the two of them looking out the window at spring in full flight, the park bursting with joyful shades of green. She wonders how she will be when she sees Russell again. She determines to be as professional as possible.

Valentina orders a cup of black Viennese coffee and a slice of *Sabarskytorte*, an intense chocolate and rum cake that she is unable to finish. She checks her messages in her phone. There is just one from Antonella inviting her to Moscow and telling her yet again that her and her lover Mikhail's fetish club is a roaring success. No other messages; not a word from Russell. She reminds herself that he doesn't have her number, but still it wouldn't be hard for him to get hold of it since he knows Marco and all his friends. Does he know that she is taking the photographs tomorrow? Part of her is embarrassed, shy almost, at the thought of running into him again – it was, after all, supposed to be a one-night stand – and yet there is a part of her that is a little glad. There was something about Russell that she found so enticing, despite the fact Marco keeps warning her that he is not to be trusted.

She takes another scoop of her cake and immediately regrets it. She is full to the brim with sweet, heavy cake. Her phone rings; she answers it immediately, expecting it to be Marco about some detail to do with the shoot. However, to her annoyance, it turns out to be her mother.

'Hello, darling,' Tina drawls. 'How are you settling into New York?'

She feels a prick of guilt that she hasn't rung her mother since she got here, but then, why should she? Her mother has never taken a great interest in her life, until recently.

'Fine; good.'

'Have you done the shoot for *Harper's Bazaar* yet?'

'No,' she says, tightly, waiting for her mother's interrogation on where they are shooting and what kind of feature they are doing. Yet, to her surprise, her mother doesn't seem to be that interested.

'I did a shoot with *Harper's* in New York once,' is all her mother says.

'When was that?' she asks her.

'Oh, years ago now,' her mother says. 'So, are you feeling any better?'

'I'm fine.'

'I mean, have you met anyone nice yet?'

'I really don't want to have this sort of conversation with you right now, Mama.'

'Sure,' her mother says, sounding completely chilled out and unembarrassed, as usual. 'Well, when are you coming to visit me?' she asks Valentina.

'I don't know . . . I mean, you don't exactly live nearby. Wouldn't I have to take a plane to Santa Fe?'

'You'd fly to Albuquerque and I can pick you up from there. I'll buy your ticket. You really should come, Valentina. It's so beautiful here. The landscape is awesome.'

'I'm not really into landscapes; besides, I'm very busy.'

Her mother sighs, knowing full well she is being brushed off. 'Well, have you gone to see Mattia and Debbie and their kids, out wherever they live?'

'It's Woodstock, Mama, and no, I haven't; I told you, I am busy.'

'Don't you think you should go and see your brother, since he is so nearby?'

'It's not that nearby . . . It's not my fault he moved out of New York City just before I came here.'

'What's wrong, Valentina?' her mother asks. 'Why are you so mad at Mattia?'

'I am not mad at him.'

But there is no fooling her mother, and it is true Valentina is still angry with her brother. Despite the age gap, they have always been very close. She had felt that Mattia always looked out for her. He had met Theo and really liked him, told her he thought he was the one. And yet, ever since Valentina found out that they have different fathers, and that Mattia *knew* this for years and never told her . . . well, she feels funny about him. They are only half-brother and sister, but that is not really the issue; it's more the fact that he hid this huge truth from her, all of her life.

'Go and see them, Valentina,' her mother says. 'It will do you good to be with children.'

'I can't believe you, of all people, are saying that.'

'Why? I love children,' her mother says, mollified.

Valentina snorts with derision. A woman, sitting at the table in front of her, turns around and gives her a cold stare.

'I better get off the phone, Mama; I'm in a café. I'll call you later.'

'No, you won't,' her mother says, and, for a second, Valentina could swear that she sounds hurt. 'Well, have fun in New York; don't do anything I wouldn't,' she says, sounding upbeat again.

'That doesn't leave too much, anyway,' Valentina mumbles.

There is silence on the end of the line and Valentina isn't sure that her mother has gone or not.

'Mama, are you still there?'

Sigh. 'Valentina, I hope one day you can forgive me; I hope you'll understand that I am not the woman you think I am.'

Click.

Valentina is furious. Always, her mother has to have the last word, and what does she mean, anyway? Forgive her for what? For being a shit mother? Or for something more specific? Like interfering in her first love affair with Francesco? Or abandoning her in Milan when she was nineteen? Or disappearing for most of her childhood on glamorous photoshoots? Forcing her to go on diets most of her teenage years? Or what about introducing Valentina to her new boyfriends every couple of months, so that Valentina gave up hoping which one might become her new father figure? And talking of fathers, isn't the worst thing her mother ever did is to let her believe that her ex, Phil Rembrandt, was her real father? But her mother doesn't know Valentina met Phil in London last year, talked to him and found out the truth. Her mother still thinks she can deceive her for ever.

She drains the dregs of her coffee and, forgetting the fact she is full, stuffs another piece of cake into her mouth. At that moment, she looks up from her table and across the café. From where she is sitting, she has a view of part of the marble staircase as it winds down into the gallery lobby. A figure catches her eye as he descends the staircase. There is something vaguely familiar about him: the height, the long, straight nose and sharp chin. Who is it he looks like? The man is wearing a baseball cap over mid-brown hair, blue jeans, a blue and white striped sweater and a pair of trainers. The clothes look like they don't belong on him.

And then something quite shocking happens. As if he can feel her gaze upon him, the man turns and looks towards her. He doesn't see her, she is surely too far away and tucked in the corner, and yet she feels he is searching for her. The blood drains from her face and her mouth is dry from sudden fear. Are her eyes deceiving her? For the man looking at her is the image of Glen. He may have brown hair rather than blond (but couldn't he have easily dyed it?) and be dressed in the kind of clothes Glen would never wear but, looking at that face, its hard, cruel lines, she is sure it must be him. How could she ever forget the man who had looked into her eyes and pulled her from the boat into the sea in the blue grotto? She still has nightmares about his octopus limbs dragging her down to a death at the bottom of the sea. If it hadn't been for Theo saving her, Glen would have killed her.

Her initial instinct is to hide. She pushes herself further into the corner of her seat, praying he doesn't see her. What if he comes into the café? It is far too small for him not to notice her. And then something occurs to her: Glen is dead. Just like Theo is dead. It was the two of them who disappeared in the blue grotto that afternoon, and the police had told her that they must have drowned while fighting each other in the sea. Yet here he is in the flesh . . . or is it really him? She has to be certain.

She jumps up from her table, but in her haste she knocks her plate to the floor and it breaks with a dramatic clatter.

'Oh, I'm sorry . . . I . . .' She tries to pick up the plate, while at the same time grabbing her bag and flinging a bunch of dollars on to the table. 'So sorry,' she says, running past the mystified waiter.

By the time she is in the lobby, he is no longer there. She runs out of the entrance of the gallery and looks up and down the street. She cannot see him. She runs towards Madison Avenue, weaving through the crowds, praying that he walked in this direction, but he has simply vanished. She has to see, make sure, look in this man's face and know for certain that he is not the man who killed her love. She swings around and runs back the other way, past the gallery again, but the man in the baseball cap and jeans has disappeared. She tries to persuade herself that it just could not be Glen. It is impossible, for how could he have survived the blue grotto and not Theo? The last time she had seen Glen, he was already half dead, gasping in the bottom of that boat, his eyes red with sea water. He couldn't have had the strength to kill Theo . . . and yet this man really had looked like Glen. Her mind is racing, her heart pounding. What should she do?

She feels devastated. It is all she can do not to drop on the ground and bang her fists against the pavement in frustration. She shakes herself angrily. That man just could *not* have been Glen. She is obsessing. She has to stop thinking about that day in the blue grotto. She has to move on. It's what Theo would have wanted.

She is fighting back the tears as she slowly crosses the road and walks into Central Park. She stops by a pink-blossomed tree that she saw from the café window and pushes her fingers into its pink petals, growing like velvet moss along its branches. It is a comforting sensation. As she clings on to that tree and what it represents – spring, rebirth, new beginnings – she makes a decision.

She is going to lock away the old Valentina for ever. She has to shut up her love for Theo and throw away the key. Because, if she can't do that, she has no chance at all.

$\mathcal{T}$ina

'OH, NO,' LOTTIE MUTTERS AS SHE AND TINA WALK INTO THE bar. 'Super creep is with her.'

'Super creep?' Tina whispers, feeling slightly self-conscious as nearly everyone in the bar turns to stare at them.

'Sabine's creepy boyfriend, Rudolf,' Lottie says. 'He doesn't like me.'

It seems to Tina that the feeling is mutual, for, as soon as they sit down at the table, Lottie clams up like a surly teenager, while Rudolf looks her punk rigout up and down in disgust.

'Are you going to a fancy-dress party, Lottie?' he asks her.

He is pleasant enough to Tina, though. He has the kind of fresh-faced complexion that makes him look as if he grew up on a farm, as if being in the big city is not his natural habitat. He shakes Tina's hand; his grip is warm and firm.

'Pleased to meet you,' he says, in very formal English. 'Sabine has told me about your visit here to our city. I hope you took some good pictures.'

'Don't worry, Rudolf; she went to all the official sights. Her camera is jammed with images of the Fernsehturm,' Lottie says, sarcastically.

Rudolf smiles, as if a little embarrassed by Lottie's rudeness.

'So, did you enjoy your day in East Berlin?' Sabine interjects, a little nervously. She is obviously not comfortable with the tension between her boyfriend and cousin.

'Very much, thank you. It has been fascinating.'

'Well, it's not over yet. Wait until you see Karel Slavik play the cello.'

'He is one of the best musicians in all of Germany,' Rudolf says, enthusiastically. 'Tonight he is playing Shostakovich's Sonata for Cello and Piano, but he also composes some of what he plays. All of Slavik's music is an expression of what we represent in our country: true brotherhood.'

Tina can feel Lottie stiffen beside her. She hopes that she will say nothing rude or sarcastic. The comment is open for derision, and yet she can see how nervous Sabine is. This young man looks the picture of jovial goodliness, but who knows what he is really like. The standard of his apartment says something about the spheres he must move in.

The same thought must have occurred to Lottie, for she manages to pull herself together. 'I can't wait to see him play. He is a hero of mine,' she says, passionately.

They knock back their vodkas, and then the three women follow Rudolf out of the bar and down the road to the concert hall. There is a steady stream of people piling through the doors and, once they are seated, Tina sees that the place is packed. She is sitting between Lottie and Sabine. Of course, everyone is looking at Lottie's outfit. Tina can't help wishing she was more subtle.

The lights go down, the curtain is raised and the audience claps. She sees the piano first and an earnest young man with blond hair sitting at it, his fingers hovering over the keys, ready to play. Beside him on the stage, his cello reclining between his legs, bow poised, is what she can only describe as the most stunning young man she has ever seen. The image of him almost knocks the breath out of her. He has an incredible face: Slavic cheekbones, thick, dark eyebrows and eyes a rich, deep shade of brown. There is a hush as the audience settles, and then he begins to play.

She wasn't expecting this sensation: to be transported by this young man's playing. She has heard Shostakovich's Sonata for Cello and Piano in D minor a hundred times. It is one of her favourite pieces of music. And yet this cellist takes her to a place with the music where she has never been. He lifts her heart out of her chest, and she sees herself flying after it, through the thick air of the stuffy theatre. This young man's playing makes her want to abandon herself. She watches his hands as he pauses to pluck some of the strings. She imagines those strong fingers touching her and, for the first time in months, she feels a little aroused. He slides his fingers up and down the neck of his cello, and then slams the bow back on to the instrument's main body, his hands and fingers working with incredible speed. Shostakovich's sonata is faster and more furious than she has ever heard it before. She imagines him playing her in the same way, sliding his hands up and down her body. She licks her lips nervously, immediately feeling guilty, as if someone could read her thoughts, but everyone is rapt by the music: Lottie leaning forward on her seat, gripping her hands, and Sabine and Rudolf holding hands. She notices that Rudolf has one of his hands slipped under Sabine's skirt and, when she looks up again, she can see the pink blush on Sabine's cheeks. Tina looks away quickly in embarrassment, but the thought of Rudolf stroking Sabine's pussy in time to the sonata has made her feel quite breathless. When was the last time she had an orgasm? She can't remember. Sometimes she thinks about giving herself one, but the whole process makes her feel depressed afterwards. Besides, she is too busy.

Too busy for pleasure? A voice inside her head asks her. *That is like being too busy to live.*

Sabine's shoulder and arm is pressed against hers, and Tina imagines she can feel that sexual energy, the excitement of Rudolf stimulating her, passing through her body, into Tina's. She shifts away, squirms in her seat, tries to cool her thoughts down and focus on the music, but the way that young man plays his cello – stroking it, striking it, plucking it, brushing it – all seems so sexual. She can feel a deep pulse beginning to throb between her legs, as if her pussy is opening out, begging for some attention. She squeezes her fists up into balls, slams her legs together and takes a deep breath as she struggles to contain herself. At the same time, she hears a tiny gasp from Sabine, and the vibration of Rudolf's hand movements against her chair stops. Tina takes a deep breath, gathers herself up and tries to paste a poised expression on her face, but her heart is running wild and, as the cellist takes them to the climax of the sonata, she can feel herself pulse, hanging on the edge, until finally he brings them down again. It feels as though it is over too fast. The young man stands to rapturous applause and bows once, before striding off stage with his cello.

Lottie turns to her with shining eyes. 'Wasn't that just amazing?' she exclaims.

They are just about to stand up and leave when a man squeezes past her in their row and stops to speak to Rudolf in German. The girls collect up their bags and wait obediently for the men to finish speaking.

'That was the Cultural Minister,' Rudolf says, turning to her and Lottie after the man has moved away to talk to another group in the audience. 'He has invited us to an after-concert party.'

'Should we go?' asks Lottie.

'Of course we should go,' Rudolf says. 'It would be a huge insult not to. Besides,' he says, almost kindly, his earlier hostility towards Lottie forgotten, 'you will get a chance to meet Karel Slavik. It's a party in his honour.'

Sabine is clasping her hands together. 'This is *so* exciting. I've never been to a party like this before.'

Half an hour later, Tina is wondering why anyone would be excited to be at such a boring party. It is being held in a dingy back room of the concert hall, with strip fluorescent lighting, Formica tables and plastic chairs. There is music, of sorts: a band playing staid and boring waltzes. It is all very sedate. She wonders if all Western pop music is banned in the DDR. Do they allow jazz? There is no sign of the star of the night, Karel Slavik. Most of the guests are overfed middle-aged men, who must be something important in the party, and young women, hanging on to their arms, who are obviously not their wives. Rudolf and Sabine are dancing to a dull tune, waltzing around the room. Lottie is stuffing her face with some of the food on offer – some kind of sausage, sliced up, and hard-looking bread that she tells Tina is disgusting. Tina wonders why she keeps eating it. The young model has already drunk quite a bit of vodka and Tina is beginning to think that they should be leaving. She is worried that, among all these important Communists (how on earth did she and Lottie end up in here anyway?), Lottie might get too outspoken, and get Sabine into trouble.

She weaves through the dancers to tell Sabine and Rudolf that she needs to go. She is not sure how to get to the border crossing from here, and would need their help. There is a stir in the room behind her, a flutter of clapping, one man even cheers. She turns around to see the cellist, Karel Slavik, standing in front of her, making his bows to the rest of the room. She has never seen a classical musician greeted like a rock star before. He bows again and, on his way up, he catches her eye. Up close, this young man is a sight to behold. It doesn't matter that his clothes are cheap and out of date. You could put him in a sackcloth and he would look divine. What attracts her the most are his eyebrows: thick, dark and almost sculpted – so expressive. His eyes are cat-like, with long lashes, and his skin is dark, as well. He is tall, with strong, lean legs and powerful arms, and an easy, languid way of moving. He makes every other man in the room seem uptight. She looks at him in appreciation, as if she is looking at a beautiful object she is not allowed to touch. He must be at least ten years younger than she.

Yet, to her surprise, this young man is looking back at her.

'Hello,' he says, in German. 'Who are you?'

'I'm sorry; I don't speak German,' she says, in English.

He looks surprised that she has spoken to him in a foreign tongue. 'Are you English?' he asks.

'No, I'm Italian. My name is Tina Rosselli. I am here with friends,' she indicates Sabine and Rudolf, who are still dancing. 'They brought me to your concert . . . It was incredible . . . I . . .'

He puts his hand on her arm and she feels as if he has sent an electric current through her body. 'Please, I would rather we didn't talk about my concert tonight.'

'Sure,' she says, not knowing what else to say now.

He takes a step towards her. 'Would you like to dance?'

'Oh!' She can feel herself blushing. 'I . . . Are you sure?'

'Of course,' he smiles at her. He offers her his hand and she takes it.

Tina cannot remember the last time she danced like this to an old-fashioned waltz. Now she is almost glad the music is so slow and boring. At first she is nervous she will step on his toes or stumble, but he is a consummate dancer and leads her around the floor so that she is practically flying off her toes. They spin around and around, and she cannot take her eyes off his. He is still smiling at her; gone is the serious and intense musician from the concert; now he is just a boy dancing with a girl. But she is not a girl. She is a woman who is considerably older than him. Why would he want to dance with her when there are plenty of pretty young women in the room, just begging for some of his attention? And yet Karel Slavik seems to have eyes only for her. Maybe it is because she is a stranger, a Westerner and this is a novelty for him. Rudolf had said he was a devout socialist – an advocate of the DDR – so why would someone like her, who represented the decadent West, be of interest to him?

Someone bangs a spoon against a glass for silence and the music stops. For a long moment, they stand, his arms still around her, looking at each other, before she steps back to see what is happening. The Minister of Culture, now red faced from vodka, is standing in the middle of the room, obviously about to make a speech. As he speaks, Tina realises that she and Karel are still holding hands. In fact, he is more than holding her hand: he is stroking each of her fingers with one of his. It is such a tiny, subtle movement and yet its impact reverberates throughout her body.

'We are here tonight to celebrate the talents of our young musician, Karel Slavik,' the Culture Minister begins to say. 'Tonight, my friend, your rendition of our great Soviet composer Dmitri Shostakovich's Cello Sonata in D minor was superb.'

Everyone claps at this point, and Karel bows again, yet still holding her hand in his. Does everyone else notice? she wonders. She spies Lottie sitting on a chair at the back of the room, her head flopping from side to side. She has to get her back to West Berlin; she is obviously twisted drunk. She can't see Sabine or Rudolf anywhere now, and wonders where they disappeared to.

'I am taking this opportunity to say how excited I myself and my colleagues – and, indeed, the party – are that Karel has completed his new work, entitled *Wir-Gefühl*, We-feeling, which is an expression of the spirit of our people: our fortitude, our industriousness and our socialist ethic. I am even more delighted to announce that we have given Karel a permit to tour this work internationally, to show the rest of the world one of the jewels of Eastern German culture and the talent of our German Democratic Republic.'

The Minister makes a toast and everyone joins in, clapping at the same time. Tina pulls her hand out of Karel's to applaud him. She senses his discomfort, that behind the easy smile he is not enjoying all this attention. He is different from me, she thinks. He wants to practise his craft without all the accolades. Yet he cannot avoid being centre stage. His breathtaking beauty makes him hard to miss.

A surge of people pushes around Karel to congratulate him and he and Tina are cut off from each other. Just as well, she thinks. She should grab Lottie and get out of here. She looks at her watch. It's ten minutes past midnight. They still have time – nearly two hours – before their passes expire.

'Come on, Lottie,' she says taking the young model by the arm and helping her stand. Lottie trips over the undone laces of her Doctor Marten boots. Damn those stupid boots, Tina thinks, as she tries to guide the girl out of the room without too much attention being drawn to them. She scans the crowd for Sabine and Rudolf, but she still can't see them.

'I need the toilet,' Lottie mumbles.

'OK,' Tina says. 'I am sure there must be one out here.'

She brings them through the door of the room and out into a cold corridor with pockmarked linoleum flooring. They wobble down it and, sure enough, there is a little wooden closet. Tina shoves Lottie into the closet.

'OK, I'll be back in a minute,' she says. 'I am just going to find Sabine and Rudolf so they can show us how to get back to the border crossing.'

'I know the way,' Lottie slurs from inside the toilet.

'Yes, well, I think tonight you might need some help.'

Tina can hear voices. She continues down the corridor and peeks around a door into an empty room. There is no light on, so it takes a moment for her eyesight to adjust in the darkness. What she sees makes her mouth drop open in shock. Sabine is bent over a table, her eyes squeezed shut, as Rudolf fucks her from behind. It doesn't look very loving. Rudolf is speaking to her in harsh German; Tina doesn't know what he is saying, but Sabine is repeating, '*Ja, Ja, Ja.*' She is saying, 'Yes, yes, yes.'

Tina pulls the door shut and steps back out into the corridor, her heart pounding. Rudolf's wholesomeness is completely deceptive, not that Sabine seems to mind.

She makes her way back to the toilet. She supposes she had better leave them to it, and she and Lottie will try to get a taxi back to the border crossing.

As she is waiting outside the closet for Lottie to finish up, the door of the party room opens and she is face to face with Karel again. She can feel a blush creeping up her neck to her cheeks, especially when she thinks about what Sabine and Rudolf are doing just down the corridor.

'Hello,' he says. 'I was looking for you. What are you doing?'

'I'm waiting for my friend,' she says. 'We have to go.'

'Go where?' he asks.

'We've got day passes. We have to go back to West Berlin.'

He frowns when she says this. 'So you were only here for the day?' he asks. 'You're not coming back?'

She shakes her head. 'No,' she says, feeling ridiculously sad about it, for some reason. 'I live in Milan. I am returning to Italy tomorrow.'

'Ah,' he says. 'You know, I dream about Italy.'

'Have you been there?'

He puts his head on one side, smiling at her as if she is a fool. 'Of course not,' he says. 'I was born in Czechoslovakia, and my family moved to East Berlin when I was three. I have travelled a little within the Eastern bloc – for instance, I went back to Prague and to visit Budapest – but I have never been to the West.'

'But you will,' Tina says, 'when you go on your international tour?'

'I can't wait . . .' he whispers, taking a step closer to her, so that his warm breath sends shivers up her spine. 'It is Italy I want to see the most,' Karel continues. 'I want to see if Florence is as exquisite in real life as it is in my dreams.'

'It is,' Tina tells him.

'How do you know what Florence looks like in my dreams?' He grins.

'Because Tuscany is more beautiful than you can imagine,' she tells him.

She hears the toilet flush, and Lottie struggling with the door.

'Are you OK?' she calls to her.

'A little stuck; just coming.'

The door bangs open and Lottie falls out, practically into Karel's arms. She gives a small scream. 'Oh my God! It's you!' She starts gabbling to him in German, but Karel stops her.

'I think we should speak English, so that Tina understands us,' he says.

'Oh, sure, yes. You were amazing,' Lottie gushes.

'Thank you,' Karel demurs, although Tina senses he is embarrassed by the praise.

She decides she should rescue him from Lottie, who is now clinging on to his shirt, asking for his autograph. 'Well, we had better be going,' she says. 'It was nice meeting you.'

'We have to go, now?' Lottie asks, woefully.

'Yes,' Tina says, firmly.

'Where are you crossing from?' Karel asks them.

'Friedrichstrasse station. Is it far from here?'

'A little way . . .' He pauses; licks his lips. 'I tell you what: this party is very boring; no one will notice if I disappear for a while. I can drive you to the crossing.'

'You have a car?' Tina asks him.

'Well, for tonight, I have use of a car,' he corrects. 'I have a driver.'

He must be important, Tina thinks, as they sit in the back of the big black Volvo. Nearly as soon as they set off, Lottie conks out in the seat next to her, her body slouched against the car window. Tina is sitting between Lottie and Karel. He has his arm around the back of her shoulders and she can feel his body pressed against hers. His proximity to her is making her feel hot and anxious; why is he having this effect on her?

'I wish we could have danced for longer,' Karel says, looking

109

at her in the dark car. His face is in shadow, but she can see the glint in his eyes. It is not her imagination; he *is* flirting with her.

'Me too,' she hears herself say.

'Tina,' Karel asks her, 'do you think you might come back and visit me again?'

'In Berlin?'

'Yes.'

'I don't know,' she says, truthfully. Once she is back in her real world, she should forget about this beautiful young man. He is out of her league.

'Please,' he whispers, bending down to kiss her on the lips. She cannot stop herself from kissing back. He is irresistible. He pulls her to him, away from the sleeping Lottie, and her whole body curls in towards his. He lifts her left leg over his lap, and she can feel his hands running up and down her thigh, beneath her black dress. She has no idea how long they have; at any moment they could arrive at the border crossing or Lottie could wake – let alone the driver watching them; what must he think? But all these rational thoughts are swept away by the power of her passion. It is as if she is forgotten kindling, left to dry for so long that, now Karel has set a match to her, she is aflame in a second. She is on fire, and nothing can put her out now.

As they kiss more deeply, his hand moves up her thigh, higher and higher, until his fingers are over the edge of her stockings, up further, and pushing beneath her panties. His fingers begin to stroke her clitoris, and she feels a corresponding vibration deep within the pit of her belly, as if her primal self is waking up, calling to her again. It has been so long since she felt like this. It is not just about feeling aroused, it is about feeling truly sensual in her own body, about knowing that this man she is kissing desires her more than anything else at this moment in time.

110

She feels the hardness of his cock pressed up against her body and imagines how it would feel to have it inside her. Yet the power of his fingers as they play her leave her unable to move. He has her captive as his hand makes strong strokes through the lips of her pussy, opening her out, softening her. He pulls her in front of him, opens his legs so that she is sitting between them, her skirt pushed up around her waist and the hardness of his cock in his trousers pressing up against the small of her back. He kisses the back of her neck as he brings his hands round to undo the buttons of her top and pushes them into her brassiere to caress her breasts. He drops one of his hands back down between her legs, again stroking her. Now she senses him pushing two fingers into her, touching a place that has been dormant for two years. He begins to rub gently in circles, while bringing his other hand to her clitoris.

She is in his hands, just like his cello between his legs. He takes control of her essence, her sound, as if he knows every nuance of how her body feels, despite the fact they are practically strangers. He brings her closer to the edge. She opens her mouth, moans with longing, leans her head back against his neck as she orgasms, her whole body vibrating against those strong, elegant fingers. She feels as if a bolted door inside her body has been unlocked and all the tension and stress of the past two years flood out. She is halfway between tears and laughter.

As if sensing her emotion, Karel wraps his arms around her, pulls her on to his lap, smoothing her skirt down again, and holding her within his arms, protectively. She puts her head on his shoulder and breathes him in. She doesn't know what to say, she is so overcome. Neither of them speaks as the car speeds through the dark and deserted streets of East Berlin.

Eventually, she sees the lights of the watchtowers and the

merciless neon floodlights pouring across the Berlin Wall as they approach Friedrichstrasse station. The car pulls in by the entrance to the crossing. She slips off his lap, and they turn to look at each other. To her surprise, he seems just as dazed as her. She was thinking that maybe he did this all the time . . .

'Come back tomorrow,' he whispers to her, his eyes blazing.

'I am going back to Milan tomorrow,' she protests.

'Just one day,' he whispers.

She feels confusion flood her. She is actually considering it.

'I can't . . . I have a family . . .' she stutters.

He doesn't bat an eye. 'I don't care,' he whispers. 'This is just you and me, for one day only. Can't you feel the connection between us?'

She wants to say, *No, what are you talking about?* But she knows exactly what he is talking about: the incredible chemistry between them that makes her want to fling herself upon him, pull him deep inside her.

'OK,' she says, hoarsely. 'I'll try.'

His eyes light up. 'Meet me at Palasthotel at fourteen-hundred hours.'

She leans forward to kiss him, but he puts his hand to her lips to stop her.

'Tomorrow,' he promises.

$\mathcal{V}$alentina

RUSSELL IS SITTING ON THE TOP STEP OF THE STAIRCASE AT THE Neue Galerie looking every bit the male model. He is leaning back, his long, jeans-clad legs stretched out in front of him, his white T-shirt taut against his muscled body and his dark auburn hair curling seductively around his perfectly symmetrical face. He is grinning at her. It is quite clear that he remembers exactly who she is. She feels back footed and self-conscious. Has he told anyone else about their one-night stand? Do all the other models and all the creative team know? Even sour-faced Taylor? The thought of such exposure of her private life appalls her. Yet, despite her irritation at his blatantly cheeky appraisal of her as she walks up the stairs towards him, she can't help hoping that he still finds her attractive. She is wearing one of her killer outfits: a minidress in geometric black and white stripes that once belonged to her mother, and thigh-high boots. She can't deny that she dressed with Russell in mind today. This is the new Valentina, and she wants to be appreciated again.

'Good morning, Valentina,' Russell says, cheerfully, getting up from the step and walking beside her as they enter the main gallery, the location for the first series of shots.

She gives him a sidelong glance, beneath her eyelashes. 'You never told me you were a model,' she says.

He shrugs. 'I find it puts women off me,' he says, raking his hand through his curls. 'They think I am going to be more interested in how I look than how they look.'

'Can I ask you something?' she says, turning to him, trying to appear as cool and indifferent as possible. 'Did you know who I was when you chatted me up the other night?'

He cocks his head on one side. 'Sure I did; as soon as you said you were from Milan, I reckoned you must be the photographer for the *Harper's* job.'

'And why didn't you tell me that we would be working together?'

'Because I thought it might ruin the moment . . . because I guessed you might bale out if you knew I was going to be one of your models . . .'

She pauses beside the portrait of the woman with the black feather hat and looks up at her disdainful expression. 'You're right . . . I generally don't sleep with my models,' she says with a hint of irony.

Russell leans forward and puts his hand on her arm. His touch sends an involuntary shiver through her body. 'You see . . .' he whispers. 'I did the right thing, didn't I? Maybe you might break your rule once more, just for me?'

She blushes, shaking her head, but already she can feel her resolve weakening.

After an initial battle with Taylor over the final selection of settings for the shots, the shoot goes surprisingly well. In the end, they decide to take pictures in front of the painting of the dancer in the main Klimt gallery; on the top-floor landing; at the bottom of the sweeping staircase; in the bookstore, using its shelves of books as a backdrop for one of the models perched

114

on a ladder; and two shots in the café, with Russell and one of the girls. She has decided to go for loving rather than fighting shots between the couple.

Focused as she is upon her work, Valentina can't help feeling a tiny bit jittery. What if she sees that man who looks like Glen again? Will she approach him and ask him who he is? She shakes herself angrily. She has to forget about the mystery man. It can't really be Glen. In any case, what are the chances of her seeing him again in the vastness that is New York?

Once they have completed the pictures in the upstairs gallery and landing, the team is all action: the models change their outfits, Marco styles them, Lori, the make-up artist, and Shannon, the hair stylist, get to work. Since Russell wasn't in any of the previous shots, he is already dressed and ready for the café location. Valentina is sitting on the floor of the landing, looking through the previous series of photos in her camera, when he brings her over a coffee.

'Thanks,' she says. 'How did you know I prefer it black?'

'From the other night . . . at my apartment . . .'

'Of course.' She tries to stay composed; after all, he is working for her today. She has to maintain some professional distance. Yet the proximity of Russell, squatting on the floor next to her, is undeniably having an effect upon her. She can feel her stomach fluttering a little; her hands shake as she changes the lens on her camera. She is crouched right by the top of the staircase and, as she looks up from her camera, she sees that she has a perfect view of its sweep, through the fancy ironwork of the balustrade. It is as if she is looking out of a cage. As is her wont, she has a sudden, spontaneous idea for a shot. What if she takes a picture of this powerful young man through the bars of the balustrade? Is he caged like a tiger, yet untameable? Or is the viewer the one who is trapped in *his* cage? She loves the idea of this ambiguity.

'Russell, would you pose for me on the staircase?' she asks him.

'With one of the girls?'

'No, on your own.'

'But I didn't think that we were doing any shots of me on my own,' he says, looking at her curiously. 'Aren't I just an accessory for the girls? My clothes complement their clothes.'

'It's not just about the clothes,' she tells him.

'Cool,' he says, getting up, not questioning her any further. 'Just tell me where you want me.'

She takes the pictures in black and white, Russell walking down the staircase and then twisting round and looking up at her.

'Look at me as if you are going to leave me for good, but you're hurt too,' she calls down at him. 'Like Rhett Butler in *Gone with the Wind*. You know the line . . . "Frankly, my dear, I don't give a damn . . ."'

The look Russell gives her is searing. He could be an actor, she thinks.

Valentina is so preoccupied that she doesn't notice the rest of the team gathering to watch until Taylor comes storming over.

'What do you think you're doing?' she says.

'A little ad-libbing,' Valentina replies, trying her best to ignore the titan woman.

'But it's not one of the scheduled shots . . . We are predominately featuring the women's clothing.'

Valentina turns to Taylor. 'Trust me, please.'

And, as she looks into the stern grey eyes of the art director, she is distracted by something else: a tall man in a baseball cap and jeans, with his back to her, passing between the two galleries.

He looks like the same man from yesterday. The Glen lookalike. She freezes, all her attention pulled towards the doorway of the gallery, waiting for the man to emerge.

'Valentina, are you listening to me?' Taylor's voice pierces her trance.

'Sorry, what were you saying?' she says to the art director, yet at the same time she begins to walk away from the group.

'Where are you going?' Taylor demands.

Valentina turns to her. Taylor has two red dots on her cheeks, and is frowning at her, arms crossed. It is clear Valentina is rubbing the art director up the wrong way, but it can't be helped; she has to investigate. What is this strange man doing in the art gallery today, when it is closed to the public? Does he work here?

'I just need to check something out in the other gallery... for a shot ...' she mumbles. 'I'll be back in a minute.'

She doesn't even wait for Taylor's response and scurries into the main gallery, yet the room is empty apart from Lori making up the Ukrainian model. She heads towards the smaller gallery with the Klimt drawings. He must be in there. But to her surprise when she walks into the space it is empty apart from the security guard. She circles the tiny room, her head pounding. Did she just imagine that man? No, he was real. She *did* see him.

'Excuse me,' she asks the security guard. 'Did you see where the man in the baseball cap went?'

The security guard starts out of his stupor. She notices beads of perspiration on his forehead, and yet it is cool inside the gallery.

'There was no one in here,' he tells her.

'But I just saw him come in,' she says, her eyes hunting around the space. She notices a narrow, almost invisible door in the

117

corner of the room. 'Did he go through there?' she asks, pointing at the door.

'Ma'am, you're mistaken; no man came into this room. That door's for staff only,' the guard says. But Valentina ignores him, and heads for the door. She has to check, make sure she isn't losing her mind.

'Ma'am, you can't go through there,' the guard tells her but Valentina takes no heed, pulling at the door. It's locked.

The guard is at her side now. She notices he is sweating profusely; big damp semi-circles beneath his arms stain his navy uniform.

'Ma'am, please step away from the door,' he says.

'Can you just unlock it?' She asks the guard. 'I'm sure I saw someone come in here . . . a member of staff, maybe?'

'No one came into this room, I told you,' the guard insists, but he won't meet her eye.

'Why are you lying to me?' Valentina asks him, continuing to tug at the door.

'Ma'am,' the guard says beginning to sound angry. 'Let go of the door.'

But she is frantic. She pulls at the door, hoping it might spring open. She has to find out if the man who looks like Glen is really him or if it is all in her head. If she could just hear him speak, for she has never forgotten his voice – the way it slid into her dreams at night; the dark things he said to her.

I will take you.

Glen has come to personify her guilt.

'Just let me look,' she demands, pulling at the door.

The guard puts his hand on her arm and she reacts without thinking, slapping it off.

'Ma'am, I am going to have to restrain you.'

But instead of being reasonable Valentina feels a flare of rage surge up inside her. How dare this sweaty security guard lie to her? How dare he touch her? She attacks the door again.

'Just let me look!' She knows she is losing it. She can see herself from above. How insane she must look to the security guard, to anyone else who might enter the gallery, and yet she is so sure she saw that man come into this space.

She bangs against the door futilely.

'Ma'am! I'm warning you!'

But before he has a chance to arrest her, she feels herself being yanked back, strong arms restraining her, pulling her into the shelter of a powerful body. It is Russell. He pulls down her arms and pins them to her, hugging her into his chest, as she attempts to break free.

'Valentina,' he whispers into her ear. 'Calm down.'

She feels like a spooked horse, about to bolt. What just happened to her? She looks from the closed door to the security guard, his face shiny with sweat, his eyes dark and angry.

'Sir, I am going to have to ask you to remove this woman from the building,' the guard says. 'She is a threat to security.'

'What's going on?' Taylor says, striding into the room. 'What are you doing in here, Valentina?'

Russell still has his arms around her. She can feel herself shaking. She doesn't want him to release her, she is afraid she might collapse if he does.

'Valentina was just looking at one of the pictures for inspiration,' Russell says lamely.

Taylor arches an eyebrow, looking at Klimt's erotic drawings.

'We are not shooting porn,' she says sarcastically.

'Ma'am, this woman was trying to get through this door, which is strictly off limits. Her behaviour was aggressive. I am going to have to ask you to remove her from the building.'

Taylor puts her hands on her hips, and surveys the security guard. She gives him a withering look. Clearly she is a woman used to getting her own way.

'Well, that just isn't possible . . . sorry, what's your name?'

'Wayne Datcher.'

'You see, Wayne, this woman is the photographer on our shoot for *Harper's Bazaar*. You have heard of us, haven't you?' She pauses, confident he will back down. 'I am sorry if we have caused any disruption but we are going downstairs now anyway, so we'll be out of your hair up here, okay?'

The guard looks doubtful, but Taylor continues to stare him down.

'OK,' he says eventually. Then turning to Valentina he says, 'Don't let me see you in here again.'

Taylor tells them to take five before they move down-stairs. Valentina can't stop shaking. Everyone is looking at her strangely. They obviously all think she is crazy. Russell gets her another coffee, while Marco leads her to a corner of the landing to sit down.

'What was that all about?' he whispers.

'I thought I saw Glen . . . the man who was in the boat with me and Theo in the blue grotto.' Her voice cracks. 'I really did. I was so sure he went into the gallery. He must have gone through that door.' She grips Marco's hand.

'Darling, are you sure you saw someone?' Marco looks at her, his eyes filled with concern. 'The gallery is closed to the public today. It's just us, and gallery staff. Maybe you've been over-doing things, and the pressure of the shoot . . .'

She is shaking her head, swallowing down her emotion,

trying to stay calm. 'No, Marco. I'm sure I saw someone.'

Russell appears with her drink. 'You probably need something stronger,' he says, handing it to her.

She takes a sip of the hot, bitter coffee.

'So what was that all about with the door and the security guard?' Russell asks them. 'Was it some ex-lover you were chasing?' He grins.

Marco looks at Russell distastefully.

'I just got a bit confused,' Valentina mutters. She is not in the mood for explanations now. The whole team must think she is a mad woman. Her first New York fashion shoot and she has ruined it. After her little scene, will she ever get another job with *Harper's*? Yet, to her surprise, Taylor is all polite concern when she comes over to check on her.

'Are you ready to start again?' she asks her, tapping her gently on the arm.

'Of course.'

Valentina switches her emotions off and suppresses her confusion. She has to stop thinking about the Glen lookalike for she has a job to do. She takes some shots of one of the girls downstairs in the bookstore and then they move into the café and take pictures of Russell with the other model. Her favourite is one of Russell looking out of the window, and the model behind him, leaning her head on the back of his shoulder and looking into the camera. It is a look of feeling safely in love.

There is no such thing! Valentina wants to scream out. Yet these dreamy images of perfect love between beautiful people are what sell fashion. How many times has Valentina had to defend her profession, not just to strangers but even to friends, like her artist friend, Antonella, who is always trying to persuade

Valentina to give up fashion photography because she says it is feeding the sickness of consumerism in society. But Valentina doesn't see the fashion industry in that way. She sees it as a place you can be truly creative, even subversively so, sometimes, with the bonus of being paid well for your creativity. She and Marco share this passion, this ability to see the subtleties of images and clothes. As she watches Marco working, pinning the clothes on the models so that they hang in exactly the right way for each shot, and making sure every single teeny tiny detail is to his highest standards, she knows that there are some who would ridicule her friend and call him obsessive about a world that is shallow, all about how you look and what you wear, but what Valentina sees is a man with as heightened a sense of detail as the finest oil painter or craftsperson. Styling is his craft, as photography is hers.

They are packing up when Russell catches her hand. She starts to see him, back in his civilian clothes. For some reason, in those café scenes, when he was dressed in brocade suits and ornate jackets, his hair slicked back and looking like a Russian aristocrat, she was able to detach from the man she had slept with. He had been a subject, a component in her composition, and she had been able to focus on the shot without worrying about what he or anyone thought of her. Now, however, she is jolted back into her present: his hand touching hers, sending tremors down her spine.

'Hey,' he says, 'want to go for a drink? You probably need it after that encounter earlier.'

She shakes her head. 'No; I'm beat,' she says. 'I'm going home with Marco.'

'Oh, OK.' He doesn't look too disappointed, and yet she can see by the look in his eyes that he is still keen.

'How about Sunday?' he asks.

'Sunday?' she repeats. 'I haven't really thought that far ahead. I'm going to be busy processing all this work over the next few days.'

'Well, let me book you now,' he says. 'I want to take you to an exhibition at MoMa.'

She finds herself saying yes, purely because she can't think of a reason to turn him down. There is something about his physical presence that has an impact on her. She has a sudden image of their naked bodies in bed together.

He will expect her to have sex with him again, and she is not sure now if this is what she wants too. She has watched him flirting with all the other women on the set all day. Marco had been right: Russell is not to be trusted. And yet it was Russell who had taken control when she lost it earlier and, when he had pulled her into his arms, held her down, she had felt a certain kind of peace for the first time in months.

Back out on the street, Valentina can't help feeling a little on edge. She looks about her, half expecting to see the Glen lookalike again, but there are no familiar faces among the bustling New Yorkers on their way home from work. As she and Marco walk towards the subway she tries to make sense of what happened today in the gallery. She had been so certain that she saw a man the image of Glen and yet it seems that no one else saw any strange man at all. Could she be wrong? Did she imagine the whole thing? And yet the way the security guard had been . . . she had felt sure he was lying. Why would he do that?

When Valentina and Marco arrive at the *Harper's Bazaar* offices the next morning, the place is in uproar.

'Did you hear?' Jilly, the receptionist, almost yells at them as soon as they walk out the lift.

'Hear what?' Marco asks.

'There was a break-in at the Neue Galerie last night,' she says, breathlessly. 'One of the Klimt's was taken.'

Valentina and Marco lock eyes as she feels the blood drain from her face.

Could she have been right all along? Had Glen really been in the gallery yesterday? A theft would explain his presence. But why did no one else notice him?

'Oh my goodness,' Marco says, putting his hand to his chest. 'It's like that movie, *The Thomas Crown Affair*. Did they catch the thief?'

'Not yet,' Jilly says. 'There were two of them. They both worked in the gallery. One was the security guard.'

Of course, she feels her heart begin to race. She hadn't been imagining anything. She knew there was something dodgy about that security guard.

'They're both missing now' Jilly continues to gush.

Marco turns to look at her, his eyes wide open. 'Valentina, I'm sorry I didn't believe you . . .'

She shakes her head, shows him it's OK. Maybe she would have thought he was mistaken, if it had been the other way around.

'The cops are here interviewing everyone,' Jilly says, dramatically. Valentina looks at the newspaper lying on the coffee table in the reception area:

Million-dollar Klimt stolen from Neue Galerie, New York

How could she and Marco have missed this on the way in today?

Marco picks up the paper and reads aloud: 'New York police are on the hunt for the perpetrators of the daring theft of two pieces of art by the Austrian artist Gustav Klimt, the painting *Black Feather Hat* and a drawing of a child from the Neue Galerie in New York last night.' He looks up at Valentina. 'Do you remember those pictures, Valentina?' he asks her.

She nods. That was the drawing of the child that looked like her, and the painting had been one of her favourites. Yet its sombre tones were not usual for Klimt. She is surprised that this is the painting the thieves would have chosen.

Marco reads on: 'The police believe that at least two professional criminals were behind the thefts. Police are currently seeking the whereabouts of the security guard, Wayne Datcher, last seen leaving the Neue Galerie at approximately nine o'clock last night, and Peter Clarke, a curator at the gallery, who was last seen at around the same time, in Mr Datcher's company.'

Peter Clarke, so not Glen. And yet that man had looked so like her old adversary. Was it possible he had changed his name? Could he have been in the gallery when she left last night? 'The cops want to interview you all,' Jilly says. 'Especially you, Valentina, because of what happened . . . you know, at the shoot, when you went for the security guard—'

'She didn't "go for him",' Marco says, tartly. 'There was just a little disagreement. Would you kindly refrain from spreading that nonsense around the office, Jilly.'

The girl blushes. 'Oh, sorry . . . It's just everyone is talking about it . . .' She looks nervously at Valentina.

But Valentina isn't listening. Her mind is racing. What should she tell the police? That she thinks the thief is Glen, that if it is him, he must be a murderer too? Her hands tremble with the idea of it. If Glen is alive, he killed Theo. Could it really be true?

The phone begins to ring at the reception desk. Jilly picks it up. 'Yes, she's just come in,' she says, putting down the receiver.

'That was Taylor,' Jilly tells them. 'The police are looking to talk to you. They are waiting for you in her office.'

She tells the cops everything. What harm can it do Theo, now that he is dead? She tells them that she thinks there is a possibility that the man they are looking for, this 'Peter Clarke', could be Glen, an international art thief who worked in competition with her deceased fiancé, Theo Steen. They had run across him in Milan and in London. The police take her seriously, nodding and writing down copious notes.

'I guess you could be right,' the one called Delaney says. He has a booming voice and red hair. 'We've no record of a Peter Clarke from Cambridge, so I suppose there is a chance it could be this Glen guy you are talking about. It's certainly a professional job.'

'So do you think this robbery was planned over a long period of time?'

'Probably. These professionals are perfectionists. They take their time setting up a job,' says the other policeman, Detective Balducci. An Italian, Valentina thinks, although he doesn't look or sound Italian.

'But why would they steal such a famous painting?' Valentina says, knowing full well that this painting by Klimt has nothing to do with Nazi hoards – the only reason she knows Glen had for stealing art. 'How can they ever sell it and get its worth, without being caught?'

'A lot of these guys do it for the prestige – to show us they *can* do it,' says Delaney.

'They like to make us run around a lot,' Balducci adds. 'They never actually sell the painting. It's a game to them.'

'It's not a game to Glen,' she says, remembering Glen's demands for compensation when Theo had stolen a painting right under his nose and given it back to its rightful owner. Glen had lost out on big money. It had been what prompted him to attack them, that day in the blue grotto.

'He's a killer,' she says.

'Can you elaborate, Miss?' Delaney asks her.

She tells them more about Theo.

'So let's get this straight,' Balducci says. 'Your boyfriend stole pictures that he returned to families who had lost them as part of the Nazi hoard during the Second World War?'

'Yes, but in the end it wasn't stealing . . .' Valentina emphasises. 'Once he spoke to the owners and told them the real story behind the pictures he had taken from them, most of them gave them up no problem. They dropped all possible charges. They were ashamed of the provenance. Not all were taken by Nazis you see; some had been stolen by Allied soldiers at the end of the war, as well.'

'So how does this Glen fit into the picture?' Delaney asks.

'He was a competitor, as I've told you. But the difference was that he was getting paid, sometimes millions, to return these paintings to families desperate to get them back.'

'What I don't understand is why these people didn't go through the legal channels. Surely they could claim the pictures back through the courts?' Balducci asks her.

'Not always. And, besides, it takes years. Many of the original owners of this art had survived the war and were very old. They just wanted their stuff back.'

'But why did your Theo do this, if there was no money in it for him?' Delaney pushes.

'Because he was trying to right a wrong.' Valentina pauses, taking a breath. 'His family is originally from Amsterdam. His grandfather worked for the Jewish art collector, Albert Goldstein, in the thirties. At the beginning of the war, many Jewish families and other refugees left their work with Goldstein to keep it safe, but, when the Nazis invaded Holland, Goldstein himself had to flee. He left the paintings with Theo's grandfather for safekeeping, but he was forced to sell them for a pittance to the Hermann Goering Divison.'

She pauses, clenching her hands in her lap. She can't believe she is telling the police about the Steens' private quest. She has an image of Mrs Steen's face for a moment: those piercing blue eyes and the soft chin, the motherly smile. Will she get them into trouble? She has already been the cause of the loss of their son. How can she hurt them further? Yet her need for vengeance against Glen is stronger and, if she has to work with the police to get him, she will tell them as much as she can so that they will help her.

'Theo's grandfather spent his whole life trying to return these pictures to their rightful owners. Theo was trying to help him.'

Balducci whistles. 'Wow! I didn't know men like that existed any more.'

'What do you mean, pal?' Delaney asks him.

'You know, doing something for the good of others at the risk of his own liberty. This Theo sounds like quite a guy.'

'Yeah, he was . . .' Valentina whispers, taking a deep breath.

Both cops look at her inquiringly.

'He's dead. If the thief really is Glen, then Glen must have killed him.'

Delaney raises his eyebrows.

'We didn't take this fellow for a killer,' Balducci comments.

'Believe me, he is. I was there.' She takes another deep breath.

She tells them about the blue grotto – how she and Theo had rowed into the little cavern, only to be followed by Glen, who attacked her, dragging her into the sea. She tells them that Theo saved her, and that he had insisted she row back out – on her own – to the fishing boat they had come in on, and get the skipper to help her. He had promised he would be following her in the other rowing boat, with Glen.

I won't let you down, Valentina. But he had. Because neither Theo nor Glen emerged that day from the blue grotto.

'The Italian police thought that they had fought again and drowned each other, but they never found any bodies. If Glen is walking around in New York then it only means one thing: he killed Theo,' Valentina says, in a shaking voice.

'Or there is one other alternative,' Delaney says, so quietly she barely hears him.

'What do you mean?' Valentina asks him, suddenly feeling a cold dread creep into her heart.

'You say they didn't find any bodies in the blue grotto? So maybe they struck a deal.' Delaney speaks up: 'This Klimt theft was a big job. It required experts to deal with the alarming system in that place. What if Glen and your Theo are working together?'

She stands up, sending her coffee mug flying on to the floor. 'No way!' she says, vehemently. 'Theo is dead! Glen tried to kill me; Theo hated him . . .'

'OK, darling, calm down,' Delaney says, surveying her calmly. 'It's just an angle . . .'

Balducci shoots his partner a warning look. 'Don't mind him –' he turns to her – 'he's always mouthing off crazy theories.'

But she sees the look Balducci and Delaney give each other; she knows that they are considering Theo's involvement.

'No, it's not possible,' she repeats. 'Theo wouldn't have just disappeared like that without contacting me. He loved me.' Her voice shrinks to an emotional whisper and she is embarrassed to be so stripped bare in front of these two men. She knows what they are thinking: it happens all the time; people run away from each other, even when they are in love.

$\mathcal{T}$ina

TINA FEELS EIGHTEEN AGAIN. SHE HAS SPENT A SLEEPLESS NIGHT on her own in the hotel room in West Berlin, her heart thumping in her chest, her head in a spin. A voice of reason keeps screaming at her. *Go home. Back to Phil, your life in Milan; back to safety.* And yet she just can't think straight. It is as if Karel Slavik has turned a switch on inside her, and suddenly, after two years of lying dormant, her spirit is alive again. The last thing she wants to do is hurt Phil and yet she can't stop herself. All she can think about is walking into that hotel in East Berlin and seeing Karel waiting for her, and wanting her. She needs to know that this beautiful young man really desires her. She tries to convince herself that she is going to teach herself a lesson because, of course, Karel won't show up and she will go home with her tail between her legs, and appreciate Phil all the more. Yet she can't help remembering the look Karel gave her when they said goodbye last night. They had made a promise.

She dresses in a blur: a brassiere corset in midnight blue with black lacy trim, and matching tiny knickers in black lace. She cannot deny that her underwear is being worn to be seen. Over this she puts on a Diane von Fürstenberg wrap dress. It is a simple jersey-knit wraparound dress with a swirling pattern in

131

emerald green and blue. As soon as she puts it on, she feels feminine and sexy. She chastises herself as she carefully applies her make-up. What has happened to her? One young man has taken an interest in her and she is behaving like a lovestruck schoolgirl. She has to pull herself together. It's not too late to go home. She can still make her flight. Yet, instead, she finds herself reaching for the phone.

'Oh, that's a shame,' Phil says.

'I'm sorry, but we have to redo some of the shoot; it just didn't work out yesterday.' She looks in the mirror at her lying face, before looking away.

'OK, well, don't get too stressed out. I know what a perfectionist you are. Try to relax tonight.'

She winces at the irony of his words.

'Phil, I'm really sorry.'

'It's OK, darling; it's hardly the end of the world. See you tomorrow.'

After she puts the receiver down, she stares at herself in the mirror.

You lying bitch.

But another voice reminds her that Phil didn't say he loved her. In fact, he didn't sound that upset she wasn't coming home, so what might he be up to? They haven't had sex in months . . . How long can a man go without sex? Maybe he is glad she is staying away another night; maybe he can cheat on her . . . She knows this is all nonsense. She trusts Phil implicitly, although she doesn't trust herself.

It is the moment of truth. She is standing outside Palasthotel – the River Spree, dark and churning behind her – looking every inch the Westerner in her Fürstenberg wrap dress. She still has the chance to turn around and walk away, but her instinct takes over and, without hesitating for another moment, she walks through the doors and into the lobby.

Karel is waiting for her. He stands up when he sees her, and she can see relief flooding his face. It occurs to her that he, in fact, thought she wasn't going to come. Today he is dressed better than yesterday, in svelte dark trousers and a crisp white shirt, but she doesn't care about his clothes: he looks stunning, no matter what – even better than how she remembers him. Again, his face reminds her of a Russian prince: pronounced cheekbones, glittering cat-like eyes that she has always found incredibly sexy in men. He looks exotic and dangerous.

'You look beautiful,' he says, taking her hands in his and giving her a chaste kiss on the cheek. 'I thought we could go for a meal first in the Domklause restaurant; it is the best restaurant in the DDR. Would you like that?'

She is not hungry in the least, but she could do with a drink. 'Yes, sure.'

The restaurant is all wood panelling and hushed voices. They are shown to a table in the corner. She is glad there is dimmed lighting; she is wondering if she looks any older to him today than she did yesterday.

She reads the menu and doesn't understand a word.

'What do you want?' he asks her.

'I don't know . . . What do you recommend?'

'Jägerschnitzel is very good,' he tells her. 'It is sliced-up sausage in bedcrumbs with tomato sauce, or you could have the signature dish, Broiler, which is chicken.'

'I'll take the Jägerschnitzel,' she says.

'And how about a beer to drink? The Berliner Bürgerbräu is very good.'

'I am not really a beer drinker,' she says, 'but I'll try it, I suppose.'

'Today you are getting a real East German experience,' he says to her, and she blushes at the irony of his words.

Once the waiter has taken their orders, they sit in silence for a moment. She is beginning to wonder whether this is such a good idea but, just as she is thinking this, Karel picks up her hand and looks into her eyes with a dreamy expression on his face.

'You are the most beautiful woman I have ever seen,' he says.

She feels another blush rising in her chest. 'That can't be true,' she protests.

'As soon as I saw you, standing in front of me last night, I just wanted to sweep you away. I could have danced with you all night.'

'I hadn't danced in ages,' she admits. Her mouth has gone dry and she takes a slug of her beer as soon as it arrives; it is surprisingly refreshing.

'But then you had to dash away in the night like Cinderella, leaving me nothing, not even a glass slipper . . .'

'I left you a promise,' she says.

'Indeed.' He gives her a jaw-dropping smile and she feels herself melting beneath her wrap dress.

The food arrives. Its smell and look don't appeal to Tina, yet she politely picks at it, while taking sips of the beer. 'I like the beer,' she comments.

'I told you it's good,' he says, cutting into his Jägerschnitzel with gusto. He eats like a man who hasn't eaten properly in weeks.

'Did you grow up in East Berlin?'

Karel nods. 'Mostly; my father is from Prague and my mother is East German. Her family moved to Prague for a while in the fifties. They met at college. They lived in Prague until I was three years old, when we moved to East Berlin.'

'And the Wall has always been there?'

'Yes; by the time we moved to East Berlin, it had been up a year.'

'What did your parents think about it?'

He stops eating and looks at her as if she is crazy. 'You do know where we are?' he whispers. 'Do you think your average DDR citizen eats in this place?' He widens his eyes and speaks to her silently.

She blushes, her face feels hot and shiny with embarrassment. 'Sorry; that's stupid of me.'

'I think it's safer if we talk about you, anyway. My life is boring. It is me and my cello and my music. I believe in the DDR. That is it. Simple. But you . . . I would guess that you are full of complexities and complications, like most Western women . . .'

'Have you known any other women from the West?' she asks him, wondering if he does this all the time.

'No,' he says. 'You are the first. I always found women from the West rather smug and superficial . . . that is, before I met you.'

She can tell, by his earnest look, that he is not lying.

'I am a fashion photographer,' she says. 'I work hard; I travel a lot . . .'

'So you have been all around the world,' he says, looking at her with hunger in his eyes. 'Tell me what countries.'

'Well, I live in Italy and I have been to France, Spain, Portugal,

America, Hong Kong, Singapore, India, Yugoslavia . . .' She pauses.

'There's more!' he exclaims.

'Yes: Holland, of course, and Belgium, Greece, Austria, Egypt, Morocco . . .'

'Are they all very different?' he asks.

'Yes, very.'

'And do you always go on your own?' he asks her.

She pauses, looking down at her Jägerschnitzel, which she has stabbed several times with her knife, but not actually eaten.

'No.' She takes a breath. 'Sometimes I bring my boyfriend . . . and my son.'

She looks up and he holds her gaze. He doesn't look surprised in the least.

'I guessed as much. I noticed you didn't have a wedding ring but, I mean, what woman like you would be single?'

'We've been together a long time.'

'And how old is your son?'

'Twelve.'

'But you don't look old enough?'

'You're very sweet,' she says, 'but I am sure I do.'

Karel stares at her for a moment, taking her in.

'So why are you here with me, if you have a partner?'

'I honestly don't know,' she says. 'I just had this urge to see you again,' she whispers.

She feels his leg push between hers under the table, rubbing her thighs and charging her body with desire.

'Do you want to see where I live?' he asks her.

She nods.

'It's not very fancy,' he says.

'I don't care.'

* * *

He leads her through the streets of Berlin, up and away from the river. To her right is the enormous Fernsehturm, which she had taken pictures of yesterday. The futuristic, state-of-the-art TV tower piercing the Berlin sky is in contrast to the drab streets that Karel is bringing her down. She recognises the area from yesterday. Nearby is Lottie's family house and her punk friends, yet Karel's district is a little less run-down. He takes her hand as they walk and she feels a frission of energy ripple through her as they walk side by side. She doesn't feel like a thirty-five-year-old mother and wife; she feels like herself when she was young again, looking at the world, wide open to what adventures it has to offer her.

When she walks into Karel's apartment, she feels like she is home. It is nothing like the utilitarian apartment block in which Sabine and Rudolf live, and neither is it like the derelict ruins of Lottie's punks; in fact, it is more like her own apartment back in Milan. The walls are lined with bookshelves, stuffed with books. She is sure that, if she took the time to analyse what books lined his shelves, she would find that some classics deemed too bourgeois might be missing. By the window, there is a record player and stacks of records. She leafs through them. They are all classical and favourites of the Eastern bloc: Shostakovich, Beethoven, Bartok, Hans Eisler. He has the full repertoire, although she is sure again that some non-approved composers are missing. Karel stands beside her and hands her a small glass of vodka, before selecting a record from the pile and putting it on. The second movement of Beethoven's 'Emperor' Concerto wafts through the room.

'How did you know that I would like this?' she asks him.

'What woman with a romantic soul doesn't?'

137

There is one second when she is on the verge of putting a stop to this, when she is about to put her drink down and walk out, but then he brings his glass to her lips, and she opens her mouth as she gulps the vodka down. It burns her throat, stoking her courage. He takes her glass from her hand, knocks it back in one and then puts it down. He places his hands on her waist and pulls her to him, bending down to kiss her. It is a long, slow kiss – a kiss that has been building up between them since she walked away last night. He parts her lips with his tongue and licks all along her bottom lip and teeth. He flicks his tongue up to her top lip and licks her there as well. She feels as if he is a large panther, tasting his prey, so that she is completely in his power. His tongue pushes further inside, until he is licking the roof of her mouth.

She is already weak at the knees. She can feel herself beginning to hum between her legs, coming alive again. It seems that her libido has well and truly returned. As he kisses and licks her, she imagines how it might feel to have his tongue elsewhere. It shocks her that she has this thought, for she has never let Phil go down on her, and lately she has avoided giving him blow jobs. However, now she is dying to put her lips around Karel's cock, to suck him deep and long and hard. What is happening to her?

'I like your dress,' Karel comments.

He has stopped kissing her and is now pulling on the tie of her wrap dress. It opens and falls away to reveal her lacy lingerie.

'Oh my God!' he almost hisses under his breath. 'Is that what Western women wear *all* the time?' he asks.

She grins. 'No; just me.'

He takes her into his arms, burrows his face in her neck. 'You smell so good,' he says, before kissing her again.

The passion between them accelerates. The fire they lit last night never went out. It has smouldered through the night and now it is has flared up, blazing between them again. They cannot hold back any longer. She rips his shirt off, not even bothering to unbutton it, as he undoes his trousers. They tumble on to the rug in his living room as the music swells with equal passion. He unlatches her lacy brassiere as she wiggles out of her panties. She reaches forward and boldly pulls down his underwear so that his cock springs free. She bends down and licks its head. It tastes bittersweet, and she longs to feel it deep within her.

Karel leans forward, suddenly scooping his arms under her knees and raising her hips off the carpet. He is kneeling between her legs, bringing his body right up against hers. She can feel his beautiful cock pressed against the soft cheek of her bottom. She reaches down with her hands and holds his cock between them. She is going to do it: make love with another man for the first time in fifteen years. She is going to break everything she has with Phil. It is so supremely self-destructive, and yet Tina is in her element. She has never felt so vital, so sexy, so young. She pushes Karel up inside her, not even thinking about contraception, despite the fact that, with Phil, she is fastidious about protecting herself from getting pregnant again. What has possessed her?

She is hypnotised by Karel's muscular arms as, with every thrust he makes, he lifts her hips towards him. His cock slides deep inside her, touching her in a place that she had forgotten existed. She is vibrating, humming right from her core. She never thought she would feel like this again. He lowers her hips to the floor, bending over her, still inside her, and presses his whole body down upon her. Now they are cheek to cheek, kissing again, the passion building between them. He is grinding into her, his breath quickening, deepening as she feels him bringing her closer and closer. He takes her over the edge. She is crying and laughing, flying out of herself as the two of them orgasm at the same time. She feels that her very being is split in half, as if she will never be whole again.

This is just the prelude. They lie on the rug for a few moments, devastated by their mutual release. After a while, Karel gathers her into his arms and carries her into the bathroom with the ease and grace of a strong young man. He turns on the tap in the bath and, while it fills, he showers her neck and shoulders with little kisses. They climb into the bath together and wash each other. As he lathers her breasts with soap, massaging them with tenderness and dexterity, she watches his cock growing in the water, imagines it to be like a magical snake, its seed filling her with life and youth. She wraps her legs around him as he slides himself forward, entering her smoothly. They fuck in the bath, water splashing over the side, soaking the tiled floor, laughing like children at the abandon of it.

From the bathroom, they move into the bedroom, and this is where they take their time. Now they have got the initial craving for each other out of their systems, they start to explore each other's bodies more, to nourish and nurture each other sensually.

She kisses her way down his body, from his mouth to his chest. She licks his nipples and then moves further down his chest to his stomach, flat and firm as a rock. His erect cock brushes her cheek, and she catches it in her mouth, twirling her tongue around its tip. Meanwhile, he is playing her with his powerful cellist hands, thrumming his fingers between the lips of her labia, pressing gently on the bud of her clitoris with his thumb. She drapes herself upon him, as if she imagines she could sink into him. She licks his cock down its length, brings her lips up and down, every few seconds squeezing it tight between her lips. Before she knows it, he has lifted her up by the hips so that she is practically sitting on his face. She stiffens for a moment, but Karel has no idea that she doesn't like this. He begins to lick her and, to her surprise, she relaxes, forgetting that this is too vulnerable a position for her. They caress each other with their mouths. They are primal, and yet they are innocent, pure passion, with no agenda or expectations, just being in union together, sharing sublime sex. She begins to understand why so many women love a man to go down on them. She has never experienced such a subtle passion, such deep yet fragile vibrations deep within her.

After they both climax, they cling to each other like two survivors at sea. And, really, his bed and his bedroom could be viewed as a sanctuary from the hopelessness of their situation. Without saying it to each other, they know that this can only be one night together, and not even a whole night. She must return to Italy tomorrow, and he must remain behind the Wall.

They sleep; they make love; they tell each other childhood stories; they make love again. Tina tells Karel the story of her grandmother, Belle, in Venice – her double life as a courtesan and her dramatic affair with the adventurer, Santos Devine.

'Is that a real story?' he asks her, incredulously. 'I mean, did it really happen?'

'Of course; my mother was their child.'

'Why are all the best love stories so sad?' Karel asks. 'Do none of them have happy endings?'

'Of course there are love stories with happy endings, tons of them: "Cinderella", "The Sleeping Beauty", "Rapunzel", "Snow White" . . .'

'They are fairy tales,' Karel interrupts. 'I am talking about real love stories. Can you think of any two people that you know that loved each other absolutely their whole lives? That had each other always? Circumstances never got in their way or jealousy or miscommunication? Can you think of a couple who were loyal and true to each other from beginning to end?'

For a moment, Tina thinks of herself and Phil, but now she has broken that. They are imperfect through her doing.

'My parents,' she tells Karel.

'Are you so sure? I used to think my parents were the happiest couple, but then I found out one day that my father was having an affair with a woman where he worked . . . My parents ended up getting divorced when I was fifteen. I was in shock for about two years.'

'I can promise you that my father was absolutely devoted to my mother.'

Tina sees her father's gentle face for a moment, the way his eyes lit up every time her mother came into the room.

'Yes, but what about your mother?'

'Oh, God, she would *never* have cheated on my father. She was very religious, for a start.'

'So your parents are still together now, after all these years?' Karel asks her, with curiosity.

'No, they are dead . . . Well, that's together in a way, I guess. They were both killed in a plane crash nine years ago.'

Karel's eyes fill with concern for her. 'That's terrible for you; I'm sorry. You would have been so young when you lost them.'

Tina turns to lie on her back, staring at the ceiling, her cheeks burning. 'Actually, I would have been about your age,' she says.

Karel leans over her, begins to kiss her gently on the lips.

'You see, that's another tragic love story,' he says, between kisses. 'Your parents didn't have a happy-ever-after, either.'

* * *

The night comes upon them fast. She sees the hours passing on the little clock upon his locker by the bed. They make love every way they can. She sits on top of him, raising herself up and down his shaft by gripping on to the bedstead, then she turns around, sits with her back to him, pressing her body into his, sliding herself along his body with every thrust, and moving her hips backwards and forwards. As he comes, she grips on to his feet and he rocks forward, the violence of his orgasm almost propelling her off the bed.

They slow things down, lying on their sides, facing each other at opposite ends of the bed. She hooks her leg over his and pulls him closer, sliding him in. She holds him inside her, with no thrusting or deep penetration, just cradling the head of his cock within her soft, receptive pussy. They begin to play with each other's feet, sucking each other's toes, as she reaches down and caresses his balls. In response, Karel begins to play with her clitoris, rolling his fingers around it, plucking at it, as if it is a string on his cello. This goes on for what seems like hours, until she is so longing to feel him penetrate more deeply, snaking up within her. Suddenly, he flips her on her back and twists himself up so that he is kneeling above her; he pushes deep down inside her. She raises her knees and rocks back, opens herself up further to him. She clasps her hands around his neck and they gaze into each other's eyes. Neither of them looks away, closes their eyes or even blinks as they lock together in every way possible: body, heart and mind.

She is lying in his arms as he plays with her hair. She feels languid and loved, like a purring cat. Her body feels amazing, throbbing with spent passion, open and confident. She hasn't felt like this in years. She looks over at the clock. It is one a.m. It is time for her to leave.

'Karel,' she whispers, 'I am going to have to go.'

He holds her tighter within his arms. 'I wish you could stay,' he says, and she can hear a crack in his voice. He really means this. She is something special to him.

'What would happen if I stayed until morning? Would I get into trouble?'

'Yes,' he says, his voice serious. 'A lot of trouble. You have to cross back over by two a.m.'

'Prison?' she whispers. She would rather be dead than trapped in prison.

'I don't know, to be honest,' he says, 'but all I know is that you don't want to miss the border deadline.'

She sighs. 'Do I have time for a shower?'

They make love one last time in the shower. As the water cascades around them, Karel begins to speak to her.

'Promise me, you'll come back again,' he says.

'I can't. I have to go home to Italy tomorrow. My son will be back from school. His father is expecting me.'

'Don't talk about your husband, please,' Karel says, lifting his head to the spraying water.

She stands up on her tiptoes and kisses his neck. 'He is not my husband – he is my boyfriend – and no one, not even him, has made me feel this way, Karel,' she says.

He looks down at her. 'I love you,' he says.

His words shoot through her body, rocking her.

'But we only just met,' she protests.

'I know, but I feel like I have always loved you . . .'

'Like we lived together in another lifetime before?'

'I never believed in that. I don't believe in God. I think religion is evil . . .'

He shakes himself so that droplets of water spray her; she opens her mouth, catches them upon her tongue.

'What do you believe in?' she asks, as he lifts her leg around his waist and slams into her, pushing her back against the tiled wall.

'The common good,' he says, between gritted teeth. 'Socialism.'

'Do you believe in a wall that stops you from seeing me?'

'Yes,' he says. 'It's there to protect us from the depraved, shallow, corrupt West . . . Life is better for everyone this side of the Wall.'

She takes his face in her hands as she squeezes her leg against his firm buttocks. 'You're lying,' she whispers. 'You don't really think that.'

He shakes his head, says nothing more, but she can see in his eyes his hunger, like before, when she spoke about all the countries she had travelled to.

She places her cheek alongside his and whispers into his ear as the water cascades around them. 'I'll come and see you play in Vienna . . . I'll help you defect . . .'

Running, hand in hand, back along the dark, deserted streets of Prenzlauer Berg towards the border crossing, Tina imagines she sees the shadows of those subversive punks, Hermann and Simone. Their images are imprinted on the film inside her camera. What kind of future are those kids facing? At least Karel has a chance to go for freedom. He will have to turn his back on everything he has in East Berlin, but he is so talented that she is sure he will make it in the West. What is motivating her to help him defect? Does she want to break up with Phil, start a new life with Karel? The idea of banishing Phil from her life terrifies her, and yet, as she runs with Karel through the streets of Berlin, she is young and in love again. Despite the fact they will be separated soon by the brutal laws of this institutional regime, she feels free, as if she is floating on air, as if there are stars shining in her hair. She is so lost in the elation of these moments that she fails to notice the dark car trailing them all the way to the neon spotlights illuminating the cruel concrete Wall.

Valentina

'ARE YOU SURE YOU WANT TO GO OUT WITH THIS RUSSELL GUY?'
Marco questions her as they jostle in front of the bathroom
mirror.

'It was you who told me to get laid,' Valentina points out, as
she and Marco look at their reflected faces.

'Yes, I know. I said you needed sex – a one-night stand is fine
– but I don't think you are ready to date yet,' Marco says,
reaching over and tucking Valentina's hair behind her ears.

'What's the difference?' she challenges him.

'Plenty,' Marco says. 'Russell is not dating material. You
can't get hurt or let down right now. You're too vulnerable.'

Valentina wonders if Marco is right. Well, it is too late now. It is
Sunday and she is already in the foyer of MoMa with Russell.
Where is the harm in it? They can look around the gallery and
hang out for a few hours. Anything is better than the waiting.
Since her interview with Delaney and Balducci on Wednesday,
she has heard nothing from either of the detectives. She and
Marco have been following the news avidly – in between doing
the postproduction on the *Harper's Bazaar* shoot – but it seems
that there have been no further developments on the art theft or
any word on the disappeared curator and security guard. Could

Glen still be alive? Living and breathing in the very same city as her, right under her nose? She needs to stop thinking about it. The whole thing is beginning to make her feel slightly unhinged. A flirtatious afternoon with Russell could be just the thing to take her mind off it.

Since it is a Sunday, the gallery is packed. Russell and Valentina weave their way through the crowds, up to the third floor, to the photography galleries.

'Ever since we did those shots on the staircase, I wanted to show you these pictures,' Russell says, leading Valentina into an exhibition by the photographer Bill Brandt called 'Shadow and Light'.

'I love his portraits,' Russell continues. 'There is a quality about his work that reminds me a little of what you do.' Valentina is surprised that Russell would even be familiar with her pictures, but then, when they first met, he did tell her he was an artist. She follows him around the exhibition, which charts Brandt's work from studies of Britain in the thirties and during the Second World War – she recognises some of his iconic pictures of London in the Blitz – through to portraits and a series of intriguing high-contrast nudes, taken in the fifties. It is not so much that these nudes are erotic; it is more that they objectify parts of the naked body in a way that makes them seem like beautiful moments in nature. She particularly loves the pictures of the abstracted body parts, taken on the East Sussex coast. Some of the nudes are distorted, and Russell explains that Brandt often used large, wide-angled fixed focus – like in crime-scene photography. It gives the images a certain dramatic narrative, like the nude of the topless woman sitting at a table and offering her hand, or the shot of a woman's back, which is cropped in such a way that it reminds Valentina of a cello.

They spend hours in the photography galleries so that, by the time they are finished looking, they are both hungry and thirsty.

'Let me treat you to lunch at The Modern,' Russell offers.

'Thank you,' she says, slipping her hand in his as they make their way to the staircase, her heart racing a little at the audacity of her action.

Russell swirls the wine around in his giant glass. It gleams like honey, and catches the same shade in his brown eyes. They have had a delectable meal and several glasses of wine, and talked their heads off about art. She's learned that, apart from modelling, Russell really is trying to be an artist. He tells her that he paints portraits.

'That's why I love Brandt's portraits; despite being photographs, they are more than just mere representation.'

'I read something he wrote,' Valentina says, 'about how the photographer has to wait until something between dreaming and action occurs in the expression of a subject's face.'

'Yes, precisely,' Russell says. 'That's what I am trying to do in pictures, too.'

Russell suddenly leans across the table and picks up her hand, as if to examine her fingers. 'I would love to paint you one day; will you let me?' he whispers, looking up at her slyly.

She shakes her head.

'No, I like to be behind the camera, not the centre of attention.'

'Well that's not exactly true is it, Valentina?' Russell asks her looking amused. 'I saw those famous erotic images of you in Venice, the ones that were exhibited in London.'

'You did?' she says, astonished, her cheeks burning with self consciousness.

'Sure, they were on the gallery's website.' He licks his lips. 'I looked you up on the internet after we met.'

He holds her with a blazing stare, and she looks right back at him, all of sudden feeling brazen. Russell knows nothing about Theo, or Glen. She is brand new with him. He even wants to paint her.

'Come on,' he says, laying down the money for the bill and offering her his hand as he stands up.

'Are you ready for some more?' he asks.

'More what?' she asks but Russell only answers her with a mischievous grin.

They walk hand in hand out of the restaurant and down the corridor, back into the main gallery. This simple gesture feels so good. To be holding the hand of a man, once again.

'Would you like me to tell you what to do, Valentina?' Russell whispers into her ear, his voice slightly different from before.

'Yes,' she whispers back, surprising herself. It reminds her of Theo, Russell's command and his confidence at this moment. He leads her to the lift and, still holding her hand with one of his, he presses the call button.

'Where are we going?' she asks him.

He puts a finger to his lips and says nothing.

They get inside the lift and move to the back as it fills. Russell stands behind Valentina, his arms around her waist and pulling her into him. She can feel his cock hard against her back, and the sensation of its promise makes her heart begin to race, her insides soften. She feels conflicted. How can she have truly loved Theo, if this man is turning her on so much?

They ride all the way up to the top floor. Russell says nothing, only kisses her delicately on the nape of the neck, pausing to surreptiously lick the bump of bone at the top of her spine. No one seems to notice – or, if they do, they are ignoring them. She feels her nipples harden, the arousal of her body, the shift and slide of her silk dress against her skin as Russell holds her waist.

On the top floor, he steers her out of the lift, his arm still around her waist. They walk slowly through the gallery space, but she is not looking at the paintings. She can feel his fingers tracing down her spine under her jacket, causing her to shiver. All sensation is concentrated within her back, her hips, her bottom, as she feels his hands moving down. She feels like one of those Bill Brandt images: one part of her, close up and intense.

The third room they come to has a large, black boxroom within it. Russell leads her inside. A film is being projected on the far wall: black and white images, on a loop, of a young man running. The space is empty apart from them.

Russell sits down, and pats the seat next to him. She sits beside him, her heart beginning to race. She has a feeling that they are not in this dark room merely to look at the art. She turns to look at Russell, but he has directed his gaze towards the video installation, a studious look upon his face. She looks at the screen as well. The black and white image has changed to a naked woman, swimming underwater, but Valentina is not really focusing on what it means to her, for all she can feel is the sensation of Russell's hand as it slides beneath her skirt and begins to stroke her thigh. It is a teasing, pleasant sensation: naughty but not too dangerous. He brings his hand higher and higher up her leg, as it brushes her hip bone, and then comes to rest on her panties, his palm flat against her pussy. Her chest tightens, her whole body tenses with the thought of discovery, and yet at the same time she is excited.

The images upon the video screen become a blur as her desire thickens. She places her hand on Russell's lap. In the darkness, she cannot see it, but she can feel the hard outline of his cock, and she imagines it deep inside her. The wine they drank at lunch curls inside her belly, giving her courage. All reason and all reserve abandons her as she suddenly stands up, and grabs the very hand he was touching her with, dragging him out of the gallery. They charge through the other exhibition spaces. She hardly knows where they are going. All she wants is to feel like the old Valentina. The girl before Theo. The free spirit who answered to no one. She spies a ladies' toilet in the corner of the top floor foyer. She pulls Russell in with her, before he has a chance to resist. They are in luck; the space is empty. They pile into one of the cubicles, the two of them giggling like naughty children.

She has never had sex in a toilet before. She always believed it was the cheapest thing to do and yet now it just feels illicit, dangerous and incredibly sexy. She faces the door of the cubicle, pressing her palms against it, and pushing her backside into Russell's groin. He pulls her panties down, feels how soft and wet she is with his fingers.

'Quick,' she whispers. 'Before someone comes in.'

He pushes into her. It is fast hard sex. It is what she needs at this moment, all her confusion over Glen, and Theo, spiralling into a point of tension.

She squeezes Russell tight, holds him there, his tower of strength within her as she scatters all around him like glass blown out of its window. She presses her lips together, for it takes all her strength not to cry out.

Russell comes just after her, kissing the back of her neck. He puts his arm around her and clasps her body to his. He says nothing. She wonders if he can feel her heartache through the vibrations of her body.

* * *

Nothing lasts for ever.

Valentina reminds herself of her mother's words every time she meets Russell. She tells herself that this is the last time they will have sex. She needs to stop seeing him before she gets hooked; yet, when he rings her each day, she can't say no.

You see, sex with Russell is no ordinary sex.

At the bottom of Russell's bed is a large chest, somewhat like a pirate's treasure chest, but painted with black lacquer and decorated with red Chinese dragons. It is locked with a big padlock, and sometimes Russell wears the key on a chain around his neck. Russell calls this his toy chest. On their second night together, he showed her the contents: an array of handcuffs, blindfolds, gags, paddles and little whips, double ended with leather tassles and fluffy black feathers. None of this stuff had been new to her. At Leonardo's old fetish club in Milan, she was introduced to just about every kind of S&M toy there is. She wonders what her friend would make of Russell's hoard. These days, Leonardo seems to have no interest in S&M, having closed down his club and turned into some kind of Tantric yoga guru, judging by the content of his intermittent emails from India.

That very night, after they had had illicit sex in MoMa, Valentina gazed into the chest for the first time and her eyes were drawn to a twist of soft white rope lying innocently amid all the dark paraphernalia. As they went on to indulge in their first S&M fantasy, they slipped easily into the roles of submissive and dominant.

He had tied her, spreadeagled, to the bed with the soft white rope. It had been an almost pleasant sensation to feel the length of rope against her skin, restraining her. She was supine, exposed to him. Completely his, relief coursed through her. All she had to do was receive what he had to give her.

As Russell leant over her and looked into her eyes, gone was the boyish mischief from MoMa; instead, he looked at her sternly.

'I'm going to use you tonight,' he said, his eyes darkening from brown to black. He paused a moment, before tying a black scarf around her eyes. 'Like you used me today,' he added.

'I—' But, before she could speak, he put a finger to her lips.

'Do you want to play this game, Valentina?' he asked.

She nodded.

'Well, then you must be silent. The only word you can say is the safe word. OK?'

She had no intention of stopping him, for she wanted him to take her all the way to the edge of her reason. She was excited by his powerful aura. If she was playing a game with Russell, she could hide from the confusion of her real life.

He had left her then. She lay on the bed, blindfolded and spreadeagled, her excitement and a little anxiety slowly mounting. But, just when she was considering calling out, she felt his weight on the mattress beside her. He began to stroke the inside of her thighs, bringing his hands higher and higher until he was fingering her.

'Ah, I see your wait has made you soft, supple, compliant . . .' he whispered.

It was true, she was damp with anticipation. What was he going to do to her? Was he going to fuck her roughly, or tease her slowly?

'I have a little treat for you, Valentina,' Russell said.

She sensed him bending backwards and returning quickly to lean over her. She started as something hot was pressed against her left nipple – so hot it almost burnt her, yet not quite. It felt hard, like glass, and it was searing against her breast as he spun it around, first one nipple and then the other. Just as quickly, he removed the hot implement and she cried out in shock as a freezing, ice-cold replacement was pressed against her hot breasts. He rolled the cold glass against her nipples while, at the same time, she sensed him bend backwards again. She felt heat between her legs.

A part of her was coming alive, a wild and abandoned part, that wanted Russell to go on. She loved the fact that all his attention was focussed on pleasing her, finding the exact levels of heat and cold that would turn her on. It seemed to her that he understood how close to the edge she liked to go. She wanted to feel this heat inside her. Slowly, Russell twirled the hot glass implement around her clitoris – she imagined it to be some kind of wand – while removing the cold one from her breasts and moving himself down her body so that she sensed him concentrating on the most tender, most vulnerable part of herself. He took away the hot wand and retraced its path around the tip of her clitoris with the cold wand. Now, ever so gently, he began to insert the hot wand into her pussy.

'Is it too hot?' he whispered.

She shook her head.

'Go on,' she said, as she felt her insides melting. She was in a fever, the contrasting sensations of hot and cold were making her sweat and shiver all at the same time, fuelling her desire. When he had brought her so close to climax that she was about to disintegrate, he suddenly removed the glass wands.

'Not so soon, baby.'

She was panting, gasping for release, but Russell had moved on the bed. He untied her ankles from the bedposts, and then her arms, while still leaving her blindfolded. And now she felt his weight pressed down upon her, and his mouth against her lips.

He slipped inside her hot pussy, and she felt the length of his cock inside her even more intensely. She wrapped her legs around his waist and raised her hips to his so that it was as if they were melded together. They fucked hard and fast just like in the art gallery, this time both of them climaxing at exactly the same time.

After he put away all the toys, safely stowed and locked in his black chest, they lay in each other's arms. Valentina was spent. All she wanted was to remain tucked tight within Russell's arms the length of the whole day to come – not to have to face the outside world and think about the lack of news on the art theft, or confusion over whether Glen was alive or not. She could forget about it all in her lover's bedroom.

The next morning Russell confesses that what really turns him on is to take their role-playing outside of the bedroom.

'What do you mean?' she asks him as they share a post-coital cigarette in bed. Her pussy is still throbbing, her backside smarting from the rough sex they have just had. 'Like in the art gallery?'

'Yes just like that. And you like it too, don't you?' he says.

She inhales, passing him the cigarette.

'I'm talking about what we call "edgeplay",' he says, turning to lie on his side, facing her.

We? Valentina thinks. Who are we? But, instead, she asks, 'What's edgeplay?'

'I guess it's pushing the BDSM boundaries of we are doing, Valentina.' He leans forward and gently strokes her forehead, while passing her back the cigarette.

'Like what?' she asks him.

'We make an agreement, that you have to submit yourself to whatever erotic demand I make of you, wherever that might be.'

'Anywhere?'

He nods, grinning at her. 'That's what makes it so sexy . . . the danger of it. I might ask you to masturbate while we are at dinner with friends, or fuck me in the restrooms at Grand Central Station, or walk around Manhattan all day with no panties on . . . It can be anything at all, but the agreement is that you *have* to agree to submit before you even know what the request might be . . . That's what makes it erotic. Do you like the idea of that?' He asks her. 'It only works for me if it turns you on as well.'

He is pushing against her body now, and she can feel his cock hardening against the side of her leg. She has to admit that the sound of all these dangerous, exhibitionist acts excites her a little.

'Just thinking about you doing these things is turning me on,' Russell says.

It is exactly a week since the theft of the Klimt painting and there have still been no new developments on the case. The Glen lookalike, Peter Clarke, the missing curator at the Neue Galerie, has not been sighted, and nor has the security guard. There seem to be no trails left to follow, according to Delaney and Balducci. Valentina tries to convince herself that she must have been confused. Glen is dead. He has to be. She has to put her past behind her, and try to move on. Isn't that why she is playing around with Russell after all?

It is her first free-day since the shoot. Valentina has just about wrapped up the selection of the pictures. She has a meeting with Taylor the next day to fight it out over the final selection of photographs and then she is moving on to do another job with Marco for *Elle* next week. She can't wait to be busy again.

She is sipping her morning coffee in Marco and Jake's empty apartment, since her two friends have gone away for a couple of days, when her phone rings.

'Hello, darling,' Russell says in his easy voice. 'Are you busy today?'

'Actually, no,' she says.

'Great, so how about a little picnic in Central Park?'

'Sounds good.'

'Meet me outside the Met in one hour,' Russell instructs her over the phone. 'Wear something long and floaty.'

'OK,' Valentina agrees, a little surprised by his request.

She is not a floaty kind of dresser, and she did not think that Russell, being such a fan of S&M, would be keen on flowing, flowery dresses either.

'Oh, and one last thing,' Russell says playfully. 'Please do forget to put your panties on!'

He hangs up before she has a chance to question him further. Her heart begins to race a little as she takes in what Russell has asked her to do. Does she have the courage to go out into the crowds of New York City wearing absolutely no underwear? Do other women ever behave like this? Russell has told her that plenty do. Apparently all around them are couples taking part in edgeplay.

She ends up putting on a long silky red skirt and matches it with a little black silk mandarin top she bought in Chinatown the day before, with red embroidery on its collar and red buttons, and a pair of black wedge sandals. She brushes her hair until it is glossy, black and shiny as crow's feathers: a neat, smooth bob, just like her heroine Louise Brooks' hair, and she paints her lips red. Last of all, just before she leaves the apartment, she slips off her red lacy briefs, and slips them into her handbag. Already she feels deliciously wanton: a mixture of fear at being discovered, and arousal at the idea of being naked underneath her skirt.

Outside Valentina is immersed in the optimism of a summer's day. For the first time in ages she feels a lightness in her step as she walks the sunny streets. She slips her sunglasses on and luxuriates in the heat of the sun on her bare arms, a prickly but also pleasant sensation. Maybe this thing she has with Russell really can work out, and she could stay here in New York. She could move in with him.

Are you crazy? she can hear her mother say. *Never be dependent on a man . . . That is the road to despair.* A little overdramatic, but her mother has a point.

The whole front façade of the Met is a mess of scaffolding and boarding. Russell waves to her from the far corner. He is carrying what looks to be a picnic hamper. So he is a romantic, as well. She pictures them feeding each other strawberries and champagne under the shade of a willow tree, like a couple from an impressionist painting.

They walk for ages, off the main path and into the heart of the park. Her red silk skirt billows around her in the gentle breeze, and she enjoys the sensation of the material brushing against her nakedness. There are plenty of people in the park, yet Russell manages to find a quiet corner, circled by trees and looking over one of the lakes. He puts down the basket and pulls out a blanket, spreading it on the grass.

'Can I tell you that you look absolutely exquisite in that skirt?'

She blushes.

159

'I thought you might prefer rubber and Lycra . . .'

'Ah, that is just a cliché, Valentina.' Russell grins at her, indicating for her to sit down on the blanket. He pulls out an ice-pack bag from the basket. 'Would you like a glass of champagne?' he asks her.

'Love one,' she says.

She tries to keep her voice light, but she hears an involuntary tremor. Something about this scenario unsettles her a little. Up until now there has been little romance in her liaison with Russell and that has suited her. They have been motivated by a mutual desire for sex. She has striven to retrieve the old Valentina, carefree and adventurous – the independent girl. Yet this picnic in the park feels a little too familiar. It was one of the things Theo used to do; bring her on romantic picnics, not only in the parks of Milan but further afield, too. She has a fleeting image of herself and Theo wrapped around each other in the swaying grasses beneath the honey walls of a Tuscan village. She takes a gulp of the champagne and pushes the image out of her mind. She has to stay in the present, the here and now with Russell.

He has stretched his legs out, and is looking at her.

'What are you thinking about?' he asks her.

She shakes her head.

'Nothing,' she says, taking another sip of her champagne, savouring its cold delicious fizz inside her mouth.

'Well, that's a lie. You looked so serious.'

She turns to him, leaning forward, and letting her voice drop to a husky whisper.

'I was just thinking how much I like wearing no panties.'

Russell's eyes darken, and she can see his erection already pushing against the fabric of his trousers.

'Well aren't you a naughty girl?' he says. 'Why don't you come over here and sit on my lap?' he grins.

Valentina knocks back her champagne, discarding the empty glass on the blanket as she crawls towards Russell stealthily. She wants to feel all animal, like a sleek cat. She wants to live purely by instinct, banishing all thoughts of love from her mind.

She climbs onto his lap, and he brings his hands up to hold her by the waist. It feels good to be in his grasp; to feel his strong hands on either side of her, holding her in place.

Russell rocks beneath her, and then sits up and starts arranging her skirt around him. It billows like a red sail, settling on the ground like a pool of blood upon the verdant grass. The lips of her labia are pushed up against the zip of his trousers. The cold metal is a dangerous sensation upon her vulnerable flesh, and yet it is turning her on.

'Undo me,' he whispers. Locking eyes with him, feeding him with the desire in her gaze, she slips her hands under her skirts and unzips his trousers, pulls down his waistband and releases his cock. It immediately presses against the rim of her vagina, as if seeking her out.

He stares at her, his eyes widening, smiling softly. This is their little game, then. Illicit passion in public. The idea of exposure frightens her, and yet at the same time excites her. She takes a breath and still holding his gaze, she slips him inside her. She takes her hands out from under her skirt, and smoothes it around her again to make sure that all is concealed. They sit like this for a while: him inside of her, growing, and her squeezing him. Their eyes locked in tight complicity.

'Slow,' he breathes.

She gives him three slow squeezes with her pelvic floor muscles, before he whispers, 'Fast.' She makes three short, sharp squeezes. 'Now slow again,' he says. Three controlled slow ones. 'Now rock,' he tells her, his voice a hiss through his closed teeth, his eyes burning into her. She grinds him gently back and forth, just the slightest movement, before giving him three short squeezes. She can feel him hard inside her, and pushing up, deeper into her. Her heart is racing with the risk and recklessness of their picnic. Her body is one whole urgent need to fuck this man, to be fucked by him.

Valentina squeezes Russell tightly inside. One, two, three; slow and steady.

'Fast,' he whispers, closing his eyes, losing himself in the sensation of his cock buried within her soft pussy. One, two, three short sharp squeezes. One. Two. Three. Slow.

By instinct she knows that they have to be careful, that all movement is hidden beneath her red flowing skirt so that if anyone were to come upon them it would be hard to tell what they are really up to. She feels his cock inside her pussy, pulsing relentlessly, as if it is her possession. She keeps up the rhythm, her heart thumping with the idea of their imminent discovery, the fear and danger of that turning her on further. She can sense Russell falling back, on the edge of his orgasm. She closes her eyes and to her shock she imagines she sees Theo. He is coming for her, pulling apart the undergrowth. He has been looking for her for so long. He will pull her off Russell and take her in his arms. He will run away with her, crashing through the woods of Central Park, running across the water like a god, and she will be weightless, as if she were a child, as if he were her saviour. No water in the world could drown their love.

'Oh my God! Valentina!' Russell whispers, his voice thick with passion.

She feels him come inside her, their slick juice running down her thighs. At the same moment, she has lost Theo; he disintegrates in front of her eyes.

'Valentina, are you OK?' Russell asks her softly.

She says nothing, yet she cannot raise her eyes to his. He pulls her down on to his chest and wraps his arms around her, and at last she feels a little better to be lying on his belly, taking in his warmth and feeling his heart beat against hers. They stay like this for a couple of minutes until his phone begins to ring. She waits for him to ignore it, but to her disappointment he gently pushes her off his chest, and she slides onto the blanket. He pulls his phone out of his trouser pocket and looks at the screen.

'Sorry,' he says, getting up and beginning to walk away from her. 'I have to take this call.'

He disappears into the bushes and she sits on her own waiting, hugging her red skirt to her knees. She feels exposed and a little foolish now. She pulls the champagne bottle out of the ice pack and pours herself another glass, gulping it back almost in one.

When Russell comes back he is different. His face is flushed and he avoids looking at her as he hastily packs away the picnic things.

'I'm sorry, something has come up,' he says. 'I have to dash off.'

'Oh, but we haven't eaten yet.'

He pauses, turns to her.

'Well, you can stay and eat,' he says, offering her the basket. 'But I have to go. It's important.'

She shakes her head. The idea of eating the romantic picnic on her own appals her.

'Is it work?' She ventures.

'No,' he says giving her a cold stare. 'It's personal.'

163

She feels as if he has slapped her face. The way he has switched so fast from attentive lover, to almost a stranger.

'Sorry.' Russell's voice softens as he notices her crushed expression. 'I really am, for running out on you like this, but I'll call you later, okay?'

After he has gone, she walks down to the edge of the little lake, watches couples rowing boats upon the water, against the backdrop of the New York skyline. Her cheeks are burning with humiliation. She feels hurt that Russell has abandoned her like this, right after making love; isn't that just bad manners? Yet she knows that the reason she is upset is more than this. She is angry with herself for being such an idiot. Marco had warned her, after all. Russell is a womaniser, and that was probably one of his other lovers. Valentina had thought that she didn't care. Yet it is obvious she does.

$\mathcal{T}$ina

IN THE WEEKS THAT FOLLOWED HER TRIP TO BERLIN, TINA viewed her experience there as a kind of fever. It was like she had been struck down, her body taken over by desire and passion. She had done a terrible thing to Phil, and yet, in a perverse way, whatever Karel did to her, had been good for their relationship. She feels racked with guilt every time she looks at Phil, and yet, at the same time, she is switched back on to sex. So had it been a good fever? A sickness that was able to heal? Is that heartless of her? Karel had told her he loved her. She can't really believe it. He is a sensuous, sexy young man. They have an amazing connection, and an unbelievable sexual chemistry, but love? Maybe, like Karel said, they had loved each other in a previous lifetime, but all that counted was the present world, and it was Phil who she loved now.

The night after she returned from Berlin, she and Phil went out for their delayed anniversary meal in a swanky Milanese restaurant. It had been a romantic evening, one that reminded her of their early years. Phil had been so attentive, telling her how beautiful she looked and that she was the centre of his universe. The food had stuck in her throat. She felt so bad. If only she hadn't done what she did! How could she ever look him in the eye again? At the end of the night, Phil presented her with a ring. It was a beauty: a huge ruby set in gold, with tiny diamonds encircling it.

'Oh my God, Phil!' she exclaimed, guilt slashing across her heart.

'You deserve it,' he said. 'After all, we're not married and I reckon, at this stage in our lives, you've earned this ring.'

'I love it,' she said, feeling almost teary as she pushed it on to her finger and held it up to sparkle in the candlelight.

Her body was still glowing with all the after-effects of Berlin. She felt so tactile. She couldn't wait to be touched, to touch. She felt desire for her old love blooming within in her again.

Back home, she went into the kitchen, took a bottle of champagne out of the fridge and, with her other hand, led Phil into the bedroom by his tie. He looked at her with expectation, his eyes widening with delight when he saw what her intention was.

She sat him on the bed as she popped open the champagne and filled two glasses, which she had left by the bed earlier. 'This is my gift to you,' she announced, taking a sip of her champagne, letting its fizzy luxury slip down her throat.

Her body was her own again. It was as if, after being with Karel, she had stepped back inside who Tina really was. She felt sultry and seductive and desired.

'You can look, but you cannot touch,' she said. 'Not yet, anyway.'

She walked over to the locker and turned on the tape cassette, which she had also set up earlier. The guitar strains of Jimi Hendrix blasted out of the little machine: 'Foxy Lady'. Phil grinned from ear to ear when he heard the music, for he remembered, too. The first time they met, this had been playing on the car radio as she had driven like a lunatic through the evening traffic into central Milan.

She began to swing her hips to the music, looking him directly in the eye, and caressing her body over her clothes. She pushed the skirt of her dress up her thighs to show him the top of her stockings, and pulled her straps off her shoulders. Slowly, she unzipped her dress and let it slide down her body until it was on the floor, and she stepped out of it. Phil looked at her with such longing she nearly jumped on top of him, but she wanted to tease him for a little longer, build this up into something special. She was wearing exactly the kind of lingerie he liked: a black, lacy bra and tiny panties, with suspender belt and stockings, and high heels. She danced in front of him for a moment, showing off her breasts, her bottom, in expert rhythm, in her sexy lingerie. She walked right up to him, and turned her back to him.

'Take off my bra,' she ordered him.

He unclasped the bra, with fumbling fingers.

She turned around, holding her bra on with her hands, and then letting it fall, pushing her naked breasts towards his face. He reached out, but she stepped back.

'No touching!' she chided him.

She danced away for a few steps, and then she started pushing her fingers down the top of her panties a little way, dragging them down, bit by bit, so that he could see a tiny bit more of her each time. She looked down at the ground, pretending to be shy, imagining that this was the first time between them once more. She spun around and turned her back to him again. Keeping her legs straight, she bent over, pushing her bottom up into the air, pulling her panties off in one go, so that he was looking at her offering herself to him. She heard him groan and, when she turned to look at him, he had pulled his trousers down so that

167

his cock was free, erect and yearning for her. She smiled coyly, dancing over towards him in just her stockings and high heels.

Finally, she let him touch her, and he pulled her face down to his so that he could kiss her. His longing flowed into her through his lips, and she realised she had denied herself her man's love for too long. She couldn't understand why. She sat astride his lap, so that his cock was tapping her belly button, and let him touch her. He embraced her with such emotion it almost knocked the breath from her. He held her for a while and then she pulled back, slipped off his lap. He looked a little panicked for a moment, as if she might stop. But who could blame him? How many times over the past couple years had she turned her back on him in their bed?

She smiled at him reassuringly, taking up her glass and filling her mouth with champagne. Then she knelt down and took his cock into her mouth so that champagne fizzed around it as she licked and caressed him. He gasped and, as she pulled her mouth away and looked up at him, she saw him looking down at her bent head with adoration. She stood up again and this time she took hold of his cock, stroking it firmly with one hand as she leant over and took a condom from the bedside locker with the other. Kissing his cock with her mouth again, she ripped the packet open and gently sheathed him. Then she sat down upon him, pushing him inside her. As she looked into his face, she could see tears in his eyes.

'Oh, Tina,' he whispered. 'I've missed you so much.'

His love for her, his need for her, fanned her heart and fed her love for him. She couldn't understand why she had rejected him for the last two years, but now she wanted to make up for it. She sent a prayer of thanks to her young Berlin friend. He had done this for her – opened up her body again and made her feel confident and sexy, and attractive to Phil. It dawned on her how important sex was to show her man how much she loved him.

They fell back on to the bed as she brought his cock up deep within her, and together she and Phil rolled back the years, back to the first time they made love, when their hearts were brimming with hope and expectation, and into the future, towards a dream, as ethereal and illusive to every couple as to them. Could they last for ever?

When she looks back, Tina calls those few blissful weeks after she came back from Berlin their second honeymoon period. She and Phil made love every day, sometimes first thing in the morning, sometimes at night, sometimes during the day, if they were both home. Overnight, he seemed to be a new man, laughing in the mornings rather than disappearing into his office for a smoke, taking time off from his writing at the weekends to take her and Mattia on trips – one time to Venice, one time to Florence and even taking them both all the way to Rome one weekend. He was so attentive, buying her flowers and little gifts of sexy lingerie, constantly telling her how beautiful she was, how much he loved her. She had been completely wrapped up in their ecstasy. She couldn't get enough of him. There was the odd time when she might think of Karel and look to see when his concert was on in Vienna. She hadn't forgotten her promise to him and, when the time was right, she would tell Phil that she had a young friend from East Berlin who needed their help to defect. She was certain Phil would help him. What happened after Karel got out, she didn't want to think about. For the least she could do was help him to his freedom. She owed him that.

* * *

169

Within one day, their harmony falls apart. It has been just over a month now since she returned from Berlin. She is flicking through the morning papers when she reads a headline that makes her stomach lurch:

DDR cellist refused right to travel.
International tour cancelled.

She knows immediately that it must be Karel. She reads on. The article is short, stating that the DDR has banned one of their most celebrated socialist prodigy musicians, Karel Slavik, from travelling outside East Germany to perform in Vienna on 17th October. The journalist writes that the ban is to last for seven years. It is believed that the East German state authorities suspected him of planning to defect to the West.

She feels sick when she reads the article. She has never mentioned her proposition to Karel to defect to anyone else, of course, and when they had spoken about it in his apartment, the water had been running in the shower. Even if he was being monitored, surely they couldn't have heard her whispered suggestion over the thunder of running water?

She slowly stirs her cup of coffee again, and again, and again, trying to think of a way she can help him, but she knows it is hopeless. Poor Karel. She had seen how much he desired his freedom, despite his pretence that he was a devoted advocate of the socialist regime in the DDR.

She takes a bite of her brioche and a sip of coffee, and immediately it repeats on her. She tries to swallow it down, but to her shock she finds herself retching. She runs to the bathroom and throws up, just in time. She sits back on her haunches and feels her forehead. She doesn't have a fever. She just feels nauseous. It is probably the shock over Karel, she reasons. What else could make her so sick, just like that?

Suddenly, she sits down with a thump on the bathroom floor and brings her hand to her mouth in horror. She tries to remember when she had her last period, counting back the days. But she knows, even without having to go to the doctor, that she is pregnant, because she feels exactly how she did when she was pregnant with Mattia: nauseous, with sore, swollen breasts. The baby must be Karel's, for she and Phil have used contraception every time they have made love since she came back from Berlin, and, before Berlin, they hadn't had sex for months.

She starts to shiver with dread. What should she do? How will Phil react if she tells him? How can she not expect him to reject her? Could she hide it from him and have an abortion? No; despite the fact she might destroy the family she already has, Tina cannot consider aborting this baby. She realises that she wants her (already she feels it must be a girl). She just hopes that Phil can accept the baby and what she means: that Tina is not the woman she pretends to be – a devoted partner and lover. No; she is neither of these things. She is a woman who breaks things and hurts the ones she loves. She hopes he can forgive her, because she cannot imagine life without Phil.

$\mathscr{V}$alentina

RUSSELL CALLS HER RANDOMLY. SHE MIGHT BE IN THE MIDDLE OF a shoot and he will ring her up, whispering down the phone how he would like to tie her up and fuck her right at that very moment. Or in the middle of the night her phone will buzz and she will receive a text.

'Come fuck me now.'

It is so dirty, and yet irresistible to her. She tells herself it is all a fun game; a distraction from her heartache over Theo, and the intrigue concerning the Glen lookalike and the art theft. She finds herself getting out of bed and falling into a taxi, speeding across town to Russell's apartment. There he will greet her silently, leading her out onto his dark terrace, crammed with luscious plants creating a protective barrier between them and the outside world. He will lead her to the old velvet armchair, positioned with a perfect view of the High Line and the Hudson River beyond. They fuck on that chair. She sits on his lap, her head tipped back and staring at the crescent moon, not caring if anyone can see them, wondering how many other women he has done this with.

Sometimes Valentina visits Russell in his studio on West 27th Street. For some reason she expects him to be an expressionist, but his paintings surprise her by being almost photo-realist. And they are all portraits, mostly women, young like her. He tells her that his inspirations are portraits by Dutch Masters such as Vermeer; the intense study of the subjects' expression and all that it reveals of who they are. He asks to paint her yet again, but always Valentina refuses. So instead they have sex. He ties her to one of the support beams in his warehouse studio and makes love to her. It is fast, urgent and primal, and yet it never satisfies her. Each time they make love she wants more. Her body is slipping out of her grasp. Longing consumes her need.

Often when Valentina leaves Russell's studio she wonders how he affords his lifestyle. He never seems to be short of money, whipping out credit cards and cash every time they go out. He has a huge studio and a fancy apartment in a prime area of Chelsea. He doesn't seem to do that much modelling work (indeed he admitted to her that the *Harper's Bazaar* job was the first one he had done in a long time) and yet he can afford to paint full time. She considers the possibility that he is a roaring international success as an artist. But if she searches for his name on the internet she can't even find a website, let alone a gallery representing him. He has tons of unsold paintings in his studio. These portraits of women, stacked against the walls, getting dusty because no one is buying them. She can only assume that he must have very rich and supportive parents.

After sex with Russell in his studio Valentina is always hungry, yet her lover is keen to get back to his painting. He tells her that she inspires him. Thus she often finds herself alone again, walking down 16th Street and into Chelsea Market. Each day she chooses something different to eat. Despite her best efforts she can't help thinking of Theo at these times. Imagining that if things had been different, the two of them might have

173

been together in this market. Sometimes she'll go to Lobster Place and eat fresh oysters, slipping them down her throat with pleasure, imagining Theo feeding her. Other days she wants something sweet, and will go to the bakery and indulge in raspberry muffins and English breakfast tea. She sits at a table for two, wrapping her legs around her chair legs, imagining they are Theo's legs, and that he is leaning over the table opposite her, kissing sweet crumbs from her lips.

After her refreshment she starts walking again. Theo leads her downtown into South Manhattan, through SoHo, Tribeca and Chinatown until she has reached South Street Seaport. She gazes at Brooklyn Bridge. She can sense him nudging her to cross it. She knows that Theo's parents are expecting another visit but she cannot face them yet. She ignores her dead lover's call, and turns on her heel back into Chinatown, and towards East Village and Marco's apartment. All the while she repeats the words like a mantra.

Theo is gone. Theo is gone.

She tries to let him go.

Tonight Russell and Valentina are playing one of their favourite games. Valentina's arms and legs are tied together behind her back with the soft silken white Japanese rope. It is loose enough that she is not in any discomfort, yet she is captive. She feels an enticing mixture of fear and arousal. Russell walks around her. He is dressed smartly in a pinstriped business suit; the only naked part of him, his bare feet. He is surveying every inch of her naked body. He is standing behind her now, and she is charged with expectation. He tips her forward so that her chin is brushing against his sheepskin rug and her backside is in the air. He bends down and she feels him trailing his fingers beneath her, from her clitoris and into her vagina, searching for her most vulnerable point, her doorway to ecstasy.

'I adore you, Valentina,' he says.

His words thrill her. He makes her feel like an object of beauty, a sensual creature, all primal, and craving his touch.

He pushes her on to her belly; her knees are still bent and her lower legs are in the air, her hands still tied to her feet. Russell doesn't even undress. She feels the brush of the woollen suit against the back of her thighs as he pushes into her. She squeezes her eyes shut as he circles his hips, churning inside her. He presses against her thighs and she feels him going deeper. Suddenly, Russell is gone as he withdraws. She gasps and, before she can protest, he is in her again, thrusting hard and forcefully. He withdraws again and then, just as suddenly, slams into her, rocking her forward. Again and again, he bangs in and out of her, until she is almost hopping off the floor with frustration. Each time, she tries to hold him tightly with her pelvis, draw him into her, and each time he pulls out, leaving her dangling. She moans with frustration.

'I'm sorry, darling,' Russell whispers, delicately trailing his finger down her face. 'Do you want to say something?'

'Oh please,' she whispers.

'Please what?'

'Fuck me!' she gasps.

In response Russell presses his thighs against her again, pushing deep, up inside her, letting her hold him, but not for long. He is moving again, this time at a different pace, fucking her with rhythmic, rapid thrusts, his cock staying firmly inside her pussy. She feels the urgency within Russell's body. Valentina is hot, so very hot, as if in a fever. She squeezes his cock, raises her buttocks as high as she can as she hears him panting, the heat of their passion carrying him with her. Oh, come into me, my darling, she cries silently, and at that moment she is shocked by the ache in her heart. Who is her darling? Russell? Or is she still calling to Theo?

'How can you afford this apartment?' Valentina asks Russell, as she lies tucked within his shoulder, sharing a cigarette, and surveying the vast expanse of his bedroom. 'Does it belong to your family?'

'No,' he shakes his head. 'It belongs to –' he pauses and takes a drag on the cigarette – 'a friend of mine.'

'Oh, so it's not yours.'

'It is mine. She gave it to me.'

Valentina raises herself on her elbows and looks down at him. '*She*?'

Russell sighs, rolling his eyes. 'I have always been clear, Valentina, have I not, that our relationship is not exclusive?'

She cannot speak for a moment. Again she feels as if he has slapped her, and that it is she who is unreasonable.

'Sure,' she finally speaks, as lightly as she can and looking away so as not to betray her feelings. 'We are not even dating, as far as I'm concerned. It's just I'd like to know who *she* is.'

'She is a lover, a rich lover.' He pauses, taking another drag of the cigarette before leaning across her and putting it out in the ashtray. 'She is married, but her husband knows all about us.' He gives Valentina a cheeky grin. 'Actually, he likes to watch us.'

'He *watches* you having sex with his wife?' Valentina asks incredulously.

'Yeah, it turns him on,' Russell says. 'Sometimes I invite a girlfriend along as well. He likes to watch his wife with other women too.'

'And where are they now?' Valentina asks, licking her lips nervously and wondering whether Russell would ever ask her to take part in a threesome for this odd couple.

'They live most of the year in LA. They are seriously rich, Valentina . . . So I caretake their New York pad. They sort of gave it to me, as long as I play ball. It's a win-win situation.' He leans back against the headboard of the bed, giving her one of his magnetic, model smiles. She is not shocked by what he has told her. Hadn't Marco warned her so many times about Russell being a womaniser? And yet she feels a little hurt. It is ridiculous of her, she knows, for she is far from in love with him, but she just doesn't like the idea of Russell with another woman. It isn't her way to share her man.

Valentina wonders if it was this wife who rang Russell up the other day, and the reason he deserted her during their picnic in Central Park. Is Russell in love with her? Is he a slave to her and her husband's demands? It dawns on Valentina just how fucked up her relationship with Russell is. Yes they have amazing sex, but it is not enough. She realises she will never again be the girl she was before Theo. He changed her intrinsically for ever more and if she stays with Russell, despite herself, she will develop feelings for him. She can't let that happen since she knows they will not be reciprocated.

Valentina gets out of bed, begins to hunt for her clothes around Russell's bedroom.

'Where are you going?' Russell asks her, frowning.

'Home,' she says.

'But it's the middle of the night,' he protests.

'I'm sorry, Russell.' She pauses, turning around and looking at him. She takes in his glorious face, the thick auburn hair, the rich brown eyes, and the appealing smile. She steels herself. 'I don't think we should see each other again,' she says.

He looks more surprised than she thought he would.

'Is it because of what I just told you? Are you judging me?'

'I'm not judging you . . .' she licks her lips. 'But yes, I guess it is because of that. I'm just not into it.'

Russell gets out of bed. She tries to look away from his naked body, its ripe pleasing contours, and how a part of her just wants to fall back into his arms and make love again.

'I never asked you to take part. You would never have to meet them or do anything you wouldn't want to do,' he tells her.

'It's not that,' she says. 'It's just I don't want *this* any more.'

She opens her arms wide, taking in his bachelor pad.

'Well, what do you want?' he says, sounding a little impatient.

'That's just it, I don't know,' she says desperately.

As the cab hurtles across New York Valentina stares out at the dark still city, her eyes so sore it feels as if there is sand in them. She wishes she could cry. Waves of loss roll over her. She has been so stupid. How could she have let herself develop feelings for another man, particularly someone like Russell, when she is not even over Theo yet? She feels as if she is on her knees, broken and so very alone. She tries her best to cheer herself with the thought that at least Marco and Jake will be back from their trip when she gets home. She can let her friends scold her gently for being so foolish, and comfort her with hot sweet tea and love.

Valentina hears voices and sees light coming from the living room as she slips her shoes off and walks down the entrance hall of Marco and Jake's apartment. Thank God they are still awake. She could not bear to go to bed without seeing them first. Yet as she enters the room, she stops dead in her tracks, her heart soaring. She cannot believe her eyes, for, sitting on the couch between Marco and Jake, sipping from a giant cup of tea, is Leonardo.

'Leonardo!'

He looks different: thinner, older, his hair shorter and darker. Gone are the plush, Mediterranean looks and in their stead is a lean, tanned, rugged man. He looks as though he has been around the world several times, not just once.

'You're back at last!' He beams at her.

'We've been waiting hours,' Marco chides her. 'I sent you several messages.'

'I'm sorry; my battery went,' she says, rushing over to hug Leonardo as he stands up to greet her. She pulls back and looks into his face. It is the same smile; the same eyes that gather her into their warmth and make her feel so safe.

She has an urge to kiss him, properly, on the lips, which of course she doesn't do.

'What are you doing here in New York?' she asks him.

'I thought I'd try it out for a while . . .' He pauses. 'Marco suggested it.'

'He never told me!' she says, shooting Marco a look, surprised that he and Leonardo have been communicating. She wasn't even aware of the fact that they knew each other in Milan.

'Valentina,' Leonardo says. 'I am not in New York by chance. I am here for you.'

'What do you mean?'

'Marco wrote me, he is worried about you . . .'

'I am perfectly okay,' she says, giving Marco a fierce look which he pretends not to notice, while neatly stacking cups off the coffee table and bringing them into the kitchen, followed by Jake.

'You're lucky he didn't call Antonella and get her to come over!' Leonardo says.

'I am not a child that needs to be looked after,' she pouts.

Yet, as she looks at her friend, she remembers all the times he has been there for her; how he looked after her the week Theo went missing; how he has always been right by her side when she really needed him. Just like now.

'It's so good to see you.' Her voice suddenly breaks against her will, and she feels a lump in her throat. She tries to stifle her emotions. The last thing she wants is for Leonardo to see her sobbing right now. And yet she feels as if a weight has lifted, and her heart is already lighter. She is back on her feet again.

$\mathcal{T}$ina

AS SOON AS SHE PASSES THROUGH THE HEINRICH-HEINE-STRASSE border crossing, it starts to snow, as if to mark her entry into a colder, crueller world. She knows that is not how all the citizens of the DDR see it. In fact, they think the West is a more brutal place: a dog-eat-dog society. Here in the DDR the state protects them. They will always have work and a home. They are looked after. But, to Tina, the state's way of looking after is a form of control. And, if you want to be different, express your thoughts, your doubts, freely, then no one is going to look after you. You are out in the cold.

She hopes that Karel is OK. She is worried about the reasons behind his cancelled tour and him being banned him from leaving the DDR for seven years. The last time she was here, he was the darling of the DDR – treasured (chauffeur-driven cars, after-concert parties) and supported. Had his contact with her encouraged him to speak out? Could he even be in the Stasi prison? The thought sickens her. Yet she has heard nothing from him, and nor can she find out anything about him. She had got hold of Lottie's address through the model agency *Vogue* had used in Berlin, and wrote to her, asking her to ask Sabine for news of Karel, but Lottie had written back saying that she no longer sees her cousin or visits her in East Berlin. She doesn't elaborate, but the message is clear: she and Sabine have fallen out and Lottie can't help her.

Tina is four months pregnant – not showing yet but, even so, it's time she told Karel he is having a child. When she first found out she was pregnant, she felt it was best he didn't know, but it was, in fact, Phil who persuaded her she should tell him. She can't believe how amazing her partner has been about the pregnancy – prepared to take on some other man's child and raise her as his own, without once suggesting there might be another option.

Of course, when she first told him, about a week after she found out she was pregnant herself, when she couldn't bear to conceal the truth from him any more, he went wild. He called her every name under the sun: whore, slut, bitch. He had stormed out of the apartment and she had truly believed she would never see him again. It was the worst she had felt in her entire life. She had crawled into bed and curled up under the covers, sobbing.

But he came back. Five hours later. He was pale and emotional as he sat down on the end of the bed and confessed that he too had slipped up – just the once. It was the previous year, when they hadn't had sex in so long and he was really frustrated. One night, he had got drunk with a visiting PhD student from America, and one thing had led to another. He had been devastated that he had cheated on Tina, and had been feeling guilty ever since it happened.

'Are you angry with me for being such a hypocrite?' he asked, with worried eyes.

She grabbed him and hugged him fiercely. 'No, not at all; I am just relieved. I am not the only sinner then!' She kissed him tenderly on the lips. 'How can I blame you when I was rejecting you all the time? You had needs.'

He looked at her coyly. 'You make me sound very primitive,' he said.

'We are all primitive when it comes down to it,' she said.

'Well, at least I didn't get anyone pregnant,' he said, a little peevishly. 'I can't believe it, Tina; you are always so careful.'

She hugged herself, looking at him with sorrowful eyes. 'I don't know how I could have been so stupid . . . I am so sorry, Phil.'

He put his arms around her. 'I'm sorry I cheated, too,' he whispered.

After she told Phil the whole story about Karel, she had a feeling that her lover felt sorry for his rival, rather than jealous.

'Poor boy, he obviously didn't know what hit him when he met you.'

'What do you mean?'

'You have no idea the impact you can have, do you?'

'Come on, Phil; I am no femme fatale. I am just like any other woman.'

He had pulled her to him, wrapped his arms around her tightly and looked at her with deep sincerity. 'Tina Rosselli, you are far from any other woman, in my book.' He kissed her on the forehead, and then looked thoughtful for a moment. 'Tina, you should tell him he is having a child. It is his right to know.'

She had wanted Phil to come with her to visit Karel, but he refused. He said it wasn't fair for him to just turn up as well.

'But do you trust me?' she asked him, curious that he was so relaxed about her visiting Karel.

'What's the point of loving you, if I don't trust you?' he had replied.

* * *

She doesn't know Karel's address, but she is certain that she will remember the way. If she walks up to Alexanderplatz, she can then follow the route they took to his apartment that day. Yet, once she is standing in the middle of Alexanderplatz, she is not so sure she does remember. She takes a breath, closes her eyes. Snowflakes flutter on her chilled face and lace her eyelashes, so that, when she opens her eyes again, they leave icy tears on her cheeks. She thinks back to that golden day in September and, sure enough, she can imagine the streets as they were without the snow. She looks at the TV tower and remembers it was to her right and behind her the day they walked to his apartment. She sets off, confident that she is going the right way.

The snow is slippery on the pavement. She walks carefully, not wanting to fall over, pulling her coat tightly around her. The morning sickness has gone now, but she isn't as energetic as she used to be. She trudges through the dour streets. It seems to take her twice as long to get to his apartment as it took the time she was here before. Eventually, she is in a street she recognises. This is it, surely. It was the building on the corner. She stops at the gateway, gripping her gloved hands. She is wondering if she should be here now, but it is too late. She has to go through with it.

She walks up to the front doors and opens them, entering the hallway of the building. It is not much warmer than outside. She climbs up to the first floor. If she remembers, his door was on the left. To her relief, she sees his name on it. He is still here. He has not been whisked away. She rings the bell, waits. What if he is out? She hadn't thought of that. It is too cold to stand on his doorstep, waiting. Yet she can hear him. Feet shuffling down the corridor and, before she has a chance to panic, the door swings open.

Karel is speechless. His mouth drops open, and he stares at her in shock. She had been worried that he might have forgotten her, but his reaction tells her that he knows exactly who she is.

'Tina! Oh my God!' He grabs her and pulls her inside the apartment. 'Here, take your coat off; come in by the fire. You must be freezing.'

She is shivering, but it isn't just from cold. She is frightened of what she has to tell him, of how he might react. She doesn't want to hurt him. As soon as he opened the door, she remembered what it was she had been attracted to. It wasn't just his beautiful Slavic face, his height, his potency; it was also this reckless, wild quality he has about him, mixed with an irresistible vulnerability – a quality that he had the sense to guard in public, living as he did in the DDR, but in private it is so clear. He is a romantic.

He takes her wet, heavy wool coat off her and hangs it up, leading her into the sitting room where a fire is blazing in the grate. Outside, the snow has got heavier; in fact, it is a blizzard of white, giving her the feeling that they are encased, caved in.

'A drink? Coffee?'

Since she has become pregnant, she cannot bear the taste of coffee. 'Do you have any tea?'

'Sure; yes, of course. I'll dig around.' He disappears into the kitchen. 'It's so great to see you,' he calls out.

She squeezes on to the end of the couch, which is littered with musical scores and notebooks. The room is a mess, but cosy. Again, she has that sense of belonging – the same feeling that she had the first time she was here. She blushes when she remembers that they made love on this very rug at her feet. That was probably when she conceived. Imagine, the very first time you sleep with someone and you make a baby!

He comes out of the kitchen carrying a steaming teapot and plonks it on the coffee table, going back to bring out cups and saucers.

'No milk, I'm afraid,' he says.

'That's fine.'

'Plenty of sugar, though,' he says, offering her the bowl. She takes three spoonfuls and stirs it into her tea before taking a sip.

'So how are you?' he asks, cheerfully, as if they only saw each other the other day.

'I'm fine.' She crosses her legs, leans forward. 'But, Karel, why was your tour cancelled? Why have you been banned from travelling for seven years?'

He looks alarmed when she says this. 'It's a misunderstanding,' he says, tensely. Then, taking a notebook and pencil from the sofa, he writes something down, before handing it to her.

Don't say anything about the tour. I am being monitored.

She takes the pencil from him.

Why?

He balances the notepad on his lap and writes:

After our tea, let's go for a walk, OK?

She looks out at the blizzard of snow. Walking in that doesn't appeal, but she supposes they have no choice if they want privacy.

Karel takes her to the park. He puts his gloved hand in hers as they walk along the snowy paths. There are few out, apart from some children rolling in the snow. As soon as they are far from any eyes or ears, he speaks.

'It's safe now to talk,' he says.

'My God, Karel,' she says. 'What's happened? Are you in danger?'

'No, no,' he reassures her. 'I am just under surveillance.'

'But what did you do?'

He puts his hands in his pockets and faces her. 'I made the mistake of composing a love song,' he says, looking almost proud of himself.

'What?' She is confused. 'What is dangerous about a love song?'

'I wrote some music that was ... well ... romantic. They didn't like that.'

'What's wrong with romantic music?'

'It's self-indulgent, sentimental, bourgeois – I could go on. I was told, in the words of the great man, Lenin himself, that art belongs to the people. My music doesn't belong to me ... therefore, I have to write what they want.'

'So what happened?'

'They told me I couldn't perform it. I said no.'

'Oh, Karel ... it was just one piece of music.'

There it is again, that glitter of something reckless in his eyes.

'Not to me, it wasn't. It was about you.'

She says nothing, looks at him in astonishment. No one has ever written music for her before.

'I didn't think it was such a big deal,' he says, looking a touch regretful, 'but apparently it was, because they cancelled the tour ... banned me from travelling. I think the real reason is

187

nothing to do with the music; I think they saw the seed of discontent in me and maybe the temptation of being in a foreign country would push me over the edge and their prize musician would defect.'

'Would you have defected?'

He looks around him furtively, but the only sound is the creaking of the trees under the weight of the fresh snow. 'Yes, of course.' He sighs, taking her hands in his. He faces her. His eyes gleam like onyx against the white background of snow. 'I am so glad to see you,' he says. 'I have thought of you so many times over the past few weeks. I have hoped you would come back.'

He tries to gather her to him, to kiss her, but she pulls back. He immediately picks up on her resistance. 'What is it, Tina?'

She shakes her head, unable to know how to begin.

'Why have you come to see me, if you don't want to be with me?'

'You wrote music about me?' she whispers, avoiding his question. 'I can't believe it.'

'Why wouldn't you believe it?' he challenges her. 'I told you that I loved you.'

'But I just thought you were saying it in the heat of the moment.'

He looks at her, his head on one side. 'It is not something I have said to any other woman.'

The impact of what he has just told her hits her with full force. She shouldn't have come. She is filling him with false hope.

'That night – please, don't deny that it was out of this world.' He continues to speak, looking worried now.

She closes her eyes, takes a breath. She is not going to lie to him. 'It was the most amazing night of my life, Karel,' she says.

His expression relaxes as he grips her gloved hand tightly. 'Why don't we go back to mine and make up for all these lost weeks?' he says.

'Can't they hear us?'

'Who gives a fuck about them? Let them hear us! I don't care.'

He begins to drag her down a snowy slope on a short cut back to the park entrance, but Tina digs her heels in, forces him to stop.

'Please . . . stop . . . I . . . need to tell you something.' She stumbles over the words but she has to get this over with.

He turns around, looking at her expectantly. She hesitates, trying to find the right words and yet, just by looking at her, without her saying anything, he seems to know. He looks at her stomach and then back up at her face, his expression a question. She nods. He stumbles back to her over the snow, he is beaming, overjoyed. He gathers her up in his arms and hugs her fiercely, before pulling away and delicately placing his gloved hand on her belly.

'You're having our baby,' he whispers. 'Our love child!'

It is not the reaction she was expecting. She had imagined he would question her, doubt that the baby is his. She had thought he wouldn't want anything to do with the child, especially when he finds out that she and Phil are going strong. She had convinced herself that this trip had been her duty, to inform the father of her child of that fact. She had not expected this joy and excitement.

'I thought you should know,' she blurts out.

He steps back and looks at her, his face drawing in. Snow is piling down upon his bare head, covering his dark hair with a white cap.

'I thought you should know that I am having your baby,' she repeats, not knowing how else to explain herself.

'So that is why you came to see me?'

'Yes, and I was worried about you.'

He looks pensive for a moment. 'And this baby that you think is so important for me to know about, will I ever get to see it, let alone take part in its life?'

She can hear the raw emotion in his voice. She should never have listened to Phil. She should not have come here today. Phil thinks that Karel is a regular young guy, irresponsible and probably relieved to know that someone else would take care of his problem. But Karel is far from ordinary.

'Of course you will,' she says, feebly.

'And how do you propose I do that, Tina? Remember, I can't leave the DDR for seven years. Somehow, I don't think you would want to live here . . . so where does that leave me?'

'I could visit you with the baby . . . and you could write and apply for a permit to travel because of family reasons. I would never deny you your rights as a father.'

Karel is shaking his head. He turns to her with blazing eyes.

'Why did you have to tell me? Can you not see that this will torture me?'

'I'm so sorry . . . I just thought you should know . . .'

He clenches his hands into fists and pushes them into his eyes. 'I can't bear it, Tina. I feel like all the life is being stifled out of me. I am a prisoner in my own home.'

She is filled with compassion for him. She goes to him, pulling his fists from his eyes. 'Don't lose hope,' she whispers, as she uncurls each one of his fingers. 'That Wall cannot stay up for ever.'

'It's been up for twenty-three years already; what makes you so sure it won't last another twenty-three? How old will my child be then?'

'Karel, I will tell our child all about you . . . We will come to visit . . .'

He is shaking his head, and she is not sure whether his face is wet with melted snow or tears.

'No,' he says. 'Don't tell the baby about me. Don't come. Promise me. It will just make it worse if you do.'

'But—'

'Are you still with your boyfriend?' he suddenly interrupts, his cheeks blooming red.

She looks down at the snow, mashed between their feet. 'Yes,' she says in a small voice.

'And he knows?'

'Yes.' She coughs. 'He's OK about it.'

'Good,' says Karel. 'Then at least I know our baby will have a father, even if it's not me.' He turns on his heel and begins to walk away from her, ploughing through the snow.

'Karel, stop! Wait!'

She slithers after him and, in her haste, loses her footing, screaming as she lands with a thump on her back in the snow. She feels a sharp pain in her back and she cries out again. He is back to her in a moment.

'Are you all right?' he says, bending over her.

'I've a pain in my back, but yes, I think so,' she says, sitting up.

He bends down and gathers her in his arms.

'It's OK; I can walk,' she protests.

'You're not walking anywhere until I get you back to my apartment and we check that you are OK. You're carrying something precious now. We can't take any risks.'

She looks up at his serious, beautiful face as he carries her through the park, his expression intent as he focuses on not slipping on the snow. It breaks her heart to see him thus, not for herself, but because she can see what kind of father he would be. He would be the best kind, like her own father, like Phil. She buries her face into his chest, trying to commit his scent to her memory.

Back in his apartment, he knocks all the musical scores off the sofa and lies her down on it, tucking a blanket in around her. He builds the fire up and then disappears into the kitchen to make more tea. By the time he reappears, she feels warm and safe again.

'I think I am quite OK,' she says.

He comes to sit beside her, starts prodding her back and asking her if it hurts anywhere.

'No, I'm fine.' She begins to giggle as he tickles her.

'Good, I don't want any damage done because of my little tantrum.'

'It wasn't a tantrum,' she defends him,' you were upset.'

They look into each other's eyes for a long moment.

'Before you go,' Karel says, breaking the silence, 'do you want to hear the music I composed for you?'

'Can you play it for me now?'

'Of course I can,' he says.

He takes his cello from its stand, sits down upon a chair and puts it between his legs. She remembers the way he had held her between his legs when he made love to her, and those fingers playing her. It feels like a dream now, that it happened in another lifetime, not just four months ago. He fiddles around with the cello for a few minutes, tuning it.

She is filled with an urge to document this moment. It suddenly seems tremendously important that she has a picture of him. She leans across the sofa and pulls her bag towards her, taking out her camera.

'Can I take a picture of you?' she asks.

He stops tweaking his cello, looks up at her with surprise. 'Sure.'

'Imagine I'm not here. Just keep on doing what you are doing.'

He continues to tune the cello and then he sits still, taking deep breaths as if he is preparing himself to go for a run up a mountain. She catches it perfectly: the moment he looks up and out at her just before he brings his bow down to strike the strings. She knows it will be one of her best portraits, even before she develops it.

Karel begins to play, and she lays aside her camera now. At first she doesn't hear the music. It is all she can do to watch him, his whole body swaying as he plays the cello, the passion articulated in the sweep of his arms, the deep concentration on his face. He is something sublime, so intensely beautiful that she feels a deep fear for his survival, as if he is a rare species. And as her vision widens, she begins to hear. The sounds of his love for her infiltrate her heart and bring her back to the moment that they first met. It *had* been love at first sight. And, no matter how much she denies it, it was love for her as well as him. This realisation confuses her, for she loves Phil too. Is it possible to love two men at the same time?

Her dilemma is swept away by the sound his cello makes,

thrilling her deep down, and stirring her, as powerfully as any mating call. Tina imagines the child within her reaching out as she gets up from the sofa and walks over to stand in front of him. And, as he plays, she uncovers herself – pulls off her sweater and drops it to floor; unbuttons her blouse. She unzips her skirt and lets it drop, so that she is in her boots, tights and bra. He doesn't pause, but continues to play, now looking into her face with such unbridled yearning. He knows her music by heart. She wonders how many times he has played it, willing her to return to him. Now she is here, and her instinct is to feel that closeness with him once again, to become one: her, him and their baby. She unclasps her bra and lets it fall from her breasts; she pulls off her boots and tights. The room is hot from the fire but she is shivering.

She never gets to hear the end of his song for her because, at the sight of her naked in front of him, Karel drops the bow to the floor, the cello making a harsh twang as he puts it aside and scoops her up, carrying her into the bedroom.

Karel and Tina enter another lifetime again – one where it is just the two of them in a place where they are free. He buries himself deep within her and touches her in a place so sacred, so sensitive, that she cries with him when he comes.

Afterwards, as they lie in each other's arms and watch the snow still falling outside, she knows that this time she will not tell Phil. It is the least she can do for Karel.

'When the Wall comes down . . .' she whispers.

'If it comes down,' Karel corrects her, tracing patterns on her arm.

'If the wall comes down, I will come to you. I will bring her with me.'

'You think the baby is a girl?'

'Yes.'

'How will we find each other?'

'If they open the borders and the Wall comes down, then I will meet you five days after the first border crossing opens, at that very crossing, at midday. I will be there, waiting for you with your daughter, no matter what.'

'I told you not to tell her about me . . .' he says, looking away from her again, his voice breaking.

'I won't . . . You can tell her when you meet her, five days after the Wall comes down.'

'You do know that might never happen,' he whispers, turning back to her with doleful eyes.

'Yes, but we have to hope. Don't stop hoping.'

'I will find a way,' she hears him whisper as she dozes off, so that later she is not sure whether he really said it or whether she imagined it. 'I will find my daughter . . .'

$\mathscr{V}$alentina

SHE WAKES EARLY, HER BODY STILL NOT QUITE ADJUSTED TO THE
New York time difference.

She slides out of the bed and looks at the clock on the beside
table. It is six in the morning. There is a sudden flash of lightning
outside the window, which makes her heart jolt, and a few
seconds later she hears a roll of thunder. Rain spills out of the
sky, a dense curtain of water. She looks at Leonardo sleeping
through the storm, oblivious of the dramatic weather. She
reaches out and gently touches his forehead. She cannot believe
he is really here, asleep in her bed. Last night, they had fallen
asleep together, like they often had in the past – she and
Leonardo, as two old friends, sharing a bed together. No sex and
no agendas. It had been such a relief after the intense sexual
demands of her relationship with Russell

Her affair with Russell is already distant to her. She is not
missing him and nor is she upset any longer. It surprises her.
Looking at Leonardo now, she realises she needs him. She
decides that she is not going to let him run off to India again.

Valentina tiptoes out of the bedroom, grabbing her silk
kimono dressing gown and slipping it on. In the kitchen, she
pours herself a big glass of water from the jug in the fridge. The
chilled water tastes sweet, coursing through her body. She yawns

and stretches. She feels better today than she has felt in a long time.

'Good morning!'

She nearly jumps out of her skin. Leonardo is standing behind her, looking devilishly sexy in his underpants and nothing else.

'Goodness! I thought you were fast asleep,' she says.

He grabs her half-empty glass of water and takes a slug. 'Time for my morning practice,' he says.

'Yoga?'

'Would you like to join me? Do you want to ask the others?'

There is another flash of lightning outside as the rain intensifies.

'Oh, I don't know . . .' Valentina says. 'I wouldn't disturb Marco or Jake, they like to get up late.'

'Whatever you wish,' he replies, strolling into the sitting room and lighting some incense that he has produced from one of his bags in the hall.

She follows, watching Leonardo spread out his yoga mat on the Turkish rug. She can't help noticing how much more toned he has become since she last saw him. He is thinner, too, but he is all muscle. She can see the strength in his legs and his back as he bends down.

Impulsively, she pulls off her dressing gown and discards it, grabbing one of Leonardo's T-shirts from his bag and slipping it on.

Her friend looks on approvingly. 'You can use my mat, if you like, and I'll use the rug. Have you ever done a full sun salutation before?'

She shakes her head.

'Just follow my lead.'

He speaks softly, giving her instructions, emphasising her

need to breathe deeply and slowly from her belly. He mentions locks – the root lock, the pelvic lock – but she doesn't quite grasp what he means. The yoga is far more physical than she'd imagined. He does sun salutation after sun salutation and before long she is in a sweat. Yet, despite her struggle to follow him, it feels good and she is so busy focusing on what she is doing, she has no chance to let her mind wander to thoughts of Russell or Theo, or even the mystery surrounding the Glen lookalike. She has to stay in the present.

He takes her through a series of postures, barely pausing between each one. She thought that yoga was slow and gentle . . . Not this yoga, anyway. Eventually, he brings them down to lie on their backs. He tells her to close her eyes and relax her whole body, limb by limb, bone by bone. She feels as if she is sinking into the floor of the apartment, as if her body is without any solid matter, but purely liquid. She drifts.

Valentina is not sure how long she has been lying on her back, but when she comes to, she hears music: a woman's voice, singing softly – some kind of spiritual chant. She sits up to face Leonardo, who is sitting on the couch in the lotus position, eating an orange and watching her.

'Do you feel better?' he asks, offering her a segment of orange.

She nods, standing up and taking the orange, sucking it until its sweet juice explodes inside her mouth.

'You're very tense,' he comments. 'I've never seen you like this before.'

'Like what?' she asks him.

'So –' he struggles for the right word – 'out of your body.'

'You're right,' she says, picking up her dressing gown and wrapping it around herself again. 'I have been trying to be how

I was before I met Theo,' she sits down next to him. 'I was seeing this guy, purely a sexual relationship, but it turned out it wasn't enough for me.'

'So what happened?' Leonardo asks her.

'I ended it, last night actually, before I came home.' She pauses. 'Thank you for coming to New York, for me.'

'You're welcome,' he says, pulling her to his side so that the two of them are snuggled up together on the couch.

They listen in silence to the music for a while.

'Do you like it?' Leonardo asks her. 'It's Deva Premal.'

'Yes, it's very relaxing . . . it calms me.'

She lets the soft chant of Deva Premal lift her up.

'Tell me how you are?' she asks Leonardo. 'How was India?'

'Amazing,' Leonardo says. 'I feel like a different man.'

'Did you do lots of yoga?'

'Yes; I mean, I am a trained teacher now in *vinyasa* yoga, and Tantric.'

'What is Tantric, Leonardo?' she asks, with curiosity.

'Apart from a type of yoga, it can also be a different way of making love,' he tells her. 'It's not just about the act of sex; it's about opening up your heart again, and you do that by unlocking your body, sensually.' He offers her another segment of orange. 'When you experience Tantric sex, it is like the most intense ecstasy you will ever experience. S&M doesn't even come close.'

She rests her head on his chest. He smells of oranges and the exotic, tangy aroma of the incense he was burning. She thinks about this Tantric sex. Maybe this could be a way of healing her heart and opening up possibilities of love again in her life.

'Will you unlock me?' she whispers to Leonardo's chest. 'Will you show me the keys to Tantric sex?'

He pulls back and looks at her. 'I didn't come here to sleep with you, Valentina. I came here because I care about you as my friend. Everyone is worried about you.'

'I know.' She nods. 'But, Leonardo, I need you to help me learn to love again . . . please.'

He looks at her in silence, his eyes widening. She can see his attachment to her – love, even – glowing from within. She needs this love. She wants to feel again.

'OK,' he says, slowly. 'If you really want me to.'

She gives him a kiss on the cheek. 'OK,' she says, snuggling up against him again. 'So what do we do now?'

He laughs. 'Well, we don't just jump into bed and have quick-fix sex when we feel like it . . . We start at the beginning. I want to take you back inside your body, so that you are aware of yourself, you love yourself, for that is the best way to give and receive love from another.'

'OK,' she says. 'So how do we begin?'

'We begin,' Leonardo says, gently removing her from his chest, 'by taking a walk.'

'We are going out?' Valentina asks him, surprised. She looks out of the apartment window; the storm is over and it has stopped raining. Now, the sun is blasting fiercely outside. She can almost see the steam rising from the streets, and she can smell a powerful aroma of wet leaves and full blossom.

'Yes,' says Leonardo, emphatically. 'Are you free today?'

'Yes; Marco is busy on another shoot. We are not working again together until Thursday.' She turns back to Leonardo and picks up the orange peelings from the couch. 'We are going to do a shoot at the High Line. I was planning to check it out today.'

'Perfect,' says Leonardo. 'Let's go there.'

200

* * *

'Did you hear about the big bank heist?' Leonardo asks her as he sits down on one of the broad wooden sun loungers on the High Line.

'No,' she says, sliding on next to him. His body is warm next to hers, and he still smells of oranges.

'Apparently it's connected to the art robbery at the Neue Galerie,' Leonardo says.

It is the first time he has brought up the subject directly since he arrived.

She feels herself stiffen. She has heard nothing more from Delaney and Balducci. It is as if the trail on the stolen Klimt painting has gone dead.

'In what way?' she asks him.

'Well, the gang hacked into several banks' systems. During the exact hour after the theft of Klimt's painting, hundreds of the gang's members rushed around the city making withdrawals of cash from ATMs, which totalled four million dollars,' Leonardo tells her.

'So robbing the painting was a ploy to distract the police from noticing the bank heist?'

'Exactly,' says Leonardo. 'They never actually wanted the painting. In fact, it will probably be found in a dumpster in some back alley in SoHo before the week is out. It's worthless to them. They could never sell it.'

Valentina frowns. 'It all seems rather over the top,' she says, thinking of the mystery curator again. Could he really be Glen? She is not surprised that he might be mixed up with some criminal gang. Despite his smooth manner, she had always thought he was a thug underneath.

'Yeah, but think about it . . .' Leonardo says. 'They stole

EVIE BLAKE

millions that day, and all the cops were running around trying to find the painting. It worked.'

She looks out at the greenery of the High Line. She can't resist framing a shot in her imagination. She pictures one of the models, a tiny girl from Vietnam, standing among the old railway tracks, greenery shooting up around her, the slightly out of focus highrises behind her.

She nudges into Leonardo, feeling his hipbones jutting against her soft flesh as they lie back next to each other on the sun lounger. She feels languorous and sensual lying in the sun. It is good to feel a man's body lying next to hers. Now would be the time of day she would call on Russell. She is so close to his apartment; he is just a block or two away. Thank God Leonardo is with her. She is not sure, otherwise, whether she would give in to her temptation or not.

She turns to Leonardo. 'Are you going to tell me Tantra's secrets? Are we going to fuck all day, all night, and all day again, without coming?'

Leonardo smiles at her indulgently. 'I love it when you talk dirty, Valentina.' He winks at her. 'But, seriously, there is so much more to Tantric than slow sex . . . When you practise Tantric, sex can become a vehicle for you to contact your core, your inner world and your silent self.'

Valentina gives a fake yawn. 'Sounds a little bit boring, darling.'

Leonardo leans over and gives her waist a squeeze, and she yelps in surprise; then he begins to tickle her under the arms.

'Stop . . . Stop . . .'

'I am teaching you not to be so disrespectful, you naughty girl.'

202

She squirms beneath him, but he doesn't give up tickling her. Passers-by look over at them, but Valentina doesn't care because Leonardo is making her laugh. The release of tension within her body is euphoric. Suddenly, he stops tickling her and leans down, kissing her very briefly on the lips. She looks up at him, and Leonardo is serious now.

'I am going to look after you, Valentina.'

'You know I don't need looking after, Leonardo.'

'And you know I don't mean it literally.'

She sits up, shimmies back on the sun lounger and twists her legs around his.

'Go on then, give me the first key to unlock my Tantric self.'

'First of all, I have to tell you the secret of Tantra.'

He crosses his arms and she examines his skin, brown and glossy as polished walnut from all those months in India.

'The secret of Tantra is that sexual energy is encouraged to stay inside your body. It is not released in orgasm, as is normally the habit.'

'But isn't that the whole pleasure of sex? To climax?'

'Let me explain. This sexual energy stays within the body and is revitalised, and through this we reach a more intense ecstasy.'

'I still don't understand. You are talking in riddles.'

'Look, in Tantric we can direct sexual energy in the usual way by orgasm, of course, or we can redirect it to give us more energy, more love. It is about *being* rather than *doing*. So, through relaxation rather than tension, we open and expand. Sex can become an all-over rapture, a total body, mind and spirit ecstasy, whereas regular sex usually focuses on one point of release.'

Now she *is* curious.

They walk along the High Line, among the fragrant spring blossoms and young grass, along the wooden slats and above the relentless streets below them. It feels almost like an analogy for what Leonardo is telling her. All the rushing to get to a destination below them is like the goal-obsessed sex of the modern age. Sex is not really sex unless we 'come'. And yet who says so? Are there other paths to rampant passion? The High Line symbolises Leonardo's Tantric: a place of inner peace and external motion; energy flowing up the body of Manhattan along the old tram lines; something old, stark and urban, transformed into something new; an opulence of gorgeous greenery.

Leonardo takes her hand in his, interlaces his fingers in hers. 'So this is the first key,' he says. 'When you make love the Tantra way, you usually keep your eyes open. The eyes are a powerful channel for sexual energy.'

'I find it harder to get turned on if my eyes are open,' Valentina tells him. 'It is easier to lose myself if I close them.'

'You said it yourself . . . You are losing yourself. But, in Tantra, that is the last thing you want to do. You want to be more aware, more present for yourself and your lover.'

Valentina thinks of her sessions with Russell, how she nearly always wanted to be blindfolded so that she didn't have to see his face – so that she could lose herself in fantasies.

'Making eye contact with your lover is an art in itself,' Leonardo says. 'You have to change the way you look. Normally, we look from in to out, but in Tantra you try to look from out to in; your eyes are like windows simply open and receiving. When you look at your lover in this way, you are allowing yourself to be seen.'

Leonardo stops walking. They are standing in front of a young sapling, its leaves pale green and juicy.

'Look at this tree,' he says. 'Really look at it – the fresh green of its leaves and its vitality.'

Valentina looks at the tree. It is swaying slightly in the light breeze on top of the High Line.

'Now close your eyes,' Leonardo says.

She closes her eyes.

'When you open your eyes again,' Leonardo says, 'imagine that you are no longer looking at the tree, but that the tree is looking at you.'

Valentina opens her eyes; immediately, she imagines that the tree is looking at her; the notion is ridiculous and yet Leonardo is right, everything feels and looks different. She feels its green vital energy filling her, she imagines she is absorbing its sweet, living juice.

'That is amazing,' she whispers.

Leonardo is grinning.

He stands in front of her, blocking the vision of the tree, and puts his hands on her shoulders. She looks up at him.

'Now look into my eyes in the same way, softly. Allow yourself to "be" and be seen. Invite me into yourself, through your eyes.'

Valentina looks into Leonardo's eyes. At first, she focuses more on his left eye, she concentrates on receiving its warm nut-brown shades, then she looks to his right, noticing that it is a slightly different shade of brown – paler, with dark-green flecks within it. This eye is not as kind as the other, and yet she finds it has more of an impact on her. The two of them stand just a few inches apart; they are as if stone, the sea of people rippling around them and washing away, and yet Valentina feels they could be standing on their own tiny cloud in a sky of desire. She has slept with Leonardo many times – he was always her 'friend who fucked' – but never has she felt such desire for him as she does now, just looking into his eyes. She doesn't need to tell him how much she wants him. He can read it in her eyes. How long they look at each other like this, Valentina cannot tell. They are in their own circle of light. Finally, Leonardo takes his hands from her shoulders and drops his head, breaking the link between them.

'Can you see now, Valentina, how making love face to face, with your eyes open, brings incredible sensuality into sex?'

She nods, a little thrown by the sexual tension between them all of sudden. How could just looking into Leonardo's eyes make her want to have sex with him so much?

'What has all this got to do with unlocking me, Leonardo?'

'Because you have been making love with your mind, and that is why you are hurting so much at the moment. I want to return you into your body, Valentina, for that is the way to healing your heart.'

'So that is the first key . . . the eyes?'

'Yes, that's it. Simple, and yet more erotic than we give them credit for. Look into your lover's eyes.'

They take a cab back to Leonardo's apartment. He tells her that it is owned by his uncle, who is living in Dubai at the moment and has more or less given Leonardo free use of it. Valentina is pleased to see that it is barely a five-minute walk from Marco's place, close to Gramercy Park. The apartment is sparsely furnished. Leonardo explains that his uncle moved all his stuff out to make room for his nephew. At the moment, there is a futon mattress on the floor in one room and orange silk curtains, with gold embroidery, hanging from the windows. Upon the futon are red sheets and, covering these, are red towels. Beside the futon are two big, black ostrich feathers in a vase, like the feathers in the Klimt painting.

'So, Valentina,' Leonardo asks her, 'I am going to make some tea and, afterwards, would you like a yoni massage?' He indicates for her to sit down on the futon mattress.

'What's a yoni massage?'

'Yoni is the Hindi for the vagina, so I think it's self-explanatory.'

'Oh . . . I'm n-not sure . . .' she stutters.

'It's very healing,' he reassures her, 'and gentle; it won't hurt.'

'It's not that; it's just, well, I feel a little exposed . . .'

'But we have made love so many times? I have seen *everything*, my friend.'

'But you won't be getting anything out of it. All your attention will be focused on me. It makes me feel a little selfish.'

'Believe me, I will be getting something out of it, Valentina. When I give a massage, I am not worrying about technique; I am focusing on myself, and the joy of touching and giving. It is as pleasurable for me as for you.'

He is looking at her in such a way that she knows he isn't lying to her. He loves me, she thinks. And, instead of this fact worrying her, it makes her feel stronger. She needs Leonardo's love.

'So,' he says, handing her a cup of mint tea five minutes later. 'Are you ready?'

Spring sunshine is cascading through the open windows of Leonardo's Tantric den. He sits in its direct beam, and stretches like a panther. The feeling returns that she had on the High Line: she wants him – not to make herself feel better, or to escape into a fantasy about Theo, but just for him.

'I'm ready,' she tells him.

* * *

She is lying supine on Leonardo's red bed. The curtains are closed, although a little sunlight sneaks in through the cracks. Leonardo has candles burning around the edges of the room. Beside the bed is pot of fragrant oil upon a little burner. Its exotic, spicy aroma fills the room, making her relax further.

She is wrapped in a red silk sarong, underneath which she is naked. Leonardo is kneeling beside her on the bed. He too has a red sarong on, tied around his lean waist. She looks up at him, feeling a little nervous, wondering quite what a yoni massage will entail. She is worried that she won't be able to control herself, that she will orgasm too soon and ruin the whole Tantric thing.

'Should I keep my eyes open – look at you?' she asks him.

'It's up to you, although maybe this first time you should close them and just concentrate on yourself, nothing else. Open up the sensations within your own body; don't worry about me.'

She closes her eyes and Leonardo begins. He pulls her silk sarong off her shoulders, as if he is unwrapping her, sliding it away from under her body, and now she lies naked before him. He massages her shoulders. His hands are slick with the hot, fragrant oil. He works down both of her arms, pulling the tension out of her hands, finger by finger. He massages her feet, her legs, her thighs, passing over her pelvic area to her stomach and up to her breasts. She imagines him scooping handful after handful of hot, scented oil into his palms, for her breasts are thick with oil, and she feels herself opening out from the heart, as he massages each of her breasts, moving his hands swiftly between the two of them. For a moment, she starts to enter a fantasy, a dream of her and Theo on a honeymoon in Morocco and her new husband massaging her with oils, but then she pulls herself out of it. She counsels herself: stay in the moment, with your body, Valentina. Take in all the sensations.

She doesn't know how long Leonardo massages her breasts but, by the time he asks her to turn over on to her front, she is entirely relaxed. His gentle massaging touch has penetrated her loneliness more than all the S&M sessions she had with Russell.

Leonardo massages her back, working his way down her spine, from the nape of her neck right to the tip of her tailbone. She senses him moving around and the next thing she feels is the most exquisite stroking sensation. He must be using the two big ostrich feathers on her. She never imagined that feathers on her skin could feel so intense, full of power. He strokes them one at time across the skin of her back, speeding up so that her skin is tingling beneath the sensation of the fluttering feathers, as if they are thousands of butterfly kisses assaulting her naked body.

He removes the feathers and pours more heated, scented oil on to her back, starts working it into her skin. This is no ordinary massage. It is as if she and her masseur, Leonardo, are in unity, as if all the sensations of her body are working through him in a circle back into her again. He presses down upon her back with his hands, and then he lies, full length, upon her back, lightly, so as not to crush her. It is a wonderful sensation to feel his naked skin upon hers, the weight of his body pressing into her, the surprising softness of his skin.

He slowly peels his body away from hers, and now all trace of tension within her has vanished.

'Turn over again, please,' Leonardo says, softly.

She opens her eyes for an instant as she turns over on to her back, and she sees him looking down at her in a way she has never seen him look at her before. It is a look of deep love and understanding. She closes her eyes, a little shaken by his expression.

Leonardo is on his knees beside her. He gently strokes her breasts again, her stomach. He takes her left leg and lifts it at the knee, bending it slightly and propping it on his lap, so that her leg is turned out. Now she is revealed to him completely. He bathes her pelvis with warm, fragrant oil, pours it on to her vagina, so that she is no longer afraid of how she looks to him. It all merges into one delicious sensation – the sliding oil and her own juices.

She can feel him massaging the mound and outer lips of her yoni. He doesn't rush, gently squeezing the outer lips and then sliding up and down the entire length of each lip. He repeats the process with the inner lips of her yoni. It is an incredible sensation: slip, slide, up and down, again and again. She has never experienced this before.

Gently stroking the clitoris in clockwise and counter-clock-wise circles, he squeezes it, just like he did with her pussy. She is drifting, but not into an unconnected fantasy; she is drifting into her own bliss, her own rapture. She feels golden.

He pours more oil on to her and then she can feel him, ever so carefully and gently, inserting his finger into her yoni. It is as if he is tentatively exploring her inside, massaging each cell of her, internally. There is no feeling of an end to this massage, no outcome or climax. He is taking his time, feeling her up, down and sideways, varying depth, speed and pressure. Her body is humming, like a song from her soul that she has never heard before. And now she knows he must be massaging what Leonardo calls her sacred spot: her G-spot. He moves side to side, back and forth and, at the same time, she can feel him circling her clitoris again. She is throbbing deep within herself, trembling, her insides fluttering like the beating wings of a humming-bird. She cannot control herself any longer as she orgasms beneath his touch.

'Keep breathing,' Leonardo whispers to her.

She has this urge to stop now – it is enough – and yet Leonardo continues to massage her.

'Don't give in,' he says. 'Keep breathing.'

She sinks back into the sensation of his touch, slows her breath. He is continuing to massage her sacred spot and clitoris at the same time. She gasps, a deep, gut-wrenching gasp from deep within her belly, and orgasms again. Still he doesn't stop massaging her. She tries to steady her breath, but she is a riot of sensation and emotion. She climaxes again, this time even more intensely than the first two times. Now she cannot stop herself, and yet, each time she comes, it is even more ecstatic than the time before. It feels like a pure orgasm, coming from the root of her own sexuality, with no need for S&M fantasies to turn her on, or even thoughts of Theo and her love for him. This is all about love and acceptance of herself.

Gradually, gently, Leonardo removes his finger from inside her, stroking her all the time on her thighs and her belly. She is still vibrating from deep within. She opens her eyes, and he is looking down at her, smiling softly. There is no need for words. She sits up and hugs him.

'Thank you,' she whispers.

It is later. The sun must have gone down, for the room is dusky and full of shadows. The candles flicker – some have already gone out. The room is full of the aroma of the scented oils that Leonardo used on her body. She feels languid, and yet also extremely aroused. They lie on the mattress together on their sides, facing each other, their bodies slightly apart, with no actual physical contact.

'Do you want to know the second key, Valentina?' Leonardo asks her.

She nods, drawn into the dark glitter of his obsidian eyes.

'It is the breath; breathing slowly and deeply while you are making love, rather than shorter and faster. This has a profound effect on your sexual energy.'

She has never thought about the way she breathes before, not until Leonardo's yoga session that morning. Now she feels open to trying anything new.

'What I want you do now is to forget I am lying here, looking at you, and to close your eyes. I want you to pull your attention inward and downward, feel your breathing, breathe into the diaphragm.'

Valentina closes her eyes. In Milan, she would have teased Leonardo for telling her to 'feel her breathing' and yet the yoni massage has had a profound effect open her. She feels like a doorway has opened on to a whole new world: a secret garden full of the bliss of lovemaking that sometimes she and Theo had stumbled upon, but only by accident. She wishes he were here now to share this.

Stop thinking; just breathe, she instructs herself. She listens to herself, feels her belly moving in and out, the soft hush of her breath as she imagines it following a circular route in her body, starting from her bottom, all the way up her spine, over her head and down the front of her belly, to between her legs. After a few minutes, she feels herself relaxing further, her face softening, her jaw relaxing, her mouth opening to make a soft 'O'.

'Open your eyes, Valentina,' Leonardo says.

She looks across at Leonardo again and she imagines she sees his breath coursing through him like a swirl of smoke twisting through the interior of his body. By instinct, they inch forwards towards each other, little by little. She looks into his eyes the whole time. They press their fingertips together – just that – before slowly pressing their palms together. Her breasts touch his chest; their legs meet; her forehead touches his nose. She can no longer look into his eyes now they are so close, but she is acutely aware of each part of her and his body, as they begin to wrap around each other.

Now she understands what Leonardo was saying about *being* rather than *doing* sex, for they don't have to 'do' anything. As if by a natural force, their bodies are pulled together, like two magnets. She can feel his hard cock against her. Her pussy is still pulsing with sensation, soft and receptive from all the hot oils and massage. She opens up to him, and it is as if he is sucked within her.

He holds her tightly and they roll so that he is lying on his back and she is above him. She sits on top of him and, her fingers still interlaced in his, pulls him up so that he is sitting too, his legs opening up into the lotus position as her legs embrace his pelvis. Their eyes are open as they look at each other, and she softens her gaze to receive him. She imagines Leonardo breathing in through his heart and out through his cock, as she takes his breath and brings it into her pussy and out through her heart. It is as if the breath is a golden light, moving in a circle. He breathes in, she breathes out, and they are forming one rapturous body. It is sublime to feel such intimacy with a man for the first time since she lost Theo. Yet, despite the peace this lovemaking gives her, there is still something missing – a sensation that, at times, makes the breath stick in her throat for second, a sensation that makes her want to swallow the breath back down again.

By the time she leaves Leonardo's apartment, it is dark. She takes her time walking the few blocks back to Marco and Jake's apartment, pausing outside the gates of Gramercy Park to inhale the scent of all the spring blooms. The yoni massage, and the lovemaking afterwards, has altered her. She now understands what women mean when they talk about 'riding the wave' in Tantric sex; she never thought that she could experience such multiple orgasms.

She is a little worried about Leonardo. The last thing she wants to do is hurt him, but he has assured her that his intention is to set up a Tantric healing centre in his new place and that she is his first proper client. He intends to give yoni massage to other women in need of sexual healing. He told her that a woman's yoni, or vagina, can hold lots of fear and trauma, so the yoni massage is extremely healing for any woman with problems to do with her sexuality, or relationships – particularly those who have been abused or raped.

'But surely many of these women won't feel comfortable having a man massage their private parts?' she had challenged him.

'You would be surprised,' he said. 'Besides, I will have a female therapist working with me, if they prefer a woman.'

As Valentina crosses First Avenue, she thinks about her friend, Leonardo. He has changed. He is more thoughtful, yet, in a way, he is less serious. She remembers how he was in London last year, just after he'd broken up with his girlfriend, Raquel. He had been quite intense at that time, telling her that he was going to be celibate until he had got himself together. That was yet another occasion when Leonardo had just turned up when she'd most needed him. Despite the fact she hasn't seen him for a whole year, Valentina feels closer to him now than she ever has before. Maybe it's because of the Tantra. Whatever it is, there seems to be a growing connection between them. Is it possible that she and Leonardo might take their friendship one stage further? Is she falling in love with him?

It is way past midnight when she gets home. She lets herself in as quietly as possible, tiptoeing through the hall and down to her room. She can hear one of the boys snoring, and wonders who it is. She will have to tease them over breakfast.

On her bed, there is a package. She picks it up and examines it. It is a tube, the type you might put a poster or print in. She looks at the postmark: Manhattan. Her address is typed. Could it be hard copy of some artwork from one of her fashion shoots? She tears off the brown paper and then pulls off the top of the tube. Inside, she sees a roll of thick paper. She pulls it out and unrolls it. What she sees makes her almost cry out in shock. For in her hands is the Klimt drawing of the child that she so admired the afternoon she went to the Neue Galerie on her own. It is the portrait that looked just like her and is the very drawing that she had heard was stolen alongside the painting of the Black Feather Hat last week. It can't be the real one, she thinks, sitting down on her bed and examining the picture. But the more she looks at it, the more she knows it has to be. Her suspicions are confirmed when a slip of paper falls out of the poster tube. She picks it up. Each letter of each word has been cut out of a magazine or a newspaper to make up the collaged message:

YOU ARE NOT ALONE, VALENTINA

She drops the slip of paper on her bed, her heart beating frantically. The note has to be from someone who knows her, and wants to frighten her. There is only one possibility she can think of.

Glen.

She had been right. He is alive.

She had always known, deep down, that the man she saw in the Neue Galerie was him. She just didn't want to believe it because of what it meant. Now he is making it impossible for her to forget about him. She clenches her fists. He wants to gloat over her, rub her nose in the fact that he killed Theo and has managed to get away with yet another crime. Well, she *won't* let him get away with it. She is not sure how she is going to do it, but she pledges that, no matter what, she is going to make sure that Glen gets his just deserts. Her anger flares within her brightly and self-righteously, yet, beneath this emotion, she can't help tasting the fear in her mouth – for she has no doubt that, if she goes after Glen, she is risking her life.

$\mathcal{T}$ina

1985

IT IS DIFFERENT WITH VALENTINA, THAN MATTIA. AS SOON AS HER daughter is born, Tina changes. It's not that she loves Valentina any more, of course not. Mattia is her first born, her son. He is special too. It's just that she feels this incredible connection with Valentina, right from the beginning. She understands her.

Valentina never needs to cry to tell her she is hungry or needs her nappy changing. Tina just knows, instinctively. Mattia was a laughing baby, full of chatter and smiles. Valentina is different. She speaks with her hands, spends hours clutching and releasing her mother's fingers, staring at her with serious eyes – Karel's eyes. She may be a tiny baby, but her grip is ferocious. Tina imagines Valentina is speaking to her through her hands.

I need you, she is saying. *Don't leave me.*

That is why she calls her Valentina: because the baby feels like a part of her, and thus she gives her own full name. It has always been abbreviated to Tina, even by her parents, but she wants her daughter to be better than her, to be a Valentina.

To everyone's surprise, including her own, Tina extends her maternity leave from three to six months.

'You didn't want to take that much time off with Mattia,' Phil comments, looking at her thoughtfully.

'I was younger; I didn't appreciate this time with the baby back then,' Tina defends herself.

Valentina murmurs in her crib, and Phil leans over and takes her in his arms. A part of Tina is dying to take her off him, but she controls herself. Phil has been so good with Valentina from the moment she was born. Not for one minute has he treated her any differently because she is not his own. It makes Tina love him all the more. And yet he has been different with her.

It's been six months since Valentina was born and still Phil and Tina haven't made love. At first, Tina was too tired and sore, anyway. She was so taken over by Valentina's arrival that, possibly, she neglected him, but after a couple of months she missed his touch, craved to feel him within her, to be one with him. However, as the weeks passed and Phil still didn't make a move, it began to hurt her that he would turn away from her in bed every night. Now he has moved into the spare room, saying that it is better if she and Valentina have the bed to themselves, so that he can get a good night's sleep.

'After all,' he claims, 'if you are still breast-feeding, I can't feed Valentina in the night. What's the point of both of us being disturbed? Especially as I have to get up for work.'

He is right, of course. But she can't help feeling rejected. It makes her pull away from him a little. She pours all her love into Valentina instead.

In the mornings, Phil is usually gone before she and Valentina emerge. Mattia is away at school and so it is just her and her girl for the day. Tina can spend two whole hours just lying on the couch with Valentina, singing to her, playing with her, sleeping with her on her belly, her little head tucked beneath her chin.

Her previous life as a fashion photographer seems like a hazy memory of rushing around, stress, noise, and all for what? Here, in the sanctuary of their Milanese apartment, she has all that she needs. At these times, she no longer misses Phil because Valentina fills up her heart and all her longing. Each flutter of her tiny eyelashes, each sigh and murmur, Tina collects and stores. She regrets that she never paid such attention to Mattia when he was a baby. She was too busy trying to resume her career.

At these times, on her own in the apartment, she sometimes imagines she can see the ghost of her mother, Maria. For the first time in her life, she stops resenting who her mother was. She almost feels like she can understand her. Her mother put all her creativity into nurturing her family, and why not? Tina always fought against her mother's lessons, but in the end she was right. There is nothing more important than your children. They must always come first. She wishes now she had learnt more of her mother's homemaking skills, but she had been so resistant as a teenager, claiming it was all boring rubbish.

Tina attempts now to emulate her mother, but the truth is she can't knit a stitch, sew a button on a shirt, even, and she is a woeful cook. As for cleaning, despite the fact she is home every day and has, consequentially, let their cleaner go, she finds it impossible to maintain the apartment. Surely it is better for Valentina if she plays with her, rather than put her in her crib and abandon her to cry while she hoovers the carpets or polishes the hall floor or any of that nonsense? And when Valentina sleeps, Tina needs to sleep too. Even the laundry seems an overwhelming task, so that Phil ends up having to do it all when he gets home in the evening, which is getting later and later these days.

At first, he tries to cook for her, but Tina is not interested in eating with him.

'You're getting too thin,' he says. 'Breast-feeding takes a lot out of you. Tina, you must eat more.'

But she has no appetite.

'It's good I'm losing all my pregnancy fat,' she tells him.

He says nothing, but she can tell by the look on his face what he is thinking: *What is happening to you?*

When she looks in the mirror, she hardly recognises herself: her pale, unwashed, unmade-up face, her hair sticking out all over the place and her gaunt, skinny frame. She spends the whole day in her pyjamas, sometimes.

One evening, she is sitting up in bed, breast-feeding Valentina, when Phil comes into the bedroom and sits down on the end of the bed. He says nothing for a moment, just watches Valentina as she suckles her mother's breast. Tina gently brushes a stray hair from her daughter's forehead.

'Isn't she perfect?' she whispers to Phil, looking up at him.

'Yes, she is,' he says, but she can see he is frowning.

'What is it?' she asks.

'Tina,' he says, 'I think you need to go to the doctor.'

'What on earth for?'

'You're getting too thin,' he says. 'You're not eating. I don't think you can cope, Tina.'

She feels a flare of anger. Does he think she is a bad mother? Hasn't she shown him how devoted and diligent a mother she is?

'I am perfectly fine,' she says, tightly.

'No, you are not.' He sighs. 'Tina, you're depressed. I don't think it's good for you not to be working, and to be home every day. It's not you.'

He is jealous of Valentina, she thinks. He doesn't want me to spend time with her.

'But you thought it was a good idea, at first.'

'Yes, I did, I admit, but I've been watching you go down.'

'I am fine!' she says, hotly. 'What new mother isn't a little tired sometimes? It's a full-time job . . . You have to put her first . . .'

'Tina, you haven't left the apartment in weeks. That is *not* normal.' His voice cracks. 'I can't live like this,' he whispers. 'You've changed.'

'It's because she isn't yours, isn't it? You don't want me to love Valentina as much as you or Mattia, do you?'

He gives her a disgusted look and gets up. She can see he is angry, but he says nothing, just storms out the room.

She didn't mean to say such a hurtful thing, or to bring up the fact Valentina isn't his child. The words had just spilled out of her mouth like a reflex. The truth is she is scared to go back to work and face the real world. It is safer here, with Valentina – this bundle that belongs solely to her, that needs her.

The next morning, Tina looks in the mirror and sees herself with Phil's eyes, and she is appalled. He is right. She does have to make more of an effort. She decides that she will dress herself and Valentina up for the day, and that they will surprise Phil at the university at lunchtime. They will go to one of their favourite restaurants for lunch. She imagines how pleased he will be with her. She will make herself eat and she will say sorry. He is right. She misses him, and she wants him back in her bed. Tonight, she promises herself, Valentina will sleep in her crib, and she will make love to Phil. She wants so much to feel his arms around her yet again. How can two people live together for over six months and feel like strangers when they were once so close?

Tina puts on her red jersey dress – one of Phil's favourites – which used to be figure-hugging, but now, to her shock, is way

221

too big for her and she looks like a scarecrow. She takes it off, feeling wretched already, and puts on a pair of black trousers and her smallest blouse, which still manages to hang off her. Her face is all dark shadows and pale skin. She does her best to conceal the tiredness and brighten her face, but it feels like her blusher just makes her look like a painted doll. Even her hair, usually her crowning glory, is dull and scraggy. It needs a cut and some deep conditioning. She realises gloomily that, for the past six months, she has neglected herself completely. To compensate, she makes Valentina look like a darling. She dresses her baby girl in a lemon-yellow frock with white, lacy trim, tiny little white socks and yellow shoes, and a white bonnet, tied under her chin with a yellow ribbon.

She is excited as she strolls down the street, Valentina tucked beneath blankets in the pram. It is a warm day for November, the sun filtering through golden leaves, a fresh breeze brushing against her cheeks. Milan seems full of sunshine, people smiling and greeting each other. She is happy to be outside again. She can't wait to see Phil's delight when they surprise him.

By the time she reaches Phil's university building, she is a little later than she expected. She hopes he hasn't left for lunch already. She turns the corner, glancing at her watch, and, as she does so, she suddenly sees him leaving the art block. He doesn't see her. She is about to call out, but, just at the exact moment she raises her arm, she sees that he is not alone. A voluptuous young woman, with long blond hair, is walking beside him, carrying a pile of books. She is probably a student, Tina tries to convince herself, and yet there is something in the way she sees the girl move beside Phil – does she actually brush his arm with her hand, or is Tina imagining it? – that makes her think otherwise. She pulls back with the pram and hides around a corner, peering out at them as they walk away from her, out the other exit of the university and on to the street. She trails behind them, keeping a good distance, for she doesn't know how she would explain herself to Phil if he turned round and saw her. She feels stupid and foolish, like a pathetic, jealous wife.

At the corner, Phil and the blond girl stop to cross the street. Tina watches like a hawk as the girl turns to talk to Phil, and she sees her lover's face looking at his companion. He is smiling in that warm, sexy way. He hasn't looked at her like that in months. Tina has seen enough. She doesn't care whether he has slept with this girl or not. It is enough to know that he desires her. She looks again at her rival: she is curvaceous, with large breasts and a soft, plump bottom. She is everything Tina isn't: young, healthy and glowing.

When she gets back to the apartment, Tina sits Valentina on her lap, facing her. Her baby girl looks back up at her with wise, old-soul eyes, her lips pursed into a tiny red rosebud.

Tina feels the first cut, a little stab of pain in her heart. Having a child is a series of separations, she realises. She wasn't conscious of this so much with Mattia, but now she sees that, with Valentina, she has been trying to retrieve the months she lost away from her baby son, immersed in work and not facing her motherhood. Yet she has gone too far in the other direction. She has been neglecting not only poor Mattia, away at school, but also her man. If she is not careful, she will lose him.

Tina gets up off the couch, carrying Valentina in her arms. She has to create a little space between her and her baby, otherwise she will smother her, like her mother did to her. Valentina will end up resenting her, just as much as she resented her own mother as young woman. She wishes she could speak to her mother now – tell her that she understands. But it is too late. Maria Rosselli is gone from this world.

She puts Valentina down to sleep. She winds up the clockwork motor on the mobile of little blue birds above her crib, watching them for a moment as their tiny wings flap up and down in time to the tinny music. For the first time since she was born, Tina doesn't rock her baby to sleep. She waits for her to cry out for her mama, yet Valentina never does. 'Good girl,' Tina whispers.

In the hall, she picks up the phone and makes three calls. One is to the editor at *Vogue*, informing her that she is available for the shoot in Rome next week, the second call is to her cleaner, begging her to return as soon as she can, and the final call is to an au-pair agency.

When Phil returns home that evening, Tina is waiting for him, an open bottle of red wine on the table and two bloody steaks (the one thing she can cook) already plated. Tina eats every single morsel of her steak, watching Phil look at her approvingly, and when her belly is full of meat and wine, she takes her man by the hand and leads him out of the kitchen and into their bedroom.

'Where's Valentina?' Phil asks her, surprised.

'She's asleep in *her* room,' Tina says, kissing Phil on the neck and shoulders.

'She's not sleeping with you any more?' he asks.

'No; you are,' Tina says.

Valentina

VALENTINA WAITS UNTIL MORNING TO PHONE THE POLICE. IN fact, she puts it off until after she has had breakfast with Marco and Jake.

'I never asked how your trip went,' she says, joining them at the table.

'Just fabulous,' Marco says, offering her the pot of coffee.

'We're planning our house in the Hamptons as soon as we make our first million,' Jake says, grinning at her.

'More like first five million,' Marco says, sighing.

Should she tell them about the Klimt print? That, currently lying on her bed, there is an artwork probably worth the price of a house in the Hamptons? Not that you could ever sell it, and, of course, she never would. For some reason, she keeps her mouth shut about the picture. She doesn't want Marco freaking out about Glen being alive, and not only that, sending her threatening notes. Better just to tell the police and leave it at that.

'Marco, I have a bone to pick with you,' she says instead, leaning over and stealing a triangle of toast from his plate.

'Oh, really, darling?' he says, looking a little shifty.

He knows what I am going to say, Valentina thinks.

'Why did you tell Leonardo that I wasn't OK?'

Jake tactfully starts clearing up the table and taking the plates over to the sink.

'Well, honey . . . you're not—' Marco starts to say.

'How the hell do you know?' she says, sounding more angry than she feels.

'Because of what was going on with that Russell guy,' Marco says.

Jake swivels around, his hands sheathed in Marigold gloves. 'Russell has a reputation, Valentina,' he says, defending Marco. 'He preys on vulnerable women . . .'

'Well, why didn't you just warn me from the start?'

'I thought I did,' Marco says, exasperated, 'but you wouldn't listen to me. I know how stubborn you are. The only person I could think of that you would listen to was Leonardo.'

She shrugs, trying to still look a little annoyed, but she knows that Marco is right.

'I thought he was just going to call you up – I never thought he was actually going to turn up in New York. When I contacted him he was in the middle of some yoga training in India. He told me he couldn't drop it just like that.'

'Well,' says Jake, 'it seems he did. He must be very fond of you, Valentina.'

He loves me, she is thinking, but she doesn't say that to her friends.

'So he is your knight in shining armour!' Marco declares, clapping his hands together. Yes, I guess he is, Valentina thinks, chewing her lip. In that moment, she decides she can't tell Leonardo about Glen's threatening note. The last thing she wants is another man she loves being hurt by that evil bastard.

'And he is going to rescue you from that awful Russell,' Marco says gleefully.

'Well he doesn't need to now. I have already broken up with Russell,' Valentina says.

'And are you OK about it?' Marco asks her, suddenly looking concerned. 'Did he hurt you?'

Valentina shakes her head. 'No; I'm fine. I ended it with him. I don't know what I saw in him, really . . .'

'Some affairs can be like that,' says Jake, knowingly. 'Intense, but short lived. They are more obsession than real love.'

He comes over to the table and dots a soapy finger on to Marco's nose. 'Just like you're obsessed with me, chicken.'

Marco laughs, flicking his lover's hand away. 'In your dreams, darling,' he says.

But Valentina sees the quality of their love. It is built to last.

Once her friends have left for the day, Valentina takes Balducci's business card out of her camera bag, where she had slipped it the day he and Delaney interviewed her. He answers on the first ring.

'Mike Balducci.'

'Hi – it's Valentina Rosselli here,' she says.

'Yes?' She can tell he can't remember who she is.

'You interviewed me over the robbery of the Klimt pictures . . .'

'Oh, yes . . . Dark-haired girl – the photographer?'

'Yes, that's me.'

'Do you have any more information for us?'

'Actually, something rather strange has happened,' she says. 'I think you should come over to my place.'

Balducci and Delaney sit on the couch, both wearing black gloves. Delaney has the print rolled out in front of him, and is examining it, while Balducci is looking at the note.

'So, you think this is the original,' Delaney is asking her, 'and not some stupid joke?'

'Well, I can't say for sure, not until it's looked at by an expert, but it's the sort of thing Glen would do.'

'You really believe this character is still alive, despite the fact the Italian police say he drowned over a year ago?' Balducci asks her.

'Yes,' she says. 'I think so. I mean, who else would do this to me?'

'You know this Glen well?' Delaney snaps up his head.

'No; I don't know much about him at all, except that he is a perfectionist, and very dangerous. He would never send me a fake picture.'

'We'll get it checked out . . . Hopefully there'll be some prints on it . . .'

'And this note, Miss Rosselli,' Balducci says. 'Why do you think it is a threat? I mean – "You are not alone" – that's what he has written. It seems a bit ambiguous.'

'It means he is watching me,' Valentina says, patiently. Are all cops as stupid as these two? 'He stalked me in Milan and in London. He has always had a sort of *thing* about me,' she says, unwillingly.

'Why didn't you tell us this the other day?' Delaney asks her, sharply.

'I didn't think it was relevant.'

Delaney shakes his head and rolls up the print.

'OK, well, we'll have someone in a car outside this apartment, keeping an eye on things. If he really is trailing you then that's our chance to nab him, although I doubt he is still in New York.'

'Do you know any of his associates? Anyone at all?' Balducci asks.

228

'No.'

'And what makes you so sure that this note *is* from Glen?'

'Well, who else could have stolen that picture?' Valentina says, exasperated.

The cops look at each other. 'We have to consider every possibility.'

They suspect Theo is behind this, Valentina thinks.

The idea that they think Theo could possibly be alive and not contact her makes her furious, let alone that they could imagine him doing such a robbery in league with the man who tried to kill her. 'I keep telling you, Glen killed Theo.'

'We've no evidence to support that theory, Miss Rosselli,' Delaney says.

She clenches her fists. 'Can you not believe me?' she says.

'Of course we believe you,' Balducci says, softly. 'Come on, Al,' he says, getting up. 'We'd better take this stuff back to the station to get it looked at. Thanks for calling us, Miss Rosselli. If there is anything else at all, just give us a shout.'

'I recommend you stay close to home for the next while, until we are able to pick him up,' Delaney adds.

'I'm working on a shoot tomorrow,' she says. 'At the High Line.'

'OK, well, don't go wandering off on your own . . . just in case,' Balducci says, patting her arm.

After they have gone, she sits on the couch, hugging her knees to her chest, rocking back and forth. She wants so badly for Glen to be caught and to bring an end to it all. But what can she do to make that happen? She needs to draw him out and, to do that, she needs to do the exact opposite of what the police have told her to do.

* * *

229

Valentina spends the next three hours walking around Manhattan. She walks uptown, right into the heart of the island, amid the jostling tourists, her eyes turned skyward as she passes the Empire State Building and the Rockefeller Center. She heads west, back into Chelsea, and down through the Meatpacking District, until she is in Greenwich Village. She meanders among the boutiques and cafés, making it easy for anyone to follow her. Yet, every time she turns around, there is no sign of Glen. In the end she decides that, for this day at least, she really is on her own. She misses Leonardo. She wants to be with him and to forget all about Glen and revenge. There is still a small hope that it is all in her imagination. That the art thief the police are looking for is not her old nemesis. On the spur of the moment, she flags down a taxi, asking it to take her to Gramercy Park. She wants Leonardo to teach her more. She needs to feel his love.

They are on top of Leonardo's bed. Today the sheets are sapphire silk, with mounds of purple brocade cushions scattered upon them. Leonardo is burning some of his Nag Champa incense, and has filled the room with candles. The atmosphere is calming yet sensual. They lie on their sides, several inches apart, and make eye contact.

'I want you to tune into your body for a moment,' Leonardo says. 'Use your breath like I showed you yesterday.'

Valentina closes her eyes and begins breathing deeply and slowly from her belly. She hears Leonardo's voice in her ear.

'Now be aware of my body, and how close it is.'

She carries on breathing but, on the other side of that sound, she can feel warmth radiating from Leonardo's body. She opens her eyes again and he is looking at her with the same expression of love and understanding that he had the day before.

'I want you to stay with the sensations inside your body and tell me how it is feeling,' he whispers. 'We are only to talk about what is happening to our bodies and hearts now. We are not going to start a conversation, or ask each other questions; we are not going to work out why we are feeling how we feel – we are just going to feel it. Do you understand?'

She nods.

'OK; you start. Tell me how your body is feeling today.'

'Cold. There is a shiver in my belly and I cannot still it,' Valentina says.

'My heart is pounding,' Leonardo says. 'I feel fear.'

It is on the tip of her tongue to ask him why, but Valentina pulls herself back into what she is feeling in her own body. She remembers his instructions: no questions; no analysis. 'My toes are freezing,' she says, 'and yet my head is burning. I feel as if I have walked on ice. I feel alone.'

'There is a fire in my belly,' Leonardo replies. 'I can feel it spreading across my stomach and on to my chest; my skin is tingling. I am frightened still, but also excited.'

'I feel some of your heat,' Valentina says, 'in my chest.' She brings her hand to rest on her breasts. 'I am not so cold any more.'

'And you are cooling me, turning my fire liquid – it is spreading across my loins,' Leonardo says, 'making my legs feel lithe, strong, like I could run for miles.'

'Your warmth makes me supple; my cold, brittle bones are softening.'

All the words that spill out of Valentina's mouth are purely instinctive. She feels as if she is reciting some kind of pleasure poem. And, as they describe to each other how their bodies are feeling, she feels her body energy becoming dynamic as she becomes more and more physically attracted to Leonardo.

231

Instinctively, at exactly the same time, they embrace. Leonardo puts his hands over her eyes and she inhales his scent: he smells of his incense – rich, musky spice. He covers her face in tiny, fleeting kisses. Next, she feels him licking her lips, forcing them to part. He begins to suck her bottom lip, delicately drawing it into his mouth. He runs his tongue over it again and then licks his way up to her top lip, and gently sucks that, too. The sensation of his tongue licking, kissing, sucking her mouth is stoking the warmth that is spreading between her legs. She opens her mouth, and he sucks her tongue into his mouth ever so gently.

He takes his hands away from her eyes as he rolls her on the bed so that she is lying on her back and he is above her, pressed against her body, his hands cradling her head, still kissing her deeply. She begins to part her legs – she wants to feel him inside her – but, to her surprise, Leonardo shifts his body up and forward, so that the base of his shaft is pressing against her clitoris rather than inside her. Now he begins to rock forward and backward; all the time his cock is locked against her clitoris. She realises that all Leonardo wants to do is pleasure her. He is sliding his cock up and down her clitoris. She feels herself merging with him, hears their breath in unison. With eyes open and a sense of awe at all that Leonardo wants to give, she finds herself climaxing against him. It feels as if something has opened at the base of her spine, as if all that cold hurt is blowing out of her, and his loving is filling her up with sunshine. And yet, despite the bliss, the healing Leonardo gives her, she cannot quite silence the words that keep spinning inside her head: *You are not alone, Valentina.*

For she realises that it is something Theo used to say to her, too.

Tina

1988

IT IS APRIL IN BARCELONA AND TINA IS ON A PHOTOSHOOT FOR *Elle* magazine. The feature is inspired by fashion of the fifties, and Tina has immersed herself in perfecting period details. She has decided to focus on Europe rather than America in the fifties, so her two models reflect that. One looks like Sophia Loren, with generous curves and wavy dark hair, and the other model is more reminiscent of Leslie Caron, the French dancer, with short black hair and a pretty snub nose. She dresses them in a combination of classic cocktail dresses, pillbox hats, and gloves, contrasting with colourful pedal pushers and bolero jackets.

It is St George's Day, and the streets are filled with booksellers and vendors selling red roses. Tina fills her models' hands with bunches of roses, and takes one shot of her Leslie Caron lookalike, in cute bottle-green pedal pushers and stripy top, stopping to peruse some of the books. Octavia tells Tina that St George's Day is the Catalan version of Valentine's Day, although – far more romantic than tacky cards and fattening chocolates – the man buys the woman a red rose, and the woman buys the man a book.

'I would like the rose *and* the book,' Tina comments.

'Well, that is typical of you,' Octavia teases her. 'You want it all.'

The shoot goes really well. She is definitely feeling that she has got back into her stride. It had been hard at first when she went back to work. It had been such a wrench to leave Valentina behind with the au pair, that the first few shoots she did she had felt like a nervous wreck, jumping every time there was a phone call for her, anxious to be finished and home as soon as possible. Now, at last, she has begun to relax a little.

Their lives are busy. Phil has begun to branch out into more journalist work, so he is not home so much, and, the weekends Mattia is back, he is out and about with friends in Milan, seemingly as sociable as his father. Tina herself is in constant demand. Her work is taking her abroad more and more often. Every time she goes away, she feels guilty about leaving Valentina, but then she knows that soon Valentina will be old enough to come with her. We'll have fun, she thinks, me and my little girl, exploring the cities of Europe. Besides, Valentina is such an easy child, each au pair she gets falls in love with her instantly.

Tina's friends had warned her not to get an au pair.

'A nanny is better,' Octavia said. 'They are usually older.'

Isabella was even more emphatic. 'Mamma mia!' she had declared on the phone to her from London. 'Are you crazy? Do you really want some hot nineteen year old from Sweden waving her big tits around in front of your man?'

'Phil isn't like that,' Tina had protested, although she was still haunted by the image of him with that blond girl at the university. Had he slept with her? Tina had decided never to ask him. She didn't want to know.

234

Tina ignored her friends' advice and, two weeks later, Inger from Norway arrived. She was anything but the Scandinavian stereotype: short and slight, with dark curly hair and almost olive skin.

'You don't look very Norwegian,' Tina had commented when she met her for the first time.

'Not all Norwegians are blond. I'm from Bergen, on the west coast – a seafaring port for hundreds of years. Sailors from all round the world have mixed their genes with the Bergenese.'

Tina likes Inger. She is efficient, considerate, and excellent with Valentina.

Often, she will sing to her – Norwegian folksongs – and the sound of her sweet voice makes Tina glad that she is minding her child, filling Valentina with sweetness and hope, rather than her own frustrations and guilt.

Phil had not been keen on the idea of an au pair, at first. He had claimed that the apartment was too small, but once Inger arrived, he changed his mind. The Norwegian was taking a year's break from university and media studies. She was very tuned in to current-day politics and she and Phil would have after-dinner debates at the kitchen table, over the Palestinian situation or glasnost. Tina watched the two of them for hints of attraction, but she never got any sense of something going on. Inger was half Phil's age. And yet, sometimes, Tina felt excluded by their passionate debates.

Lately, Phil has become involved in investigating some Mafia crimes in the south of Italy. She hears him chatting to Inger about it a little, telling her about some of the horrific things these gang members will do, just to get control of the drug trade. It stresses Tina to hear him talking about it and, when he starts speaking to her, she asks him to stop. He claims she isn't interested, but it's not that. She is terrified he will get hurt. Phil isn't Italian, and she feels he doesn't realise how vengeful these people can be. She wants to know as little as possible about it. The more she knows, the more she worries.

Some evenings, she hides in her dark room, sifting through pictures longer than is necessary. She cannot bear to look at Inger in her tank top and tiny shorts, her slim brown legs and flat belly, and she dreams of getting back her own body from before she had children. When she was the same age as Inger, she remembers wearing tiny miniskirts and hot pants, and having so much fun with Isabella. They got a lot of male attention. Surely Phil must desire this girl?

When Tina returns to the hotel in Barcelona after the shoot, there is a message for her. It is from the editor of French *Vogue*, a Vivienne Aury, asking her to call her.

Vivienne Aury is a legend in the magazine world. One time editor of *Harper's Bazaar* in New York, she moved back to Paris in the seventies, where she has been editor of *Vogue* ever since. She must be nearly seventy years old, surely? Tina feels a tiny thrill of excitement. To be left a message from the editor of French *Vogue* is a huge honour. She wonders if she has an exciting job for her.

She calls her as soon as she gets up to her room.

'Tina Rosselli?' The Frenchwoman speaks to her in heavily accented English, despite all the years in New York. 'I am so glad you received my message.'

'I was very excited to receive it,' Tina says.

'I have been following you for many years, my dear,' Vivienne Aury says. 'Your star has been rising steadily. I am sure your mother would have been proud of you.'

Tina frowns. The last person she can imagine being proud of her photographic career is her mother. It is an odd thing for this woman to say.

'Well,' Vivienne continues, 'when I discovered we were both in Barcelona at the same time, I thought that it must be serendipitous. I wonder, would you be free this evening to share some tapas with me?'

They meet in a little over an hour's time at a chic tapas bar just off Las Ramblas. Vivienne is already waiting for her. She is a tall, elegant lady, with snow-white hair, cut into a short pixie style. She stands up when Tina walks into the tapas bar, and looks quite moved by her appearance; Tina can't think why.

'*Mon Dieu,*' she says, staring at Tina so hard it makes her feel a little uncomfortable. 'I have seen pictures of you, but nothing has prepared me for seeing you in the flesh.'

Tina feels a little confused. She doesn't think she looks that remarkable.

They both sit down and order some wine and a few plates of tapas, although Tina is not hungry. Her curiosity is piqued. She has a feeling that there is more to this meeting than the offer of a shoot or a discussion of the fashion industry. Even so, they chat pleasantly enough about the world they both inhabit. Vivienne, despite her age, is witty and sharp. Tina likes her instantly.

Maybe she is going to offer me a job, Tina thinks, and we could all move to Paris? The idea suddenly appeals. More than anything in the world, she would like to get Phil away from that Mafia stuff.

'Well, my dear,' Vivienne says, dabbing the corners of her mouth with her napkin. 'I am sure you must be wondering why

I called you up and asked to meet you. It is evident you have no idea who I am.'

Tina frowns. Well, of course she knows who she is. Vivienne Aury is one of the top magazine editors in the world.

'Let me explain,' Vivienne says, seeing Tina's confusion. 'I am an old friend of your mother's.'

'My mother's!' Tina exclaims, unable to conceal her astonishment.

'When she lived in Paris, we knew each other, not for a long time, and yet we became quite close.'

'I'm really sorry, but I think you must have me confused with someone else. My mother never went to Paris in her life.'

Vivienne looks surprised; she gives Tina a piercing look. 'Your mother is Maria Rosselli, daughter of Belle Brzezinska, from Venice?' she asks Tina.

'Well, yes, that is her name, my grandmother's name, but—'

'She studied dance in London, and then she came to live in Paris in 1948,' Vivienne tells her.

'No, that cannot have been my mother,' Tina insists. 'She wasn't a dancer. She lived in Italy all her life until she . . .' Tina stumbles. 'Until she took a plane to America . . . and . . .'

Vivienne leans forward and puts her hand on Tina. 'I know,' she says, softly. 'She was killed in a plane crash.' She pauses. 'She was finally coming to see me in New York. I am so sorry, Tina. I should have written to you at the time to offer my condolences, but I wasn't sure if you knew about me, and Maria's past . . . It is now clear you know nothing.'

Tina takes a swig of her red wine. She wants to tell Vivienne that she is terribly wrong. The woman she thinks is Maria Rosselli just could not be, but then she has a flicker of memory – a moment when she was a little girl. She remembers opening a door and seeing her mother dancing. She was on her own, a duster in hand, in her apron and with her hair up in a scarf, spinning in the sunlight spilling in from the dusty windows, motes like glittering gold around her. Her mother had not seen her, and Tina had been spellbound. Her mother had been a princess in that moment. She had forgotten all about it until now.

'Please,' she says, 'tell me who my mother was.'

'Maria Rosselli was a very talented young dancer, although at the time I knew her, she never told me. I found that out later,' Vivienne says. 'What can I say about your mother? She was a true free spirit, a woman ahead of her time, a libertine. She inspired me to follow my dream and go to New York and become a magazine editor.'

Tina drops her jaw open in shock. The description Vivienne has given of her mother is the opposite of how she would have described her.

'She wasn't like that when I was a child,' Tina says. She thinks back, remembers her mother constantly nagging her, or on her knees praying all the time. She had seemed so old and grey to her, but now she realises why. 'She was very sad,' Tina tells Vivienne. 'To be honest, I was closer to my father.'

Vivienne looks away, her cheeks colouring slightly. Tina picks up on it immediately.

'What is it? Why did my mother change?'

'She had a lover when we were in Paris. That is why she went there,' Vivienne says.

'A lover?' Tina repeats, incredulously.

'Yes; we were all part of this scene in a little area called Saint-Germain-des-Prés, in Paris. We would dance all night listening to jazz, and hang out in cafés discussing art and politics, you know, with characters like Jean-Paul Sartre, Simone de Beauvoir,

Juliette Gréco, Albert Camus and Jean Cocteau.'

Tina is speechless. The idea of her mother, in her clogs and blue dress, wearing the black headscarf come rain or shine, sitting in a café discussing feminism with Simone de Beauvoir seems preposterous.

'Her lover, Felix Leduc, was part of that scene. He was a film-maker, a surrealist like Cocteau.'

'I can't believe it; this is incredible,' Tina says.

'I am sorry it is a little bit of a shock,' Vivienne says. 'When I moved to New York, I left my old life – my life during the war, when I lost so much – behind.' She coughs, clears her throat and takes a drink of her water before proceeding. 'But since I have returned to France, I have met up with some old acquaintances. Felix is one of them.'

Tina has heard of Felix Leduc. She thinks she may even have seen one of his films. To think that he had been her mother's lover . . . What had happened to Maria Rosselli to change her so much?

'I am here, actually, on behalf of Felix,' Vivienne says, catching Tina's gaze and holding her with her own green eyes, still bright, despite her age.

'Really?' Tina asks.

'Yes; he would very much like to meet you, but he is old and frail. We were hoping you might have the time to accompany me to Paris and visit him.'

It seems like a bizarre request.

'Oh, that's very touching, but – sorry, I don't mean to be rude – but why would he want to meet me? He obviously lost contact with my mother years ago.'

Vivienne looks awkward. Tina is sure that she is probably the only person who has seen the editor of *Vogue* tongue-tied.

Something is beginning to bother Tina; she feels a nudging sickness in her stomach.

'Maybe if I explained that, when your mother left Paris, it would have been August 1948 . . . and, well, probably the best thing is if I show you this.' She opens her bag and takes out an old black-and-white photograph. Tina takes the picture and stares down at it. It is of a group of young people in a semicircle, with their arms all around each other.

'That's me,' Vivienne says, pointing to her younger self, still recognisable with the same short hair. 'And that's your mother,' she says, pointing out a beautiful young woman with curly hair tumbling around her shoulders.

Tina feels winded. Her mother looks so happy. She never saw her smiling like this her whole childhood. She is laughing, not into the camera, but looking up at the man who has his arm around her. He is looking into the camera: a steady, sure gaze.

'That's Felix,' Vivienne says, softly.

Tina looks at his face and she gasps. The photograph drops from her hand on to the table. Vivienne says nothing more. Tina takes a breath. She picks up the photograph again and looks at Felix Leduc's face. There is no mistaking the comparison. She has no need to look in a mirror. No wonder she didn't look like her father, Guido.

'Oh my God,' she whispers.

'Felix is your father, Tina,' Vivienne tells her. 'It's plain to see. He wants to meet you.'

'No,' Tina says, shaking her head. 'He may be my biological father, but my real father was Guido Rosselli.'

'Tina, think about it,' Vivienne urges. 'It may be your only chance. Felix has cancer; he is dying.'

Tina looks back down at the picture of her mother, arm in

arm with this Felix Leduc, and she wants to scream with rage. She controls herself, takes a breath. She stands up stiffly. 'I am sorry, Vivienne; I really can't meet him.'

She turns on her heel and walks out of the restaurant. She has just walked out on one of the most powerful women in the fashion world and yet she doesn't care.

Outside, she runs down the street, her heart pounding in her chest. She feels as if she is about to have a heart attack. This must be some kind of nightmare. How on earth could her mother have been that man's lover? This is not the woman she knew: shy, reserved and devoted to her family . . . But, worse still, worse than anything, is the fact that that photograph of her mother with that arrogant film-maker has just destroyed her father – her darling father, Guido Rosselli.

How dare Felix Leduc want to know her now that he is dying? He didn't want to know her his whole life. He's had nearly forty years to make his introductions to her. Her parents have been dead fifteen years now, so – even if her mother hadn't wanted him to see her – he could have found her after they had gone. If Vivienne knew her mother had died, then she must have told Leduc. It is unforgivable.

Back in her hotel room, to her shame, Tina begins to cry. She has lost her father all over again. He was not hers, ever. She is not sure who she is crying for, really – herself or Guido. She needs to hear Phil's voice, and tell him all about it. She picks up the phone and rings the apartment in Milan. Inger answers.

'Good evening, Tina; how is Barcelona?' the Norwegian asks her.

'Fine.' She can hear music in the background. 'How's Valentina?' she asks the girl.

'She's asleep now, missing you. I read her a story – the one about Goldilocks and the three bears.'

'She loves that one.'

'Yes.' Inger pauses. 'Do you want to talk to Phil?' she says. 'He is just here.'

What does she mean, 'just here'? Tina thinks. Is he standing right behind you? Are you naked? Is he about to fuck you?

'Hi, Tina; how'd it go today?' Phil says.

She wants to tell him everything, but she can't speak. She is doing her best to swallow back the tears.

'Tina, are you OK?'

'Yes,' she manages to say in a husky voice.

'Is everything all right?' he asks, but he sounds distracted, as if he isn't really listening to her.

'I miss you,' she whispers.

'No, not like that; you'll cork it!' Phil suddenly shouts. 'Sorry, Tina; that silly Norwegian girl was about to ruin a good bottle of Ripasso. What did you just say?'

'Nothing,' she says, her tears suddenly dry, her heart hardening.

'OK, well, I'll let you go,' he says. 'I am sure you're busy.'

They are drinking wine, she thinks. They are going to get drunk together, and fuck each other.

'Tina?' Phil is still speaking to her. 'Take care, honey. I love you.'

'Love you, too,' she whispers back, but the words feel like crumbs upon her lips.

Tina sits on her own at the hotel bar, watching the bartender clearing away the glasses, and finishes her gin and tonic. He is whistling away to flamenco guitar music as he works. Her head is spinning with all the revelations of the day. Suddenly she is furious – so angry. Why didn't her parents tell her the truth? She had a right to know who her real father was. It hits her then about Valentina, for she is doing exactly the same thing to her own daughter. She is letting her believe that Phil is her real father. Will that end in pain and fury one day, when Valentina finds out the truth?

Her anger deflates; she feels lost and abandoned and she wants to be made to feel good again. She has a sudden urge to get drunk and go wild.

'Are there any places to go dancing near here?' she asks the bartender.

'There's a club right across the road,' he tells her. 'The music is a good mix.'

She promises herself that she will only go for one drink and one dance. Despite the fact it is a Thursday night, the club is packed, yet the atmosphere is relaxed. It seems to be a young, free-spirited crowd. Most of them are probably students or artists.

She buys herself a drink at the bar, and leans back, watching the people dancing. Already, she feels a little better. The music is a little too popular for her taste. but then one of her favourite songs comes on: 'Kashmir' by Led Zeppelin. She just has to dance to this. She knocks back her drink in one.

She feels good: free and unbound. Dancing on your own in a nightclub full of strangers, where you don't know anyone and you don't care what they think of you, is the best therapy, Tina thinks. She banishes the image of Phil and Inger sharing the bottle of wine, and lets go completely, whirling like a dervish on the dance floor. Young men come and go, dancing with her for a short time before moving on. It feels wonderful to have this freedom, just to enjoy dancing with strangers. She is feeling a sense of her own body return, how she can move herself sensually, how she can feel the music inside of her.

A young man keeps returning to dance with her. He has shoulder-length, curly dark hair; he is muscular but not too tall – about the same height as her in her heels. They begin to really dance together. He takes her by the hand and twirls her on the dance floor; she pushes her body up close to his, enjoying the sensation of his young, firm body against her. They gyrate on the dance floor together, grinding their hips, all inhibitions gone. She feels wanton and sexy. Is this what dancing did to her mother, Maria? Vivienne had told her that she was free spirited and a libertine. Maybe being the way I am is something I cannot help, Tina thinks, as she lets this young man pull her tightly to his body, feels the sinew of his leg muscles pressing against the softness of her thighs.

Half an hour later, they tumble through the door of her hotel room, kissing all the while and shedding clothes. She kicks off her heels as he pulls off his shirt. For one so young, he has a hairy chest, and she pushes her fingers into it, pressing her nails against his skin so that his breathing becomes more rapid. They tear their clothes from each other. His eyes glitter darkly as he leans down and kisses her neck; she lifts her throat to him and he kisses her there, then works back down to the sides and nape of her neck. He begins to bite her, gently squeezing and teasing the skin of her neck with his teeth. Spikes of pleasure and pain course through her body, feeding her with longing laced by fear. She should stop him – he could really hurt her; he is most certainly marking her – and yet she can't. She loves how it feels.

He backs her to the bed and she falls on to it, with him on top of her. Her young Spaniard alternates between kissing, nibbling and biting all along her shoulders and down the sides of her body. He kisses and gently licks her nipples. The sensation of his lips on her breasts is driving her crazy. She wants him to fuck her so badly.

Suddenly, he clamps his teeth around her left nipple and she gasps as he bites it – not too hard, but hard enough that she feels the dual sensations of pleasure and pain. This is dangerous – and yet, despite the fact she doesn't know his name, even, she craves this erotic combination of fear and fervour. It makes her feel so much better; the pain of his biting takes away the heartache inside her.

He moves down her body, biting around her hips and thighs. She opens her legs now, desperate for him to be inside her. She feels his lips upon her vulva and her breath quickens with anticipation. He licks once, twice, and then he gently bites her, moving his mouth up to her clitoris and delicately nibbling it. The sensations upon her body are driving her wild; she can feel herself getting closer and closer to the edge. He suddenly thrusts his tongue up her pussy. My God, this man is an animal, Tina thinks. He is bringing out the primal in her. She is squirming, about to come. As if sensing this, he pulls back and gets up off her body. He gives her a long look, while she stares at his erect cock – surprisingly big for such a small man. They don't speak. She lies back on the bed, spreading her legs wider, begging to be fucked.

He picks up his jeans, ripping open a condom packet with gusto. She thinks he looks somewhat like a matador, a man full of macho prime. She knows even before he enters her that he is going to fuck her hard and rough. It's what she wants; it's what she needs.

* * *

He is still asleep in her bed when she gets up the next morning. She gathers her things together, trying not to make too much noise. He is sleeping on his stomach and curled to the side. He looks so innocent and childlike in repose. He is very young. She guesses from the quality of his clothing this he is probably a student.

She leaves him a note on the bedside table, explaining in Spanish that she had to get an early flight home and that he should stay in bed until check-out. All is taken care of. Then she leaves him some money. She is not sure why she does this. Does it make what she did any better?

She checks herself in the mirror of the wardrobe before she leaves the room. She cannot bear to look at her cheating face. How could she have done this to Phil? What was she thinking of? She can't explain the jealous rage that possessed her last night. She was so certain that Phil and Inger were up to no good back in Milan, yet now it is a nonsensical idea. They were just sharing a bottle of wine, which they all do most nights. To her horror, she sees that her neck is covered in several large strawberry bite marks. How on earth is she going to cover that up when she gets home? She valiantly covers her neck in foundation, but it doesn't work. She can feel herself panicking. Phil will see them. How can she explain herself? She pulls a silk scarf out of her case and wraps it around her neck several times, yet what will she do later when she has to take it off?

While Tina is sipping her coffee at the airport, trying to restore herself to calm, she can't take her eyes off the departure board. She is not looking at the flight to Milan, but the flight to Paris. She watches as the minutes creep forward, the opportunity for her to meet her father diminishing.

Boarding.

Final Call.

Gate Closed.

It is at that moment that her own flight to Milan is announced. She picks up her bag, rearranges the scarf around her neck, and steps forward. Her body is still sore from the night before, and her heart heavy. Yet she wants to go home. More than anything, she wants to spend the night in Phil's arms. He is the one true love of her life.

$\mathcal{V}$alentina

'MOVE IN WITH ME?' LEONARDO ASKS HER.

They are sitting on cushions in his front room, eating take-out salad. Valentina is so shocked, she nearly chokes on her falafel.

'What did you say?' she asks him.

'I asked you to move in with me,' Leonardo says, quite calmly, taking a sip of his beet and carrot juice. She can tell by the expression on his face that he means it.

'But why?' She knows her answer isn't very polite, but she is, quite frankly, stunned by Leonardo's offer.

'Because you need to give Marco and Jake some space . . .' He gives her a shy smile. 'And I want you to.'

'Are you sure you want me around all the time?' She scoops some hummus out of its box using a corner of pitta bread.

'I would love nothing more than to have you hanging around all the time,' Leonardo says with feeling.

His words frighten her a little. If she moves in with Leonardo, this will be no quick fling. This could be something big – possibly permanent – in her life. She chews her lip, wondering what to say in reply.

'You don't have to give me an answer now,' Leonardo says. 'Think about it.'

'I don't need to,' she says. 'Yes. I will.'

She feels a surge of emotion, a bittersweet sensation of pain and hope. She is finally taking those steps towards trusting another man.

The food has been cleared away and a bottle of Prosecco drunk. For the first time in months, Valentina feels really good – relaxed, yet excited. Her life is changing and she has no idea what direction it is going in, but just this fact lifts her spirits. Nothing is worse than predictability. She is going to move in with Leonardo . . . What might happen next?

The two of them are sitting opposite each other on the futon mattress, listening to Sigur Rós, the dreamlike melodies spinning a seductive web around them.

'Do you remember how you felt when I was touching you, massaging your yoni?' Leonardo whispers to her.

Valentina had felt like she was melting beneath Leonardo's hands. It had been one of the most sensual experiences of her life.

'Yes,' she says. 'It was amazing.'

'I wanted to show you that there are so many ways of using the simple act of touching when you are making love.'

'What do you mean?' she asks him.

'Of course we touch each other when we make love, but we often don't experiment enough with the erotic effects of touch. In Tantra, you try to touch lovingly, with awareness in your hands, so that, when you are being touched, you let yourself receive the touch. You absorb the warmth into the body.'

'So, in a way, you giving me a massage was not just you doing something to me?' she asks.

'Exactly; you are not passive . . . You are actively receiving my touch and that, in turn, affects me.'

She understands what Leonardo is saying now: that he had felt as if they had been bound together in a sensual interaction when he had massaged her.

'Valentina,' Leonardo whispers, trailing his fingers down her face and looking at her with such devotion that it makes her heart race. 'Tonight, I want you to make love for yourself, not for me.'

She frowns. 'I want to make love to you,' she says. 'I want to make you happy.'

'Oh, Valentina, you do,' he says, smiling at her. 'You have no need to try so hard.'

He draws her into his arms and they kiss slowly. As they gradually peel their clothes away, she becomes conscious of every point within her body that is touching every part of Leonardo. Her fingertips against his cheeks, her breasts pressing against his bare chest. Instead of falling down on the bed, Leonardo sits up, pulling her into his lap as he sits in the lotus position.

Valentina puts her legs around Leonardo's waist and her arms around his back as Leonardo hugs her in his arms at the same time. She raises herself up so that she can feel Leonardo's cock tapping against the lips of her pussy. She feels a thrill, a trembling inside her womb.

'Just relax,' Leonardo whispers, still looking into her eyes. She consciously relaxes her pelvic floor, imagining herself opening up to Leonardo's cock. Slowly, ever so slowly, he penetrates her, and in response she feels herself opening up further, yielding, receiving his cock into her. She feels his cock jerking in her, not thrusting, but snaking more deeply into her pussy. It feels to her as if Leonardo's cock has an intelligence all of its own. It is controlling their love making, as if, by instinct, it is telling them when to move and how much to move.

Looking into Leonardo's eyes, she feels safe and loved – protected. And yet, despite the deep bliss she is experiencing, the sensations building and building, she cannot help wishing that she had shared this experience with Theo.

She and Leonardo are one breathing entity, they rock back and forth, and then with a deep, shuddering breath, he climaxes. She holds his gaze, as her body responds, beginning to vibrate, and she joins him in his rapture, orgasming again and again.

They lie in each others arms, neither of them speaking. Valentina looks up at the ceiling at the shifting lights from the city bleeding through Leonardo's curtains, reminding her of the chaos that is her life. The world outside the sanctuary of Leonardo's bedroom is constantly spinning. Thoughts of Glen and the danger she could be in are all out there, and yet in bed with Leonardo she feels safe. She has found some stillness. Valentina feels a surge of gratitude and love towards her friend and all that he has given her.

'Leonardo?' she asks, turning to him, and tracing her finger down his face.

'Yes, darling, what is it?' He looks up at her, concerned.

'Is there a male equivalent of the yoni massage?'

'Of course, there is,' and she can see that he is now smiling. 'It's called the Lingam massage.'

She puts her hand upon his chest and presses down against his firm skin.

'Will you teach me how to do it?'

He puts his hand upon hers, squeezes it tight, and pulls her deep into the richness of his eyes.

'With pleasure.'

Valentina and Leonardo are kneeling on his bed. The sun is beginning to rise, and the room is infused with pink peachy tones as the dawn infiltrates his bedroom. They hold hands, looking into each other's eyes. She takes one of Leonardo's hands and puts it on his heart, placing her hand over it. She feels the beat of him, hears his breath, and whispers to him, 'Lie down on your stomach on the bed.'

Valentina takes a small bottle of coconut oil from the shelf beside the bed and pours a tiny pool of it into her palms. The exotic and enticing aroma of coconut wafts up from her warm hands.

She begins to massage Leonardo's shoulders. She swirls her hands on his back in broad, swift movements, as if they are two birds, dancing together. Like Leonardo has told her, she can really feel him through her skin touching his skin. His pleasure becomes her pleasure. She pours a little more oil on to his legs and works all the way down to his feet, then up again, until she has reached his buttocks, firm and strong. She lies down on top of Leonardo's back, pressing her body into his. It feels wonderful to have her breasts pressed into his back, her pussy against his butt, to inhale his coconut, male scent, and to look at Leonardo in repose, his eyes shut, completely trusting her, completely hers. She feels a deep sense of freedom, for there is no agenda in Leonardo's bedroom, no expectation of performance or perfection.

She peels herself away from Leonardo, ever so slowly, revelling in the bliss of their slippery skin coming apart.

253

'Turn over,' she whispers to him.

Her eyes are immediately drawn to his erection. She looks at his cock in a different way. It is not just a part of his body that can do something to her; it exists in its own right. She adores it. Valentina fills her palms with more coconut oil, so that it is dripping through her fingers, pattering on to Leonardo's torso. She advances the massage, slowly, from his chest down towards his inner thighs and pelvis, until she can hear that Leonardo is breathing deeply from his belly, and his body is fully relaxed. She leans down and kisses him gently on the lips. She hears him murmuring: just her name, nothing else.

She pours a small quantity of the coconut oil on to Leonardo's cock and balls. She rubs the oil into his skin, from the top of his thighs up to his pelvis, using slow, steady motions. As she massages her lover, she feels his rapture. She is turned on just by touching him, just by feeling his erotic sensations. She begins to massage just above his cock, rocking her hand on the pubic bone, and then moving down to his balls, very gently pulling and kneading them. She traces her hands down to massage just behind his balls, but not as far back as his backside. Valentina puts her whole body into the movements that her hands make: strong downward strokes, all the way from his cock to his butt, and then alternating these with circling in between, pushing a particular point with her finger.

She places her hand on Leonardo's cock, holds it lovingly, embraces it in her hand as if it something precious. She begins to massage the shaft, gently squeezing the base of the cock with her right hand, and then pulling up and sliding her hand completely off. She pours more oil on to her hands and then does the same thing with her left hand, squeezing Leonardo's cock at the base, pulling her hand up and then sliding completely off. She does it again with her right hand, and then with her left again; right and left; right and left. She changes direction, sliding alternating hands from the top down to the base. After a few minutes, she takes his cock between both hands and rubs her hands quickly back and forth, as if she is starting a fire. Valentina wonders if Leonardo *is* on fire. His eyes are closed, his lips parted; she can see the pink of his tongue resting on his teeth. She takes Leonardo's cock by the head and gently shakes it back and forth, before cupping the head in her palm and twisting her hand and wrist. She hears Leonardo give a tiny gasp, and she knows he is so close to the edge now. It excites her to feel that she is bringing him there, and he is letting her. He is giving his whole body up to her direction. She can feel the deep inner vibrations within Leonardo's body. She can sense when she is bringing him close to climax, and yet she pulls back and slows down at just the last moment. At these points, Leonardo breathes so deeply that he sounds like a low roll of thunder. Several times, she feels he is going to climax and yet it is as if he is able to bring all that bliss back inside his body, rather than spill it out. Eventually she takes him all the way, and she watches him intently as he orgasms in front of her. He looks so vulnerable and yet so magnificent at the same time.

Valentina leans over Leonardo and kisses him on the lips, and he opens his eyes, looks right into the heart of her. She flinches and looks away, for she feels he has seen the truth.

$\mathcal{T}$ina

1989

SHE HAD THOUGHT HE WAS DEAD. WHEN SHE FIRST OPENED THE door and saw Garelli, Phil's police friend, standing on her doorstep, looking sombre, she had thought Phil had been killed. Tina was not a woman for hysterics, but she had cried out instinctively. It had felt like her punishment. She deserved to lose Phil.

Inger had come running then, asking Garelli in her broken Italian what had happened.

'Signor Rembrandt has been shot,' Garelli said. 'But he is OK. It's just a shoulder wound.'

'He's OK?' Inger checked, while Tina stood speechless, trembling.

'He saved my life,' Garelli said. 'He is a hero.'

'I don't want a hero,' Tina had snapped. 'I want my man alive and well.'

It had only been a matter of time before something happened. Ever since she had got back from Barcelona, Phil had been working nonstop on the piece he was writing about the violent crimes of a particular Mafia gang, based near Sorrento. At first, she hadn't complained. She felt so guilty about what she had done in Barcelona that she was just glad he was still with her, that he didn't know about her betrayal. Yet, as the weeks went on, she almost felt as if Phil was two-timing her – not with another woman, but with this case.

'You're going to get hurt,' she warned him. 'Phil, these people are very dangerous.'

'I know,' he said. 'But they have to be stopped. I'm trying to help Garelli and the police build up a case.'

'Please, Phil, just let the police do their job. You don't even have a gun.'

'Why would I need a gun –' he had laughed at her – 'when I have the power of my pen?'

She hadn't thought it funny. 'This is no joking matter,' she said.

'I know,' he replied, suddenly serious. 'Not when a young girl is murdered brutally and her body dumped in a bin in Naples, just because she happened to be in the wrong place at the wrong time, or when a young boy is overdosing on heroin, drugs supplied by these bastards, which make the same bastards so rich that they pretend to be respectable.'

Tina shook her head. 'They are a force unto themselves, Phil. You can't change it on your own.'

'I can try,' he said. She had never seen him so mad. 'That guy, Caruthers, thinks he's a king. He has his son in the most expensive private school in England and is bringing him up to be some kind of little lord so he can run his empire. And it's not just drugs, Tina. It's everything: prostitution, robbery, murder. It doesn't stop.'

By September, Phil was working day and night, obsessed with the case. He said they were close to a breakthrough. One morning, when Valentina had been in kindergarten, he had persuaded Inger to go with him to take some photographs of one of the gang members in a café, since they all knew what Phil looked like. Tina had been furious when she found out.

'How dare you endanger that girl's life?' she had flared up at him, shocked at her own protectiveness towards the young Norwegian. 'She is a complete innocent.'

'She offered to come with me,' Phil said. 'She found it exciting.'

'I don't care if it was the most thrilling event of her life. She is only twenty years old. You are *not* to take her with you ever again.'

Yet, now he is shot and, as she races to the hospital in her car, Tina doesn't care about whether he was asking for it or not; all she wants is to see him and to check he is OK.

'There's my girl,' Phil says, sitting up in bed, his arm in a sling, his shoulder covered in bandages.

She bursts into tears. She cannot help it. He looks so vulnerable, all bandaged up. She can see he is in pain, despite his smile.

'Hey!' he says. 'Come here, you silly cow.'

She flops on to the bed and buries her face in his chest. He strokes her head.

'I'm OK; it's only a minor wound,' he tells her.

She pulls back and looks at him. 'I thought you were dead,' she hiccups. 'When I first saw Garelli, I thought they had killed you.'

'No, they can't get rid of me that easy.'

'Don't joke,' she begs.

'OK, love,' he says, gently. 'Come here.'

She climbs on to the hospital bed with him and snuggles up to his unbandaged side. He puts his good arm around her. She realises it is the first time in weeks that they have had a proper cuddle. He has been so busy with his work.

Phil kisses the top of her head and she raises her face to him. They kiss each other softly. She can feel her pulse quicken. She wants so much to slip into the bed beside Phil and make love to him.

'You know, I have always had this nurse fantasy,' Phil teases her.

'Don't get any ideas now!' she teases back.

'I wouldn't dream of it; you're the only woman for me, Tina Rosselli.'

She winces when she remembers how she has betrayed him. Twice. She doesn't deserve Phil's love. She wants everything to go back to the way it was before he started on the Mafia case, when Valentina was a baby and Mattia was still at school. Now her son is in America and feels so far away from them. She had not wanted him to go – surely seventeen was too young to go to the other side of the world? – but Phil insisted that Mattia needed the experience of a gap year.

'I called Mattia up,' Tina says. 'He's going to get a plane back tomorrow.'

'There's no need,' Phil says, 'that will cost a fortune.'

'Phil, you're his dad. Of course he's coming back.'

'How's he doing over there?'

'Good; he's got a job moving furniture in New York. And a girlfriend. Her name's Debbie.'

'And where's our little girl?'

'She's with Inger in the park. They've gone to feed the ducks. She wants to know where Papa is.'

'I'll be home soon. They said just a day or two and I'll be right as rain, a little sore, but—'

'Phil, you have to stop,' Tina says.

'But we nearly have him, Tina,' Phil says, his eyes flashing with excitement. 'I am going to bring Caruthers down.'

'Listen to me, Phil,' Tina says. 'It's too dangerous.'

'It's going to be fine,' he reassures her. 'It's nearly over now.'

'I'm worried about Valentina, Inger, all of us . . .' Tina says.

'OK,' Phil says. 'You're right.' He frowns, thinking for a moment. 'Why don't you and Valentina stay with Mattia for a while in New York, until the whole thing is over? Inger is due back in Norway in a couple of weeks, anyway.'

'But what about you?'

'I'll stay here,' he says. 'I have to finish it, Tina.'

'No,' she says. 'I'm not leaving you.'

Phil smoothes the hair back on her forehead with his one good hand, and kisses it. 'You know I love you, Tina, more than my very own life, don't you?'

She nods.

'You need to trust me.' He sighs. 'I can't let it go now. That would be worse. We need to make sure Caruthers is locked up.'

She shakes her head. 'Please, Phil—'

'I want you all to be safe, too,' he interrupts her. 'So maybe *I* should go away for a while, until it's all over?'

'No,' she says, her heart filling with panic. 'Don't leave me.'

He grins at her. 'Don't be crazy; of course I won't be leaving you . . . It will just be temporary.'

'No,' she whispers. 'I can't live without you.'

She knows it is the sort of thing lovers tell each other all the time. But it is true. For, the moment she had seen Garelli on her doorstep, when she thought she had lost Phil, she felt as if she was dying inside, too, as if her body was falling away from her heart, as it dropped like a stone and cracked beneath her.

'One day, maybe you'll have to, Tina,' Phil says, tipping her chin with his finger. 'We are all alone in the end.'

$\mathcal{V}$alentina

VALENTINA WATERS THE ALOE VERA PLANT ON LEONARDO'S
kitchen sill. She squeezes its plump, juicy leaves between her
fingers and tests the soil to check it is moist enough. Sunlight
spills through the open window; already spring has turned to
summer. She wonders if she will remain in New York for the
whole summer. Marco has told her it gets unbearably hot, but
then so does Milan. When she told him about moving in with
Leonardo, Marco had been pleased for her.

'I thought you felt I wasn't ready to date yet,' she challenged
him, as they packed up her stuff, 'let alone move in with
someone.'

'Leonardo is different,' Marco said, folding up one of her
shirts more carefully than Valentina ever would. 'He will take
care of you.'

She has been living with Leonardo for just under a week and,
so far, it has been a dream. She has managed to put to the back
of her mind all thoughts of Glen and his sinister note. She has
not heard a word from the police on anything to do with the art
robbery, apart from to confirm that, indeed, the picture had
been the original Klimt drawing and, unfortunately, there
had been no fingerprints or other DNA evidence found. They
had examined the tube it was posted in, found the post office

on 76th 9th Avenue in the Meatpacking District and looked at the security cameras, but everything came up with a dead end. Valentina has finally decided to let it all go. Everything. Even her desire for revenge on Glen. It is too dangerous. It's not worth it. That is how Leonardo makes her feel. Besides, she could still be wrong. The man she believes is Glen might not be him at all. And whoever it is, he is surely no longer in New York. The man would be crazy to stay in the city, seeing as every cop is after him.

Each morning, Valentina is woken by her lover with a cup of Kusmi detox herbal tea. She sips this cleansing brew while Leonardo massages her feet. Sometimes, if they are in no hurry, Leonardo graduates to massaging the rest of her body, unfolding her so that eventually they begin the morning making love.

Today, as they lay in bed together, their toes kissing, Leonardo had tried explaining a little more about Tantric sex.

'With Tantra, an orgasm is no longer the all-important goal that has to be reached through effort and tension every time,' he had said to her. 'When it happens, it is good, and when it does not happen, it is good.'

'I find that hard to grasp,' Valentina admitted, trailing her finger down the inside of his arm. 'I have often had sex without climaxing in the past, but it has always left me feeling a little unsatisfied and, if my partner doesn't come, I feel like a failure.'

'That is because you are putting some kind of goal or aim on to the sex. You are focusing on pleasure rather than esctasy.'

Leonardo strokes her face.

'What I want to try to show you is how to bring relaxation, in the true sense of the word, into sex, so that it becomes a

263

magical revelation rather than a pattern that you follow every time.'

'How do you mean, "relaxation"?'

Leonardo stretches his arms above his head. He looks cat-like: tranquil yet alert. 'I don't mean a state of exhaustion or collapse; I mean true relaxation, when you pull your attention from without to within, from activity to rest, doing less and being more. It is about releasing control over how we make love so that we don't conform to habits.'

She turns on her side and looks down at him, planting a kiss on his forehead. 'I feel pretty relaxed now.'

'You would be surprised how tense you really are. You have to consciously release that tension. Next time we make love, try to find those areas of tension in your body. For instance, if you relax your jaw, you can immediately feel it having a softening effect on your pelvic area; or, if you relax your feet, squeezing and releasing your toes, it can relax your vagina.'

'So when *is* the next time we make love?' Valentina asks him, propped on her elbow, a cheeky grin on her face.

He gives her a long look, smiling slowly. He looks even more like a cat now, as if he is about to purr. He pulls her down on top of him, kissing her lips softly. She kisses him back, putting her hands on either side of his face and treasuring him. She is tempted to close her eyes, to lose herself in a fantasy, but Leonardo holds her gaze and, as she fights this urge, keeping her eyes open, she finds that she is more keenly aware of her body opening up to him. She sits up on top of him and pulls back; for a moment, they hold this position, their hands on each other's hearts, breathing in unison.

She can feel his cock growing beneath her, unfurling, and yet she brings to mind all that Leonardo has taught her. She needs to be as conscious of her body as of his. She needs to make love to herself as well as him. In this way, she can love him the best. She bends down to kiss him as she feels his cock, as if by instinct, pushing up inside her slowly. She holds him and opens up further, so that he is sucked deep within her. She feels as if his tip is now touching the most sacred, most sensitive part of herself, yet she determines not to think about the outcome. Instead, she concentrates on how her body feels. She relaxes her jaw and, sure enough, she feels her pelvis opening out further, pulling him in even more.

For the first time in her life, she thinks about the power and strength within her. She imagines a yellow diamond in her diaphragm, and it is shining brightly. She wills that light to spill out, to relax. To her surprise, she feels a sudden wave of nausea, a lump in her stomach as all the pain, the heartache from the last year, begins to surface. She is frightened for a moment, but Leonardo is holding her tightly, looking into her eyes, silently healing her with his love. They are making love without effort, without tension. It becomes a dance, a sensuous winding of their bodies, as if they are two snakes wrapped around each other.

They make love for two hours. If someone had told her before that she would be having sex for two hours straight without climaxing, she would not have believed them. She would have viewed it as frustrating – embarrassing, even – that neither of them could come. Yet, by the time their passionate dance slows down and the two of them unwind again upon the bed, she feels euphoric, her body radiating with bliss, all thoughts of past pain and future insecurities blanked out by the rapturous present. She feels like she is gathering Leonardo into her, all his healing love and positivity. She feels valued and treasured, and surprisingly unafraid. All of these Tantric sex keys are helping to unlock her fears of intimacy.

She wants to bring this feeling with her into the rest of the day, but, as soon as Leonardo leaves for his yoga class, she begins to feel a little edgy again. Everything would be perfect if it wasn't for Glen and the Klimt picture. She tries to push it to the back of her mind yet again. She is booked for a shoot this afternoon: a model, called Sophie, wanting her do a series of more experimental pictures for her portfolio. They have decided to use a variety of New York locations: Central Park, the Guggenheim, Times Square and the top of the Rockefeller Center. Valentina is looking forward to the project. She plans to play around with some digital processing techniques, such as multiplicity and compositing.

Just as she finishes putting together all her props for this afternoon's shoot, her phone rings.

'Hello, darling, it's Tina.'

Why didn't her mama just call herself Mama, like other mothers? She hates the fact that she wants Valentina to call her Tina all the time. For a start, they have the same name, more or less.

'Oh, hi.'

'How are things going?' her mother asks. 'Are you getting plenty of work?'

It is always about the job, Valentina thinks, when it comes to her mother.

'Yes, actually, I'm really busy.'

'Good,' her mother says. No advice for once.

There is a pause on the line.

'Well, I'm in New York,' her mother suddenly announces.

'Oh, really?' Valentina says, cautiously. What does her mother want?

'Yes, you see . . .' There is another awkward pause. This is most unlike her mother to be lost for words.

'What is it, Mama?'

'I'd like to see you, as soon as possible,' she gushes. 'We need to talk.'

'What about?'

It seems about ten years too late to Valentina. She is done trying to get on with her mother. She will tolerate her, but they will never be close.

'I've been speaking to Phil,' her mother says.

Valentina doesn't say anything. Her heart begins to sink. She had hoped that this was a conversation she could avoid with her mother. She had laid the ghost of her absent father to rest when she met Phil Rembrandt and he explained that, in fact, he wasn't her real father. She had decided when she was in Sorrento with Theo that she didn't want to know any more about her real father, and that she would never bring it up with her mother or Mattia. She had been angry with them for lying to her, but what was the point of talking about it now? She didn't want any more pain in her life; besides, when she lost Theo, finding her real father seemed very insignificant compared to her heartbreak.

'Why didn't you tell me that you knew . . . about Karel?' her mother says.

'I didn't see the point . . . I was waiting for you to tell me.'

'I was never going to tell you,' Tina says, matter-of-factly.

'Precisely,' Valentina says, in a cold voice. 'So what was the point?'

'But now you know,' her mother says, 'I need to tell you about him.'

'Why?'

'Because Phil made me realise what I did was wrong. I'm sorry, Valentina.'

Valentina is stunned. She cannot remember a time when her mother ever apologised to her.

'Look,' her mother continues, 'I don't want to have this conversation on the phone. Can we meet somewhere?'

Valentina glances down at her watch. She has arranged to meet Sophie in a restaurant called Steak Frites at four this afternoon. It is only twelve now.

'OK, do you want to meet for lunch at a place called Steak Frites? It's a French restaurant on Eighteenth and Fifth.'

'See you there at one,' her mother says.

Steak Frites is decorated in the style of a Parisian bar in the twenties, with decorative wallpaper, mirrors, and vintage hats adorning shelves. It has become a favourite place to eat or drink for Valentina just because it reminds her of that era. She also told Sophie she thought it would make a good location for one of their pictures. It is a quirky place, the lights hung from shades made out of bowler hats. The restaurant is full of theatrical details and vintage allusions.

She arrives just a few minutes before her mother. Last year, after Theo disappeared, she saw her mother for the first time in nine years. She was surprised by how little she had changed. In fact, if anything, she looked better. Today, she still has jet-black hair in a bob, and her skin is pale and soft. She has relatively few wrinkles for her age, probably because she has been so careful to protect her skin. For Tina Rosselli, personal maintenance is a priority in her life. She is her usual svelte self, not quite as thin as she used to be, but still slender, dressed simply in skinny jeans and a white shirt, with black high-heeled boots. Valentina feels like thunder thighs next to her, in her short skirt and ankle boots. Why has she dressed up for her mother, anyway?

They take a seat near the front window of the restaurant, ordering a 'Steak Frites' salad each, and fries on the side, between them. Her mother selects a bottle of red wine to go with it.

'You look better,' her mother comments. 'You've put on weight, but it suits you.'

Valentina is not sure whether to take this as a compliment or an insult.

'You look amazing, as usual,' Valentina comments.

Her mother nods, as if she knows this already, and Valentina instantly wishes she hadn't complimented her. Already Tina is irritating her. She takes a deep breath. She needs to try and not get too wound up and angry.

'So, how are you feeling?' her mother asks, after the waiter has brought the wine. 'Has moving to New York helped you get over that guy?'

Valentina takes a swig of her drink. She feels fury building up inside her. 'He was not just "that guy", Mama. His name was Theo and he was my fiancé.' She can hear her voice rising. 'We were getting married.'

Her mother looks at her in alarm. 'OK, calm down; I never realised it was that serious. You mentioned marriage to me last year, but I thought you were fantasising . . . You see, you never told me you were getting married or that you had even got back together with Theo. The first thing I knew was the accident . . .'

'He was the love of my life, Mama,' Valentina blurts out, emotionally, the truth of this statement searing her as she says it. It is true, and yet, by saying it, she feels like she has betrayed Leonardo is some way.

Her mother looks appalled. She is speechless for a moment. She leans across and takes Valentina's hand. 'I know how that feels – to lose the love of your life.'

Always her mother turns everything she says, no matter how personal, into a conversation about herself. Valentina looks at her mother and wonders who was her great love: Phil or her father, this mystery Karel, or maybe there was some other man in her mother's life she never knew was the love of it.

'I didn't think you believed in such things, Mother.'

'Every girl believes in *the one*, Valentina. All of us – secretly, deep down – are waiting for our prince to come.' She gives a sad laugh, takes a slug of her wine. 'I know my mother had a secret love, before she met my father,' she continues. 'And, of course, my grandmother, Belle, had Santos. For everyone there is someone. Some of us are lucky to keep hold of them, and some of us are not so lucky.' She pauses, takes another sip of her wine. 'But we should be grateful for that time we had with them and we should never close up to love again, just because of a broken heart. It may not be the same, but it is still love.'

Her mother is beginning to sound like Leonardo. Their food arrives. Valentina is suddenly ravenous. She takes a handful of chips and dips them into the bowl of ketchup.

'So have you come all this way just to talk to me about my father?' she asks, bluntly.

'Actually, I'm on my way to visit Mattia and his family,' she says, 'but I wanted to talk to you first.'

Of course, her mother wouldn't come to New York just to see her. It had to involve some other reason as well.

'Why don't you come with me to see Mattia?' Tina suggests.

Valentina shakes her head. 'I'm busy.' She wants to add,

falling in love. Knowing her mother, if she met Leonardo, she would insist he give her one of his healing yoni massages. The idea of that horrifies her.

'Come on, Valentina; you know Debbie and I don't get on that well. You can be my cushion. And you haven't met the kids, either. Mattia is quite hurt.'

'He can come and see me in New York; why doesn't he come here?'

'You know it's harder for him since his work relocated upstate. Why can't you make the effort for him? He has always looked out for you.'

She shrugs, trying not to show her true feelings, but her mother is no fool.

'Are you angry with him?' she asks.

'He knew about Phil and Karel, and he never told me.'

'That's not his fault; that's my fault, Valentina. I was the one that wanted to keep it secret. I made him promise not to tell you.'

'Why, for God's sake? Why did you let me grow up believing that my father was Phil and that he didn't want to know me? Can't you see how damaging that was?'

'I do now. Phil is very upset I let you think so, too. He feels guilty that he didn't play a bigger role in your life.' Her mother pauses and takes a delicate sip of her red wine. 'But, Valentina, I have to take the blame. I took you away from Phil. I wouldn't let him back in my life. I was so *hurt* by him.'

'Why? Why would you be hurt? You're the one that went off and had a child with another man . . . From what I can see, it is Phil who was the wronged party.'

Her mother sighs. 'It is so much more complicated than that, Valentina. Maybe, when you are older and have been married to

271

someone for a few years, you will understand how things were between Phil and me when I went to Berlin.'

Valentina forks some of her steak into her mouth. It is tender and bloody. She washes it down with some more red wine, trying to drown the bitterness, the anger she tastes in her mouth.

Her mother takes a chip out of the bowl and dips it in the ketchup, but, rather than eating it, she holds it between thumb and index finger, as if it is a little wand. 'I met Phil when I was so young, Valentina. I was very inexperienced,' she says, waving around her chip. 'We were together for twenty years in total. Phil was very preoccupied with work when I went to Berlin . . . I felt very alone . . . I . . .' She drops her uneaten chip on to the plate.

'I don't want to hear the reasons why,' Valentina snaps. She knows she is being hard on her mother, but she had liked Phil when she met him in London. In a way, she is furious that he is not really her father. It occurs to her that one of the reasons that she doesn't want to see Mattia is that she is jealous. Her brother has a father, and a relationship with him, whereas she has neither.

Tina looks chastised. She plays with the food on her plate. To her annoyance, Valentina notices she is not actually eating. This game with food that her mother has always played drives her mad: ordering big fancy meals and leaving them untouched. It makes Valentina want to overeat, stuff every single one of those greasy chips down her throat.

'Just tell me about my father. Who is he?'

Her mother coughs, looking a little uneasy. 'He was a very talented musician. In fact, in the Eastern bloc, he was a celebrity cellist. His name was Karel Slavik. His father was Czech and his mother was German. He lived in East Berlin. He had the most beautiful hands, such incredible, strong fingers . . .' Valentina's mother looks away from her, out of the restaurant, at the busy sidewalk outside. 'He was younger than me,' she says.

'How much younger?'

'Ten years. He was twenty-five. He had been a child prodigy in the DDR. Already, by the time I knew him, he had made several famous recordings. He was a staunch advocate of socialism.'

'And how did you meet him?'

'I went to see him play in East Berlin. I was over in West Berlin on a fashion shoot and one of the models had a cousin who lived on the other side of the Wall. I was curious to see what it was like . . . Well, more what the people were like.'

Valentina tries to picture her glamorous, consumerist mother in East Berlin with this Communist musician, ten years younger than her. Maybe it's because of her love of the film *Wings of Desire*, but she always imagines East Berlin in black and white. That young man would have been living such a different life from her mother. He would have been innocent to the corruption of the West. And yet Tina Rosselli had just swanned in there and taken what she wanted from this poor Karel Slavik. The picture is becoming clearer to her now.

'How could you have been so irresponsible?' she says to her mother.

Tina flinches as if she is the child being told off by her parent.

'How could you let yourself get pregnant by an East German man, someone you knew would never be able to see his child grow up, unless of course you suddenly became a Communist and moved in with him,' she says, sarcastically, for the idea of her mother ever giving up any of her freedoms is unbelievable.

'It wasn't like that, Valentina. It was an accident. These things can happen.'

I know, a voice inside Valentina speaks, and suddenly she is overwhelmed with the desire to tell her mother about the time she got pregnant by accident, how she miscarried, and how Theo got her through it. His love had saved and sustained her. If she could tell her this then maybe her mother might understand what Theo had meant to her. But now is not the time. Her mother is finally coming clean about her father. She has to listen through to the end.

'He was going to defect,' her mother tells her. 'He was going on an international tour, all approved by the party. The first concert was to be in Vienna. I had promised that I would go there and help him defect. But then, all of a sudden, the Minister of Culture cancelled his permit. They said that a piece of music he had composed was antisocialist and self-indulgent, but Karel believed that someone had found out about his plan to defect . . . someone betrayed him . . .' Her mother's voice wavers. She stops for a moment and takes a swig of her wine.

Valentina looks at her curiously. She has never seen her mother so emotional before.

'I only found out I was pregnant after his tour was cancelled.'

'Did you ever see him again?' Valentina asks, leaning forward.

Her mother nods. 'Once. I felt he should know I was having his child. I was about four months pregnant when I went back to see him in his apartment in East Berlin. He was under surveillance then, but I didn't care. I told him I was going to have his baby. I shouldn't have . . . It was stupid of me . . .' Her voice trails off. She takes the bottle of wine and fills up her glass again with a shaking hand.

'Valentina, I admit the reason I have never told you this story before is that it is hard for me to talk about it. I have tried my best to forget it. My affair with Karel ended in tragedy, and not only that – through it, I lost Phil. The only man in my life who loved me unconditionally, and yet I threw him away because of Karel. It was a mess.'

'But the Berlin Wall came down in 1989,' Valentina says. 'Did you never hear from Karel again, or didn't you go and find him?'

'Of course I went to find him. The last time I saw him, I promised him that, as soon as the Wall came down, I would bring you to meet him. He never really believed it would, but I always hoped. Then, quite suddenly, it began to happen.' Tina pauses, swirling her fork among the lettuce leaves on her plate. 'Don't you remember?' She looks up at Valentina. 'You would have been about five years old. I brought you to Berlin with me.'

Valentina frowns. She remembers Phil had told her that her mother brought her to Berlin with her, that Tina had wanted him to come too. But Valentina really cannot remember where she was with her mother specifically, just a place that was not home and where she was very cold. 'Did you find him?' she asks.

Was it possible that Tina had found Karel and he had turned his back on them? Had he not wanted to know his five-year-old daughter? The thought hurts her, she tries not to let it, but she feels so wounded for that little girl.

Her mother looks up from the table with sorrowful eyes. 'Yes, Valentina; in a way, I did find him.'

The way her mother says this sends a chill down her spine.

'How do you mean?'

'Do you not remember my friend, Lottie, and where she took us that day?'

Valentina shakes her head.

'She took us to a cemetery . . . to your father's headstone. I found out that he was dead, my darling. He was dead because of me. So now do you understand why I never wanted to tell you?'

Valentina stares in horror at her mother, for Tina Rosselli is crying. She has never seen her mother cry before. The sight of it fills her with panic. She doesn't know what to feel: anger to discover that her father, after all, is dead, anyway, and that she will never know him? Or pity for her mother, who blames herself?

Valentina sits, frozen, on the other side of the table. She doesn't comfort her mother, or touch her, even. She is beginning to remember. A memory that she had buried deep is emerging out of the fog of her mind. Lottie. Yes. She sees that woman, with thick black hair, tall, like a witch. She had scared Valentina. And she remembers now a graveyard, how it had been so cold and she had not wanted to go in. She remembers Lottie holding her hand tightly and turning her away, but she had already seen her mother falling on her knees in front of a grave, her mother wailing so loudly it had terrified her. She knew someone important was dead. She just didn't know it was her father.

'How did he die?' she asks, mercilessly, clenching her fists upon the table.

'He was killed, trying to get over the Wall,' her mother says, looking at her desperately through her tears. 'Shot in the back. He was trying to get to you, Valentina. He wanted to see his baby girl.'

Valentina's heart cracks open. She thought that she had hardened it to her mother, that Tina could no longer hurt her. Yet she is thawing fast. Maybe, before the love she felt for Theo, before Leonardo's healing presence and all that he has done to unlock her, Valentina would have taken this news calmly, almost cynically.

He wanted to see his baby girl.

Could it be true? Had her father died because he wanted so badly to know her? She stares at her mother disintegrating in front of her, and something happens. Her mother had *tried* her best for her. Face to face with the sight of her weeping, Valentina's own feelings fly out of her violently, like a bird that has suddenly been set free from its cage.

'Oh, Mama!'

Her voice breaks, she feels her eyes begin to water. Tina Rosselli leans over and grabs her hands. They cling on to each other as, finally, Valentina understands who her mother is. It has taken nearly thirty years, but it is not too late to begin again.

'Forgive me, Valentina,' her mother whispers.

'I already have,' her daughter tells her.

$\mathcal{T}$ina

1990

EVER SINCE SHE ARRIVED IN LONDON ON MONDAY, FOR THE fashion shoot for the French edition of *Marie Claire*, Tina has found it hard to focus. The shoot is on London street style, with the aim being to bring a more edgy look to the French readership. She has chosen the East End, around Bow and the canal, as her location, as well as moving into more well-known spots in the City of London, such as some of the old Wren churches. Yet, despite the fact she is working long hours, each evening she takes the Tube to Finchley Road, where she never makes it past the Underground entrance before she turns around and returns to the city centre.

Tonight is her last night – her last chance to see Phil. She knows exactly where he lives. She got the address off Mattia weeks ago. She made her son promise not to say anything, pretending that she was going to write to Phil about something to do with Valentina. To be honest, she doesn't think Mattia cares that much what she is up to, anyway. He never came back from his gap year and has his own life in America with this girlfriend, Debbie, and her family. He seems to have shed Tina and Phil, and started anew.

278

'It's just his age,' Isabella counsels her.

'How do you know?' she asks her friend. 'You don't have kids.'

Isabella shrugs. 'I know I don't,' she says, 'but I do know that there is nothing you can do about it.'

She has been staying with Isabella and her current lover in her swanky apartment in Kensington. The night before, over several glasses of wine, she had asked her friend if she should go and visit Phil. She had expected Isabella to tell her to forget Phil, enjoy being single and go out with her clubbing for the night, since her lover was out of town, but, to her surprise, Isabella had encouraged her to go and see him.

'You two are the real deal,' she told her.

So here she is, already halfway up Finchley Road, further than she progressed all those other nights. How had she let their estrangement go on for so long? She never meant that to happen. When she returned from Berlin, devastated at what she had found out, she should have rung Phil up, told him they were back in Milan. Yet she had been so confused. For months, she blamed herself for Karel's death. She didn't deserve Phil. There was also a part of her still angry at his abandonment, although she knew in her heart that he had only left to keep them safe from the same men who had shot him. He had always intended to return, that is until she told him she was going to Berlin to meet Karel.

And then Phil went off the radar. Tina asked Mattia about him, but her son told her that Phil had changed his number and that even he couldn't get hold of him. The next thing she knew, it was all over the news. Caruthers had been arrested, Garelli was the cop in charge of the arrest, and a massive exposé by Phil was in all the major newspapers. He had finished the job, just like he had promised.

By the time Phil had contacted Mattia again, Tina had buried herself in work. Every time she thought about Phil, it hurt, so the best thing to do was to keep working. She knew she was becoming obsessive, even bringing Valentina with her on most of the shoots, but she couldn't help herself. Anything was better than sitting at home on her own, feeling unwanted.

Yet, now she is here in Phil's home city, she can't resist the urge to see him – if only to ask him how he is, if only to shake his hand and wish him well. They had ended things so badly.

She looks at the address in her notebook and checks the street name. This is the one. She turns the corner and counts down the houses. Darkness has already fallen and, as she walks down the street, she can see inside all the houses. Most are lit up. It is dinnertime and she watches couples and families eating around tables, or watching TV. We used to be a family, she thinks, sadly. Me, Phil, Mattia and Valentina. It is all broken up now. And who is to blame? Her or Phil?

She stands with her hand on the gate leading to Phil's front door. The house is dark and she is just about to turn away when a light in the front room clicks on. There are no curtains on the window and she has a perfect view of the room. She can see the Phil-ness of it: walls crammed with bookshelves, old furniture and potted plants. And then, suddenly, she sees him. Her heart almost stops in her mouth as Phil walks into the room, carrying a bottle of red wine and a corkscrew. He looks more divine to her than ever: taller, his hair streaked with grey, but his face still young. She takes a step forward, pushes the gate open and then she stops in her tracks. For Phil is not alone. Following him into the room is a woman carrying two wine glasses. Phil says something and the woman laughs. She is quite beautiful, Tina thinks, as her heart begins to chill. The woman is curvaceous, almost plump, with curly red hair, and a big smile. She is nothing like Tina. She brings the glasses over to Phil, who has opened the wine and put it down on the coffee table in front of the couch. He turns to the woman and she leans towards him. They kiss.

The sight of it feels like a firebrand on her heart. Tina turns on her heel and walks away. Each step she takes feels like walking on fire. Her heart is freezing, her body burning with regret, with self-loathing.

You left it too late, she berates herself. You have lost him for ever.

The next day, she is walking through King's Cross train station, on her way to get the Tube to the airport, when she takes a wrong turn. Instead of entering the Underground station, she finds herself standing on a station platform. She has plenty of time before her flight to Milan, so, instead of rushing, she decides to have one last cup of English breakfast tea at the station café before she leaves England – a country she never intends to return to, now that she has lost all hope for her and Phil.

The café is empty apart from another woman, sitting in the corner, reading a newspaper. Tina can't help noticing how striking the girl is. She spends her professional life taking photos of beautiful women, and this girl would never make a model, yet there is something about her that is so alluring. She is elegantly voluptuous with lustrous red hair – just like that of Phil's lover last night – that cascades over her shoulders. The more Tina looks at her, the more she reminds her of the woman she saw with Phil last night. Her plush, sculpted lips are like a Da Vinci angel, and she has the most extraordinary eyes – when she glances up and looks at Tina, she notices that one of her eyes is brown and one is blue, just like a cat she used to have when she was a child. The look the girl gives her is unsettling, as if she is undressing her. Tina knocks back her cup of tea and wanders out on to the concourse.

She looks up at the departures board as she makes her way to the Underground entrance. She notices that the Orient Express is leaving in just five minutes, and going all the way to Venice. How she would love to be in Venice now! It has always felt more like home than Milan, which she supposes makes sense, since both her mother and grandmother are from Venice.

Something crazy possesses her. Before she knows it, she has blown all her money from the shoot on a ticket for the Orient Express and is now sitting in one of the vintage nineteen-twenties carriages, glass of complimentary champagne in front of her, looking out the window as the train begins to pull out of King's Cross train station.

What on earth is she doing? She has to go back to Milan today, to Valentina. She can't abandon her daughter. Yet she hadn't been sure how long the shoot would go on for when she left Italy, and she had told Natalia, her new au pair, that she could be away until the weekend. Tina decides she needs this little interlude in her life. She will go back to Milan refreshed, full of positive energy. She will be able to put Phil and his new woman to the back of her mind. Surely that is better for her daughter than how she is feeling at the moment, sad and lonely?

Venice. Already her spirits are lifting at the idea of arriving in her city of dreams. Meanwhile, she has the whole experience of the Orient Express to behold. Her compartment is exquisite, all dark wood and vintage décor, with a little table and a proper table lamp. And, what luck! In her case, she had brought some of her grandmother's vintage clothes from the twenties for her nights out with Isabella and her lover in London. She can really go to town and dress up.

Nearly all the other travellers on the train are dressed in evening clothes from the twenties and thirties as they make their way to the dining carriage. As she walks down the shunting corridor in one of Belle's silk evening gowns with her hair styled just like her grandmother's once had been, a white ostrich feather curled around her black Brooks' bob, Tina feels like a glamour puss. It doesn't matter that she is forty-one years old. She feels svelte and sultry, every inch the young siren. Gradually, the nightmare vision from last night begins to ebb away.

She slides into a seat at an empty table, wondering who might choose to join her. A waiter takes her drink order: champagne – how could it be anything else?

She makes a silent toast to her grandmother Belle in her head, and takes a delicate sip of the champagne. It is ice cold, and intoxicatingly fizzy. The restaurant car begins to fill, and then she sees her: the redhead from station café. She is looking right at her with her strange brown and blue eyes. It is no surprise when she makes a beeline for her table. She is dressed in a sapphire-blue silk gown, with diamonds dripping from her ears.

'Can I join you?' She speaks in an upper-class English accent.

'Yes, please do,' Tina says.

'Lucinda Grey,' the lady says, offering Tina her hand.

'Tina Rosselli,' Tina replies, shaking her hand, which is soft and supple as a newborn's.

'I hope you don't mind if my husband joins us,' she says to Tina.

'No, not at all.'

They make small talk until Lucinda's husband arrives. She tells Tina that he is the English Ambassador to Italy and that they are travelling back to Venice on their way to the eternal city of Rome.

'I always dreamt of going on the Orient Express, so Rudi surprised me with a weekend in Venice, plus the tickets, for our first anniversary present.'

'You've only been married a year?'

'Yes – newlyweds!' She smiles. 'How about you? Are you married?'

'No,' Tina says, quickly changing the subject. 'I live in Milan. I work as a photographer.'

'Wait a minute,' Lucinda says, 'are you Tina Rosselli, the fashion photographer?'

'Yes, that's me.'

'Oh, I have a book with some of your pictures in it. I am a big fan.'

'Thank you,' Tina says, suddenly distracted by the appearance of one of the most stunning men she has ever seen, entering the restaurant car.

'I am guessing by the look on your face that my husband has just walked in,' Lucinda comments, smirking slightly.

'I'm sorry,' Tina blushes. 'I didn't mean to be so rude.'

'It's fine; in fact, I am very flattered *and* used to it. Heads turn when Rudi enters a room.'

He is nearly as beautiful as Karel, Tina thinks, but not quite. No one has matched the beauty of her lost cellist. Rudi saunters down the restaurant car, obviously looking for Lucinda. He is all chiselled cheekbones, big brown eyes, dark olive skin and sexy stubble. He is wearing a full tuxedo, complete with bow tie, and still manages to look cool.

'Ah, here you are,' Rudi says as soon as he reaches their table. Up close, he is even more jaw-dropping.

'I'd like you to meet Tina Rosselli, Rudi. She is my new friend.'

They share two, three, four bottles of champagne. The food is exquisite, but Tina, as usual, only pecks at hers. Everything becomes a dizzy blur; all she knows is that she is enjoying the company of Lucinda and Rudi immensely. After dinner, they totter down the corridor in the train.

'Would you like to come to our berth for a drink?' Lucinda asks her.

The vintage compartment has been turned into a luxurious bedroom. Tina glides her hands on the dark wood furnishings that are so highly polished she can almost see a reflection of her face in them.

'What's this?' Tina asks, as Rudi hands her a brown, fizzy drink.

'Pimm's Royale,' Lucinda says. 'It's Pimm's, topped with champagne. My favourite tipple.'

'It's all very English,' Tina says.

'Well, that's what we are,' Rudi comments.

She tastes it. 'Mmm, I like it.'

She sits down on the bed and Lucinda sits down next to her, while Rudi sits on a footstool in front of them. He undoes his bow tie and the top button of his shirt.

'I can't believe I am sitting next to Tina Rosselli,' Lucinda says. 'And you are *so* pretty, too.'

Tina looks at Lucinda's angelic face. Her skin is all peaches and cream. Her eyes flicker a million different shades of blue and brown. She is sitting so close to her, she can smell her. She smells of lavender and vanilla: an intoxicating combination.

Afterwards, she cannot reason how it began, but suddenly she is kissing Lucinda. She has never kissed a woman on the lips before and it feels so surprisingly different: soft and fragrant, like licking open the succulent petals of a flower. They move in closer to each other, unable to stop, and, when Lucinda pulls the straps down on Tina's gown, she doesn't stop her. She is aware of Rudi sitting perfectly still, as if he is a cat watching its prey, but instead he is watching his wife seducing Tina. The whole situation is bizarre and extremely sexy.

The two women strip down to their underwear, still kissing. Lucinda pulls her up on to the bed and straddles her, so that Tina is lying supine. Lucinda kisses the length of Tina's body and, as she goes, she pulls off the rest of Tina's underwear so that, eventually, she is naked. This young woman is all soft, voluptuous curves, her breasts brushing against Tina's own, her mouth all over her, caressing her and melting her into submission. Lucinda sits back on her haunches; her breasts are fulsome, her nipples big dark berries. She shifts her body to the back of the bed as Rudi gets up from his stool and stands over Tina.

'Do you know what makes my wife happy, Tina?' Rudi asks. His voice is low and husky, like the taste of mature malt whisky.

'What?' Tina whispers, feeling exposed, yet turned on by her naked presence in front of this beautiful man.

'She likes to watch me fuck other women; it pleases her very much.' He licks his lips, surveying her. 'Would you like to please her, Tina?'

'Yes,' she hisses, almost under her breath.

He grins with satisfaction as Lucinda clambers off the bed.

'Touch yourself, Tina; I want to see all of you.'

She bends her knees and opens her legs, revealing herself to him.

'Oh, you have a beautiful pussy, Tina – doesn't she, darling?' Rudi says.

But Lucinda is busy undressing her husband. She pulls his shirt out of his trousers and unbuttons it; then she undoes his trousers and pulls them down, along with his pants. She takes his clothes and folds them on to the chair; they are both standing naked in front of her, now.

Lucinda looks at Tina touching herself. 'Oh my; oh, yes, Tina, you have a very pretty cunt.'

For some reason, their flattery turns her on further. Tina strokes the lips of her pussy with one hand, while circling her clitoris with the other, all the while looking at the naked Rudi, his cock erect and ready for her. She imagines him inside her. Despite the fact his wife is right there with them, somehow it doesn't feel wrong.

'I think you should fuck her, darling,' Lucinda says, producing a condom packet and ripping it open with her teeth. She sheathes her husband with the condom and then sits back on the bed, crawling behind Tina to watch.

Rudi pulls Tina's hands away from her body, holding them above her head, gripped around the wrists with one of his hands. With his other hand, he guides himself into her: a hard, deep thrust. She gasps. It feels so good to have a cock inside her again. She hasn't had sex since Phil left. Phil. She squeezes her eyes shut.

Don't think about him, Tina. Nothing lasts for ever.

Rudi begins to move in and out of her, slowly at first. She can hear little gasps beside her and she looks to her side; she can see

Lucinda touching herself as she watches her husband inside Tina. She turns back to look at Rudi, but his head is turned away from her, for he too is looking at his wife. It is surreal, for, despite the fact he is inside her and fucking her, he is quite clearly connecting to his wife in his passion. It is the strangest thing. Tina closes her eyes. She doesn't care. She just wants to feel the sensation of this man's cock pounding into her and imagine she is back with Phil.

Rudi pulls out, flips her over on to her front, and starts to fuck her from behind. The rocking motion of the train adds to the sensation of his cock thrusting in and out, and grinding side to side within her. She can feel herself gathering up all the tension that she has stored inside her over the past year, building to the moment last night when she saw Phil with that other woman. She needs to let go of him, to be released. At the very same moment that Rudi comes inside her, she is climaxing as well, gasping with relief. She lies on her front, her face buried in the pillow, as she feels him withdraw.

She rolls on to her back to see Rudi remove the condom and then gather up his wife, who is still touching herself, her red hair blazing against the white sheets. He kneels in front of her on the bed and, amazingly, Tina can see that he is already hard again. He pulls Lucinda on to his lap, and she sits on top of him, wrapping her legs around his waist. They are gazing into each other's eyes, rocking together, as if she is no longer there. She waits and waits, and yet still they are making love. It occurs to Tina that she was the starter for their five-course sex feast. She slips off the bed and creeps around the room, gathering up her things and putting them back on. She pauses by the door to the compartment.

'Well, goodnight,' she whispers.

Rudi has his back to her, but Lucinda waves an arm, her eyes half closed. 'Thank you,' she mouths.

Tina steps out into the corridor of the train and takes a breath. What the hell just happened inside that compartment? She remembers Lucinda telling her that she was flattered Tina had found her husband attractive. Obviously she was not the jealous type. But then she had said she was used to it. Maybe this was her way of keeping hold of her husband. Rather than him cheating on her behind her back, she actually organised it herself. She was in control. Smart lady, Tina thinks, as she walks back down the corridor to her room. Although, perhaps, a little too clever for her own good. Was it really worth it? To watch your man have sex with another woman, just so you can keep a ring on your finger . . . ? Or did Lucinda genuinely find it sexy? She touches her lips and remembers how the girl had kissed her. There were so many different ways of looking at the scenario.

She slips into her berth and gets into bed, her body still humming; yet she feels better than she has felt since Phil left. The sex has calmed her, made her feel good, almost as if it were a tonic. She falls asleep and doesn't wake until they are pulling into Venice.

She never sees Lucinda and Rudi again. Yet she comes to view that night on the Orient Express as a turning point in her life. Like taking off one of Belle's vintage costumes, she sheds her old skin and becomes a new Tina – the Tina her daughter comes to know: a fiercely independent woman who guards her heart as if it were her very own child. Despite the many boyfriends Tina Rosselli has over the years, she never falls in love again.

Valentina

BEFORE THEY PARTED, HER MOTHER HAD GIVEN VALENTINA A small brown package. Inside was a CD with a picture of the Berlin Victory Column on the front, its golden angel raising a hand to her.

'When I returned to East Berlin in 1989 and discovered what had happened to Karel,' Tina told Valentina, 'Lottie gave me a record he had made. She told me that it was music he had composed especially for you.'

Valentina had gripped the CD in both her hands. 'For me?' she repeated, in shock.

'It is called *What Valentina Sees*,' her mother told her. 'You would have been exactly one year old when Karel died on 17th May 1986. If only he had waited a few years . . .'

'Would you wait indefinitely to hold your child for the first time?' Valentina had asked her mother.

'No,' Tina said, shaking her head. 'I would have tried to escape, too, of course.'

Valentina looked down at the cover of the CD.

'I took that picture, at the time I knew your father,' her mother told her. 'I got the record transfered on to CD for you.'

Valentina opened the cover. She was not prepared for what she saw inside. For on the inside cover of the CD box was a picture of the man who must be her father. He was sitting in a chair, holding his cello between his legs, his hands (those beautiful hands, as her mother described them) resting on the neck of the cello, as if it were a tender girl. He was looking directly into the camera, his image mesmerising. He looked impossibly young, with thick black hair and a feline face. He was beautiful. Valentina could see why her mother fell for him.

'That's Karel,' her mother had said, sadly.

Now she is back in Leonardo's apartment, her shoot with Sophie completed, although she felt the whole time she was not really present, just taking pictures with her instincts, rather than her mind. She tells Leonardo everything as she sits between his legs on his futon mattress and he puts his arms around her, silently listening to all she has to say. When she has finished telling the whole story, Leonardo squeezes her tightly before speaking.

'It's incredible that your father was this man,' he tells her.

'I will never know him, though. He's dead. My mother blames herself for telling him about me. She says that's why he tried to get over the wall . . . but, Leo, is it terrible that a part of me is so glad he knew about me and that he wanted to see me?'

'Of course it's not terrible – it's natural. He had a father's instinct, an instinct that was so powerful, it ended up getting him killed.'

'Because of me, he is dead,' Valentina says.

Leonardo hugs her tightly. 'Of course not; it's neither your nor your mother's fault. It's the fault of the border guard who shot him in the back. It's the fault of those who gave the guard the orders to shoot. It's the fault of the Communist regime in East Germany that denied Karel Slavik the right to travel to the West.'

'Now I know why Mama is the way she is,' Valentina says. 'I just wish she had told me before.'

They sit in silence for a moment or two, listening to the sounds outside the window: New Yorkers calling to each other, music playing from a car across the street, a police car racing by.

'Do you want to play the music, Valentina?' Leonardo asks her softly.

She turns around to face him and nods. It is the only thing she has of her father. Her only chance to know him, yet, at the same time, she is frightened that the music will mean nothing to her.

Valentina closes her eyes as the strains of Karel's cello wash over her. She had expected music that would make her feel sad, particularly since cello music is naturally melancholic, yet this composition that her father has created for her makes her feel different. It is almost joyous. She realises that Karel is trying to depict the world through the imagined eyes of his baby daughter. He is playing to the child within and what he conjures is something magical and light, a music that sends her heart fluttering, that makes her want to smile.

He is alive in this music. She pictures the serious young man she saw on the inside cover of the CD, furiously playing his cello, his whole body dancing with the comely body of the cello, his strong, long fingers plucking the strings with all the intensity of his frustration. In his music, he is playing all the lullabies he never got to play her, singing her all the nursery rhymes he never got to sing, telling her all the fables and stories from his homeland and his family that he will never get to share with her.

She opens her eyes again and sees Leonardo watching her, reading her face for her feelings. She does something so rare: she smiles. It is a smile that starts right in the pit of her belly, spreads through her chest and heart, and lights up her face.

They play the music again and again, lying naked in each other's arms on Leonardo's futon mattress. Early evening sunshine spills through the open curtains as she is cradled within her lover's arms, feeling safe and wanted. Leonardo pulls himself up to lie on his side next to her, bringing his pelvis close to hers. He wraps his legs around hers so that they create a scissors; now they are brushing together. Leonardo takes her hands in his and brings them down to his cock. She sees it, silky and curled in his lap. She fights the urge to stimulate his cock, watch it grow hard; instead, she lets him show her what to do. The idea of this makes her breasts tingle, her nipples erect, and, between her legs, she is already softening.

With her hands within his, he folds away all of her fingers, apart from the second and index finger of each hand, which he turns into two forks. Then he places one of her finger forks around the base of his cock, and one behind the rim of its head. He needs to give her no more direction. Instinctively, she draws him into her, taking deep breaths and opening herself out to receive him, relaxing her pussy, so that she is drawing him into her. Now he is inside her, softly, but neither of them moves; they look at each other and the nakedness of their union. It has to be the most honest sexual moment of her life. She begins to feel his cock and her pussy buzzing together without need for either of them to do anything. It feels like something magical is happening inside of her. She is empowering his cock as it hums inside her. Leonardo puts his hands on her breasts, circling the nipples with his palms, while she strokes his buttocks and his thighs. She can feel his cock vibrating more strongly now, as slowly and steadily it grows, pushing up high inside her, dancing and jerking upward. It is the most thrilling penetration.

They are united like this – for how long, she cannot tell – but, after a while, Leonardo begins to rotate, pushing deeper inside her. Her body responds with heart-shuddering vibrations as she twists with him so that he is now kneeling above her, still inside her, and her feet are resting on his shoulders. They pause in this position for a moment, as she feels him going deeper and deeper inside her, then she opens and drops her legs as he pushes into her.

She feels unravelled by Leonardo, open and yielding. Without intention or effort, the two of them climb. She imagines she is at the top of that cliff, and below is the shimmering Mediterranean ocean. Before, this scene had been a nightmare, one that reminded her of death and loss, but now she wants to dive into it – with Leonardo – swim to the bottom, hand in hand. They climax together, in absolute synchronicity, their eyes still open, all pretence stripped bare.

Afterwards, they lie spooned in each other's arms. She can feel Leonardo's cock, soft again, curled against her back. She wants to kiss its tip, yet she stays where she is. She feels protected from everything outside of Leonardo's room, as long as she stays within his arms. She is so grateful to him for all that he has done for her. And yet, despite the revelation of this new sexual language, she knows deep down that what they have is not the same as what she had with Theo. She loves Leonardo, of course she does, and he loves her, but is she in love with him? Is there a difference?

Her mother had spoken about being open to love, even if you lose the love of your life. Valentina cannot punish herself for ever. She deserves to be loved. What more can she ask for than to be loved by Leonardo?

* * *

The next morning, Leonardo rises early, telling her he is attending a seminar on Tantric sex. 'I'll be gone all day,' he says, putting her cup of Kusmi tea on the locker beside the mattress. 'Is that OK?'

'Of course it is,' she says, stretching sleepily. 'I can have a lazy day off.'

'Are you not working? Are you sure you don't want to come with me?'

She shakes her head. 'I said I'd meet my mother again, later on. She is staying on in New York a couple more days. She is trying to persuade me to go to see Mattia.'

'You should go,' Leonardo says.

She turns on her side. 'Maybe,' she says.

Once Leonardo is gone, she puts on her father's music again. Each time she listens to it, she loves it even more. It is like a balm to her heart. My father made this music for me, she thinks. She feels special and, at the same time, so very sad that he died. He was younger than she is now when he lost his life.

Her phone starts ringing. She almost considers turning it off. She wants to be left in peace to listen to her father's music and to think about him. In the end, she picks it up. It could be work, especially as she sees Marco's number coming up on the screen.

'Valentina,' Marco says, sounding serious.

'What is it?' Valentina asks, already tensing. 'Is everything OK?'

'Did you hear the news?'

'No,' she says, holding her breath. She can tell by the tone of his voice that it is something bad.

'They found the security guard from the Neue Galerie,' he says.

Valentina has a momentary image of the guy's sweaty, stubbled face.

'What do you mean, "they found him"?'

'In the Hudson River . . . Valentina, he's dead.'

Her heart begins to race; her mouth goes dry.

'Christ,' she whispers.

'They have DNA that links the murder to Glen. You were right, Valentina. He is alive.'

She paces around the apartment. She has already left two messages for Balducci but he hasn't returned her calls. She guesses he is thinking, *What more can she add to the investigation?* Since she moved to Leonardo's, the cops had stopped their surveillance of her, not believing her conviction that Glen was alive. But now . . . Well, now . . . it is clear they should have taken her seriously. Her enemy is still in New York. All of the calm, loving security that Leonardo has built around her comes crashing down. It's no good. She can't give it up. She has to find out where Glen is. She convinces herself that it is so she can help the police, but really she knows, deep down, it's because she wants to find out the truth. What did Glen do to Theo? For a moment she considers ringing Leonardo, yet, in the end, she drops her phone into her bag. She tells herself that his phone would be switched off, anyway, if he is at the seminar, but she knows that's not the real reason she doesn't call him. He would tell her to let it go.

She thinks hard. Her chances of finding Glen in New York are ridiculously slight. She has only one lead, the post office in the Meatpacking District from where he posted the Klimt picture to her. The likelihood she will succeed where the police have failed are remote and yet she *has* to do something. She can't just sit at home and wait any more.

* * *

She walks from Leonardo's apartment along East Twentieth and down to Fourteenth Street and Union Square Subway station, taking the train to Fourteenth Street and Eighth Avenue. She heads into the Meatpacking District, noticing that many of the buildings are old warehouses converted into galleries. Isn't this the perfect place to hide stolen art?

After an hour of wandering around aimlessly she realises her search is fruitless. The only way she will find Glen is if he comes looking for her. She knows he will. She can feel it in her bones. The fact he sent her the picture and the threatening note proves this. She should ring the police again and insist they set up surveillance, and then all they need to do is sit tight. Wait.

Valentina strolls back along West 15th Street. She passes a café, and the aroma of freshly roasted coffee beans draws her in. She will take a quick coffee break before she rings the police. After all, she has been walking around for hours. She needs to re-charge.

She sits on a high stool, watching the people passing the café window, going in and out of Chelsea market. She has only been in New York a few weeks but already she feels like she belongs. Milan is special, of course, but she loves New York. It occurs to her that the feeling she has here is the opposite of what her father must have experienced in East Berlin in the eighties. She feels liberated and open. She particularly loves New Yorkers, the way anyone will just strike up a conversation with you and say what they feel. In East Berlin you risked your liberty if you told a stranger your real thoughts on something.

Just as she is sliding off the high stool she sees him. Glen. Striding bold as brass down West 15th street. Her heart almost stops. What were the chances of that? He has dyed his hair again, almost black, and he has grown a scraggy beard, but Valentina would recognise that walk anywhere: the menacing march of Glen. She slips out of the café and follows him down the street. He is heading back into the Meatpacking District from where she came. She drops her head, afraid he will turn around and see her, but Glen seems to be in a hurry. She almost has to run to keep up with him.

He criss-crosses the streets until he is walking down by the side of the Hudson River. It glints in the sunshine like a sheet of rippling steel. Suddenly, he turns in sharply to the left. She walks cautiously to the corner of the street, and peers around the corner. He has stopped in front of a large warehouse.

Valentina watches Glen as he pulls back the door. She restrains herself; she wants so much to run up to him and smack him over the head with her bag, but the notion is ridiculous. He could overpower her in a second. This is the moment she should call the police, yet she cannot let him out of her sight. She knows it's idiotic of her, and yet Valentina can't stop herself from following him down the street, and very, very carefully opening the door to the warehouse. She slides in through the door, looking around her. Glen has disappeared. She is in one big space, with graffitied walls. She grips her bag to her chest, as if it will protect her from what evil lurks inside this factory.

She is just debating whether she should leave and call the police, when suddenly she hears voices. It is too late to go back out the door. She dives behind a pile of packing cases. The voices are getting louder, and she now notices a hallway at the back of the space, and hears footsteps. She squats down, leans her back against the packing cases and holds her breath, still gripping her bag. She is terrified now. What the hell did she think she was doing, following this crook, Glen, to his gangster den? How many of them has she now stumbled upon? How on earth will she get out of here?

She can hear the men are now in the room, talking. She can't make out exactly what they are saying, as she is too far away. She steels herself, and peeks around the packing case. What she sees freezes her blood and makes her heart drop like a stone. She hears a rush in her ears, as if her head is in its own private storm, as her throat goes dry and she becomes speechless. For, in front of her, facing her so that she is looking right at his face, and deep in conversation with the man she believed killed him, is the love of her life, Theo.

$\mathcal{T}$ina

1993

IT SEEMED A GOOD IDEA AT THE TIME TO COMBINE THE FASHION shoot with a pre-Christmas trip with Valentina to see the land of the real Father Christmas. There is more snow than Valentina has seen her whole life, but more exciting than that are the reindeer, the husky dogs, the arctic foxes, and all the sled rides. Her daughter is in her element, never complaining that she is cold, but delighted by the joy of jumping off the roof of the little woodshed by their hotel into the mounds of snow beneath it, building snow caves and making angels in the snow.

Tina, however, had not realised how much she hates the cold, and the long hours of darkness. It is the shortest day of the year and, here in the Arctic, there is hardly any light at all. The sun never makes it above the horizon, although, as it lurks just beneath it, the snowy landscape is transformed to dusky-blue pastel reflections upon the snow. She is lucky there is so much snow, for it reflects what light there is and makes it possible to take the photographs.

The shoot had focused on an antifur campaign. They had decided to shoot the feature on fake-fur coats in an Arctic environment to show that you didn't need to wear real animal skin to stay warm. She had picked Scandinavian models. There was a tall, fit-looking Swede called Berit, with long blond hair, which gleamed against the snow like sheaves of gold. Berit was in her natural environment, sliding through the snow on her skis, rather than trudging around in snow boots like the others. She told Tina that she had grown up north of the Arctic Circle in Sweden. The other model, Tove, was from Finland, with straight, jet-black hair and Slavic eyes. She was terribly tall and terribly thin, and taciturn – that is, until she started drinking vodka; then she became the most animated and chatty model Tina had ever met.

Tina had enjoyed the shoot part of the trip, despite the cold, because she felt she had produced some of the most beautiful images of her career, and the team had had fun drinking and chatting in the hotel lounge each night. The winter light was quite amazing, creating challenges she had never faced before. One night, the northern lights danced for them. Valentina was beside herself with excitement. She told her mother they were princesses dancing in the sky. Tina had taken some shots of Berit and Tove against the backdrop of the lights. The swirling green and purple curtains of light contrasted with the girls in their fake furs in cream and black.

They had finished up twenty-four hours ago and everyone else had gone home to prepare for Christmas. Tina was itching to get back to Milan. Why had she decided to do this trip with Valentina? They were staying in a quiet hotel on the outskirts of Tromsø, a small city in northern Norway. Once Valentina was in bed for the night, Tina couldn't go anywhere or do anything. All she could do was sit in the hotel lounge, drinking a bottle of local Mack beer, bored out of her mind. At least if she was in

Milan, she could get a baby-sitter and go out. She has been doing quite a bit of that lately.

After her Orient Express trip from London, Tina had decided that life as a single woman wasn't that bad at all. She can do as she pleases, and live exactly how she wants, without constantly having to think of the needs of a man.

'Yes, but don't you get lonely?' all those smug married women ask her.

'No,' she counters, 'of course not. If I need company, it is not hard to get it. I can always have sex, whenever I want. I am a free spirit,' she claims.

Being single means that Tina stays on her toes. She looks after herself, makes sure she is always groomed, fit, looking good.

'It is such an amazing feeling when you know you can still attract the attention of a young man,' she tells her married friends. 'And, when you make love, they make you feel like a goddess.'

'But what about love?' they ask her.

'I love myself,' Tina argues. 'I love my son. I love my daughter. That's enough love for me.'

What she doesn't tell them is that she also has days when she hates herself and regrets losing Phil, and that she is aching with longing for something more in her life. It is an ache that nothing – and no amount of hugs from her little daughter – can ease. The only thing that makes her feel better is going out and getting laid. If she is down, instead of sitting in front of the telly and eating ice cream, she calls up the baby-sitter, dresses up and goes out on the prowl. She has heard of the term 'cougar' – an older woman who picks up young men – and she guesses that is what she has turned into. But none of these young men is a victim. They love the freedom of sleeping with a woman like Tina, who knows what she is doing and expects no commitment from them whatsoever.

She is beginning to feel down, sitting in this boring little hotel in Tromsø. She knows what she needs to pick herself up, but is stuck here with Valentina. As she is resigning herself to another dismal night watching downhill skiing on the television, the door of the room opens and a young man walks in wearing the most ridiculous Christmas jumper she has ever seen. He has short, bristly dark hair, broad cheeks and the brightest blue eyes. He is not tall, but she can tell he is all muscle beneath the big jumper covered in red, black and white zigzags with little silver buttons at the collar.

'*Hei*,' he says, in Norwegian.

'Hello,' she says back, in English.

'Where did you get your beer?' he asks her, reverting to English.

'It's mine,' she says. 'I bought it in the shop; help yourself.' She indicates a bag by her chair. 'They might be getting a little warm now.'

He takes a beer and snaps off the lid with his bare hands.

She raises her eyebrows. 'You've strong hands,' she says.

'Yes, I am working outside with reindeer a lot; I need to be strong.'

'Are you a reindeer herder?' she asks him, incredulously.

He nods.

'So you are Sami, then?'

She has always been interested in the Sami, an indigenous people who live on the northern edges of Europe, in land that straddles Norway, Sweden, Finland and Russia.

'Yes, that's right. I've lived here all my life.'

'My God, how can you? I mean, all this snow, and the cold and dark – how do you stand it?'

'It's all I've ever known; actually, I love it. When I go away, I miss the North. I think it's something in the blood.'

'Well, I am definitely a southerner,' she says, snuggling into her chair. 'I don't mean to be rude, but I find this place cold and depressing – and boring.'

He says nothing for a moment. They drink the beer together, watching the television.

'I can show you a side to the North that is not boring, and not cold,' the man says, quietly, under his breath. 'And it is far from depressing.'

She turns to look at him, and he is staring at her intensely. She takes him in, and she feels that urge deep within her. She needs some sex right now. But where could they go? Does he have a room in the hotel?

He stands up, offers her his hand. 'I can take you somewhere that you will never forget,' he says.

'Oh, really?' she says, coyly looking at him under lowered lashes.

'But we need to get dressed first in our snow clothes.'

'We have to leave the hotel?'

She thinks of Valentina, asleep in their double bed. She shouldn't even be down in the lounge, let alone leave the hotel, but the Sami man is standing right over her, looking at her in a way that leaves her no doubt that he wants to pleasure her. She bites her lip, undecided about what to do.

'Are we going far?' she asks.

'Not far,' he says.

She guesses that it will be OK. Valentina is asleep for the night. She never wakes up and it's not as if she is a baby any more. She is eight years old already. When will Tina get an opportunity like this again?

'OK,' she says.

She pulls on her snow trousers and jacket, hat, gloves and boots, feeling far from sexy now. They trudge out of the warm hotel and into the Arctic night. The cold slaps her in the face. It must be at least minus ten, if not colder. The Sami man is putting on a pair of skis.

'Oh, I don't have any skis,' Tina says.

'That's OK; just get on to the back of mine and put your hands around my waist. I can take us there.'

She steps on to the skis behind him, puts her arms around him, and he pushes off. Her body presses against his through her snow clothes, and her legs are forced backwards and forwards along with his as they slide across the snow. It is a thrilling sensation as he picks up speed and takes them away from the hotel and the other buildings that straggle the edge of Tromsø, and into darkness and the empty Arctic tundra. She looks up at the sky as she sees the northern lights shimmering above her, like a swaying curtain of colour and particles. She feels like she is in one of her daughter's fairy tales. It reminds her of the stories she used to love her mother reading her when she was a little girl, about faraway lands and exotic princes.

In the distance, now, she sees a light glowing in the night. He whizzes them across the snow and she begins to understand how someone could love living here. The speed, the cut and slice of the snow beneath them, is exhilarating.

She sees now that the light comes from a window in a circular wooden cabin. The Sami man pulls up outside the cabin, and she steps off the skis, her legs shaking a little from the exertion. He takes off his skis and leans them up against the side of the cabin;

then, taking her gloved hand in his, he opens the door. They step into a little outer porch, where they take off their boots and all their snow clothes, hanging them up on hooks. He then leads her into the main area of the cabin. A fire rages in the centre of the cabin and, when Tina looks up, she can see the smoke curling up through a hole in the roof. The room is lit solely by candlelight. The floor is covered with reindeer skins and sheepskin rugs, yet she forgets about her antifur principles; she is focused on the Sami man, who has taken a bottle of some kind of golden liquor and is pouring two glasses for them. He hands her one.

'What is it?' she asks.

'It's aquavit,' he says, knocking his back. 'It is a special Norwegian spirit. It is flavoured with herbs and spices. Traditionally, it gets its special flavour from being sent in oak barrels over the equator twice, from Norway to Australia and back again.'

'For real?'

'Yes, absolutely,' he says. 'It really makes a difference to the taste of the drink. Apparently, the constant movement, high humidity and changing temperatures cause the spirit to mature and extract more flavour.'

She takes a sip of the spirit. It is not unpleasant: a predominant taste of caraway seed and anise. She goes for it and knocks it back. It warms the pit of her belly and helps her relax.

'What's your name?' she asks him.

'Gunnar,' he says.

'My name is Tina.'

'Hello, Tina,' he says, taking her in his arms and giving her a smoky kiss. He smells amazing – of the crisp, snowy pines framing the tundra, and of woodsmoke from inside the cabin.

Gunnar pulls back and smiles at her. 'Have you ever experienced a sweat lodge?' he asks her.

'No,' she says, shaking her head.

'Do you like the heat?' he asks, his northern eyes blazing into her.

'Sometimes,' she says, thinking of those unspeakably hot days on the beach with Phil in Sardinia, back when she was young.

'Good,' he says, pulling off his Nordic sweater. 'At the back of this cabin, I have my very own private sauna. I prepared it before I went out and now I think it will be just right. Would you like to join me for a sweat?'

'Sure,' she says. She has never been much of a fan of saunas, but she wants to see Gunnar naked.

He strips off in front of her with no reservations whatsoever. 'Come on,' he says, grinning. 'Are you shy?'

'No, not at all,' she says, brazenly, beginning to hurl her clothes into a pile by the fire.

Despite the minus temperatures outside, the room is warm. It feels good to be naked and out of all the layers she has had to pile on to herself the past few days.

'This way,' Gunnar says, walking across the cabin and opening the door to his sauna.

The heat hits her in a wave as she steps into the tiny space. She slides on to a wooden bench next to him, which is so hot she feels it is almost burning her flesh. Already beads of sweat are budding on Gunnar's forehead.

She lies back and closes her eyes, breathing slowly and deeply. It is intensely relaxing and incredibly sensual to be lying next to this naked man in his sauna. She can smell essential oils, as if the steam is filled with eucalyptus. She opens her eyes again and Gunnar is lying back, watching her.

'Would you like fire or ice?' he whispers to her.

She looks at him with curiosity. 'Fire,' she whispers.

He sits up and pushes her down on to the wooden bench of the sauna so that she is on her back. He lies on top of her, pressing down on her. His flesh is so hot against hers that she feels that they are burning each other. He slides down her body, and brings his mouth to her pussy. He begins to lick her with his hot tongue, sliding his hand up and down her sweaty thighs.

She gives a low moan. She feels so hot, as if she is about to pass out.

'Ice,' she whispers. 'I need cold.'

He pulls her up, squatting back on his haunches, his blue eyes laughing. 'As you command!'

He stands up and, in her dizzy haze, she watches him saunter over to another door at the back of the sauna. He opens it and there is brief, sudden blast of pleasantly cooling air, before he shuts it again. She closes her eyes, feeling herself melting further in the steam and heat of the sauna.

Gunnar comes back to her. Kneeling in front of her, he lifts her by the hips, brings her pussy to his mouth and presses his lips to it. They are ice cold and she flinches, but then he opens his mouth and she feels the sting of freezing ice on her pussy. She screams in shock, as he licks ice and snow all over the lips of her vagina. She feels it melting into her instantly and, after the initial shock, the sensation is a thrilling combination of pleasure and pain.

'Oh my God,' she whispers.

'Do you like?' he asks, in a low voice.

He puts her feet on his shoulders, widens her legs further and takes a cup of something, filling his mouth with liquid. She closes her eyes as she feels warm liquid shooting all over her sensitised pussy. She wonders if it is that golden aquavit. She is quivering

308

with sensations. Gunnar is pushing her to her limits, and she is feeling possessed by something wild and primal.

He drops her hips and pulls her up by the arms, so that he is holding her sweaty body within his. They writhe together, their bodies slipping and sliding. She is desperate to feel his cock inside her, yet he is still holding back.

'Do you want to do something very wild?' he says.

'Yes,' she breathes.

He scoops her up in his arms and walks across the tiny sauna, opening the second door and stepping outside into the snow. She is naked in minus ten and yet she isn't cold. She is still burning with the heat between them.

'We have to be fast,' he whispers. 'I don't want you getting hypothermia.'

There is a sawhorse for cutting wood in front of her, draped with reindeer furs. He carries her to it and tells her to hold on to it. She presses her naked body against the furs, her nipples stimulated by their soft warmth as the soles of her feet press into the crisp, dry snow. It is not wet or freezing; in fact, it is like the finest sand, like tiny sparkling crystals brushing against her feet.

She bends over the sawhorse, her body still burning from the sauna, her pussy a riot of sensations, as Gunnar enters her. He grips her waist with his hands as he pushes deep inside her. She hears him panting, groaning, like a beast from the forest, and she loves it: this primal sex, outside, under the northern lights, upon the Arctic tundra. He thrusts into her and she feels him rubbing against the opening of her pussy, stimulating her even further. Next, she feels him raise himself behind her, as if he is standing on his tiptoes, and then he slams into her again. His cock slides right into her, touching her on her G-spot. She gasps. He keeps changing angles as he fucks her, so that she is being stimulated in every corner of her pussy. He speeds up, rapid rhythmic thrusts, his breath shorter and faster as he comes inside her. The feeling of his hot cock vibrating inside her takes her over the edge, and she is orgasming too, flung across the furs.

Quickly, he picks her up and carries her back into the sauna. He takes a towel from a pile by the door and rubs her down. It is only now she realises that she is shivering with cold, yet she had felt so very hot outside. He rubs her and rubs her, and then he tells her to lie down and relax. They stay in the sauna for another five minutes, sweating together, giving each other soft, sensual kisses.

Afterwards, he takes her into the shower, turning the water on full blast as they stand beneath its spray, washing each other's bodies. She grips his cock in her hand, squeezing gently at its base and then bringing her hand all the way up to stroke its velvet head. His eyes become slits as he gives a low moan, and then he picks her up by the waist. She wraps her legs around him and, pressing against the tiles for support, they make love again beneath the torrent of steaming water.

Now they are spent. They cuddle up in blankets in front of the fire, sipping ice-cold beer. She feels like a satisfied fat cat, sated and pampered, curled up in front of the flickering flames.

'Do you want to stay the night?' he whispers, snuggling into her.

Suddenly, she remembers Valentina. She stiffens, frozen with horror. For how many hours has she left her child alone? What if she wakes up and is frightened?

'I'm sorry, Gunnar, but I have to go.'

'Right now?' He looks at her incredulously.

'Yes . . . You see . . . I have to go back to the hotel. My daughter is in bed in our room.'

'What?' He looks appalled. 'How old is she?'

'She's not a baby,' she says, defensively. 'She's eight.'

He stands up, the mood between them broken irredeemably. He says nothing, but the look he gives her tells her he thinks she is a bad mother.

'I'll take you back on the snowmobile,' he says. 'It's faster.'

To her relief, when she returns to her hotel room, Valentina is still fast asleep. Yet, when she looks at her watch, she realises that she has been gone with Gunnar for over three hours. She sits on the bed, staring down at the pure innocence of Valentina and shocked by the thought of what might have happened to her little girl. Anything. There could have been a fire in the hotel and she would have perished in the bed. She could have woken and gone looking for her in the snow, got lost, and frozen to death. She could have been sick, and scared, and scarred for life. All the healing afterglow of her sexual encounter with Gunnar is gone in an instant. Instead, it is replaced with a numbness, followed by a slow dread realisation. If her craving for sex, her need to get laid, is so strong that she is willing to abandon her child for the night, then she has a problem.

$\mathscr{V}$alentina

PURE RAGE COURSES THROUGH VALENTINA AND IGNITES HER INTO action. She no longer cares about personal safety, but stands up from behind the packing case. Theo sees her immediately. He steps back in shock, his face draining of all colour as she marches over towards him.

'Bastard!' she screams, slapping him in the face with all her might. She is unable to say anything else. Her emotion has robbed her of speech. She turns on her heel and storms out of the factory. She can see Glen, to her left, looking as surprised as Theo at her sudden appearance.

Out on the street, she begins to run – blindly, with no direction. She is searing with anger and pain. She can't understand it. He is alive. She should be glad of that, but she is too hurt, too wounded by his betrayal to feel good about it.

'Valentina! Valentina, wait!'

She can hear him behind her. Panic begins to rise within her. She has to get away from him.

'Valentina! Stop . . . please . . .'

She feels him grab her arm. She pulls away from him with all her strength, but Theo spins her around.

'Valentina, Valentina, Valentina . . .' he repeats, like a mantra, as if he is unable to say anything else. There is colour back in his cheeks and his eyes are shining. If she were not so confused, she could swear he was jubilant at seeing her. He makes to embrace her, but she slaps him away.

'No!' she screams at him.

He struggles to hold her, but she pushes him away.

'Hey, lady, are you OK?' a man shouts from across the street. Theo drops his arms, stops trying to hold her. They stare at each other. She is out of breath, from running and from emotion. She could call over that man, get the police involved; she can see that Theo knows this. He looks down at the sidewalk.

'Please, Valentina,' he whispers, 'just let me explain.'

She watches him, his head bowed over, and suddenly it hits her. Theo isn't dead. And, despite her fury and her confusion, she can't help but feel a huge weight lift from her shoulders.

'I'm OK, thanks,' she shouts back to the concerned pedestrian, who shrugs and moves off.

Theo looks up. 'Thanks,' he says. He holds out his hand. 'Please, let's go somewhere and talk. Let me explain everything to you.'

She ignores his proffered hand. She is trembling with emotion: relief that he is alive, and anger that she has been living with her loss, her guilt at his death, for over a year.

'I thought you were dead, Theo,' she says, her voice hoarse. 'How could you do this to me? And to your parents? My God! How could you be so cruel?'

'I know, I know,' he says, raking his hand through his hair.

She notices now how tired he looks. His skin is pale and he has dark circles under his eyes – yet still the blue of them bewitches her. She cannot turn her back on him.

'But you have to believe me; I had no choice,' he says.

What can he mean? What exactly happened in the blue grotto

313

between Theo and Glen? They had been enemies, and now it seems they are partners of sorts. She looks behind Theo, but Glen is nowhere to be seen. 'How can you associate with Glen? He tried to drown me, Theo; don't you remember?'

'Of course I remember. Please, let's go somewhere we can sit down and talk,' Theo pleads.

She takes a breath. 'OK,' she says, churlishly, for she knows she cannot walk away from him now. She has to find out why he abandoned her.

They walk side by side down the street. She is tempted to look at him, touch him, to see if he is real. Deep down she had known he was alive still, hadn't she? When Delaney and Balducci had had their suspicions, she had felt a twinge of premonition. She just didn't want to believe that he had run away from her . . . She just didn't want to believe Theo didn't want her.

He takes her to a quiet bar, all dark wood and shadowy corners. They are the only people in there; it is not yet lunchtime.

'I'll have a coffee,' she says.

'Do you want anything to eat?' he offers.

She shakes her head.

They sit opposite each other. She stares into her coffee. She cannot bear to look at his face and remember the man she loved. It is the face of the person she had wanted to marry, have children with, who she thought loved her as much as she loved him, the face of the man she thought was dead and buried at the bottom of the sea. Here he is, resurrected, but in a different incarnation. No matter what his story is, he has deceived her, betrayed her, let her believe he was dead . . . How can there be any justification for that? She feels an urge to run away again, and hide in Leonardo's futon until her lover returns this evening.

Theo coughs nervously. 'My God, Valentina,' he says, with emotion. 'It is so wonderful to see you again, face to face.'

She looks up at him with lowered lids. His eyes are shimmering blue, seemingly brimming with joy.

'What do you mean, "face to face"?'

'I have seen you, from afar,' he admits, 'since you arrived here in New York . . .'

'You followed me?'

'Just once or twice, when you first arrived, then it got too dangerous. You were being watched by the police.'

'My God, Theo; did you and Glen steal that Klimt painting?'

'Yes,' he whispers. 'I had to.'

'What do you mean, you "had to"? That picture had nothing to do with Nazi hoards. Why did you have to steal it?'

'It's all to do with you, Valentina.'

'Me?' she says, in shock.

'Do you remember the last thing I said to you in the blue grotto, Valentina?'

She nods, remembering that haunted afternoon when her world had been turned upside down. 'You said, "I won't let you down".' Her voice cracks with the blatant irony of that comment now. 'But you have,' she says, fiercely. 'You have broken my heart, ruined my life . . .' She turns away, angrily swallowing down tears. She mustn't lose her cool and show him how much she is hurting.

'For what possible reason do you think I might walk out of your life, Valentina, so dramatically and so suddenly? Why did I make that decision in the blue grotto?'

She says nothing for a moment, her mind beginning to open up to new possibilities.

'It was something that Glen told you?' she asks, slowly.

315

'Yes. It was a conversation we had. Believe me, he is no friend or partner of mine, but I have been forced to work with him this past year.'

'What did he say to you about me?' she asks, urgently. 'What lies did he feed you?'

'He didn't say anything *about* you, Valentina. He told me quite clearly and plainly that your life was in grave danger, if I didn't agree to do exactly as he said.'

'But we had overpowered him . . . We could have brought him to the police and you could have told them he was threatening me . . .'

'Don't you understand, Valentina? It's not Glen who is behind all of this. Our art theft of the Klimt was specifically designed as a decoy to distract the police so that the people Glen works for could pull off a bank heist here in New York . . .'

Of course, it is just as the newspapers had said. The art theft was a front for the bank heist.

'They wanted the best thieves for the job, and Glen had told them how good I was. I was told that, if I didn't do as they requested, they would kill you.' He pauses, clasping his hands as he speaks. She has never seen him look so serious. 'The agreement was that I was to work with Glen towards stealing a masterpiece from a gallery in New York City. We had to wait for the right time, when the gang was ready to do their heist. I was promised that, once I had fulfilled my end of the bargain, once I had waited a month, I could dump the painting wherever I wished, return it, even, if I could avoid being caught, and you would be out of danger.'

Valentina sits in stunned silence. What Theo is telling her sounds as if it is out of some kind of thriller, not her real life.

316

'But why couldn't you have told me all of this? Why did you pretend you were dead?'

'Because the deal was that I went with him, right there and then. He pointed out one of the gang on top of the cliff at Capri. I could see he had a gun aimed at you while you were rowing back to the boat. The skipper on the fishing boat was in on it as well. He had orders to kill you, if I didn't play ball.'

'But afterwards, surely you could have written to me, Theo? Explained what was going on?'

'I couldn't risk you knowing anything or trying to persuade me not to do it. I knew you wouldn't want me to steal the painting. You wouldn't have valued your life as highly as I did. You wouldn't have let those people bully you . . . but, believe me, they meant business.'

Valentina thinks of the poor security guard, Wayne Datcher, at the Neue Galerie. Was Theo involved in his death? She shudders at the thought.

He takes a breath and leans across the table towards her.

'Do you see now, Valentina, why I had to drop out of your life so suddenly?' Theo says, urgently.

'But why did you do it like that? Could you not, in all this time, have sent me a message of some sort . . . let me know you were still out there?'

'At first, I thought it best I didn't; I thought it would torture you. Every time I thought about how much you were suffering, I felt wild with frustration, and I never thought it was going to go on so long. They kept making us wait to do the job until they were ready with their hacking scam. But then, when Glen told me he saw you in the Neue Galerie . . . I couldn't resist sending you the picture of the child that looked like you. I thought you would make the connection.'

'That was from you?'

'Of course it was from me. Don't you remember the note?'

You are not alone, Valentina.

'I thought it was a threat from Glen,' she tells him.

Theo shakes his head. 'It was my way of letting you know I was here and that I have always been looking out for you.'

'But you did leave me alone,' Valentina says, angrily. 'You abandoned me in Capri. I thought you'd drowned . . . You have no idea how that nearly killed me.'

He looks right into the heart of her. She feels almost hypnotised by his blue, piercing gaze. 'Yes, I do, because it nearly killed me to be apart from you . . . and to know what you were going through. I did it because I had to keep you safe. Don't you understand?'

'You should have gone to the police, Theo. You should never have got involved with these people.'

'I couldn't risk it. I saw the scope on the gun, glinting in the sunlight on top of that cliff, and Glen with his mobile in his hand, ready to call him. They would have done it, Valentina. And you are too precious to me.'

Her heart is thrumming with emotion, her mind swirling with confusion. He has told her she is precious to him. She cannot believe it, still, that Theo is right in front of her – flesh, and blood, and beating heart.

'What are you going to do now, Theo?' she whispers, hesitantly.

'As soon as Glen and I dump the picture . . . somewhere safe, where it will be found and returned . . . I am a free man . . .'

'So you really think they will let you walk away?' she snaps.

'Yes; the only one I know by name and face is Glen. Besides, if they don't let me go, I have enough evidence to put the whole gang behind bars for years.'

'They'll kill you. Just like they killed that security guard at the Neue Galerie.'

'He's dead?' Theo gasps.

'Yes; they found him washed up from the Hudson this morning. Theo, you will never be free of Glen, not now.'

He frowns, thinking hard. 'You have to trust me, Valentina; I will go to the police, I promise. I'll do a deal. I will do anything, just so that we can try again. We could start a new life somewhere else where nobody knows us.' He looks at her, his blue eyes shimmering with hope.

'No,' she says, harshly, looking away. 'It's taken me so long to get over you.' She shakes her head. 'I can't just walk away from everything here. I have my life back now, Theo.'

He looks humbled, nods in agreement. 'You're right, of course; how could I ever expect you to forgive me?' He sighs. 'I hope you have got over me, Valentina.'

She wants to slap him again. How could he possibly think that she would ever be *over* him?

She grips her hands, locking the fingers together. She is staring at the golden hairs on his forearms, thinking about how it felt to touch them with her hands. He has told her that her life was at risk, but surely, somehow, he could have let her know he wasn't dead? Just to drop out of her life like that . . . How could she possibly forgive him? And yet, deep down in the pit of her belly, there is a cry rising up: *He is alive! He is alive!* For some reason, she wonders what her mother would do in this situation, if she could see past all the pain and betrayal and take back the man who was the one true love of her life.

'Theo, I need to think . . . I need time . . .' she starts to say.

He reaches out for her hand and, this time, she lets him hold it. She can feel immediately that old chemistry begin to surface between them. His fingers are strong and warm around hers. She feels as if her hand fits perfectly within his.

'Take all the time you want,' he says.

'I'm involved with someone else . . .' she says, awkwardly.

'Oh.' Theo's face falls. 'Of course, you would be . . . Sorry . . . I didn't think . . .'

'It's Leonardo,' she blurts out.

Theo tenses. He drops her hand. 'I'm happy for you both,' he struggles to say. 'I don't want to break that up, Valentina. Leonardo is a good guy.'

'He *is* a good man,' she says, with feeling. 'And he has really helped me, Theo . . . If it weren't for Leonardo, I would have fallen apart. He has been there for me, Theo,' she splutters with emotion. 'But . . . But . . .'

'But what, darling?'

Theo looks into her eyes again. It is as if she absorbs the blue of them and she can still see his feelings for her, as clear and true as the last day she saw him in the blue grotto.

'Can we . . . ?' he starts to ask. 'Maybe we could try—?'

'It's too late,' she interrupts, shaking her head sorrowfully. 'I have Leonardo, now; I told you.'

'Are you sure, Valentina?'

She stands up, walking around the table as he stands up, too. They face each other. She can feel the synergy between them, her body crying out to touch him, be touched, but she manages to hold herself together.

'Goodbye, Theo,' she says. 'Good luck.'

He looks at her with wild eyes, panic rising. 'Please, I have to see you again. You have to understand why I did what I did . . .'

'I do understand,' she says, her voice surprisingly calm. 'I understand that you did it to protect me. I know you did it because you loved me . . . but it's taken me a year to let you go, and now . . . it's too late to start again.'

He puts his hand on her arm, and her whole being trembles.

'Just tell me you don't love me and you'll never see me again,' he says to her.

She can't. She tries to, but the words stick in her throat. She yanks her arm away from him and walks away without another word.

Valentina runs through the streets, her heart still pounding, her head in a whirl. She has no idea where she is going until she finds herself outside Central Park. She keeps running; she has to find somewhere private, where no one can see her. By the edge of a small lake, she falls on her knees, all strength gone from her body. She rocks back and forth, trying to comfort herself. She never imagined she would have to grieve for Theo twice in one lifetime.

You are not alone, Valentina.

She remembers now. How could she have forgotten? In the first year of her and Theo's relationship, she had been so afraid of getting hurt. She had tried all that she could not to be dependent on Theo. But she had fallen in love, despite her outward denials. It was the miscarriage that had changed things so dramatically between them. The night it happened, Theo had been so loving and gentle. She clenches her fists at the memory. Growing up fatherless, she had never experienced such tenderness from a man. At first, she had surrendered to his care. She had been so weak and ill, and he had bathed her, cleaned up all the blood and wrapped her up in the bed sheets, holding her all night long.

Yet, by the next day, her distrust had seeped in. She had gone to the hospital alone while Theo was out. She had denied him the chance to be with her and share in their loss. For she had lost his child, had she not? For days, she had shut him out, locking herself in her studio and sleeping on the couch. She waited for him to go away, for the door to slam and for her to be on her own yet again. For, in her experience, that was what everyone who loved her did: they left – Phil, her mother, Mattia . . . But Theo didn't go anywhere. In fact, he pulled a chair up by the door of her studio and he slept outside, as if he was a loyal hound, keeping guard.

Only when he had gone to work did she come out. All around his armchair were scraps of paper and magazines, ripped apart; a pair of scissors lay forlornly on the arm of the chair. What was he doing every night? She would touch the discarded blanket in the chair, still warm from his slumber, rim the half-drunk coffee mug with her fingertips, and she would look in the mirror and hate herself. 'Go away,' she said to her reflection. 'Leave me alone.'

On the third night, he pushed a card under the door. On the front of it was the most amazing collage in blue – all the shades of his eyes, and more. And, with these little scraps of coloured paper, he had created the image of two beautiful blue birds taking flight together, the tips of their feathery wings touching each other as they travelled skyward. She opened the card. He'd written just one line, creating the words by cutting out individual letters from the magazines and papers.

YOU ARE NOT ALONE VALENTINA.

Those words had changed her. For the first time, she had realised that she didn't have to face all the challenges of her life on her own any more. She could choose to face them with Theo.

They would share not just the highs, but also the lows. That was true love.

She feels a searing pain in her gut and leans over, gripping her sides.

'It's too late,' she whispers.

Life with Theo is complicated, intense, and yet euphoric. Just being in his presence for that past hour has made her feel alive again. Yet it is too frightening. She is too vulnerable and exposed when she is with Theo. The love that Leonardo has for her is different. He heals her.

She sits up, straightening her back. Finally, her life is back on track. Her career has taken off in New York on a whole new level of productivity; she is in a nurturing relationship with a caring man and she has even made amends with her mother. Why would she run away with Theo into a life fraught with danger and difficulties?

Her phone rings inside her bag. She pulls it out to see that, finally, Balducci has returned her call from this morning.

'Miss Rosselli? Mike Balducci here. Sorry I didn't get back to you sooner. Do you have something for us?'

She pauses; she doesn't know what to say now that she knows Theo is involved in the robbery.

'I heard about the security guard,' she says.

'Yes; not good,' Balducci says, matter of factly. 'Can you help us out with anything? Have you heard from this Glen guy?'

If she tells the police where the warehouse is, they'll catch Theo. *Well, why shouldn't they?* a voice inside her head taunts her. *He deserves to be caught. He is a criminal now.* Yet she can't do it. She can't give him up.

'No, but I think Glen is still in New York.'

'OK, thanks for that, Miss Rosselli.' He pauses. 'And is everything OK with you? Are you sure there is nothing else you want to tell me?'

'No,' she says. 'That's it.'

Afterwards, she cradles her phone in her palm, staring down at it blankly. Is she now obstructing the course of justice?

The phone buzzes in her hand and she picks it up. It is a message from an unknown number:

> Valentina, please meet me at 47–50 Strts, the Rockefeller Centre subway station, southbound island platform tonight at 20hrs. If you come, you will see how much you mean to me. Theo.

She stares at the message mutely, her heart pounding in her chest again. She stands up and begins to slowly trail her way back out of the park. She doesn't reply to the text. But she knows she will go. She cannot resist. She frowns, thinking hard. She can't keep Leonardo in the dark any longer. It's not fair. She calls his number, but of course his phone is switched off. He told her that his seminar wasn't over until eight tonight – the same time Theo wants to meet her. She knows he won't check his phone until then; even so, she leaves a message.

'Hi, Leonardo. Something amazing has happened.' She pauses, licking her lips nervously. She can hear her voice shaking. 'Theo is alive. I know . . . it's . . . well . . . I can't believe it . . .' She stumbles over the words, imagining Leonardo listening to them, wondering how he will react. 'Look, I am going to talk to him tonight. I am meeting him at the Rockefeller Center subway station, southbound platform at eight. If you want to see him too, meet us there as soon as you can, when you're finished.'

She has done the right thing. She refuses to deceive Leonardo, and yet now it won't be just her and Theo when they meet. Deep down, she knows she has told Leonardo because she is afraid of being on her own with Theo, afraid of breaking down, afraid of showing him that she still loves him.

She walks out of the park and up Fifth Avenue. The Guggenheim appears before her. She has seen pictures of this building, but nothing prepares her for its beauty in the flesh. It is so bold, and yet so simple. The main body of the building, a white cylinder that widens as it rises in bands, breathes serenity and calm. She walks inside the building and stands beneath the glass dome, looking at an installation of plastic hammocks filled with coloured water.

It occurs to her that how the Guggenheim looks from the outside – self-contained, peaceful, almost like a modernist temple – is very different from the inside. Yes, there is the calming sweep of each white floor spiralling into the light-filled space, but the interlacing of these plastic hammocks with their bounties of different colours is like all the threads of life: a sort of kaleido-scopic web, she thinks, some colours bouncing of each other and connecting, others at odds with each other. It is a game, Valentina thinks, as life should be. Why do we all make it so heavy, so desperate and dark, when love should make us laugh? She remembers Theo's famous motto – *Have fun* – a phrase she had always thought flippant. Now it takes on a whole new meaning.

Valentina still doesn't know what she will say to Theo and Leonardo tonight when they all meet in the subway station, or where they will go, but there is one thing she is sure of: she is going to be true to herself.

Tina

2004

SHE STARES AT HER DAUGHTER AND SUDDENLY SHE SEES HER AS A woman for the first time. She is no longer her little girl, who needs protecting and looking after. She is a person in her own right, a ferocious young woman. She looks at her in awe as her daughter's words echo in her ears:

You've driven my father away; you've driven away every man who loved you; you even drove your own son away. No one can stand you for long . . .

She feels as if her daughter has punched her in the stomach. To her surprise, emotion begins to rise in her chest. She can feel a lump forming in her throat and her eyes begin to water. She wants to leap up off the couch and grab Valentina. She wants to hold her tight and tell her she is sorry. She wants to beg her not to leave her as well. But, before she has a chance, Valentina shouts, 'I'm moving out!' and storms off down the corridor and into her bedroom, giving the door a loud bang.

She sits, paralysed, on the couch. She doesn't know what to do. Tears begin to trail down her cheeks. She can't let Valentina see her like this – undone and broken. She gets up and goes into the bathroom, grabs a load of tissues and shoves them into her eyes, forcing the tears to stop. She goes back into the living room and drinks her glass of wine down in one. What has she done that is so terribly wrong?

All she had wanted was revenge for her daughter. It was dreadful to see her suffering so much. When they were in Greece, she'd hated that man, Francesco Merico, so much, she would have happily plunged a knife into his heart. Within a few months, he had transformed her daughter from a composed young photography student to a hysterical mess. He was a married man with a *pregnant* wife, he was Valentina's tutor at college and he was a heartless bastard who'd seduced her virginal daughter and broken her heart. She had to get him out of Valentina's life, so she had spoken to a few people that she knew on the board of the university and had got him removed. They did not look kindly upon tutors who seduced their students. In a way, it had been cathartic for Tina, bringing her back to her bad treatment by her first lover, who – ironically – had also been a professor at her college.

Yet Valentina is furious with her about it, accusing her of interfering in her life. Tina feels that her daughter is being unfair. She has always been so careful about not smothering Valentina and she gave her plenty of space when she was growing up. She starts to feel frightened. She has always counted on her daughter's love, but now it seems she hates her. Is Valentina right when she tells her that she has driven everyone away? Phil left her. Mattia grew up. And, as for all her boyfriends over the years, well, yes, she supposes most of them left her, but secretly she had wanted them to. She tires easily of them. She has always prided herself on not being possessive, but maybe that is the problem: she doesn't let her lovers know how she feels about them. She hasn't

327

been able to, not since Karel. Look what loving her did to him! She still feels responsible for his death.

Maybe she should sit Valentina down and tell her all about her real father – that he had died because he had wanted to see her so much. Tina pours herself another glass of wine and takes a sip. No, that would just upset and confuse her. It is too late to tell Valentina the truth now, especially as it seems that she is driving her daughter away, as well. What the hell is wrong with her?

She has been feeling so low recently. She knows it's to do with what happened before she went to Greece with Valentina. She should talk to someone about it, but she is too ashamed.

Tina had slipped into her old bad habits. It was partly because, as she got older, she had found it harder and harder to meet a man who was genuinely into her. As well as that, her fame was against her. The last couple of boyfriends she had were only with her because of who she was. They were sycophantic young men without personalities, and expected her to pay for everything. How could she get turned on with a man that? So, after the last disastrous affair, she had decided to stay single and celibate for a while. It was no problem being single, but the celibate part she found hard.

At first, she pleasured herself. When she went on a shoot to Sweden, she found a sex shop and bought all sorts of goodies: a little pink vibrator for her clitoris and a rabbit vibrator for the works, plus some erotic literature. Yet it was no good. Of course she could give herself an orgasm, but that is not why she craves sex. She needs that intimacy with another human being. It crossed her mind that maybe she should try women. She remembered that she had enjoyed kissing that girl, Lucinda, on the Orient Express all those years ago. But that had led to screwing her husband. The truth is Tina loves cocks. She craves deep penetration, and the scent of a man upon her skin.

In the past, when she had the desire for sex, she had always waited until she went abroad for work. Too many people knew who she was in Milan. Yet this one particular Saturday night a couple of months ago, she was desperate for intimacy. Valentina had been staying with her old school friend, Gaby, so Tina had the place to herself, which was a relief. She had tried her best to be good, and not go out. She poured herself a big glass of red wine, watched some porn while masturbating, but she just ended up feeling more frustrated. In the end, emboldened by the wine, she decided to go out.

Maybe that night she had not been so careful about how she looked. Maybe she put on a dress that was a little too tight and too young for her, or her eye make-up was too heavy, her lips too red. She tries to find a reason for what happened, but, each time she thinks about that night, she feels a mixture of rage and shame. How could she let something like that happen to *her*?

She went to a bar in a part of Milan she doesn't normally go to. Initially, it seemed like a good idea. The place was packed with good-looking young men. She sat down at the bar and it wasn't long before someone bought her a drink and started chatting her up. He had blond hair, she remembers that, and very white teeth. The last thing she remembers is dancing with the blond man on the tiny dance floor, lights flashing around her and the music pounding in her ears, speeding up her heart rate. She remembers thinking that the drink he had bought her had affected her, and that she was drunker than usual. After that, she remembers nothing. That is, until the next morning.

She had woken up with a splitting headache and a lurching

stomach in a strange hotel bedroom. Stumbling out of the bed, she had only just made it to the bathroom before throwing up in the toilet. She had clung to the toilet bowl for about an hour, emptying her stomach, dizzy and frightened. What was wrong with her? Finally, she had crawled back to the bedroom. She surveyed the scene. The bed was empty, the sheets dragged on to the carpet. The room looked trashed. There was a bucket of melted ice on its side and an empty champagne bottle, smashed glasses, her dress ripped to pieces and her underwear was nowhere to be seen. She gave a little sob as she saw three used condoms shrivelled up on the carpet beside the bed.

What had happened to her? She couldn't remember anything. Yet, as she looked down at her own body, she gasped in horror. She was covered in blooming bruises and big red bites. She reached down to touch herself and winced. She was so sore. Someone fucked her all right, several times, and roughly. Her stomach lurched and she rushed back into the bathroom and threw up again. She had never been so sick in her life. She pulled herself up on to the bathroom sink with her elbows, and that's when she saw the writing on the mirror. He had used her red lipstick to write his message:

DIRTY OLD WHORE

She brought her hands to her mouth and started to cry. The words pierced her, made her shrivel up in shame. She crawled into a corner of the bathroom, drew her knees up to her chest and she sobbed her heart out. She was a little girl again, all alone in the world, with no one to love her or take care of her. She wanted Phil. She wanted him so badly to make it right and to hold her in his arms. It was years since she'd last seen him and yet still he was the one she wanted to protect her and take this dark nightmare out of her life. She didn't move for hours. She sat in the corner of the bathroom, shivering, throwing up every now and again, and then crawling back into the corner. She heard a maid knocking a couple of times to clean the room, and then going away.

She had been raped. Not just once, but three times. She didn't even know by whom. Was it the blond man in the bar? Or maybe it had been another man? Could there have been more than one man? There were two empty champagne bottles and four broken glasses on the floor. She just could not remember what had happened that night. She knows now that her drink must have been drugged. Why else would she have blacked out? That is why she was so sick. She should have rung the police. And yet she was too ashamed to do it.

Tina is fifty-five years old. What woman her age gets herself raped? She knows it's not her fault – of course it's not – and yet she just can't face the judgement of other people. She can imagine them all condemning her, even her own daughter: what kind of woman in her mid-fifties goes out to a bar on her own on a Saturday night, dressed like a young tart? A woman looking for trouble, or a prostitute, that's what. The message on the mirror had said it all: *Dirty old whore.*

She had stumbled to her feet and grabbed a towel, trying to wipe the lipstick off the mirror until it became one big red smear. She needed to get out of the hotel before they called management.

It was the final insult to discover that she was staying in the most expensive five-star hotel in Milan: the Hotel Principe Savoia, a hotel that always had a special place in her heart because it was where Phil had stayed the first night she met him, all those years ago. When she checked out – in her ripped dress and wearing a pair of dark glasses that she had, thankfully, found in her bag – to her horror, the manager addressed her by name. When she asked if the room was paid for, he told her in a smooth, sneering voice, 'But of course; you paid for it last night, Signora Rosselli, with your credit card, don't you remember?'

When she got home, she had taken three showers in a row. She had scrubbed herself until her skin chafed and bled. And then she had climbed into bed, weak from being so sick, and feeling like she wanted to die. When Valentina got home she had pretended to be ill. She could not face her daughter.

She had planned to tell Valentina about it when they went to Greece. She had wanted to share their heartache, their humiliation, together. She needed to confide in someone. Who better than her daughter? She wanted them to be friends. But Valentina had been so far away from her. Every time she tried to talk to her, Valentina said she wanted her to leave her alone. The time was just never right to open up to her.

Tina wanted to purge herself of what had happened that night in Milan. They had hiked for hours, day after day, scrambling up rocky hills and wandering through ancient ruins. She had tried to inspire herself to have some love for life in that beautiful place, diving down deep into the Aegean Sea, wishing she could go all the way to the bottom and into another world: a magical underwater kingdom, where love reigned supreme. She had spent a lot of time thinking about Karel. Maybe it was because, every day, Valentina looked more and more like him. What might have been, if he had been there at the border crossing all those years ago?

Each day in Greece, Tina strove to rub out those awful words her rapist had branded across her heart. Dirty. Old. Whore. The

332

weird thing was that the word that hurt her the most was the most harmless one: old. She had tried not to let it make her bitter or hate men. She realises now that it hadn't worked. She had taken out her own need for vengeance on Valentina's married man. She had made him pay for what happened to her that night in Milan.

Tina sits back down on the couch and looks around the room. She has lived in this apartment all her life. It has always been her sanctuary. But now it feels like a prison. She has to leave Milan. It is not just because she can't bear the thought of coming face to face with her rapist or rapists one day and not knowing it . . . but also because, if she doesn't leave, then Valentina will leave her. She couldn't bear that.

She has to give her daughter some kind of stability, so, if she gives her the apartment, it can be her sanctuary instead. Besides, she honestly believes that, for the moment, Valentina is better off without her. Maybe in a while they can live together again, but right now her daughter needs her independence, to spread her wings, come out of the shadow of her dysfunctional mother. All she is going to do is fuck her up. She knows that Valentina will think she is angry with her, especially if she goes without talking to her, but her resolve will weaken in the morning. Tina decides that she has to go now, before she changes her mind. Before she does any more damage to her daughter's life.

She will go to America. She has been there several times already, and she is due to do a shoot in New York next week. She will just go early tomorrow. A friend of hers lives in Arizona, in a place called Sedona. It sounds idyllic, full of new-age, gentle-hippy types. She could do with some peace, some quiet.

Tina makes a decision: she will go cold turkey. From this day forward, she has no intention of ever having sex again, *unless* she falls in love. She doubts very much that that will happen. She has let her chances slip by in this lifetime, and now she must learn to live with the consequences.

$\mathscr{V}$alentina

SHE ARRIVES AT THE ROCKEFELLER CENTER AN HOUR AND A HALF before she is due to meet Theo in the subway station. She stands outside the Center for a moment, staring up at the elegant skyscraper, gleaming against the dusky sky. It is less showy than the Empire State Building or the Chrysler Building and yet Valentina has always been drawn to the Rockefeller building more than the other two. It speaks of a time in New York when dreams really could be made in a day. It is a solid manifestation of that hope, in an understated way.

She has been walking around Manhattan the whole afternoon, trying to sort through her emotions. Fortunately, her mother had cancelled their coffee date, telling Valentina that she was very sorry but something had come up today, and could they meet for dinner tomorrow? In the past, Valentina would have been annoyed with her mother, read some more rejection into her cancellation, but today it doesn't bother her. In fact, she is relieved, for she has a feeling that, if she were to tell her mother everything about Theo and Leonardo, her mother would tell her to pick Theo. She is not sure she wants to hear this advice.

Valentina goes inside the Rockefeller and wanders through the empty shopping mall until she comes across the Rock Center Café. She hasn't eaten all day. She convinces herself that is why she needs to sit down and have some food, but really it's so she can look at anyone passing by. If she could corner Theo down here on the concourse of the Rockefeller, it would be so much better. She is not too keen on meeting him on a crowded platform of a subway station. She has always suffered slightly from claustrophobia and it surprises her that Theo would ask her to meet him there. What is he going to say to her? She suddenly looks down at her hands, realising she is still wearing the engagement ring he gave her in Italy. She twists it around and around her finger. Now she *has* to give it back, despite what Mrs Steen said. She wonders how on earth Theo will explain himself to his parents. Will they forgive him?

Valentina orders crab cakes and one of her special Valentina cocktails, the best thing Russell ever did for her. As she sips the fortifying concoction of sweet raspberry liqueur and tangy limoncello, she reflects that it seems like an age since she was with Russell. Now when she thinks of him she feels sorry for him. How could she ever have thought that things might have worked out between them? Russell was locked into a world of fantasy sex without substance, a world she used to inhabit before she met Theo. She had been slipping back into that life until Leonardo arrived in New York. He is the one who has unlocked her frozen heart.

At five minutes to eight Valentina enters the Rockefeller Center Subway station and makes her way to the island platform for southbound trains. The subway is one aspect of New York she isn't so keen on. It is dirty, stuffy and smelly, sometimes the stink of sewage almost turning her stomach. She feels the ceilings are too low, and the platforms are too narrow for the number of people who use them. She pushes through the crowd searching for Theo's face. Her chest is tight with expectation. She still has no idea what she will say to him when she sees him. A train pulls into the station blasting her with hot fumey air, and she puts her hand over her mouth and squeezes her eyes tight as if she is in a sandstorm. To her relief the platform clears and the train takes off, a few stragglers passing her on the way to the exit. She walks all the way down to the end of the platform and yet she can't see Theo anywhere. She feels uneasy, on edge. She doesn't like this place and wishes that Theo had picked somewhere else as their meeting point.

'Good evening, Valentina.'

His voice cuts into her like an icy blade. She spins around, her heart racing in terror, for standing in front of her is Glen. He looks down at her, all two metres of him, his eyes glittering with malevolence.

'What are you doing here?' she asks, in horror.

'I asked you to meet me here.'

She shakes her head in disbelief.

'Of course, I had to be a little devious,' he says, smirking at her. 'I knew you wouldn't come if I asked you to meet *me*, so I cheated a little.'

'The message was from you, not Theo?' she says, her voice coming out in a ghostly whisper.

'Yes, indeed,' he says, taking a step towards her, forcing her to flatten herself against one of the red pillars on the platform.

'Why would Theo bother with you now you've run off with his best friend?'

She looks over Glen's shoulder. There are plenty of people around; in fact, all she has to do is call out. And yet she doesn't. She needs to find out if Theo is okay first.

Glen takes another step towards her. His eyes are dark, his

skin so pale it is almost translucent. She imagines the cruel blood flowing through him, fuelling his spite and meanness.

'I told him, what else could he expect from a girl like you? A *slut*,' he hisses.

She feels a flare of outrage. 'Stay away from me,' she says, as calmly as she can. 'Else I'll scream so loud every cop in this station will hear me and come running.'

'Oh, no,' Glen says. 'I wouldn't do that.'

He is breathing over her. She tries to turn her face away, but he hems her in against the pillar. She feels something sharp pricking her chin and, to her horror, when she looks down she can see that Glen has a knife in his hand. It is hidden from view by the bulk of his body, which is pressing against hers. He trails its tip down her chin, on to the soft pulse of her neck. She remembers that Wayne Datcher's throat had been slit when they found him floating in the Hudson River.

'You see,' Glen whispers, 'if you call out now then you will never ever again see your darling Theo.'

She stiffens. 'What have you done to him?'

He puts a finger to her mouth.

She tries to bite back her lips, but she can't help tasting the salt of his skin.

She tries to look past Glen. Surely someone has noticed them? Yet he is so tall and pressed up so close to her that she can't see clearly around him. They could be any couple, locked together in an embrace against a platform pillar. She begins to panic slightly; maybe no one sees what is really happening at all.

'You still don't get it, do you?' Glen says.

She tries to shift away from him, but the tip of the knife blade against her chin is enough to stop her.

'It has always been about you,' he says.

338

'What do you mean?' she asks, confused and frightened. 'What have I ever done to you?'

'Valentina, it was your father who took away everything from me,' he says.

For a moment, Valentina thinks of her real father – the ethereal Karel – but, when Glen continues to speak, she realises that he is referring to Phil Rembrandt.

'My father was a great man, Valentina. If he had been a Roman, he would have been an emperor. Men followed him.'

He trails the knife further down her throat, so that it rests at the base of her neck.

'But your father brought him down, and for what reason? To sell newspapers!' He says angrily.

'Phil Rembrandt is not my father,' she says.

Glen presses the flat edge of the knife against the base of her throat so that she is almost choked. 'Don't lie, Valentina,' he says, releasing the knife.

She says nothing, she is so terrified. Please, she begs inside her head. Someone must have noticed them. How is it possible that no one has seen Glen threatening her?

'My father died a broken man, in prison. He killed himself, Valentina. All because of your father.'

'That's not Phil's fault,' she whispers. 'He was just doing his job.'

'Just like Theo was doing his job, taking away all my work? I had to make him pay. I had to make you *both* pay. So, I thought, what better way than to make you think he was dead . . . and to make him believe that, if he contacts you, you will die . . . I don't know who was more tortured, you or Theo.' He sniggers. 'Oh, sweet vengeance.'

She tries to wriggle free of him, but he just pushes his body into hers. His smell is overpowering. She can taste the crab cakes rising like bile in her mouth.

'And then the beauty of it is to let you find each other again, but not for too long – oh, no – just long enough for your hearts to click into motion again. And then, *bam*.' He slams his free hand against the pillar above her head. 'Destroy you, all over again.'

She gasps in shock and in fear.

'Shush!' He gives her a threatening look, pushing the blade against her chest now.

'Hey, what's going on here?' A cop emerges at Glen's shoulder.

Valentina tries to signal with her eyes, but Glen plunges his mouth on to hers and pulls her into his arms. She tries to pull back, but she can feel the knife against her heart and she knows what will happen if she struggles. Glen grinds his mouth into hers. He tastes of metal, and death. She wants to throw up.

'OK, you two lovebirds, but don't hang around on the platform all night,' the cop says, and she sees him retreating. She opens her eyes wide, desperate to signal to him, but he is striding away now with his back to her. Glen pulls away from her, smirking nastily.

'You taste so good, Valentina,' he says. 'It's a pity you and I never got together.' He looks behind him at the cop. 'Well, I guess it's time we got going. We don't want that guy to come back,' he says, taking her by the arm, the blade pushed into her side, and leading her towards the edge of the platform. There are more and more people arriving for the next train and yet no matter how hard she tries no one will catch her eye.

'The funny thing is that, all this time Theo thought he was protecting you, it was just my own little game,' Glen tells her.

'But he said that one of your associates was pointing a gun at me . . . that the skipper on the boat in Capri was working for you . . .' she whispers.

'That's rubbish. I just got a friend to stand up on the cliff with a pair of binoculars; from a distance, the light catches on them just like they would on the scope of a gun. And the skipper . . . Well, I didn't even know his name.'

'But the bank heist – that really happened,' Valentina says.

'Oh, I knew about it . . . Friends of my father's were working on that heist for a year. They asked me if I wanted in, but I decided not. But it was a perfect cover for the reason behind the art theft. You see,' he says, 'the police think the art theft was a decoy for the bank robbery, but actually, for my purposes, it was the other way around.'

'You'll never sell that painting,' she whispers.

'I know, and I don't care,' Glen declares. 'Although, Datcher certainly did.' He frowns. 'Stupid, greedy fool! God, Valentina, he bled like a pig – ruined my best shirt.'

'Please, Glen, let me go . . .' she begs.

He gives her a short laugh. 'Now, that is the last thing I am going to do, Valentina. Don't you see? It has always just been about you and me, righting the sins of our fathers. This whole art robbery has been a way to get to you, don't you see?'

'But how did you know I'd be in New York?'

'That was just a happy coincidence . . . although unfortunately your presence here has put the police onto me sooner than I expected.' She can feel the breeze of an approaching train, as he forces her to step closer and closer to the edge of the platform.

'Does this excite you a little, Valentina? They say that sex is like death . . . when you climax, that feeling of going over the edge.'

He forces her right to the concrete rim of the platform. She looks down at her feet, her head swaying with dizziness.

'Remember the blue grotto, do you? Our swim in the deep?'

She begins to shiver, trying to dispel those images which haunt her nearly every night.

'Did you not realise then that it was always you I wanted to destroy? I thought if I could take the daughter away from the father it would be almost equal to my loss . . . just.'

She looks up at Glen and, for the first time, she really does believe he is going to do this. He is going to kill her. She tries to pull away from him. She doesn't care about the knife any more. Let him stab her; she would rather that than be pushed in front of a subway train.

'Behave,' he hisses, trying to rein her in with his free hand. Yet at last people have begun to notice. A woman screams, someone else cries out, and she sees the cop returning, running down the platform towards her, his hand on his gun. Glen swings Valentina around to face them, still teetering on the edge of the platform so that she is facing the tunnel, and she can see the lights of an approaching train. He has the knife at her throat now, in plain view.

'Don't come any closer or I'll slit her throat,' he warns. The cop stops in his tracks.

Each second seems as if it is in slow motion. The lights of the train get closer and closer, and the stinking wind from the tunnel assaults her.

'Let her go!'

Glen's head snaps up as Valentina's heart jumps into her

mouth. It is Theo, running down the steps onto the platform, and behind him she sees Leonardo, along with Balducci and Delaney. They have come to rescue her, she thinks dimly through the haze of her fear, but it's too late for she sees the train pulling into the platform, and the shocked face of the driver as he slams on the brakes, the screeching horror of the sound. She knows what will happen next. Glen will push her off the platform in front of the train. There is nothing anyone can do to stop him.

'Drop the knife!' Balducci is yelling, his gun primed on Glen.

They are teetering on the edge of the platform, her and Glen, and all of a sudden through the blindness of her terror she feels a fierce determination. She is not going to die like this. She has to save herself. Forgetting the consequences of the knife at her throat, she rocks back on her heels just enough to unbalance Glen. He drops the knife and it clatters onto the platform as she jams her elbow back into his chest with all her might. He slips off the edge behind her. She senses him grappling to get a hold of her, and he does grasp her jacket just for second, enough to tip her back with him. It is Balducci who saves her, planting a bullet into Glen and making him suddenly release her. She hurls herself forward onto her knees, landing in front of Delaney who pulls her to safety.

It is a horrific sound, the sound of flesh and bone against metal, the scream of the man dying amid the screams of those who witness the end of Glen as the D7 for Coney Island slams into him.

She is suddenly surrounded by people: Delaney helping her up to her feet, Balducci running past her towards the stopped train, but she can't look behind her at what lies upon the tracks. There are police everywhere. She looks about her in a blur as someone puts a blanket around her shoulders. Leonardo comes rushing towards her. She has never seen him look so pale and shocked. He takes her into his arms and only then does she realise she is shaking uncontrollably. He strokes her hair, saying her name again and again.

'Valentina, Valentina, Valentina . . .'

But she doesn't feel him, she doesn't hear him. He cannot comfort her. She is looking for Theo. And when she sees him at last her whole being screams to run to him. He stands at the very end of the subway platform looking at her with such a haunted expression on his face, such a look of pain and loss, that it sears her. She wants to tell him she needs him, but the words dry up and she is so weak now she can't release herself from Leonardo's arms. Instead she sees him walk away, throwing her one last glance, and, shoving his hands in his pockets, he runs back up the subway steps before the police have the chance to recognise him. Theo is gone.

$\mathscr{T}$ina

2013

TINA IS MORE NERVOUS THAN SHE HAS BEEN HER ENTIRE LIFE. SHE can't stand still and yet she is afraid she will miss him if he arrives while she has popped off to get a coffee or go for a stroll. She has to stand right here in front of the arrivals gates so that the first person Phil sees at Newark Airport is her. She wants to catch his spontaneous reaction to her because then she'll know whether her hope is false or not.

Tina is a different woman from the one that left Milan nine years ago. She now works as a reflexologist as well as being involved in the running of an art gallery in Santa Fe along with her friends, Suki and Della. It is commercially successful, and yet also gives her time to build up her practice as a healer, and do some photography herself. She lives in a beautiful house overlooking the valley, and has many good friends, as well as a devoted dog, Sheba.

Tina moved to Santa Fe in 2011 and immediately fell in love with the city. She has always been a fan of Georgia O'Keeffe's paintings and, here in the city that became her home as well, Tina sees her landscapes everywhere. The desert soothes her. She thought it would be hard to live so far away from the sea, yet strangely she feels echoes of the ocean in the landscape. Suki explains it to her: New Mexico used to be under water, she says. If you look down upon it from an aeroplane, you can see that.

'It's like we're living on a great big dried-out seabed,' Suki tells her. 'You know, if you look hard enough, you can still find shells.'

Tina loves the idea of this. At last, she has found her way to the bottom of the sea, and, instead of drowning, she is living, getting stronger day by day.

When she first came to America, it had been tough. She was an addict, struggling not to succumb to her cravings, yet at least she was in a country that recognised her condition. After a few months in Arizona, she chose to live in California, and joined a local sex-addiction therapy group. For years, she didn't tell anyone outside of the group about her problem. She thought people would laugh at her. But sex addiction is no laughing matter. She heard such heartbreaking stories in her group sessions of families torn apart, lives destroyed.

After about two years of therapy, she finally felt better. That deep craving for sex that she would get whenever she felt lonely or down faded away and she began to hope that she could socialise again without risk. She started to travel around America. As she did so, she took pictures of women.

Tina has this long-term vision of a project that celebrates the beauty of every woman, not just the rarefied face and bodies of models, who she has worked with all her life, but women like her, with all their flaws: women of every race, colour and creed. She wants to show the beauty of imperfection – in young women, middle-aged women and old women. Finally, 'old' is no longer a dirty word for Tina. These elderly ladies are the portraits she loves the most, the faces showing women who have lived full lives, their stories written in their wrinkles, and those wrinkles making them look so majestic and powerful to Tina. It is the eyes of these old ladies that are the most startling: full of depth and wisdom, many brimming with a kind of universal love, almost all of them bright and hopeful. She wants to be like them, accepting her true nature and letting it shine forth. Tina wants to be young at heart – but, to be that, she needs her children to love her again.

It has taken years, but she has managed to build bridges with Mattia, although she still finds his wife, Debbie, difficult. She supposes that it is because Debbie is only being protective of her husband. Mattia's wife has witnessed the damage his mother did to him: years of being abandoned at home when she went away to work, and then boarding school. How did Tina end up being such a bad parent? It has been hard to acknowledge this truth, and the reason why Valentina didn't want to know her for years. Yet, now she has seen Valentina in New York, she can feel the connection growing between them again. That incredible bond that she had with her girl when she was first born is still there.

She had let Valentina down in so many ways when she was a child. And yet it seems that her daughter does still love her. She thinks about her own mother, how she struggled against her. Tina had constantly felt that Maria Rosselli was disappointed in her, despite her career success. She had always gone to her father, Guido, for comfort. And yet, despite all the conflict, she loved her mother just as much as her father. Tina realises now that, devastated as she was by her parents' sudden death, it was her mother's that hit her hardest, for they had never made their peace.

She wonders what Maria Rosselli would think of her now.

Would she be proud? She had always been fond of Phil, and disappointed that Tina wouldn't agree to marry him. She cannot believe that, after twenty-three years of silence, today she will see Phil again.

Oddly enough, it was Valentina who had unwittingly brought them together. When Tina had returned from that horrific trip to Milan last year, minus her daughter, who point-blank refused to leave Milan and all the ghosts of her missing lover (Tina couldn't refer to him as dead . . . She still wasn't so sure herself), there had been a letter for her from Phil. It wasn't a long letter; in fact, it was breathtakingly brief and she had wondered why he hadn't emailed her. Mattia had obviously given him her address, so why not her email?

In the letter, Phil had written that Mattia had told him about Valentina's loss and that he had heard that Tina had gone back to see her in Milan, and he wanted to know how she was. The whole thing was strange because, of course, Mattia could have told Phil how Valentina was himself. At the top of the letter was his address, plus his email. She couldn't bear the wait with snail mail, so she wrote him an email:

> Dear Phil,
> Thank you for your letter. I was so surprised and glad to hear from you after all these years. I won't lie to you. It was hard in Milan. Valentina is very upset about the loss of her young man. She is very angry with me, too. I have been a bad mother to her and now I have to live with the consequences.
> I hope all is well with you.
> Love Tina

348

He wrote an email back almost immediately. Short again:

> Dear Tina,
>
>   You are not a bad mother. You did your best. You love your children. That makes you a good mother, in my book.
>
>   I am well. I am living in London now. I am still lecturing, but gave up the journalistic work. It wasn't good for my heart!
>
>   Love Phil

She wondered what he meant when he wrote, 'it wasn't good for my heart' . . . Did he mean physically? Or emotionally? Was he still with the redhead she had seen that night in London, all those years ago?

They began writing to each other. At first, it was short and polite: *How are you? What are you up to?* She told him about the art gallery in Santa Fe, her healing work, and her photographic project. He told her about a history book he was writing on the Blitz in London, and tales about colleagues at London University. Then they began to reminisce –

Do you remember that holiday in Sardinia? The time Mattia broke his arm when he fell off the swing in the park? When he won the prize for best art project in school? – all the safe, early memories, before she went to Berlin, before Valentina.

One day, she couldn't bear not to know any more. *Are you single?* she had typed – just one line – and sent it off.

Yes, he replied, almost immediately.

Me too, she wrote back.

I find that hard to believe, he wrote.

It's true, cross my heart.

349

What is wrong with the men of Sante Fe? he replied.

I could say the same about London women.

Six weeks ago, he had written her another email. She noticed that he had sent it from London in the middle of the night. It was just one line – no 'Dear Tina'; no 'Love Phil' – *Why did you never tell Valentina about her real father?*

His message knocked the breath out of her. She imagined him typing the email having drunk one whisky too many, finally his justified anger at her surfacing.

She thought about trying to explain herself. She thought of writing to him about finding out that her own father was not Guido Rosselli, but some French surrealist film-maker, and what that had done to her. It had been part of the reason why their relationship had failed. She thought of trying to explain that it was better for Valentina not to know, that ignorance is bliss, but none of her explanations convinced even herself. She knew that she had been wrong and so did he.

So, in the end, she just wrote, *I screwed up. How did you find out I never told her?*

He wrote back:

Valentina came to see me in London last year, before her boyfriend died. She was very upset with me for walking out on her when she was little. I had to tell her that I wasn't her real father. Tina, if you screwed up, so did I. I might not have been her birth father, but I was the only father Valentina knew, and I abandoned her.

His email had had a devastating effect. She had sat out on her porch, with Sheba's head on her lap, the dog looking up at her with doleful eyes as she cried her heart out. What a mess it all was! And, worst of all, Valentina knew the truth and never told her. She had been with her for over a week in Milan when Theo disappeared, and Valentina made no mention of it. No wonder her daughter had been so angry at her; no wonder she had hardly spoken to her, so that, in the end, Tina had to give up and come home. Valentina had even been mad with Mattia.

After this last email from Phil, Tina decided that she should stop raking up the past. That meant she should no longer correspond with Phil. What was the point, anyway? He was in London, she was in Santa Fe, and they were so careful of each other that they couldn't even handle a phone call.

When she didn't reply, he sent her another message: *Are you OK? Did you get my last email?*

She felt she should respond. It was only fair.

Yes, I am sorry. I am very shocked that Valentina went to see you and she never told me when I was in Milan.

He wrote back immediately: *So you never spoke to her about Karel?*

All she could write was one word: *No.*

Phil replied instantly:

Dear Tina,
    I am sorry to be interfering, but I do care about Valentina. Where is Karel? Could you get him to contact her? I feel she needs to meet him.
    Love Phil

She stared at her computer screen, and reread Phil's email. She had never told a soul about what happened to Karel. Not even Mattia. It was her most shameful secret, far worse than any of

351

the things she did when she was a sex addict. She took a deep breath. It was time to own up.

> Dearest Phil,
>   Do you remember when the Berlin Wall came down and I took Valentina with me to meet Karel? Remember I wanted you to come too? She never got to meet him because he was already dead. In 1986, a year after Valentina was born, he tried to escape over the Berlin Wall. He told a friend that he wanted to see his baby girl and couldn't wait any longer. He was shot by the border guards and later died in hospital. It was my fault he died. I should never have told him I was pregnant. He would be alive today if I had left him alone.

She couldn't write any more, so she pressed send. The next minute, her phone was ringing. She stared at the screen. It was a long number with a foreign code: British. She picked it up.

'Hello,' she whispered.

'Tina.' His voice flooded over her. She felt like crying.

'Hi, Phil,' she said.

'Tina, I never knew . . . I am so sorry about Karel. Why didn't you tell me at the time? I would have come back to you.'

'I know,' she said, her voice hoarse with emotion, 'but, Phil, I just would have kept hurting you again and again. I am no good for you.'

'I think I can decide that for myself.'

It felt so good to hear him speaking, to know that the man writing her the emails was no figment of her imagination, but her love coming back to her.

'You need to tell Valentina about Karel,' Phil said, gently.

'I know, I will . . .'

'Mattia told me she is in New York.'

'I know; I've spoken to her on the phone. I asked her to visit me, but she doesn't want to.'

'You have to go and see her in New York and speak to her before it's too late.'

'I think it's already too late, Phil.'

She remembered Valentina's outburst when she had gone to see her in Milan last year. *You mean nothing to me*: that is what her daughter had screamed in her face.

'It's not too late, love,' Phil said.

His words pierced her heart. He had called her 'love', like he always used to. She knew it was an English endearment that probably slipped off his tongue all day in London, but still . . . he'd called her 'love'.

Phil had been right. After her lunch with Valentina, Tina had called him up, bubbling with joy and emotion, and sobbing down the phone.

'I think we should get together, as a family,' he said. 'All of us – Mattia and Debbie, as well. I am going to book a flight right now.'

Her heart had started to race when he'd said that. It was all very well having their safe little email correspondence, but to see him in the flesh again? She is so much older now than when he last saw her. It's been over twenty years.

She looks up at the arrivals screen. His flight landed half an hour ago. He should be through those doors any minute now. She feels sick, her stomach fluttering with a whole flock of butterflies. She tries to steady her breath. She clutches the bunch of red roses in her hands, their thorns pricking her fingers. She feels a little foolish now. What sixty-four-year-old woman gives a man red roses?

The doors open and she sees him immediately. It is her Phil, as he was when she last saw him. He may have a head of thick, white hair, be wearing a pair of glasses and have a thousand wrinkles, but he has the same smiling face, the same rich eyes and kingly bearing. She takes a deep breath and acknowledges the sight of Phil: her one true love. She waves her roses in the air like an idiot, red petals flying everywhere. He sees her, his face breaking into a wider smile and he comes towards her through the crowds.

'It's you! Tina!' He gives her a hug, and she feels like breaking down within his arms. She is so happy. She never thought that she could feel such joy again.

They pull back and she gives him the roses.

'You bought me flowers,' he says, smelling the roses. She looks into his face and she can see tears brimming in his eyes behind his glasses. She cannot say anything; she just reaches up and takes his dear face between her hands, planting a kiss upon his lips.

To the end of her days, Tina will look back at that golden afternoon with Phil and see it as the moment her life flowered. They may both be over sixty years of age, but that evening, in bed with Phil, she finally understood that her femininity and the real nature of her and Phil's deep love and sexual bond has nothing to do with outer appearances, but is ageless – a profound, powerful force that resides within them.

They made love a different way. Not with the urgency of when they were younger, or with the pressure of having to perform. Their love unfurled, petal by pink petal, until it floated within their hearts, like a lotus flower, the cause and effect of their history of love. Tina realised something: she and Phil had created their love themselves. It didn't just exist. They had made it, dismantled it and now made it again. Their spirits were the same, their unity as pure as it had always been, despite the passing of the years and the many other lovers they had each had. None of that was important any more. All that did matter was now.

They lay within each other's arms, kissing and stroking each other, reawakening their passion for each other. He slipped inside her still soft, and she opened herself to him, relaxing from deep down inside her very being. She felt Phil growing inside her, filling her with his magic, his warmth, his loving. They stayed like this for hours, joined together, in humble union, watching the sun set and then rise again over the Hudson River.

$\mathcal{V}$alentina

A HAND, COLD AS ICE, CLAMPED AROUND HER FINGERS LIKE A vice grip; death's hand, dragging her down, into the darkness. He is so strong, Glen. She sees him again in her nightmare, in the seconds before he died; she sees the pure hatred for her in his eyes, the passion for revenge consuming him like a poison and turning him into a killer. She smells the subway stink, hears the train approaching, feels the hot wind of terror on her face. Valentina is falling off the edge of the platform, she is lost, she is gone. She screams out in terror.

'Valentina! Valentina!' Marco is on her bed beside her, cradling her in his arms; Jake is on the other side of her, stroking her back.

'It's only a dream; wake up, Valentina,' Marco comforts her.

She is shaking uncontrollably, unable to speak. The two boys get into bed on either side of her, holding her safe within their love, as if she is their child. She cannot sleep now. Yet she is soothed to listen to Marco's soft snore, to feel Jake shifting beside her in the bed. She is OK, she reminds herself. It is over.

And yet, in a way, she knows it will never be over. What she and Theo had is broken for ever. And now he has suddenly dematerialised. Instinctively, she and Leonardo didn't mention him or the fact that the boyfriend she had accused Glen of murdering was suddenly alive. The last thing she needed was police snooping into her private life, and part of her wanted to protect Theo, despite his crime. Now there was nothing linking him to the art robbery – apart from the actual picture, of course – if what Glen said was true. The bank heist and the Klimt robbery had been unconnected, so the gang knew nothing of Theo's involvement. As long as they didn't run into Balducci or Delaney again, there was no reason for anyone to suspect Theo.

Hours later, after the interminable interviews, she and Leonardo had gone back to his place. She was still shaking with shock, yet she couldn't settle. Everything felt wrong, as if she was in a parallel universe, a place that was not her real life. Leonardo tried to calm her by massaging her. He bathed the cuts on her throat from Glen's knife and rubbed arnica into the bruises on her body. He tried to hold her in his arms and kiss her, yet all she could think about was the fact she had wanted Theo, not Leonardo, at the time when she thought she would die.

In the end, she had to tell him the truth.

'Dear Leonardo,' she said to him, as she lay spooned within his arms, breathing in his soothing aroma of incense and oranges.

'What is it, Valentina?'

She turned around and gazed into his eyes and, the intelligent, sensitive man that he was, he knew what she was about to say.

He nodded, as if she had already spoken to him. 'I love you, Valentina,' he said. 'I always will, but I want you to be happy more than anything else.' He paused, brought her hand to his lips and kissed it. 'Go to him,' he said.

'No,' she replied. 'I am not going to Theo, Leonardo.'

He had looked surprised.

'I need to be on my own for a while,' she told him. 'You know the way you were when you broke up with Raquel? You had to be on your own for a few months . . . Well, I think I need to do that.'

'But you and Theo . . .' Leonardo sighed. She could tell it hurt him to say these words. 'I would be lying if I didn't think you two belonged together. He loves you.'

'I know,' she said, looking down. 'And I love him, but I can't be with him. Not after what he did to me.'

'Are you sure?'

'No, to be honest, but I think I am going to stay with my mama for a while in New Mexico – get to know her again.'

'That's good, Valentina.' He clutched her hands. 'Remember, I am always here for you, if you need me.'

She raised her eyes to his, felt the warmth of his love and friendship. She wrapped her arms around him and gave him the biggest hug of their lives.

'I know,' she whispered into the back of his warm neck. 'And I will always be here for you, too.'

Valentina looks out the cab window as she, Marco and Jake travel through East Village. It is Saturday night and the streets are alive, bars, restaurants and clubs bulging with people of every colour and creed. She loves the diversity of New York, all the different cultures rubbing side by side. She wonders what it will be like living in New Mexico. She imagines deserts, red rocks (or is that Arizona?), valleys and mountains, big skies. She imagines getting lost in all that space.

'Thanks so much for coming with me, guys,' she says to her friends.

'It's our pleasure, Valentina,' Jake says.

'Besides,' Marco says, 'I can't wait to meet your mother: *the* Tina Rosselli!'

Valentina rolls her eyes. 'Oh, please! Not you as well . . .'

'Come on, darling,' Marco beseeches her. 'How can you not expect me to be excited? She is one of my fashion heroes. Why else do you think we're friends?' He gives her a nudge.

'Well, if it makes you feel any better,' Jake says, 'I've never heard of your mother.'

She pats Jake's knee. 'That's probably because you're too young, unlike Marco here.'

Marco huffs, but he is in good humour. 'What time is Antonella and Mikhail's flight getting in?' he asks her.

'About fifteen minutes ago,' she glances at her watch. 'They're coming straight to the restaurant.'

'I can't wait to hear all about their club in Moscow,' Jake says.

'I hope she doesn't get too X-rated,' Valentina mutters.

'I am sure your mama can handle it,' Marco says.

'It's not Mama I'm worried about . . . It's my sister-in-law, Debbie; she's a bit straight-laced.'

'This is going to be so interesting,' Marco declares. 'To finally meet your mother, and your brother and his wife . . . All of your family in one go.'

'Not quite,' Valentina says, for she can't help thinking of Phil, even though he isn't her real father.

They have arranged to meet in a little restaurant in Greenwich Village that specialises in making risotto, her mother's favourite dish (although, knowing Tina, she will probably only eat one forkful all night). As Valentina walks through the door of the restaurant, she immediately sees Mattia, who is standing at the bar, ordering drinks. Her brother rushes over to her, enveloping her in a massive hug. She is surprised how good it feels to be embraced by him. All the resentment she has felt against him for the past year melts away. What's the point of focusing on the fact we have different fathers? she thinks. We are brother and sister. It's as simple as that.

Mattia pulls back. 'Mama was telling me all about the dramas going on in your life.' He hugs her again tightly. 'My God, Valentina. To think . . .'

She looks up at her brother. 'I've missed you, Mattia.'

He ruffles her hair, looks almost tearful. 'And I've missed you, too, sis.'

They stroll, arm in arm, to the table, where Marco and Jake have already joined the others. She sees Debbie smiling at her, and Tina next to her. To Valentina's astonishment, sitting next to her mother is none other than Phil Rembrandt. Phil has his arm around her mother's shoulders and they are both beaming at her like newlyweds.

'Darling!' her mother gushes. 'We wanted to surprise you!'

Valentina has never seen her mother look more beautiful than in this moment. She is not the sophisticated, chic style icon, but a different woman altogether – a woman even more exquisite for her lack of guile. Her cheeks are blooming like a young girl's and her eyes are sparkling with joy.

Phil stands up and gives Valentina a hug. It feels good to be held in his arms, even more comforting than being hugged by Mattia.

'How are you?' he asks. 'You look tired,' he adds, holding her at arm's length and looking at her with concern.

'I'm not sleeping very well,' she says, as she slides into a seat next to him, while Mattia sits on the other side of her. She wonders if she will ever tell Phil about Glen, that the real reason he persecuted Valentina was all linked to Phil's crusade against Glen's father.

'You've been through an awful lot,' Phil says. 'You need to take care of yourself. You could have post-traumatic stress syndrome.'

'Did you have that?' she asks him. 'After you were shot?'

'I don't think so,' he says.

At the same time, her mother turns to her and says, 'Yes. He did.' She pats Phil's hand, looking up at him. 'Don't you remember?'

'The truth is, that time was black with stress. I don't remember much until I moved to London.'

He and Tina exchange a look. Everyone else is busy chatting, but Valentina sees the length of it, the regret and forgiveness they silently share.

Suddenly, there is a commotion as the door is flung open and Antonella, Valentina's artist friend, makes a dramatic entrance, her suave Russian lover, Mikhail, in tow.

'Valentina, my love!' she totters over to the table in her mega-high platforms. The vision of her is breathtaking.

Valentina can't help noticing poor Debbie pale in horror, and Mattia looking at her friend with his eyes on stalks. For Antonella is in the tightest, teeniest black minidress, with a plunging neckline, leaving little to the imagination. Her red hair appears even more vibrant than usual, piled on top of her head like a flaming Leaning Tower.

Despite all her eccentricities and exotic appearance, Antonella is a girl with a solid heart. Valentina feels a rush of joy at seeing her, for her friend decided to come to New York as soon as she heard about what happened.

'Antonella, it's so good to see you,' she says, as her friend squeezes in opposite her and makes her introductions to Valentina's family.

'What a wonderful creature,' Tina murmurs, giving Antonella an admiring look. 'Am I right in saying that your aunt is my old friend, Isabella?' she asks her.

'Yes, my Aunty Issy . . . She is just so crazy, isn't she, Valentina?'

Tina turns to Phil to explain. 'Remember Isabella, when you first met me in Milan? The one who invited you over for that conference? She lives in London now. Antonella and Valentina stayed with her when Valentina was over the time she went to see you.'

'*Mio Dio!*' Antonella exclaims. 'Is this *your* father, Valentina?'

There is an awkward silence at the table. Valentina can feel Mattia shift next to her; she glances at him and can see that he knows that she knows the truth now.

'Have I said something wrong?' Antonella says, picking up on the tension.

'Well, actually—' Tina begins to say.

'Yes,' Valentina interrupts, talking over her. 'Yes, this is *my* father,' she says.

She senses Phil turning to look at her, but, instead of returning his gaze, she reaches under the table and grabs his hand. It is warm and strong, squeezing her in return.

A month ago, she would never have believed it. Here she is, sitting around a table with a brother, a mother *and* a father, sharing a meal with her friends. Theo would be so proud of me, she thinks. She tries to shove him to the back of her mind. She cannot let her feelings for Theo ruin the evening.

'Well, I suppose you are wondering what we are doing here together, Valentina?' Tina says, cuddling into Phil. The sight of her mother like this with a man is strange. Valentina realises that, in all the years and with all the many boyfriends she had when her daughter was younger, Tina has never seemed as happy or as in love as she is today.

'You see, we have been corresponding a little by email and telephone. When I told Phil you were here in New York and we were going to see Mattia, he decided to come over.'

'I thought it was time we had a family reunion,' Phil says.

Valentina looks at Phil and she can't help feeling warmth for him in her heart, despite the fact he walked out on her when she was a little girl. Now she understands why, and that it wasn't his fault. It suddenly occurs to her that what Phil did all those years ago by leaving Tina and her daughter, was tantamount to what Theo has done to her. Phil left them to protect them, just like Theo did. Of course, her mother's reaction had been different to hers, but now, looking at the two of them together, it is quite clear that they belong together. How many years had they wasted apart and lonely?

'You see,' Valentina's mother continues, 'as soon as we saw each other again, at the airport, yesterday, well . . . it was like this rush of emotion . . . It was amazing.'

Phil is chuckling. 'We fell into each other's arms like two love-struck teenagers.'

'Oh, Valentina,' her mother sighs, 'we have had the most amazing night.'

Mattia holds up his hand, while Valentina groans.

'OK, that's enough information, thanks,' Mattia says.

'But I think it is so romantic,' gushes Antonella.

'It just goes to show,' Tina says, 'it's never too late for second chances.'

* * *

They are drinking their espresso when the waiter approaches their table with a large cream envelope in his hand. 'Is there a Miss Valentina Rosselli sitting here?' he asks.

'That's me,' she replies.

'This was just delivered for you,' he says, handing her the envelope.

She turns the cream envelope over in her hands, suddenly nervous. A tiny flare of hope has lit up in her heart.

'What does it say?' Antonella squeals. 'This is so intriguing!'

'Who's it from, Valentina?' her mother asks her.

There is nothing on the outside of the envelope. Valentina rips it open, and reads aloud: 'Hotel Bar, The Sherry-Netherland. Tonight, 21 hrs.'

That is all, but it is enough, for he is not giving up. She knows it must be Theo. He is not letting her go, not yet. He is reminding her of the games they used to play, the secret trysts they would have in anonymous hotels. This message is so much more than the name of a hotel and a time. It is a question: *Do you love me enough to forgive me?*

'But does it say who it's from?' Antonella is asking her.

'It's from Theo,' she says, quietly.

Marco and Jake exchange worried looks, while her mother is frowning as if deep in thought.

'What? The arrogant bastard!' Antonella declares, looking outraged. 'How dare he proposition you after what he has put you through—'

'Valentina?' Debbie, her demure sister-in-law, interrupts, but, without meaning to, Valentina talks over her.

'How did he know to deliver the letter here?' she asks the group.

'I'm afraid that was me,' Mattia speaks up. 'He called me up, begged me to help him . . . Did I do the wrong thing?' he asks her.

'No, you didn't.' Valentina chews her lip, thinking. What should she do? Should she go to that hotel? Can she trust Theo again?

'Valentina, you know it's—' Debbie starts to say again.

'Don't go, Valentina!' Antonella exclaims, drowning out poor Debbie.

'I know you are angry with him because you love me, but please, Antonella, Theo is not the man you think he is.' Valentina hears herself defending him.

Her friend shakes her head. Mikhail puts his hand on Antonella's arm, saying something in Russian to her. She shrugs, still looking cross, but says no more.

'Is Theo the boyfriend everyone thought was dead?' Phil asks Tina.

Her mother looks at her, and something quite miraculous happens. It is as if time slows down, as if every tiny part of that look from her mother is absorbed into her heart. For the first time since she was a little girl, she feels her mother's love. It breathes life force into her and it gives her courage, for she knows that, no matter what, she is safe.

'Theo is the love of Valentina's life,' Tina says, turning to look at Phil and putting her hand on his. 'Just as you are mine.'

'Valentina!' Debbie exclaims, so that finally she has everyone's attention.

'What is it, Debbie?' Valentina says, slightly irritated by her sister-in-law breaking the moment.

'You have to go, girl!' she says. 'It's almost nine now!'

To her surprise, it is her sister-in-law, the prim and proper Debbie, who shoos her out of the restaurant and into a cab.

* * *

As the taxi weaves through the dense Saturday-night traffic, Valentina glances at her watch. It is already ten minutes past nine. What if he doesn't wait for her?

The Sherry-Netherland hotel is right opposite the main entrance to Central Park on Fifth Avenue. Valentina rushes into the hotel lobby and, as soon as she sees the interior of the hotel, she can't help feeling touched. This is exactly the kind of place Theo would know she loves: vintage and very Italian in style, with its marble floors and chandelier. She looks around for the hotel bar. When she discovers it is called Harry Cipriani Bar and is a duplicate of Harry's Bar in Venice, she thinks, *Of course*. If Theo could meet her in Venice, he would, and this place is the next best thing in New York. She walks into the bar, but she can't see him anywhere. She goes up to the bar, a little self-conscious, as the place is so empty.

'Good evening, madam,' the bartender says. 'Can I give you one of our signature Bellinis?'

'Yes, thank you.'

Where is Theo? Why is he leaving her to wait now? Yet she knows that this anticipation is part of the game between them. He knows that it turns her on.

The barman hands her the cocktail.

'Would you, by any chance, be Miss Rosselli?' he asks her.

'Yes, that's me.'

He hands her another envelope addressed to her. She opens it up. Inside is a small piece of card with a room number written on it. That is all. She knocks back her Bellini and gets up. She can't waste one more minute without Theo. She walks back into the lobby, feeling dizzy. It feels like she is in a dream. She pinches herself. Is it really true? Does Theo still love her? Is he waiting for her in a room in this hotel?

* * *

She stands outside the door to the room, swallowing back her nerves, pulling on the belt of her jacket. This is it, then. She is here. It is the moment she is going to find out if her and Theo's love has survived through the pain, the hurt, the betrayal of the last year.

He opens the door, dressed in a black shirt, open at the neck, and a pair of suit trousers, with bare feet. His eyes are sizzling, burning ice blue, and his dark hair falls in thick curls around his face. She wants to leap into his arms, cover him in kisses, but she holds back. He says nothing, just pulls her in by the hand.

The room is lit by one lamp, and the curtains are drawn. There is a huge double bed in the centre of the room, its covers pulled back. She stares at it, rather than at him. She doesn't know what to say, how to say it. But it seems she doesn't need to say anything. Without saying a word, expressing any message through his eyes, Theo begins to kiss her neck and shoulders.

'Theo, what . . . ?' she starts to ask, but he silences her question with a kiss, while at the same time he reaches for the belt of her summer jacket, unbuckling it so that it falls open to reveal her in her slinky silk dress. He gives a low moan and his eyes become slits of desire as he puts his hands inside her dress to caress her breasts. He is still kissing her. She feels as if he is drinking her in. It is so different from being with any other man. All she wants is for him to be inside her, and more. She recognises that all those Tantra sessions with Leonardo have changed her sexual language. She wants Theo to penetrate her deeply, like Leonardo described to her.

Theo pulls her jacket from her shoulders and it slides to the ground. Next, he drops the straps of her dress off her shoulders; it slips down her body and she steps out of it. He prowls around

EVIE BLAKE

her, appreciating her. Her nipples push against her lacy bra, and she feels heat snaking up her, making her pussy soften and yearn for him. He snaps the bra open and catches her breasts in his hands as they tumble out. Next, he pulls her up close to his body. He is still dressed, and the texture of his silken shirt and soft woollen trousers against her bare skin turns her on further. He kisses her deeply, pushing his fingers underneath her G-string, and delicately touches her. He moans as he feels how soft and open she is for him. He makes a sudden, powerful movement, ripping the G-string from her. Now she is just in her suspenders, stockings and heels.

He pulls back and leads her to the bed, sitting her down upon it. Then he kneels before her and unclips one stocking at a time, slowly unrolling them, while at the same time decorating her legs with fluttering kisses. He picks up her right foot, brings her toes to his mouth and sucks each one. He does the same with her left foot. Then he places them both back down on the carpet. He leans over and unclips the suspender belt, kissing her warm belly before drawing back. She is sitting naked before him, as he stands in front of her.

Their eyes lock and she feels seared with the passion that speaks from his eyes. He starts to unbutton his shirt, slowly, methodically, and then dramatically pulls it out of the waistband of his trousers and flings it off. Next, he unbuttons the trousers and lets them drop. He is wearing no underwear. His cock is erect. God, her beautiful cock, *her* cock – she wants to shower it with kisses. But, when she leans forward to touch him, he gently pushes her back, shaking his head. Instead, he touches himself, holding his cock in his hand as if to show her the weight of it, and bringing his hand up and down its shaft. She wants so much to stroke Theo's cock, but every time she reaches forward to

368

touch him, he gently pushes her back on to the bed, so that now she is lying down.

He climbs on to the bed and, kneeling at right angles to her, begins to kiss her all over. From her mouth, down to her chin, her neck, and all over her breasts. Down her chest and to her stomach. On to her pelvis and then further still. She feels his tongue upon her clitoris, running back and forth; she can feel her whole being gathering, and yet she doesn't want to climax, not yet. She wants this night to last and last.

She reaches down and lifts his shoulders, forces him to sit up, and then she pulls him down next to her on his side. She lifts her leg over his and she pushes her pelvis in towards Theo, so that they become a scissors. She feels the silky tip of his cock drawn towards her pussy. Looking into his eyes and breathing deeply, she imagines her whole being opening up to her true love. He pushes into her, not thrusting, but snaking, as if drawn by a magnet to be inside her. She holds him there for a moment, feeling him grow, throb within her, as she feels herself softening and opening up to him further. Theo begins to move from side to side, not back and forth, but rather a rocking, sideways. Deeper he goes within her. She is locked in perfect harmony with Theo. She feels golden, relaxed waves of orgasm spreading through her, growing in intensity. Instinctively, the two of them begin to rotate around the central fusion of Theo's cock, deep inside her pussy.

Without him pulling out, she lifts her leg and twists around so that now she is facing away from him. He is behind her, snaking even deeper within her. She lies on her belly as he tips so deeply inside her, his weight upon her back, so that she feels she is entering a new world, a place of deep, rapturous bliss. All that she learnt from Leonardo is coming together and now she understands why, every time she made love with her friend, she felt that something was missing. It was because he was not the right man for her. With Theo, she is a perfect fit. He is the one for her.

Valentina lifts her body up on to all fours while Theo begins to lean back on to his heels, pulling her with him so that they are both kneeling on the bed, with her sitting on Theo's thighs. Valentina begins to slide herself up and down his shaft, while Theo holds her by the hips, lifting her, directing her movements. He licks her spine, her neck, strokes her whole body as they ride higher and higher together. Their breath is as one – deep, universal – and together they cry out as they orgasm at exactly the same time.

They lie in each other's arms, their naked bodies entwined around each other. Valentina feels Theo's heartbeat against her chest.

His heart beats. He is alive.

She feels a thrill of joy, despite all the complications, the deceptions; at the end of the day, her one true love is resurrected. Not many widows are so lucky. She vows she will treasure what they have found. Never again will she lose Theo.

'You're alive,' she whispers, holding him by the shoulders and looking into the deep blue lake of his eyes.

'I'm alive.' He smiles gently. 'And you came?'

She nods. 'Yes.'

She says no more, for there is almost far too much to talk about. Life is more complicated now. Theo is going to have to explain to his parents, everyone he knows, that he has risen from the dead. He is going to have to avoid being arrested for the theft of the Klimt painting at the Neue Gallerie, and somehow find a way to return it. There are so many things that could go wrong in their lives now, and yet she is still jubilant, for Theo is back with her and for good.

I want you inside me for ever, she thinks. I want us joined in body, mind and heart, for lifetime after lifetime.

'Do you forgive me?' Theo asks her, suddenly noticing his engagement ring upon her finger and bringing her hand up to his lips. He kisses the ring, his mouth plush upon her skin.

'Yes,' she says, looking deep into his eyes. 'Because, Theo, I love you. I have never stopped loving you.'

He looks at her in adoration.

'I need to take you, right now,' he whispers.

He rolls her on the bed, and she laughs in delight at his sudden assertion. He wraps her up his arms, laughing alongside her. His desire for her is a balm to her wounded heart. He lies upon her, cradling her face in his hands, looking serious again.

'I love you with all my heart, Valentina,' he says, as he enters her. Tears begin to load her eyes. He sees them and recognises how rare and precious they are, like fragments of their love, lost and refound. They move as one body, him within her, her within him, passionate, and absorbed within the present moment, floating together upon an iridescent sea of ecstasy. Together Valentina and Theo unlock the door upon a whole new world of loving.

The End

Author's Note

Although the theme of this book is about love in all its many aspects, I feel that, since Tina's story is partly set in Berlin, I would like to mention how very moved I was by the stories of all those who attempted to cross the Berlin Wall during the time of its existence. One thousand and sixty-five people died either trying to get over the Berlin Wall, at a border crossing in East Germany, or in prison after attempting to escape. Their crime: to want to choose how and where they lived their lives. Men, women and children, shot down or left to drown in the River Spree, treated with no humanity or compassion.

I would like to dedicate *Surrender Yourself* to every one of those lost people.

${\mathcal A}$ppendix I

The Valentina Cocktail

The Valentina Cocktail was invented by Andy Seach, who runs the bespoke cocktail company, Barfly UK (barflyuk.com).

The cocktail evokes the spirit of Valentina and is a powerful combination of sensations. Please drink with care. It is very strong!

Recipe

Crush ice and put in a cocktail shaker.

Pour in 35 ml gin, 15 ml limoncello and 15 ml Chambard (black raspberry liqueur) and shake.

If you want to make it slightly less alcoholic, you can replace Chambard with raspberry cordial.

$\mathscr{A}$ppendix II

Leonardo's Tantric Sex Keys

Leonardo teaches Valentina the art of Tantric sex. Here are his practical Tantric tips to make your lovemaking more intense and ecstatic!

1. Look into your lover's eyes.
2. Breathe slowly and deeply while making love.
3. Share what you feel in your body and heart, as you experience it.
4. Relax from inside to out: rather than 'doing' sex, try 'being' sex.
5. Touching, stroking and caressing are very important parts of making love. A woman's breasts are her most powerful erogenous zone.
6. Reduce the amount of tension in lovemaking. Stop worrying about achieving orgasm and try to stay in the moment with your lover.
7. Soft penetration is an easy and potent way to start lovemaking.
8. A woman's most ecstatic sexual energies are in the upper part of her vagina. Sustained deep penetration is a way of

awakening this within the woman. The penis can become a powerful magnet if the woman relaxes and receives him.

9. When making love, try to withdraw as little as possible, let the penis and vagina create one unit and rotate around it. Shifting positions while making love creates a rapturous dance of love.

If you would like to learn more about Tantric sex, I would recommend the book *The Heart of Tantric Sex* by Diana Richardson.

$\mathcal{A}$ppendix III

How to give a Yoni Massage

In *Surrender Yourself*, Leonardo gives Valentina a yoni massage. Not only is this highly erotic, but it is also a very healing experience for woman, especially those who have suffered any form of sexual abuse and find it hard to relax when making love.

In this instance, Valentina has multiple orgasms, but it is not necessarily part of a yoni massage to climax. It is more about deep sexual relaxation and healing of the vagina. There are reputable Tantric masseurs in most major cities who will offer yoni massages with either female or male therapists.

This is how Leonardo gave Valentina her yoni massage:

Begin by giving a full body massage with warm scented oils. The yoni massage can last up to two and a half hours and it is best if the experience is slowly built up for the woman who is being massaged, so that she receives the full benefits and completely relaxes. Thus, massage the woman while she is lying on her back, initially focusing on her breasts. As she turns over on to her front, massage her back, buttocks and legs, pressing your own naked body upon hers. This is an extremely sensual experience for both massaged and masseur.

When she is ready, lift her left leg, turn it out and rest it on your lap, 'opening' her up. Fill your hands with warm scented oils and bathe her pelvis with the oil, pouring it on to her vagina.

Gently massage the mound and outer lips of her yoni. Don't rush. Gently squeeze the outer lips, and then slide up and down the entire length of each lip. Repeat the process with the inner lips of her yoni. Slip, slide, up and down, again and again.

Gently stroking the clitoris in clockwise and counter-clockwise circles, squeeze it, just like with the vagina. Keep pouring more oil on to her all the time. Ever so carefully, and gently, insert your finger into her yoni. Imagine you are massaging each cell of her internally.

There should be no feeling of an end to this massage, no outcome or climax. Take your time, feeling her up and down, sideways, varying depth, speed and pressure. Work your way inside her until you are massaging her G-spot on the vaginal wall. Move side to side, back and forth and, at the same time, circle her clitoris again.

At this point, she may well orgasm, but do not stop! Tell her to keep breathing as you continue to massage her G-spot and clitoris at the same time. She may well orgasm again, but still don't stop! Let her ride the wave, climaxing again and again; each time will be more intense than the time before.

Gradually, gently remove your finger from inside her, stroking her all the time on her thighs and her belly. Give her time to come back into the room. Embrace!

$\mathscr{A}$ppendix IV

How to give a Lingam Massage

In *Surrender Yourself*, Leonardo teaches Valentina how to give him a lingam massage. Blow your lover's mind by treating him to this experience. Moreover, it is extremely sensual and erotic to give the massage as much as to receive it.

It is very important to give this massage naked, as it becomes an even more erotic experience for both of you – the masseuse and your lover.

First of all, sit opposite each other, naked on the bed. Put his hand on his heart, and hold your hand over it. Let him do the same to you. Look into his eyes and breathe together from the belly.

Now get your man to lie on his front and warm some fragrant oils. Pour oils on to his back and begin to massage his shoulders. Swirl your hands on his back in broad, swift movements. Pour more oil on to his legs and work all the way down to his feet, then up again to his buttocks. Lie down on top of his back, pressing your naked body into his. He will love feeling the softness of your breasts against his strong back. Peel yourself away and ask him to turn over.

Fill your palms with more fragrant oil, spreading it on his torso, and advance the massage slowly, from his chest down towards his inner thighs and pelvis, until you can see his body is fully relaxed.

Pour a small quantity of oil on to his cock and balls. Rub the oil into his skin, from the top of his thighs up to his pelvis, using slow, steady motions. Begin to massage just above his cock, rocking your hand on the pubic bone, and then moving down to his balls, very gently pulling and kneading them. The balls for some men can be a very sensitive area, so make sure that you are not too rough and check with your lover how much pressure he likes.

Trace your hands down to massage just behind his balls. Put your whole body into the movements that your hands make, using strong downward strokes, all the way from his cock to his butt, and then alternating these with circling in between, delicately pressing the G-spot in his butt with one of your fingers.

Now place your hand on his cock; hold it lovingly. Begin to massage the shaft, gently squeezing the base of the cock with your right hand, and then pulling up and sliding this hand completely off the head of the cock. Pour more oil on to your hands and then do the same thing with your left hand, squeezing your lover's cock at the base, pulling your hand up and then sliding it completely off. Do it again with your right hand, and then with your left again – right and left, right and left. Now change direction, sliding alternating hands from the top of his cock down to its base. After a few minutes, take his cock between both hands and rub your hands quickly back and forth, as if you are starting a fire (and you probably are!).

Take his cock by the head and gently shake it back and forth, before cupping the head in your palm and twisting your hand, as if you are squeezing a lemon. At this stage it is likely that your lover is close to orgasming, but for his experience to be ultimately more intense, pull back and slow down a little; tell him to breathe deeply.

Repeat the massaging of his cock again until he ultimately climaxes. Or perhaps he will want to make love to you . . .

Have you been seduced by Theo and Valentina?
Go back to the beginning of their love story
with this extract from

Liberate Yourself

the first book in the addictive trilogy.

$\mathcal{V}$alentina

VALENTINA PUSHES HERSELF UP ON TO HER ELBOWS AND GAZES AT her lover. Six months they have been living together. She leans over and carefully arranges her arm across Theo's back. She loves to do this while he is sleeping, when he doesn't know how she likes to imagine the two of them together, and all that could be possible. Tenderly she strokes his flawless skin, letting herself express a rare moment of affection. It is a gesture she is careful never to make when Theo is actually awake.

Valentina examines her flaxen whiteness against the sallow colouring of Theo Steen, and considers what a perfect contrast the two of them are. She is as pale and fine boned as her beloved twenties icon Louise Brooks. He is dark skinned, more sultry than any Latin lover she has ever known, yet with disturbingly bright blue eyes. It would make more sense if it were she who was dark. She is after all the Italian, while Theo is from New York, his parents Dutch immigrants. She doesn't know much about his background, but it appears very different from hers. He is close to his parents, both of them, and to Valentina's eyes his childhood was charmed. So much attention and expense lavished upon him. Theo is an accomplished cellist, equestrian and fencer, as well as speaking a myriad of languages. He could have gone into any profession he chose. He is one of those men she thought would irritate her. A privileged high-achiever who doesn't need to worry about making a living, and can indulge full-time in his passion – the study and analysis of modern art. Yet she did not dump him at the first opportunity, as she thought she might; instead here he is in her bed, lost in the innocence of sleep right beside her. He is *living* with her.

Valentina looks down at her sleeping lover. Theo is lying on his stomach, his head turned away from her. She wonders where his dreams take him. She wonders if he will wake with the memory of her touch upon his skin. Last night she wanted to make him come so much, and yet strangely she had no desire to have an orgasm herself. This is not usual for her, not very Valentina, she thinks. Even now she is not demanding morning sex. At some point does the passion fade? If you took away the sexual desire between her and Theo, would there be nothing left? Strangers before their union; and strangers again afterwards. Is it time to end it? *No, not yet*, a voice begs inside her head, and she tries to swallow her anxiety. She is panicking unnecessarily. This is just all so new to her, to be cohabiting.

She has never shared her apartment with anyone else, not since her mother left. It still startles her how easily it all fell into place, the fact of Theo moving in. She knows why she asked him. It was a knee-jerk reaction to her mother's warning. Is he using her? Instinctively she rejects the suggestion. He was so hesitant about accepting her offer. Asked her several times if she was sure. There *is* something different about him. Already he has seen her at her lowest, and he didn't leave.

Valentina knots the end of the sheet around her finger, pulls it tight. A ring of white cotton pinching her flesh, making her bite her lip. It's because he doesn't take anything for granted, she thinks; despite his easy life, he never stops trying to please her.

She lies back down on the bed and smiles up at the ceiling, studying each glinting crystal of the chandelier as she dwells on last night. She tentatively runs her tongue over her lips. She can still taste him. She savours the saltiness of her lover as she recalls how she caressed him with her mouth, pushing him as far as he could go, not stopping despite his plea to be inside her. She would not allow it. She wanted everything to be focused on him. And so she kept on going: licking, teasing with her teeth, flicking her tongue around his length and squeezing his velvet hardness tight between her lips. She needed to feel his abandon inside her mouth. His vulnerability, and her power. She had taken him over the edge. And when Theo cried out her name, it was like a flare to her heart. Burning her and yet warming her at the same time, filling her with the dual sensations of fear and satisfaction. How could that be? Normally she doesn't like her lovers to speak, let alone cry out. She always insists on making love in silence. She hates false proclamations of love, uttered in the heat of passion. Yet Theo called to her, and deep down inside her there was an answering echo, despite her conscious denial. Now the salty flavour of him lingers still upon her lips. No wonder she dreamt of the sea. She closes her eyes and pushes away unwanted images, her smile fading. But they resurface, these disjointed sensations from her dream. Sinking under water, unable to swim up to the light; darkness, suffocation.

'Hey, what's wrong?'

She opens her eyes. Theo is lying on his side, his head resting on his hand, his clear blue eyes studying her.

'I had a bad dream last night.'

He pulls her towards him, and she lets him fold his arms around her. She closes her eyes and feels his chin as he rests it on the top of her head.

389

'Do you want to tell me about it?' he asks, his voice muffled against her hair, but she doesn't reply, not immediately, and he doesn't push her. It feels so good to be held in her lover's arms; she doesn't want to take them back to her nightmares, ruin a fresh new day with her baggage.

'No,' she says.

'Okay, darling.' He kisses the top of her head. The endearment trips off his lips so easily. Can he really mean it? She finds it hard to do the same, the words sticking in her throat. *Darling*. She stiffens in his arms, wanting now to push away from him. Theo gently unravels his body from around her, as if sensing her need for distance.

'I'll make some tea,' he says, getting out of bed, studiously avoiding eye contact. She watches him in all his glorious nakedness as he strides across the room. He wraps her silk dressing gown around himself, but it only adds to his manliness, emphasising the masculine contours of his body. She feels a stirring below her navel, deeper, deeper, as she watches him walk out the door. Why did she chill in his arms? Now she would like to make love.

She glances at the clock. It's already after seven. She should be getting up; she has a busy day ahead, yet still she cannot stir from the sanctuary of their bed. She yawns and stretches, awaiting Theo's return with the tea. She is glad she didn't blot this morning with her narcissist fears.

Valentina isn't fond of the past. She has never understood the obsession amongst her contemporaries with relationship transparency, the need to dredge up your personal history and expect your lover to share it. It bemuses her how so many young women want to manipulate their boyfriends through pity. The last thing she wants is to be a victim. No, it is better to never look back, always maintain a little mystery. She believes you should keep your secrets to yourself. That has always been her motto. And yet . . .

She can't get Gina Faladi's words out of her head. Said in all innocence, of course. Gina is a sweet person, if a bit too submissive in Valentina's opinion. She has seen the way she lets her boyfriend, Gregorio, boss her around. God knows what he is like under the covers. Yet despite this, Gina is one of the best make-up artists Valentina has ever worked with. Last week they flew to Prague together to do a fashion shoot for *Marie Claire*. It was on the way home, after a couple of glasses of wine on board the flight, that Gina asked her the question that now keeps circling inside her head like a big black cat.

Where does he go?

That was what Gina said. Valentina was about to reply that she had no idea, and so what, she and Theo didn't do jealousy, but when she saw Gina's eyebrows beginning to arch, she changed her mind.

Work. She took a sip of her red wine. *Going to exhibitions. Meeting artists. Buying art*, she expanded vaguely. A good excuse, and who knows, possibly true. But the fact of the matter is that Valentina has absolutely no idea where her lover disappears to once a month and for several days at a time. Yes, there have been articles and reviews, and before he met her, two books had been published, one on German expressionism and one on futurism in Italy in the twenties, but there is not nearly the volume of work one would expect from such a globetrotting art critic. And what is he doing in Milan? His part-time lecturing at the university hardly provides a good income. Surely he could get a better position in a university back in America? Yet when she asked Theo why he was in Italy, he avoided answering her, waving his arms around like a true Italian and stating vaguely that it was where he needed to be right now. Every day she expects him to tell her he is going home. And yet here he is, still based in Milan nearly a year after she met him.

In the beginning, Valentina didn't care where Theo went. In fact during the first couple of months of living together she looked forward to his little disappearances. She couldn't help doubting her rash offer, and blamed her mother's words for pushing her into making it.

'Don't let him possess you; that's what they all want to do. And for God's sake don't move in together.'

As usual her mother had taken the wind out of her sails. What had induced Valentina to call her anyway? She had been on some kind of a high, after the first few exciting weeks with Theo, and she had had this foolish urge to share it with her mother. She had even sat up half the night to wait for a good time to call her in the States. Yet of course she should have known better. Instead of being happy for her, all her mother could see were the negatives.

'Valentina,' she warned, 'you and I, we're not able to give ourselves up totally to just one man. We need space. I learnt that the hard way, honey. Don't rush into anything.'

Her advice made Valentina furious. She was *not* like her mother, who was vain and self-centred, an attention-seeker and unable to share, even with her own children. She had to prove her wrong. So that very evening, much to Theo's astonishment, she invited him to move in with her. Why not? His landlord had just given him notice, and he needed to find a place to live anyway. Her apartment was huge and cost her nothing, since it belonged to her mother. They were to be flatmates, she told him, who happened to have sex together. The incongruity of her proposition made him laugh and call her a crazy woman. Even so, he accepted.

Yet if she is honest with herself, Valentina has to admit that she is afraid her mother could be right. She finds it hard getting used to compromising. She and Theo rarely argue, and they have similar tastes in music, food and art, yet it is the little things that get to her. She likes the bedroom door open at night, and a light on in the hall, whereas Theo prefers complete darkness and a closed door. She likes silence when she works, and he plays music. Usually it is something they both like, but occasionally he puts on music from the eighties that her mother loved – Joy Division, The Cure – way too loud so that she can hear it even when she is in her studio or in her darkroom developing pictures. It always makes her grit her teeth. And sometimes he talks too much. He is careful not to talk about himself, or push for too many questions about her mother (something other lovers all end up doing, which puts her off them instantly), but he is obsessed with discussions. It could of course be on art, or a film they might have just seen, and that is fine. But Theo also loves to get stuck into talking about current affairs, economics or history. He is constantly quizzing her on Italian politics. What do people think of Mussolini now? What happened to her family during the Second World War? Valentina has no interest. She had a stomach full of politics when she was a child. Her mother's bedtime stories of what had happened to her father's family during the war were enough to put her off for life, as well as her mother arguing over the rights and wrongs of communism with her brother Mattia, on the rare occasions she saw him. Somehow she equates the clash of her parents' ideologies with the reason why her own father left all those years ago. Valentina doesn't like idealists. Those who neglect their own families for the sake of the common good. Theo seems more pragmatic; how can he not be with his upbringing? And yet when he starts talking about the world and hope for change, it makes her edgy. Does he notice the tightness around her mouth as she sets it in an uncommunicative line, the clench of her jaw as he pushes her to give an opinion? It is no coincidence that usually the very next day Theo will announce that he is heading off on a work trip, as if he knows she needs to be on her own.

Valentina has always been used to solitude. She grew up as if she was an only child, since Mattia was thirteen and away at school by the time she was born. Her father left before she was old enough to remember him. Even Mattia claims he doesn't know where he is. So it was just her and her mother, who taught her from an early age to be self-sufficient. When she was very young, Valentina's mother took her with her on her photographic assignments, and the long hours spent waiting turned her into an avid reader.

Once Valentina was thirteen, her mother left her behind in Milan, claiming she didn't want to disrupt her education, but Valentina suspected that it was because she didn't want her teenage daughter cramping her style. All the men loved Tina Rosselli. She was an icon in her world of glamour and style. To her credit, she never hid her age, but to be accompanied by a glaringly younger version of herself was a little too much for her vanity to bear. Thus Valentina would spend whole weeks at a time on her own in the apartment, her only company her mother's sulky cat, Tash. She remembered bringing Gaby back with her one Friday after school, and her friend's complete astonishment when she realised that Valentina had been alone all week. It was a fact she was careful not to broadcast when she was in school.

'But who looks after you?' Gaby asked her, wide eyed with pity.

'I don't need anyone to look after me,' Valentina replied haughtily.

'Do you do everything yourself?' Gaby asked her. 'Your clothes?'

Valentina couldn't help but notice her friend looking down at her crumpled school skirt and blouse. The nuns were always telling her off for her messy uniform, a criticism she was careful never to relay to her mother, who was fiercely proud of her appearance and always left Valentina strict instructions to be neatly turned out.

'I don't care about how I look,' she said nonchalantly. 'It's only school.'

Gaby gingerly hung her satchel on the back of a kitchen chair. The table was littered with unwashed cups and a couple of sticky plates.

'So do you cook for yourself?' she asked Valentina.

'Sort of.' Valentina sashayed over to the fridge, feeling very grown-up. 'Are you hungry?'

'Always!' Gaby grinned at her. 'Hey, let's eat everything we're not supposed to. I'll go to the bakery while you cook.'

Valentina limply hung over the fridge door, and stared inside. There was a jar of pesto, a block of Parmesan and a container of rigatoni. That was it. Gaby joined her by the fridge. She put her arm around her friend's waist when she saw its paltry contents.

'Is that it?' she whispered in horror.

Valentina couldn't reply. She was seeing the inside of her fridge with her friend's eyes. She felt so ashamed of her mother.

'Mama's not that into food . . .'

Gaby squeezed her waist.

'I can cook something nice for you. My mother taught me how.'

Valentina bit her lip. She loved Gaby, but sometimes she couldn't help feeling a little jealous. Gaby's mother was one of those traditional Italian mamas. Plump, doting, always feeding you. It was why, Gaby complained, she was twice the size of Valentina. Yet Valentina admired Gaby's budding curves. She herself was still tall and narrow, with no shape at all. Her mother had never taught her to cook.

'Okay, I'll go to the bakery and buy us some little cakes,' Valentina offered.

'Get a selection, four different ones each!' Gaby called as Valentina went out the door.

Not only did Gaby cook for her, a sumptuous meal of pesto and rigatoni, with a rich tomato sauce (where did she find the ingredients in the chaos of the kitchen cupboards?), but by the time Valentina returned with the cakes, she had also swept the floor, washed the dishes and wiped the kitchen table. Her friend's desire to care for her filled Valentina with awe, for she knew she would not think of doing the same for her.

'Aren't you lonely?' Gaby asked her as she polished off the tomato sauce, licking the spoon hungrily.

'Never,' Valentina said, sitting back and feeling the rare satisfaction of a full belly. 'I like being on my own. Although I wouldn't mind having you as my cook.'

This love of being in her own company has never gone away. So until Gina's fateful words, Valentina had actually looked forward to Theo's short absences. Only two, at the most three, days away. Long enough to relish her solitude and to miss him, but not too long to worry about where he is or what he is doing. The fact that he has never offered an explanation demonstrates that he believes they are above the possessiveness others can get bogged down by. They really are flatmates first, lovers second. He never asks her what she has been up to.

Valentina gets out of bed and draws back the curtains, opening the French window slightly. She is cooled by the autumnal breeze, yet even though her skin is prickling from the chill, she likes to remain naked. She closes her eyes and the wind feels like a hand stroking her, all the way from her forehead, down her cheeks and neck to her throat and chest. She feels her nipples harden as the temperature drops inside the room, and wind licks between her legs. She can hear the constant stream of traffic through Milan, the heartbeat of the city, and yet she catches what peace there is as well. She visualises random images of tranquillity: a pigeon taking flight in the cloisters of Sant'Ambrogio, a boat drifting down the Naviglio canal, an empty swing in Parco Sempione rocking in the breeze. She smells the dying leaves, imagines them spinning off the trees on Via De Amicis. She likes this time of year in Milan. The city has finally cooled after the heavy, humid summer. August can be a nightmare, forty degrees and yet skies as grey as lead. Everyone tries to get away. This year she and Theo escaped to Sardinia for three weeks. Just as hot, yet the sea breezes lifted the oppressiveness of it.

She opens her eyes and feels such a longing to be back in Sardinia, outside in nature, naked on the warm sand, smelling the salty tang of the sea washing over her. As she walks across the bedroom, she imagines wading through the balmy sea. She feels the weight of her nakedness and catches a glimpse of her bottom as she passes the mirror. Men have always admired her behind. She has to admit she is rather proud of it. After being such a skinny teenager, she was pleased when her curves finally developed. She hates to see other women ashamed of their bodies. Struggling into swimming costumes behind towels at the beach; self-conscious and eyes averted when trying on clothes in changing rooms. Can they not see how beautiful they are, in all their diversity, within their curved contours: the creamy velvet of their skin, breasts of all shapes and sizes, soft stomachs, broad hips, voluptuous thighs? The only other women she knows who are as open as she is about nudity are the models she photographs. Those stick-thin girls are past any kind of self-consciousness. Sometimes when she sees models who are obviously anorexic it makes her tense, almost angry. She is, as all her friends will tell you, one of the most non-judgemental people you will ever meet. Yet anorexia brings back ghosts for Valentina. Images of her mother she would like to forget.

By the time Theo returns to the bedroom with a tray laden with teapot, cups and saucers, Valentina is back in bed, sitting up expectantly, a pillow stuffed behind her back against the iron bedstead. This is one of the advantages of living with someone. Just by making her a pot of tea, Theo makes her feel cherished.

Her lover carefully places the tray in the middle of the bed, and climbs back into bed beside her.

'Will you be mother?' he asks her.

The English phrase amuses her. The last thing she could imagine her mother ever doing is pouring tea out of a teapot like a duchess.

'Of course,' she says, looking at Theo from under her lashes. 'As you know, I like to be in charge sometimes.'

He grins back at her as she picks up the teapot and begins to pour tea into his cup. As she does so, Theo leans forward and cups her breasts, one in each of his hands.

'Don't want my property getting splashed by hot tea,' he explains, winking at her.

She swats him off nonchalantly, yet a part of her likes this. She leans back against the pillow, nursing her hot tea between her hands, and wonders if they are the image of an old married couple, sitting side by side in bed drinking Earl Grey tea for breakfast. Well at least we're naked, she thinks comfortingly.

'Are you okay now?' Theo asks her.

She nods, sipping the tea. The warm liquid comforts her, and yes, she can honestly say that her night-time fears are banished for today. Theo puts his cup of tea down on the bedside table, leans over towards her and kisses her on the neck, just under her ear. It tickles, but also sets her heart racing a little.

'I have something to ask you,' he whispers, his breath lifting her hair.

Involuntarily she stiffens with unease. No, not now; she doesn't want to talk about it this morning.

'I have to get up. I want to develop some pictures before I go on the shoot,' she says, placing her cup back down on the tray.

'It's just a little question, Valentina, don't worry.' She looks at him, and he is smiling at her, his eyes brimming with bemusement. Is he mocking her?

'Well, go on then,' she commands.

'My parents are coming to Europe,' Theo says. 'They are going to Amsterdam first to visit my grandparents but then they thought they would come and see me, us, here in Milan.'

'They know about *me*?'

'Of course they know about you!' he laughs. 'We've been living together for six months, Valentina. They are dying to meet you.'

She looks at him in horror. He is completely relaxed, as if this is something of small consequence. The fact that his parents are coming to Milan. That he wants her to meet them. Her mouth dries up for a minute and she is unable to speak.

'They're not coming until the end of November,' he continues. 'I know it's ages away, but I wanted to give you fair warning.' He hesitates, beginning to notice the expression on her face. 'I know you're not keen on family stuff.'

She shakes her head vehemently.

'No, Theo, I'm sorry. I can't meet your parents.'

'What?' He looks astounded. His mouth drops open in shock.

'I told you this before. This is how I am,' she says stiffly, pulling back the covers, straining to get out of bed. Theo catches her arm, restraining her.

'Valentina,' he says softly. 'Really, it's nothing to be worried about. They are nice people. I've told them so much about you. They just want to meet you.'

She whips her head around.

'You told them all about me!' she spits.

'Of course I did. You're my girlfriend.' Theo looks wounded.

'That's the first I knew about it,' she says cruelly.

Theo's forehead creases in confusion.

'Well what are you then, if you're not my girlfriend? We're living together, Valentina. We've already been through—'

'Don't say it . . . I told you not to mention it again . . .'

'But Valentina . . .'

She holds her hand up, stops him before he starts to speak.

'I am your lover, Theo. And that role is something very different from a girlfriend. The term "girlfriend" implies that we have some kind of vested relationship, a possible future. "Lover" is a more transitory term. It is a temporary condition.'

'Christ, Valentina!' Theo exclaims. 'You are an infuriating woman.'

'Remember, Theo,' she says calmly, and it is a good feeling, this sensation of being in control, 'when you moved into this apartment, I told you it was convenient. It suited us both. But I also told you that it wasn't going to be for ever, remember?'

She listens to her voice. It is outside of herself, and she is unpleasantly reminded of her own mother speaking. *Don't let him possess you.*

'Valentina, I am not asking you to make any big commitment. It's just my parents. I'd like you to meet them, that's all.'

'I'm sorry, Theo,' she says, climbing out of bed and looking down at him. 'I don't want to. They can stay here, but I'll go away. You'll have the place to yourselves. It's much better that way.'

Theo looks her up and down in disbelief. Just his gaze causes her nipples to harden, and she can't help noticing his reaction to her naked body in return.

'It's not better that way,' he says softly, entreating her with his rich blue gaze. A part of her wants to give in, to fall back into the bed, sink into his arms and comply. Yet her terror dominates. She can't bear the thought of meeting Theo's parents. It brings her too close to him, too much into his world. And if that happens, how will she find her way out again when it ends, because surely one day they will tire of each other? Nothing lasts for ever. She sighs deeply and turns away from him, picks up her dressing gown from where he discarded it on the floor and puts it on, tying it tightly around her waist.

'I can't talk about this right now. I have to get ready. I've a lot to do today.' She wanders over to the dressing table and picks up her hairbrush, pulling it listlessly through her hair.

She watches Theo getting out of bed, defeat still clear in his features, and she feels guilty. It's time to change the subject.

'Do you want to go to Antonella's opening tonight?' she asks, trying to sound more upbeat. Theo pauses in the doorway of the bedroom, towel in hand.

'Sorry, I can't. I have to go away. I've another job.'

'Again?'

The word slips out. Deadly. Valentina wishes she could snatch it back. She turns away quickly, yet she can still see his face in the mirror. His expression is impassive now.

'Do you not want me to go away?' he asks.

She backtracks furiously.

'No, of course I don't mind. It's just a surprise. I didn't know you were going away *today* . . .' Her voice trails off and suddenly she feels foolish, exposed.

'Would you like me to cancel?' he asks, leaning against the doorway and looking at her with interest.

'No, of course not,' she snaps crossly. 'I was just wondering where you're going. It's not that big a deal.' She tries to sound indifferent, focuses on arranging her hair.

'Are you sure you don't want me to stay?' he asks. She can feel the heat of his gaze, although she still refuses to catch his eye.

'No, I told you, I don't care,' she says harshly. 'I was just curious, that's all.' She softens her voice.

Theo drops his towel and walks over to stand behind her. As he leans over her and strokes her hand, she can feel his erection pushing against her silk-clad back. She knows he is trying to entice her to turn around and touch him. Yet she resists.

'I always thought you weren't that interested in where I go or what I do,' he says quietly.

'You're right. I don't know why I asked you really. I like mysteries,' she explains, trying to keep her voice light. 'They keep things from getting boring.'

'I see.'

He spins her around on her stool and he is smiling at her as if he knows something she doesn't.

'What is it?' She pushes her finger into his belly, which is so firm it almost springs back. What art critic has a stomach like that?

'I have a present for you,' Theo says. 'I believe it will stop you from being bored while I am away.'

'Oh really?' she says huskily, reaching towards him now. Maybe she does have time to make love before she has to go to work. She is aching to feel him inside her. The morning's conversation has made her feel unsettled. She knows that if they make love it will calm her down. Yet just as she is about to touch him, Theo steps back and shakes his head, looking at her flirtatiously.

'Now, now, Valentina,' he says, walking across the room towards the wardrobe. 'Patience.'

He opens the wardrobe and takes out a large package, placing it on the dressing table in front of her.

'But why have you got me a present?' she asks, and their eyes lock in the mirror. He hesitates for a minute, holding her with his gaze that seems to say so much. Words she doesn't want to acknowledge. She casts her eyes down.

'Because I believe it's time for you to have this,' he tells her.

So it's not something she might want, or like; it's something she should have. Why is he being so obtuse? She leans over to unwrap the package, but Theo puts his hand over hers and pushes her fist into his palm. She looks back up at his reflection in the mirror. She feels as if time has stopped as she looks into

Theo's glacial blue eyes, the only northern part of him, and for once she is inquisitive for his secrets. She sees herself reflected: tiny and naked. A little butterfly of flesh imprinted upon his iris.

'Later,' he says, pulling her up from the dressing-table stool. 'Open it when I am gone.'

He kisses her, and she lets herself succumb to his touch. His hands work at the knot at her waist, and when he has undone it, he slips the dressing gown off her shoulders so it drops to the ground. His erect penis pushes against her pelvis and she is craving him, aching to feel him within her. She stands on tiptoes and wraps one leg around the back of his. He is almost breathless as he lifts her up and pushes into her.

'Valentina,' he gasps. 'Oh my Valentina . . .'

'Shush,' she says, putting her finger to his lips to silence him. He carries her over to the bed. She is twisted around him, feeling his length going deeper and deeper inside her. They fall together as one on to the covers, and she squeezes him tight, urging him to push faster, harder into her. He raises himself above her, taking both her hands in one of his, and lifting them above her head. She is lost in the power of his passion. He pulls back ever so slowly, and as he suddenly rams back into her, she can't help gasping slightly. She joins him in force, thrusting back with all her might, and they become one throbbing entity. She closes her eyes, relaxing at last. This is what she needs. Complete abandonment. She is all sensation, her body leading her, no thoughts involved. He touches her deep within, as only Theo can, and she begins to pulse around him. She has an image of ripples in water, ever increasing, ever decreasing, to the swirling whirlpool at its very centre. They climax together and she is dragged down, as if the bed itself is the bottom of the ocean drowning them. The water is black.

* * *

Afterwards, he cradles her in his arms. She knows she needs to get up, that she is going to be late for work, and yet she is paralysed, held tight within her lover's embrace.

'Valentina?' he whispers into her ear.

'Don't talk,' she entreats him. Don't ruin our peace. He ignores her.

'Valentina, please be my girlfriend.'

She doesn't reply.

'Valentina, I want us to be more than casual lovers. Flatmates.'

She turns to face him.

'No, Theo. I don't want that.'

'Are you sure?'

She nods, and he looks so sad she almost agrees to his request. But what's the point? She is not girlfriend material.

She tries to console him with her body. She places her hands on his chest, pushes her fingers through the twirls of hair and tugs them, before raising her fingers to her lips and licking them, pinching his nipples tight. All the while he stares at her, speechless, yet his body doesn't respond. Eventually he takes her hands in his, and lifts them up and away from his body.

'Why not?' he asks. 'I don't want to change who you are. I just want to be able to call you my girlfriend.'

'Theo . . . I can't . . . you know that . . . I told you before . . .'

Her inadequate words stumble over each other. She pulls her hands away from his grasp.

'Can you not just think about it? Please try, Valentina.'

She wants to scream at him that it is no good. She can't let herself fall in love with him. And yet she finds herself agreeing to think about it. Even though she knows it isn't fair, she lets him walk away hopeful.

405

* * *

It is too late now. He has gone. Where, she has no idea, apart from the fact that it will be cold, since he took his down jacket and snow boots. She is glad he didn't push her further. *Will you be my girlfriend?* No, she could never do it. Why can't he let things just stay as they are? Casual. Fun. Sexy. But living with someone is hardly casual, she suspects. Has she been a fool to let a man move in with her? And why does he need some sort of commitment from her? She doesn't want him to leave . . . and yet she can't give him what he wants. Maybe her mother is right after all, she thinks sourly. Maybe she and her mother are the same. Inconstant butterflies, flitting from one man to the next.

Valentina shakes the thought from her head, and picks up the package on the dressing table. It is surprisingly heavy and she places it back down again. It is a plain brown-paper parcel tied with string. No label on it. No card. She is full of anticipation. What could it be? She hopes it isn't a grand romantic gesture. My God, what if he is building up to a proposal? The idea horrifies Valentina. She has no intention of ever getting married.

She steps back and stares at it. She is not sure she is ready to face what lies inside that brown paper. She has a feeling it is something important. She walks into the bathroom and turns on the shower full blast. As the steaming water cascades over her shoulders, down her back, stomach and thighs, she opens her mouth and lets it run through her. She tries to wash away her anxiety, forget the look in Theo's eyes just before he left. Why is it that all her lovers want to cage her? She hoped Theo was different. She gives him so much space, and yet even he isn't satisfied. What annoys her most is how his excursions are beginning to bother her. Sometimes she finds herself waking up in the middle of the night when he is away and wondering if he is okay. She will be on the verge of sending a text when she manages to stop herself. Their rule is never to contact each other when either of them is abroad. She hates the pestering nature of texting. The last thing in the world she wants to be is needy.

She is pulling on her stockings when she can bear it no longer. She has to know. Wearing nothing but her G-string, suspender belt and one sheer stocking, she squeezes the package and tries to weigh it in her hands. It could be a picture, or a book. It's too big to be a ring, anyway, thank goodness. She unties the string, which is knotted tightly and takes ages. Typical Theo. Then she slowly rips off the paper until it is shredded at her feet.

She is holding a black book. On second thoughts, it is an album, but old, made from some kind of black velvet that is so worn it is no longer plush, but bare cloth. As she opens the book, she is hit by a strong scent of old roses, sweet and decaying. She looks at the open book and sits down on the bed in surprise. How strange. Her present is a riddle. Attached to the first page is a negative. She can tell immediately that it is old, because it is bigger than modern-day negatives. It also has a yellowish tinge. It is attached to the thick, card-like paper by a tiny sliver of tape that she can easily remove. She takes out the negative and holds it up to the light, but it is impossible to make out the image. She flicks the page and finds another negative. She turns the next page, and the next. All of them contain negatives. Nothing else. No words. No pictures. No explanation. She feels inexplicably annoyed, and tosses the book behind her on to the bed. What kind of a present is this?

No ordinary present, that's what, Valentina.

She can hear Theo's voice inside her head. She cannot help but be reassured. She picks up the negative she peeled from the album. This is more than a gift, she thinks. This is a game. A thrill of excitement stirs inside her belly. Theo is playing with her. Giving her little fragments of . . . what? Him, her, the mystery that surrounds him? This is fun, and certainly not a marriage proposal or anything too romantic. She carefully places the negative on her bedroom bureau and pulls on her other stocking. She cannot wait to get into her darkroom to make a print and uncover the first clue in her lover's puzzle.

THE
DESIRES UNLOCKED
TRILOGY

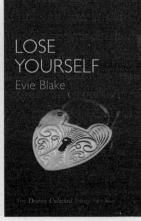
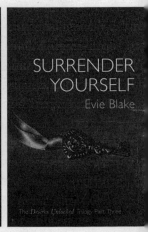